# The Highlander's Excellent Adventure

## The Survivors: Book VIII

*Shana Galen*

THE HIGHLANDER'S EXCELLENT ADVENTURE

Copyright © 2020 by Shana Galen

Cover Design by The Killion Group, Inc.

# Also by Shana Galen

REGENCY SPIES
*While You Were Spying*
*When Dashing Met Danger*
*Pride and Petticoats*

MISADVENTURES IN
MATRIMONY
*No Man's Bride*
*Good Groom Hunting*
*Blackthorne's Bride*
*The Pirate Takes a Bride*

SONS OF THE
REVOLUTION
*The Making of a Duchess*
*The Making of a Gentleman*
*The Rogue Pirate's Bride*

JEWELS OF THE TON
*If You Give a Duke a Diamond*
*If You Give a Rake a Ruby*
*Sapphires are an Earl's Best Friend*

LORD AND LADY SPY
*Lord and Lady Spy*
*The Spy Wore Blue (novella)*
*True Spies*
*Love and Let Spy*
*All I Want for Christmas is Blue (novella)*
*The Spy Beneath the Mistletoe (novella)*

COVENT GARDEN CUBS
*Viscount of Vice (novella)*
*Earls Just Want to Have Fun*
*The Rogue You Know*
*I Kissed a Rogue*

THE SURVIVORS
*Third Son's a Charm*
*No Earls Allowed*
*An Affair with a Spare*
*Unmask Me if You Can*
*The Claiming of the Shrew*
*A Duke a Dozen*
*How the Lady Was Won*
*Kisses and Scandal (anthology)*

THE SCARLET
CHRONICLES
*Traitor in Her Arms*
*To Ruin a Gentleman*
*Taken by the Rake*
*To Tempt a Rebel*

STANDALONES AND
ANTHOLOGIES
*Bachelors of Bond Street (anthology)*
*Stealing the Duke's Heart (duet)*
*The Summer of Wine and Scandal (novella)*
*A Royal Christmas (duet)*
*A Grosvenor Square Christmas (anthology)*

# Dedication and Acknowledgments

This book is dedicated to Monique Daoust. She was a tireless supporter of the romance genre and of my work. I miss her every day.

Thanks to Gayle Cochrane for two very important contributions to this book. First of all, she told me Ines needed a story and Duncan was her hero. I was skeptical, but as usual, Gayle was right. Secondly, Gayle suggested the title of this novel. She was right about that too.

Thanks as well to my writer friends who cheered me on and commiserated with me via Zoom while I finished this book, including Lark Howard, Nicole Flockton, Tracy Goodwin, Sharie Kohler, Colleen Thompson, and Kim Ungar.

# *One*

*Ines*

"She is an unmarried young lady," her brother-in-law said. "It's absolutely out of the question."

Ines narrowed her eyes in annoyance, even though neither Benedict Draven nor her sister, Catarina, could see her. She was eavesdropping. Again. She hadn't meant to—not this time. She'd been passing by the drawing room and heard her name. She'd promised herself she wouldn't eavesdrop on her sister and brother-in-law. They were married and deserved their privacy. But that promise did not apply in case of emergency. And this obviously qualified as an emergency as their discussion pertained to her future.

"We cannot keep her here, under lock and key, forever," Catarina said calmly. "She is young and wants some independence. It is not as though she is one of your fine Society ladies. She is a lacemaker."

"She's part of my family now, and I won't have her living alone above the shop. Even if I thought it was safe, you know her temperament."

Ines bristled but restrained herself from interjecting as that would only prove Draven's point.

"I was a bit wild at her age too," Catarina said, a smile in her voice. "If you remember."

Draven made a sound of dismissal. "That was war, and you were desperate."

"Yes, desperate to escape an arranged marriage to a cruel old man."

Ines nodded her head—she'd been facing a similar fate at one time. She'd run away with Catarina when, at the tender age of fourteen, their father had tried to marry her to one of his friends. She didn't like to think of how close she'd come to being trapped forever. Of course, when she'd escaped, she'd thought she was embarking on an exhilarating adventure. The reality was hours of detailed work in the back of a shop with other lacemakers. Her only excitement had been attending mass on Sundays. Ines ran a finger over a rough piece of paint on the wall and scratched at it as Draven spoke again.

"Why don't we see how things progress with Mr. Podmore?"

*Podmore*. Ines almost retched aloud. Mr. Podmore must be the most tedious person in London, if not the whole of England. Probably the entire world. He was forever going on about carriages. He was a successful cartwright, and his conveyances were known for their sturdiness and reliability. He'd once spoken for a quarter hour, uninterrupted, on the importance of wheel spokes. Ines had almost fallen asleep. She would never allow herself to be pushed into a marriage with a man like Podmore. She wanted passion, excitement…danger.

"I am afraid the interest there is all on one side," Catarina said. "But perhaps if they pursue an enjoyable activity together, it might help. I will suggest a ride in the park when he arrives today."

Ines started. Podmore was to call on her today? *Caramba!* She had to escape before he arrived or she might be trapped with him for hours, and she simply could not listen to another monologue on wheel spokes.

Ines stepped back and bumped into someone. She spun around and stared into the face of Ward, Draven's butler. He was only a little taller than she. His head was bald, but a shadow of stubble darkened his cheeks. "Ward!" she hissed. "What are you doing there?"

It was a ridiculous question. Ward was everywhere. One never knew when or where he would turn up.

The butler raised a brow. "I might ask you the same question, Miss Neves."

She blew out a breath. This was why she wanted to live above the shop. There was no privacy here. Her color rose as she realized how hypocritical that thought was considering she was the one eavesdropping.

On the other hand, Ward was eavesdropping as well... Ines straightened her shoulders. "I will pretend I did not see you, if you pretend you did not see me."

"Happily, miss."

Ines started for the front door, but Ward cleared his throat. She turned back. "What is it now?"

"Mr. Murray will arrive and knock on the door any moment. I suggest you exit another way."

Ines had no idea how Ward always knew who was coming and who was going and when they would appear, but she was too stunned by the mention of Duncan Murray to say anything.

The image of the Scotsman immediately flashed into her mind. All she had was his image as she had never been introduced to him. Ines had only glimpsed him through cracks in doorways. But those quick peeks had shown her quite enough to arouse her interest. He was tall, oh so wonderfully tall, and big and strong. She liked big men, men who had to turn to the side to fit their shoulders through the door and duck under the lintel to avoid banging their head. Mr. Murray had thick arms and legs—she'd seen his legs because he often wore a kilt. They were muscled and covered by brown hair. He had quite a lot of hair. The hair on his head was long enough to pull back in a queue, which was how he wore it when he visited. But she imagined untying the piece of leather securing his hair and running her hands through the freed locks. Then maybe he'd kiss her with those lips that always seemed to give everyone a mocking half smile. She'd feel the bristle of his two days' worth of stubble.

She didn't need to have met him to know he was a man of passion, excitement, and danger.

"Are you well, Miss Neves?" Ward asked.

Ines realized she'd been standing still, staring off into space. "Yes, why?" she asked quickly.

"Your face has gone red and your breathing has quickened."

"I am thirsty," she said, putting her hands to her hot cheeks. "I think I shall go to the kitchens and ask for a cup of tea." She walked away as rapidly as she could, certain Ward had known exactly what was causing her cheeks to color.

Once in the kitchen, she didn't see the cook, and she set about heating water to make her own cup of tea. She didn't really want any tea, but she needed something to do while she calmed her thoughts.

She had to hide somewhere until Podmore had gone. But if she left, she would miss the chance to spy on Mr. Murray's arrival. She would have to sneak around because Benedict always met with the Scot in private. Ines had once overheard—very well, *listened in*—when Catarina told Draven that Murray was wild and would be a bad influence on Ines. Benedict had said that of course he was. That was why the troop had called him the Lunatic. A description like that only made Duncan Murray more intriguing.

She *had* to find a way to meet him one day.

Ines heard a carriage stop outside the house and groaned aloud. Today would not be that day, obviously. Murray always came on a horse. Podmore always came in a carriage. He had several—a gig, a curricle, a barouche. She knew all about them. She had to escape now or she'd be forced to spend the afternoon with him, and it was such a lovely afternoon—warm and sunny and far too pretty to spend with dull Mr. Podmore. If she could avoid him today, she would be spared his company for the next few days as tomorrow her family was to travel to the country for the wedding of the sister of the Duke of Mayne.

Ines left the cup of tea brewing on the table, wiped her hands on the apron, and crossed the room to the courtyard door. She opened it, peeked out, and when she didn't see any of the servants about, stepped outside and closed the door behind her. Sheets and table linens hung on a line to dry and a half-painted chair had been abandoned in a corner. She could hide here for a little while, but a few sheets would not provide much cover. She had to find somewhere Catarina wouldn't think to look.

She heard a coachman speak to the horses out on the street, and an idea came to her. She would hide in Podmore's carriage. No one would look for her there. She could hide inside until Podmore came back, then slip out the opposite side when he returned. She would miss his visit completely.

Pleased with her plan, Ines opened the courtyard gate, slipped outside, and went around the side of the house, where she spotted the carriage. It didn't look exactly like the one Podmore had showed her last time. It wasn't as shiny and didn't have gold accents. This was much plainer, though she was certain he could make it sound like the most amazing carriage ever constructed.

The coachman had left his box and was speaking with a deliveryman nearby. His absence made Ines's task easier. She walked to the door of the coach, careful to stay low so the coachman would not see her through the windows. But even that was not a worry as the coach's curtains were closed. She opened one door, slipped inside, and closed it again. In the darkness, she couldn't help but smile at her own cunning.

She sat back, prepared to wait until she heard Podmore returning. The squabs were comfortable but not as luxurious as she'd anticipated. Where was the velvet Podmore insisted upon? Perhaps he had realized that velvet seats in summer were far too warm. The heat in the closed space was already making her uncomfortable and sleepy.

A few minutes passed, and then a few more, and she heard the coachman climb back on his box. The coach started moving a few minutes later, which was to be expected. They were looking for her inside the house, and Podmore would not want his horses to stand for too long.

Ines was rather used to riding in coaches now, though she had never even seen a coach in the tiny village where she'd grown up. But even after having ridden in coaches dozens of times the past five years, she still enjoyed the feeling of being carried by a momentum not her own. She closed her heavy eyes and waited for the horses to come to a stop outside Draven's house again. She should probably hop out as soon as the coach stopped. Podmore would have given up on her by now and might be waiting for his coach to carry him home. She would exit on the street and try to sneak back into the house via the courtyard.

Catarina would scold her, but Ines was not sorry. She had told her sister she did not care for Mr. Podmore and that she did not wish to marry any man that she didn't love. She wanted a man who could offer passion, excitement, and— Catarina usually cut her off by then. Her sister treated Ines's pronouncement the same way she treated Ines's requests to move to the little room above the lace shop: with a big sigh. Her older sister seemed to forget that when she had been only a little older than Ines, she had run off on her own and tried to find a husband to save her from the marriage her father had arranged. Not long after, Catarina had swooped in the night before Ines was to be married and offered to take Ines with her to Spain. Ines had agreed, eager to escape a life she hadn't wanted. But now, when Ines craved a little freedom of her own, Catarina still treated her like the girl of only fourteen.

The way Catarina babied her infuriated Ines, but emotional scenes did not sway Catarina. They'd grown up with a violent father who often screamed and yelled for hours. That was before he used his fists. Catarina was not impressed if Ines yelled or stamped her foot or even if she cried. Ines was not ashamed to admit she'd tried all three tactics. Now she would have to think of something else. Perhaps if she took on more responsibility at the lace shop. She could prove that she could be trusted with greater obligations. She pondered that idea for a little while.

She must have fallen asleep because when she jerked awake, she was surprised to find her muscles stiff, as though she had been in the same position for some time. Then she noticed the heat of the day had faded and the noise of London, a noise she had become so accustomed to, had quieted. At the same time, she realized the carriage was still moving. Why was it still moving? Wouldn't the coachman have just made a circle or two and returned to her home to collect Podmore? Ines snatched open the curtains closest to her and stared out into a field dotted with sheep. She opened the curtains on the other side, heart pounding, and stared at a small cottage.

This was not London.

This was not Podmore's coach.

\*\*\*

*Stratford*

Stratford Fortescue sat in a chair on a hill overlooking his family's estate, the sun on his face, and the wind ruffling his hair. He could relax now that the baron had gone inside after the picnic lunch. His mother and aunt had strolled away, heads together as usual, but his cousins and siblings and their spouses were enjoying a game of lawn bowls at the base of the low hill. He had an excellent view of the prospect of Odham Abbey from this vantage point. The building was undeniably Georgian in design, though the original structure had been Tudor. In the eighteenth century, the Tudor origins had been covered by granite and white paint and fashioned into a Palladian mansion.

Even as a child, Stratford had liked the clean lines of the house and its perfect symmetry. A year shy of thirty, he was a man of logic and reason. He'd studied the art of war and was known for his ability to develop efficient yet ingenious strategies to win even when the odds seemed improbable. Stratford liked simple elegance in a house and in a plan. His older siblings had invited Stratford to join their games, but he had declined. He'd spent the last few months in London surrounded by inane conversation. He had no desire to subject himself to more if it could be avoided. It wasn't that he didn't enjoy the company at the country house. Indeed, he only ever came if there were guests. Less risk of being alone with the baron then.

But even in the midst of a house party, Stratford enjoyed his solitude. Besides, if he joined the group, someone would want something from him. He'd long ago been designated the lowest ranking family member; he was always the one sent to fetch and deliver and squire.

Even his Aunt Harriet and his cousins ranked above Stratford in the unwritten family hierarchy. She was not really his aunt. She was related to his mother in some form or fashion—his mother's second cousin or some such thing. It was easier to call her his aunt and her children his cousins. Before her husband had died, the so-called aunt and uncle had produced four females and a male. Not a one of the distant female cousins was married, and their brother was all of ten and off at school, which meant Stratford was always taking this Wellesley sister or that one to some ball or other. He could use a moment's peace. Of course, as soon as he thought it, one of the cousins started up the hill toward him. It was Abigail Wellesley, the youngest of the quartet of daughters. At fifteen, she was not yet out, but Stratford was certain she'd be dragging him about Town next Season.

She smiled at him, her blue eyes bright against her pink cheeks. She wasn't wearing her bonnet, and Stratford motioned to the white umbrella swaying in the breeze.

"You'd better cower under that or your mother will have your head."

Abigail made a face. "I like a little sun on my cheeks." But she sat dutifully under the umbrella. When he didn't say anything, she started in. "I tired of the game. Hester kept winning, and she has a bad habit of gloating."

"Behavior not to be borne," he drawled.

"I wish we could go back to London. There's nothing to do here. Surely you wish you could go back to London, Stratford." She meant because the baron didn't want Stratford here. Even a girl of fifteen could see Stratford did not belong.

"No," he said flatly because even though things were awkward at Odham Abbey, he was used to it. And he'd had enough of Town for the moment. He had enjoyed it while Duncan Murray had been there. The Scot was always interesting company. But Duncan was probably on his way back to Scotland by now, and though Stratford hadn't really wanted to come home, when his mother requested his presence, he hadn't been able to think of an excuse to stay away.

"You're like Emmeline," Abigail announced. Emmeline was her eldest sister, the one his aunt despaired of ever marrying. She was also the other reason Stratford had come to Odham Abbey. He would not have missed the chance to spend a few days in Emmeline's company for anything.

Stratford did not take Abigail's bait, so she fed him more. "She doesn't like London either. In fact, I heard her tell Marjorie she was not returning."

When Stratford still didn't respond, Abigail said, "Can you imagine that?"

"I am certain your mother will have something to say about it."

"She doesn't know," Abigail said. "No one knows what Emmeline has planned, except Marjorie and me, because I overheard."

Stratford was not really interested in what any of the Wellesley girls had planned. But he peered down at the lawn to catch a glimpse of Emmeline—just a glimpse. He was not so far gone as to watch her constantly or follow her about. He had his pride.

Emmeline wasn't with the others. He was not alarmed. She'd probably gone inside. Except he didn't remember her being at the picnic. Come to think of it, he couldn't recall seeing her all afternoon.

"Where is Emmeline?" he asked.

"I can't tell you," Abigail said.

Stratford sat straight and gave the girl his full attention. "What do you mean?"

"It's a secret. I wasn't even supposed to have heard. Emmeline swore Marjorie to secrecy."

"Did she go to take a nap?"

Abigail smiled. "No. She's not even here." Her hands flew to her mouth, and she looked horrified. "I mean, I mean—"

"Where is she?" Stratford asked, looking directly at Abigail. The girl shrank slightly.

"I told you I can't say."

But she'd wanted to tell someone. If she hadn't, she wouldn't have come up here looking for someone to confide in. Stratford's skill was in strategy, but even he didn't have to work very hard to figure out how to make Abigail talk. "Abigail, either you tell me where Emmeline has gone or I will fetch your Mama and tell her exactly what you were up to in London."

Abigail's eyes went wide. "How did you know?" she breathed.

He hadn't known, and he still didn't know. The statement had been a calculated risk, and as usual it had paid off. "It's my job to know things like that. Now talk or I call for Auntie Harriet."

"Very well! Emmeline has run away."

Stratford frowned. "Run away? Where?"

Abigail tossed her dark curls. "To the posting house, of course. There she will catch the coach."

Stratford's heart nearly stopped. This was worse than he could have imagined. If it had been any of the other sisters, he wouldn't have believed it, but Emmeline was just bold enough to do something like that. "Which coach?"

"I don't know. Whichever one would take her furthest from London. She said she would not be made to suffer another failed Season. She'd rather die. You won't tell Mama now, will you? I told you what I know."

Stratford didn't answer. He was already striding down the hill and toward the stable. One of his brothers called after him, but he simply waved and went on. If he stopped to explain, he would surely miss Emmeline. He'd probably missed her already. Devil take that woman. He'd always known she had a mind of her own—everyone knew that— but she'd also seemed rather level-headed for a female. Why would she run off like this? Abigail must be mistaken. He hoped this was all a misunderstanding.

Stratford flagged down a groom and in a few minutes rode away from the house and toward the posting house. When he arrived, it was as he'd expected. He'd missed the coach. When he'd asked if the proprietor had seen Miss Emmeline Wellesley, the proprietor frowned. "What does she look like, sir?"

"She's beau—" he began. Then shook his head. What was he saying? She was Emmeline. Stratford cleared his throat. "She has dark hair, quite dark, almost black, in fact. It's dreadfully glossy in the right light, and she wears it draped over one shoulder with a loose curl that falls down over one…" He cleared his throat. "Er—blue eyes, medium height, Rubenesque figure."

The proprietor, a man of sixty or so, with a weathered face and red hands, drew his brows together. "What's that mean?"

"Never mind. Have you seen her?"

"I didn't see any fine ladies, but then I weren't looking for any. I did see one female. She that seemed a bit out of place."

"How so?

"It's a warm day, but she were all wrapped up in her cloak. I didn't get a look at her face."

Stratford did not want it to be Emmeline, but the description fit. A woman who hadn't wanted anyone to see her face would wear a cloak on a warm day. Emmeline was a clever woman. The proprietor told him the coach's next stop, which would be a brief one simply to change horses. But he added, "Just follow the Great Northern Road. You'll catch her."

As Stratford mounted his horse again, he reflected that he had been trying to catch Emmeline his whole life. He'd tried for years to catch her attention and her interest, but she never treated him any differently than she treated anyone else in his family. And he would rather keep his feelings to himself than be made a fool of by announcing them when they were not returned.

And so he would bring Emmeline back, preferably before his mother or aunt realized she was missing. In that case he'd be sent after her anyway, but his departure would be accompanied by much wailing and gnashing of teeth. If he could bring Emmeline back quickly and quietly, all the fuss and theatrics could be avoided. Not that Stratford believed bringing her back would be easy. She had some reason for running away, but she was generally a sensible woman. She didn't disappear onto the terrace with men at balls and didn't drink too much at garden parties or offer to show her skill at the pianoforte at musicales.

In fact, Stratford thought as he spurred his horse to a gallop in the hope of catching the coach before it advanced too far ahead, except for her tendency to be outspoken, she was no trouble to chaperone at all. She was a wallflower. What had gotten into her?

Unfortunately, at the next posting house, he was told he had missed the coach by a half hour. By now he had to change his own horse, and he thought better of continuing on without sending some word to his family. He penned a note to the baron, stating the facts and reassuring the baron (though truth be told it was his aunt he was thinking of as the baron did not deign to read missives Stratford sent) that he would bring Emmeline back safely in no time at all. He sent the horse back with the note and informed the lad he sent that the baron would pay when he arrived. Stratford was a bit light on coin as he hadn't expected to be traveling any further than the dining room this evening. And by now evening was descending. The summer days were long, the light lasting until eight or nine, but his stomach told him it was time for dinner. Ignoring that rumbling, he continued on, adding starvation to the list of grievances he would present to Emmeline when he found her.

# *Two*

*Duncan*

Duncan Murray stepped off the box of the coach he'd hired to take him back to Scotland and stretched his legs. He'd never liked being cooped up inside a coach and would have normally traveled on horseback, but he had gifts for his mother and sister from London, and he had needed a vehicle to convey them all. And now, after four hours on the box, he was rather appreciative of the coach. He hadn't slept much the night before as he'd spent his last hours in London with his friends at the Draven Club. He'd drank too much and had been late paying his respects to Colonel Draven this morning. But it might be a year or more before he was in London again, and he hadn't regretted drinking to the health of his friends— and to their wives and their horses and even to children yet-to-be-born. Finally, at approximately four in the morning, they'd run out of reasons to drink and stumbled to their beds.

He lifted his face to the setting sun. He would have enjoyed the fine summer day if the heat of it hadn't made his head ache. Soon he'd be back in the cool of Scotland, though, and that was something to look forward to—even if his return would also be accompanied by his mother's disappointment.

He'd disappointed his mother once with disastrous consequences for all, especially his father, and Duncan had sworn he would never disappoint her again. Yet here he was coming home alone when she'd ordered him to find the daughter of an English peer to marry.

"Sir, the horses are almost ready," the coachman informed him as the hired man climbed back up on the box.

Duncan nodded. "Aye. Looks like we have two or three hours of light left. Make the most of it." He wanted to cover as much distance as possible while the good weather held. Once they reached Scotland, the climate was less predictable. He started for the coach and the coachman called after him. "You won't be riding up here, sir?"

"Nae. I find myself in need of a wee nap. Wake me when the light fades, aye?"

"Yes, sir."

Duncan climbed into the dark coach and shut the door as the coachman spurred the horses forward. He raised his arms then attempted to find a comfortable position on the seat. He was far too big to lie down upon it, so he extended his legs to the seat across from him, determined to stretch out and nap that way. But his feet nudged something soft and solid. He'd thrown his greatcoat inside earlier, but this was too heavy to be a coat. He nudged it with his foot again, and it moaned.

Duncan was instantly alert, knife in hand, and in attack position. "Who's there?" he demanded, voice low. "Show yerself."

There was no response save a long…sigh? Was the intruder sleeping? Moving gingerly, Duncan lifted the shutter on the lamp slowly, shedding weak light into the interior. There was definitely someone curled under his coat. He made out a distinctly human shape. Brown hair at the top of his coat and a yellow slipper peeking out of the bottom.

A lass? Christ and all the saints!

Duncan knelt on the floor between the seats and peered more closely. With his coat in the way, he couldn't see much, so he pulled the material back slowly, revealing the fine facial features of a young lady. Her eyes were closed and her face lax as though in sleep. He pulled the coat down further, exposing slim shoulders and slender arms tucked close to her body.

Duncan sat back on his haunches. Where had she come from? Had she been in the coach since London? She didn't look like the sort of poor creature who would stowaway. She wore an apron, but under it was an expensive gown. There was lace at the throat of her striped yellow and white dress. It was one of those dresses ladies wore in the morning before they donned the afternoon and evening gowns he liked because they showed a bit of skin.

Duncan stared at her for several minutes, not sure what he should do. Wake her? Let her sleep? He'd never had a woman fall asleep in his carriage before. Of course, he didn't own a carriage, but he didn't take it to be a usual occurrence, nonetheless. The wheels jounced over a hole in the road and the woman shifted, opened her eyes slightly, then made to turn over.

Until she spotted him, and her eyes opened. With a jerk, she sat up and opened her mouth, presumably to scream. Duncan acted quickly, putting his hand over her lips before she could emit a sound. "Dinnae fash, lass. I willnae hurt ye."

She continued staring at him, her large brown eyes the size of saucers.

"Shh," he said as he slowly moved his hand away. "Dinnae scream."

His hand fell to his side, and she blinked at him. She was fully awake now. Her chest rose and fell under the thin material of her dress. Slowly, Duncan moved back to the seat across from her. Now that she was sitting and facing him, something about her was familiar. He raised the shutter of the lamp on the opposite side of the coach to view her more clearly. He could have sworn he had seen her somewhere before, but then he'd been to twenty balls or more in the last few months and countless other amusements. In his search for a bride, he'd looked at so many women, they blended together in his mind.

Since she still hadn't said anything, just continued to stare at him, he decided he had better begin the preliminaries. "Do I ken ye, lass?"

Her eyes widened further, which was truly remarkable as he hadn't thought they could open any further. "What's yer name?" he asked.

Her brow furrowed, and she opened her mouth then closed it again. She seemed to be trying to speak but could not find the words. Did he frighten her, or did she have a reason for not wanting to tell him? Let her keep her secrets—for the moment.

"Och, ye dinnae want tae tell me, is that it? Verra well. Where did ye come from? How did ye find yer way in here?"

He gestured to the coach and she followed the movement with her eyes.

Well, this was one of the more tedious conversations he'd had. Perhaps if he revealed something of himself, she would follow. "My name is Duncan Murray." He tapped his chest. "Since ye're in my coach, sleeping under my coat, I dinnae think it's too much tae ask yer name, lass."

She swallowed, her long throat moving delicately. "Beatriz," she said quietly, pointing to her own chest.

Duncan narrowed his eyes. She hadn't said it in the English way—Beatrice. In fact, she hadn't sounded British at all. "Where are ye from, Beatrice?"

"Beatriz." And then she said several sentences, none of which made an ounce of sense to him. He wasn't very good with languages. He understood the English well enough as his mother was one. But though the Highland clans had always been close with the French, Duncan had never learned it. Still, he'd heard it enough to figure what she'd said wasn't French. Maybe Italian? Or German? Christ, he didn't know.

She was looking at him expectantly, probably much as he'd been looking at her a moment ago. Now he was the one confused. He didn't particularly mind having her eyes on him. She was unusually pretty. In addition to those large brown eyes, she possessed chestnut-colored hair that fell in waves about her face. On the seat beside her was a cap that had probably confined it at one point but had been lost or set aside during the trip.

"Where are ye from?" he asked.

She cocked her head to one side.

He pointed to himself again. "Scotland." He pointed to her.

She bit her lip as she considered. He watched her small white teeth sink into the pink flesh and tried not to think of sinking his own teeth into that flesh. She was lost and alone. He needed to help her, not maul her. This was the problem with months of bride-shopping—all looking and no touching.

Finally, she looked up at him and cleared her throat. "Portugal," she said.

Duncan sat back on the seat. "Christ and all the saints."

Duncan sat silently for some time with the word she'd spoken ringing in his ears. He was a man of action—some said too much action. He often acted without thinking, and that was fine by him. He lived by his wits and his instincts, and they hadn't led him wrong yet. Sure, some might call him a lunatic—his fellow soldiers did—but Duncan couldn't see how caution and restraint had served them any better than impulsivity had served him. But now, just for the moment, he wished he had Stratford or Phineas here beside him. Those two seemed to always know the correct course of action. They'd know what to do with this lass.

Duncan looked at her and sighed. She looked back at him, her legs still curled under his greatcoat, and her eyes wide with concern. She dropped her gaze when it met his, and a blush rose on her cheeks.

"I dinnae suppose ye ken what tae do aboot this situation?" he asked, mostly to himself, but she looked up at the sound of his voice. "I can't exactly leave ye oot on the road nor can I take ye tae Scotland with me." He rubbed a hand over his eyes, which burned with fatigue. He wished he had slept last night. His mind would be clearer. "I can only think of one option. I'd better take ye back tae London."

"London?" she asked in an accented voice. "*Não. Não* London." She shook her head and looked the most animated he had seen her.

Duncan leaned forward. "What's wrong with London?"

She didn't answer, merely looked at him.

"Ye dinnae like London?"

"*Não* London," she repeated.

Well, that was a problem. He needed someone who spoke her language to find out who she was and where she belonged. A few of the men in Draven's troop had been in Portugal and knew the language—Neil was one, but he was back in London. Nash was another. Nash was a sharpshooter who had been injured in battle. Duncan hadn't seen him in a year at least, since Nash had retired to his family estate. If Duncan remembered correctly, that estate was only about fifty miles out of the way in the village of Milcroft.

"But if we go too much further north, we'll have tae dooble back," he said before parting the curtains and sliding the window down. "John Coachman!"

A moment later the driver's voice carried back on the breeze. "Aye, sir?"

"Stop for the night at the next inn!"

"Sir?"

Duncan looked at the woman staring at him in alarm. "Our plans have changed."

*** 

*Emmeline*

Emmeline Wellesley—a distant relation to the duke of that name—was beginning to realize that perhaps she should have thought through this plan of running away a bit more thoroughly before embarking on the adventure.

That is to say, she should have thought about it for more than the quarter hour it took her to gather her belongings and depart. Yes, she was weary of the Season. It was her fifth

Season, and the way things were progressing, she could envision a sixth and seventh Season as well. Emmeline had begun to wonder exactly how many Seasons her mother planned to force her to endure. Surely with three younger sisters, her mother might try to economize and cut her losses.

Emmeline was most certainly a loss in the eyes of Society. She had received only a handful of lackluster proposals from men she would not have married had a pistol been pointed to her head. The problem, as her mother had told her often enough, was that Emmeline insisted on opening her mouth when she met an eligible gentleman. And once she opened her mouth, she had the Very Bad Habit of saying what she thought. Her mother chastised her continually for her impertinence. Women were not supposed to have ideas of their own about matters other than fashion. Unmarried women, especially, were not to have thoughts about anything. They were to smile and flutter their lashes and agree with the man at their side.

Emmeline never fluttered her lashes and seldom agreed with any man. And whenever she was out in Society, she rarely smiled. Her mother always forced her into undergarments that cut off her breathing and dresses that were too small, so Emmeline could barely inhale much less dance. Added to the inconvenience of not being able to take in sufficient oxygen, her mother also did not allow Emmeline to eat, hoping that Emmeline would wither away and actually be able to fit into the too-small gowns. And her mother wondered why Emmeline did not look forward to the Season.

But this year insult had been added to injury. Marjorie, who was enjoying only her first Season, had a suitor who had asked Mama's permission for Marjorie's hand. Mama had agreed, but she wanted to keep the betrothal quiet until the end of the Season to "give Emmeline more time to make her own match."

Emmeline was the eldest of the five siblings, and it was traditional to marry the eldest before the younger. But Marjorie had accused Emmeline of "ruining everything" and "standing in the way of all my happiness" by remaining unattached. Though her sister's words had hurt Emmeline, she could not fault the sentiment. Of course, Marjorie, who was only twenty years old, wanted to publicly celebrate her good fortune. Her betrothed was the son of an earl—a younger son, but he had a good living as a barrister and had also inherited money from a doting grandfather. He seemed a pleasant enough man, though Emmeline found his conversation dull and plodding and his ideas about justice very wrongheaded indeed.

But then Marjorie's brain was also dull and plodding, full of useless information about fichus and fripperies. She never read anything beyond the *Morning Post*'s descriptions of the clothing the fashionable set wore. Emmeline's family preferred cards to literature, embroidery to long walks, and an evening at Vauxhall to the Royal Opera House. They did not understand Emmeline any more than she understood them.

But sitting in the packed coach, wedged between a woman with a baby whose nappy needed changing and an older woman whose head was drooping as she snored silently, Emmeline thought she might be more like her family than she had been willing to acknowledge. After all, running off like this was one of the more idiotic things she had ever done.

Yes, her feelings had been hurt by Marjorie's cutting words. Yes, Emmeline had wanted to shock her mother and catch her attention so that she might finally listen when Emmeline said she did not want to go to another ball or assembly or dinner party. That she could not stand another evening of her stays biting into her ribs. But perhaps this method was a bit too extreme?

Emmeline hadn't even really decided where she should go. She had a vague notion of visiting her paternal grandmother, who lived in the far north of England, but Emmeline realized now she did not really know if the coach on which she rode would take her anywhere near her grandmother's residence in Carlisle. She had known it traveled north, and that seemed all that mattered at the time.

Now she had been sitting on this coach with the smelly infant and the snoring woman and the two men across from her arguing about the price of wool for the last three hours, and she needed to use the necessary and stretch her legs and fill her lungs with fresh air.

And so it was with great relief that the coachman called back to the passengers on top of the coach—at least she was not seated up there—and those unfortunates called down to inform those seated inside that the coach would stop for a brief refreshment at the next posting house. The sound of voices caused the mother to rock her baby and shush him, though he did not cry. On her other side, the elderly woman snorted awake and looked about.

"What is the commotion?" the lady asked.

"We will be stopping soon for refreshment," Emmeline told her.

"Oh, thank goodness. I fear I may not be able to stand after such a long period of sitting, though," the lady said. "My legs are not what they used to be."

"I'll be happy to provide whatever assistance you might need," Emmeline offered.

The lady beamed at her, her eyes a pretty hazel under her dour black hat. "Thank you, my dear." She patted Emmeline's arm. "You remind me of my Lucy, now ten years in her grave."

"Oh, I'm so sorry," Emmeline said, even as the older woman's eyes filled with tears.

"She was my only daughter, you see, and a comfort to me in my advancing years. My sons pay me no heed. They hire companions for me, but what good is that when the creatures leave me to fend for myself? My last one ran off with a gentleman she hardly knew. And now I must make my way back to Derbyshire all on my own."

"My own grandmother lives in Cumbria," Emmeline said. "I will be happy to assist you to Derbyshire."

"You are most kind." The lady patted Emmeline's sleeve. "But I fear you have taken the wrong coach. This conveyance is not traveling to Cumbria."

Emmeline nodded as this confirmed her supposition. "I purchased my ticket in haste. At the posting house I will ask about making a change at some point on the route."

"My, but you speak decisively for one so young."

Emmeline had heard this criticism before. *Decisively* was another word for her mother's favorite—*Impertinent*.

The lady continued, "I have traveled on this coach many times, and I would be happy to assist you. It seems we can both be of service today."

Emmeline did not need the woman's help, but when she squeezed Emmeline's arm, Emmeline managed a smile for her. She'd been mistaken about this adventure after all. It was not exactly comfortable or pleasant, but she'd be able to stretch her legs shortly, and she could assist the older woman, who was alone in the world. This was exactly the sort of thing Emmeline was always telling her mother—there were more important things to do than finding a husband. It felt infinitely more satisfying, when they did stop a few minutes later, to help the lady down from the coach and into the small public house than it ever had to exchange words about the weather with the son of a duke.

Inside the small, dark posting house, Emmeline ordered bread and tea and paid for it and that of the older lady, who she had learned was a Mrs. Goodly. Mrs. Goodly asked the proprietor of the posting house where Emmeline should change coaches to travel to Cumbria, and though he was not certain, he assured her she would have that opportunity once they were further north. Emmeline sat at one of the smattering of tables, Mrs. Goodly across from her, and sipped her tea. She would have preferred to go outside and walk about in the sunshine and fresh air. The posting house smelled of cabbage and Mrs. Goodly had wanted to sit by the fire, which made the room much too warm. But Emmeline could not leave Mrs. Goodly alone.

Finally, the coachman came inside and informed the passengers the coach would be departing again in five minutes. Emmeline helped Mrs. Goodly rise to her feet and supported her as she walked across the room. But before they could reach the door, the young mother cried out, "Oh, no!"

"What is it?" Emmeline asked. The woman turned to look at her, tears streaming from her eyes. Emmeline knew that look. She'd seen it a time or two on her own mother's face when her brother had been a baby. It was exhaustion coupled with frustration.

"Oh, it's nothing," the mother said, dashing a hand across her wet eyes. "My little Jack has just wet his clean nappy, and I left his others in the coach."

"I will fetch one for you," Emmeline said. Really, what would these passengers do without her?

"Thank you, but they are packed at the bottom of my valise. I fear it would take too long to find them."

"Perhaps I can hold the baby while you search," Emmeline offered. "I will just see Mrs. Goodly to the coach and then return."

"Oh, but this lady can see me to the coach," Mrs. Goodly said. "Then she can fetch what she needs and return."

Emmeline did not know why she hesitated. The plan was reasonable and more efficient. She opened her mouth to reject it anyway then realized perhaps her mother was correct, and she did argue just for the sake of arguing. Emmeline swallowed her objection. "Oh, yes," Emmeline agreed. "That is a much better solution."

"The proprietor offered me this room to change him," the mother said, leading Emmeline away from Mrs. Goodly to a door in the back. She opened it, and Emmeline saw a small storage closet full of mops and brooms, but a table was cleared and that must have been what the mother used to change the infant. "If you wait in here, I will be right back. He's sleeping," she said as she handed him to Emmeline. "I've covered his face so the light doesn't wake him."

Emmeline took the small, warm bundle and stepped into the closet, rocking the baby gently. The mother gave her a hug, which Emmeline found very sweet. The door closed behind her, the motion causing the lantern to go out and casting her into darkness. Emmeline assumed this was probably for the best so the baby would stay asleep as long as possible. Come to think of it, the baby had been sleeping the entire journey. Emmeline didn't remember Robert sleeping that much when he'd been an infant. This mother was either very lucky or the baby was very tired.

From inside the closet she heard the coachman call out for any last passengers. Emmeline started. She knew the coaches did not wait for anyone, but surely the mother would tell him she needed to collect her child and Emmeline.

She waited for voices indicating someone was coming for her, but there were none. Growing even more alarmed, Emmeline tried the handle of the door. When she pushed down on the latch, it did not move. She tried it again, pushing harder. Nothing happened. The door was locked. She waited for screams or the sound of the mother running back to claim her baby, but there was only silence as the passengers had left and now the public house was empty.

Emmeline pounded on the door with her free hand. When no one came, she called out. There was no answer. The proprietor was probably outside or in the kitchen, which meant he could not hear her. But she had to get out before the coach was too far away. She had to catch up and reunite the mother and child. She was certain the mother was distraught and in a state of panic at having her child left behind.

Emmeline was certainly panicking. She could not be left here. She had no idea where she was, and it wasn't as though there was a town nearby. This posting house had been all she had seen on the road for some time.

Emmeline pounded on the door again, then realized she had better calm down or the baby would wake and cry. But the baby was already moving in her arms. Emmeline pushed the blanket away from his face and murmured some words of comfort.

And that's when the baby licked her.

To her credit Emmeline did not drop the squirming bundle. She jumped, but she managed to hold on. Shaking now with fear and uncertainty, she reached a hand back toward the baby's face.

The baby licked her again with a big, wet tongue…

That was no baby tongue.

Emmeline touched the child's face and felt a wet snout, fur, and soft, long ears.

It was not a baby at all. Further unwrapping of the blankets confirmed her suspicions that she held a small dog.

And that was the point Emmeline sank to the floor. She had been duped, played for a fool, tricked. And here she had prided herself on being the cleverest of her sisters. Well, they weren't sitting in a broom closet with a dog wrapped like a baby, were they?

But why would the so-called mother want to trick her like that? What could she possibly be after—

Emmeline set the dog down quickly and reached inside her dress for the pockets she'd tied over her petticoat. She dove into one pocket then the other. Both were empty. But how—

That hug.

The embrace she had thought so sweet. That was when the woman had reached into her pockets and taken her purse. And now poor Mrs. Goodly was trapped on the coach with the duplicitous woman.

Except that Mrs. Goodly had encouraged her to go with the mother and baby. And Mrs. Goodly had not stopped the coach when Emmeline did not arrive before it departed. Surely a woman like Mrs. Goodly could make a coachman listen to her.

It was all so clear now. Mrs. Goodly had been part of the scheme as well, and Emmeline had been very easy prey. Why hadn't she argued? The one time she held her tongue and look what had happened!

The dog licked her hand again and Emmeline stroked his head. "No wonder you were so quiet," she said. "She was probably feeding you treats to keep you happy." At the mention of the word *treat* the dog put his—or her—paws on Emmeline's knee and jumped. "I don't have anything for you," Emmeline said, sinking down to the floor. "And until the next coach arrives, we'll probably be stuck in here."

She listened for a few moments, but the room that had been so full of people a few minutes ago was silent. She leaned her head back against the wall. "What will we do? I have no money, no one knows where I am." She bolted upright, sending the dog scampering back. "I left my valise on the coach! Oh, no!"

She had nothing but the clothes on her back and the dog creeping back toward her feet. Now she'd have to slink home and admit what a failure she was—not only at securing a husband but at running away. She couldn't do anything right!

Emmeline straightened her shoulders. If she continued to think that way, she'd probably end up right where she'd been, propping up a wall at another ball. She'd made the decision to go to her grandmother's, and she would see that through.

One way or another.

# *Three*

Ines could not tear her gaze from the Scotsman seated across from her. He was like a dream—or a fantasy—come true. In the flesh he was even better than she had imagined. He was taller, gruffer, and more dangerous than she could have hoped. They sat in the public room of an inn in a village she did not know the name of. He'd told her, but she'd been looking at his hands. Large hands she suspected would feel deliciously rough on her skin. Watching her warily, he bit off a hunk of bread and motioned for her to eat. She tried, but it was difficult when she could not stop thinking about what he looked like under his clothes.

Everything about this day was surreal. Duncan Murray was looking at her, had been talking to her, was eating with her. Of course, he didn't know who she was. He thought she was a Portuguese woman named Beatriz. Ines hadn't planned to lie to him or to pretend she didn't speak English. She'd

49

been struck mute when she'd awoke to find him looking down at her. Her throat had closed up and her mind hadn't been able to think of anything except the words *I love you.* And when he had asked her name, she had been about to tell him she was Ines, but then she realized that once he knew she was Catarina Draven's sister, he would take her straight back to London. And so she'd given him one of her other sisters' names, and she'd pretended she didn't speak English so she didn't have to try and think of any more lies. Ines was not a very good liar. Catarina always said Ines's face was like an open book.

Quickly, she looked down and ate a spoonful of soup. If her face was an open book, she had better stop staring at him because he'd know right away she was lusting after him. But was that such a bad thing? If he knew, he might try to take advantage of her. She shivered at the thought of his kisses.

"Are ye cold, lass?" Duncan removed his coat and draped it over her shoulders. Ines was not cold, and though she liked the warmth of his coat and the scent of him surrounding her, she could not appreciate his chivalry. Why did he have to be such a gentleman? Didn't he want to ravish her? Didn't he want to sweep her into his arms, carry her up the stairs, and kick open a chamber door then have his way with her?

Ines sighed. Given that Duncan Murray had been given the sobriquet the Lunatic by his fellow soldiers, Ines feared that it was not propriety that kept Murray from following his baser instincts. He had taken one look at her and didn't want her. Catarina always said Ines was the pretty one, but she'd heard Murray was looking for a wife these past weeks in London. The fact that he was going home without one meant he was quite choosy, for surely he could have had any woman he wanted. He was breathtaking to look upon and exciting to be with.

Ines could only assume that whatever Duncan was looking for, it wasn't her. He probably wanted one of those pale, yellow-haired English women with blue eyes and a curvaceous figure. Ines was dark haired, dark eyed, slender, and petite. She'd been told many times she was attractive, but obviously she did not have the qualities that would tempt the Scotsman.

"Why the long face, lass?" he asked. "I ken ye miss yer family, but we'll have ye back in Town for supper tomorrow."

Oh, good. Just what she wanted. To sit across from Catarina and Benedict and explain how she ended up in Duncan Murray's carriage. The Scotsman would probably be none too pleased when he learned she spoke perfect English.

She was beginning to regret not simply telling him who she was to begin with.

Murray pushed his plate away and lifted his glass of whisky. "I do wonder how ye ended up in my coach. It doesnae make sense tae me. Why would ye climb into an unfamiliar coach?"

She wished she could tell him about Podmore. She would have climbed into the mouth of a lion to avoid the cartwright.

"But I suppose that's one more thing I dinnae ken aboot London. I went there tae find a bride."

She did know this, but she was surprised he was speaking of it. Perhaps the whisky he'd drank made him talkative. Or perhaps it was easy to talk to someone he didn't think could understand him.

"But do ye ken what I found instead? A passel of lasses who jumped everra time I said boo." He shook his head and drank more whisky. "I was an idjit to believe anything had changed. We Scots are considered little more than barbarians." He leaned closer, speaking conspiratorially. "In my case, that's nae altogether untrue, lass, but I dinnae advertise the fact." He winked, and Ines made a little sound of need, like the sound a puppy makes when waiting impatiently for her food to be set down.

The wink was roguish and unexpected from a man who had the look of a barbarian with that long hair and the scratchy beginnings of a beard. She liked barbarians just fine.

"To tell ye the truth, I wouldnae have bothered with the English if my mother had nae insisted."

Ines wanted to ask why his mother wanted him to marry an English lass—er, lady.

"She's English, and my uncle, the laird, has had nae end of trouble with the English. Lady Charlotte thinks if I marry an Englishwoman it will be a boon tae the entire clan. She'll blister my ears when I return withoot a bride."

Ines's own ears felt blistered at his words. He needed an English bride. Not only English, it seemed, but a lady. She was neither of those things. No wonder he didn't look at her. So much for her fantasies about marrying Duncan Murray.

Duncan was still speaking, something about the trouble the laird had in the past with English soldiers, but Ines was not listening again. Yes, Murray's mother, Lady Charlotte, had wanted him to marry an English lady. But it now appeared that eventuality would not come to pass. He was returning home without a bride or a betrothal. Ines had always said she wanted to pick her own husband, one with the PED (Passion-Excitement-Danger) qualities she prized. She'd already escaped one marriage and she didn't think she was so lucky as to be able to escape a second. But if she could not have Murray, a marriage for her would have to be years in the future. She wanted to experience the world a bit first. She wanted to kiss a man like Duncan Murray and perhaps a few dozen others before she decided who she would tie herself to permanently.

The problem now was how to make Murray realize he *should* kiss her. She couldn't tell him since she was pretending she couldn't understand him. Perhaps she could use nonverbal communication…

Ines made a show of yawning and covering her mouth prettily. When he didn't seem to notice, she did it again.

"But ye must be tired, lass. I'll see ye tae yer chamber."

He had secured them separate chambers. Hers was at the top of the stairs and to the right, and his was on the other end of the first floor of the inn. He'd certainly made sure he was far away from her. Now he took her arm and escorted her up the stairs. Ines's heart pounded so loudly she couldn't hear a word he said, if he even spoke. He'd drank quite a bit of whisky but didn't seem the least bit impaired. That was too bad because she'd been hoping he would stumble, and she could catch him. And then they'd look into each other's eyes, and he wouldn't be able to resist ravishing her.

They had almost reached her chamber and there'd been no sign of stumbling or hints that a ravishing was coming. Well, if he wouldn't fall into her arms, she'd have to fall into his. At her door, she took the key from her glove and inserted it into the lock. Then she opened the door. He couldn't kick it open now, but she was willing to forgo that part of the fantasy. She turned to tell him goodnight and pretended to trip and fall forward.

If all had gone as she'd wanted, she would have fallen into his arms. Instead, his hand shot out, caught her elbow, and he righted her with one easy motion. Damn his strength and agility!

"Careful, lass," he said, still holding her at arm's length. "Goodnight."

She glared at him and at his puzzled look, finally managed to parrot his "Good night." And then he was gone, and she closed the door behind her and wondered just exactly how everything in her life always went wrong.

\*\*\*

*Stratford*

Stratford had little hope the posting house in the distance would yield him any more answers than the last three where he had stopped. But the light was fading, his horse was tiring, and he could use a drink before going on. He didn't like that Emmeline had managed to get ahead of him. As a single rider, he should have easily overtaken the coach. The problem was he couldn't be absolutely certain she was on it, so he had to stop at every inn or public house the coach might have stopped at to inquire after her. So far no one remembered her.

That didn't discourage Stratford. At most of the stops, the coach would not have paused long enough for the passengers to disembark. But eventually the passengers would be allowed down for refreshment and personal needs. He simply had to find the posting house where the coach had paused and hope Emmeline had stepped out and been seen. He slowed, tossed his reins to the groom who hurried out to greet him, and ordered a fresh horse. "Did the mail coach stop here?" he asked.

"Which one?" the groom asked. "One headed north stopped about an hour ago."

Finally! Good news. "Was a young woman among the passengers? Dark hair, blue eyes…"

"I can't say, sir. I didn't see the passengers. Mr. Miller will know."

Stratford followed the groom's eyes toward the low building a few yards away. "Mr. Miller is the proprietor?"

"Yes, sir. We have another coach scheduled in a quarter of an hour, so he might be supervising in the kitchen. He'll hear if you call for him."

Stratford thanked the groom and entered the dark public house, his eyes surveying the room for any sign of a Mr. Miller. The room was empty and though Stratford thought it rather gauche, he called out for the man.

But instead of a male reply, he heard a woman's muffled voice and a pounding on the wall. "What the devil?" he muttered, moving closer to the sound of the pounding. "Who is there?"

"Open the door!" the voice called out. "Let me out of here!"

Stratford realized the sound of pounding did not come from behind a wall at all but from behind a door. A chair had been placed in front of the door, ensuring it remained closed with the occupant inside. Stratford looked about for the elusive Mr. Miller, but the man was still absent. With a shrug, Stratford moved the chair aside.

The door swung open and a woman tumbled out, followed by a jumping blur of brown-and-white fur.

What the devil had he unleashed? He had the urge to push the woman and animal back into the closet, but she stumbled right into him, and when he righted her, he looked down into the bright blue eyes of Emmeline Wellesley.

"Miss Wellesley," he said, trying to ignore the dog jumping at her side.

"Stratford?" She glanced down at the dog, which he identified as a King Charles Cavalier Spaniel. "Hush." But the attention only seemed to encourage the spaniel, who began to bark and run around them in circles. Emmeline said something else, but he couldn't hear over the din of the animal.

"Pardon?"

"I said, what are you doing here, but now I realize you must have been sent to look for me."

Her supposition was close enough to the truth. "And it seems I've arrived just in time."

"What?"

"I said—oh, for God's sake." He bent, lifted the spaniel into his arms, and the animal quieted. "Do you want to explain what you were doing locked in a"—he peered over her shoulder—"storage closet with a spaniel?"

"Not particularly," she said, crossing her arms over her generous bosom. If she'd been wearing a cloak earlier, she had shed it, and now she wore a simple white muslin dress. It was modestly cut, but it couldn't quite hide her lush figure.

"Not even a cursory explanation? After all, I've been riding all day. I think after all the trouble I went to find you, I deserve that much."

"Oh, you do, do you? Perhaps no one has ever explained to you that when someone runs away, they generally do not want to be found. So forgive me if I do not thank you for doing precisely what I did not want."

Ah, yes. This was the Emmeline his aunt complained about, the one full of fire whom Stratford saw all too rarely. The dog licked his chin and Stratford wrinkled his nose. "And to think I always said you were no trouble."

"I am no trouble because, as usual, I am not your concern." She started away from him, crossing the room of the public house, and stepping outside. Stratford followed.

"What are you doing?"

"Continuing my journey," she said, looking this way then that for a groom.

"Oh, no you are not. You are coming back to Odham Abbey with me."

She shot him a look that said over-your-dead-body, and Stratford hoped she did not possess any weapons else his life might actually be in danger. At that moment, the groom reappeared leading a horse, and Emmeline walked right up to him. "Thank you," she said. "I will take this animal."

Stratford could not blame the man when his mouth dropped open in shock. He had known Emmeline was a force to be reckoned with. He had seen her take on her mother and more than one suitor, but she was clearly in a mood now, and pity the man or woman who stood in her way.

And that man was obviously him. "Wait a moment!"

The groom, hand half-extended to give over the reins, paused.

"The lady and I need a word. If you'll excuse us."

"We do not need a word," she said.

"We do," he said. He looked down at the dog in his arms then over at the groom.

"I'll take her, sir," the groom said. "She's a real beauty."

Stratford handed the dog to the groom who immediately crooned to the spaniel and brought her over to a patch of grass where the dog seemed relieved to be able to…well, relieve herself. Aware the groom was still nearby, Stratford lowered his voice. "Listen, Emmeline—"

She sighed. "This is the part where you tell me I cannot take this horse and I must come back with you and what will people say and think and so on."

"Exactly." There. She could be reasonable.

"And what I will say to you, Stratford Fortescue, is I no longer care. I am not returning. Not with you. Not with anyone."

"Emmeline, be reasonable," he said, hoping that he could will her into behaving logically.

"*Stratford,* I am being reasonable. This is how a reasonable person behaves when she has been pushed to the brink of sanity and made to attend event after event whereupon she is maligned and insulted and ignored. What I might argue is that it is *not* reasonable for that person to keep attending said events."

Stratford could see her point, though her logic was twisted. "Then have that conversation with your mother."

"Don't you think I have? She will not listen. And of course, neither will you. You are not my brother. Our families are friendly, but you have no authority over me."

"And yet I feel as though I have an obligation to be certain you come to no harm." That was part of the reason he had come after her. The other part was the rare chance to spend time alone with her. They might have known each other for years but he could count on one hand the number of times they had ever shared a private word. "Don't be difficult."

That was the wrong thing to say. He saw it in the way her eyes immediately narrowed.

"Difficult, am I? Wanting my freedom makes me *difficult?*"

"Emmeline, I thought we were friends." He would explain and appeal to her reason. "There's no reason for all this trouble."

"Do you know why I was never any trouble when you escorted me about Town?"

Stratford did not like the look in her eyes.

"Because I felt sorry for you."

"Don't be ridiculous." Hot anger flooded through him. *She* felt sorry for him? The perpetual wallflower, the spinster of three and twenty, the woman who couldn't secure a beau if she tried, felt sorry for *him*?

"I did. Because you did not want to be there any more than I. And you were as pathetic as I because we both did whatever we were told and dutifully followed the rules. Well, sir, I am done following the rules." She made a move toward the horse, and Stratford grabbed her arm.

"Oh, no you don't." She gave his hand on her arm the most disdainful look he had ever seen. He could almost feel the heat of her loathing. "You are clearly distraught." That seemed to be putting it mildly. "Therefore, I will ignore your insults. But I draw the line at allowing you to take that horse and ride away."

She stepped closer to him, so close he could smell the lemon scent he always associated with her. Her eyes were so brilliantly blue that he almost needed to squint. "Oh, yes, I am."

She snatched her arm from his grip and made an unsuccessful attempt to put a foot in the horse's stirrup. The horse shied away.

"And just where will you go?" Stratford asked, clasping his hands behind his back to resist the urge to shake her until she listened. "It will be dark soon."

She didn't look at him, but her shoulders stiffened.

Ah, he had hit a chink. Now to exploit it. "Do you have blunt to pay for a room at an inn? Not that any inn will accept you. A lone female? Any decent inn will assume you are a fallen woman and not want you under their roof."

She still did not turn to face him, but he could almost hear her thinking.

"I'll stay here then."

Time to wrench a crowbar into that chink and open it wide. "This is not an inn. There are no rooms to let, and if you haven't coin to pay for food and drink, the proprietor will not let you stay."

"We'll see about that," she said, and Stratford had no trouble believing she would bend the proprietor to her will. His strategy teetered on failure.

"Emmeline," Stratford began. She glared at him over her shoulder. "Miss Wellesley," he said sharply. "Clearly this is not a decision to make without more consideration and discussion."

She rolled her eyes.

He ignored her. "I propose we inquire as to the location of the nearest inn, stop there for the night, and discuss this further in the morning, when we are both feeling refreshed and clear headed."

"I won't change my mind," she said.

But she already had. When he'd arrived, she wanted to escape him as soon as possible. Now she was tacitly agreeing to go with him. "Of course not, but at least you will be rested and fed. Wait here while I secure another mount and inquire about the inn."

He started toward the groom then realized he didn't trust her not to mount his horse and ride off while his back was turned. He took the horse's reins and brought the animal with him.

The groom was more than happy to give him the location of a good inn, which was not the nearest but was close enough to reach before full dark. But before he went to saddle another horse, he gave the dog he'd been playing with a baleful look. "What will you do with the dog, sir?"

Stratford stared at the spaniel. He hadn't considered the dog in his plans. But, of course, if this was Emmeline's dog, they must take her with them. "She can ride with me," he said.

The groom nodded and gave the dog one last affectionate pat on the head. Stratford made his way back to Emmeline and informed her of his plans.

"That's not my dog," she said.

Stratford frowned. "I assumed she was yours since you were trapped in the broom closet with her."

Emmeline's cheeks colored and she looked down. Now this was an interesting development. He had rarely if ever seen Emmeline blush. "It's a long story. She was—er, foisted upon me."

"Then you don't want the dog?"

The groom was leading another horse toward them and gasped. Emmeline gave him a look from the corner of her eye. "I did not say that. I can't leave her to fend for herself."

"Oh, miss!" the groom began. "If the dog isn't yours, might I have her? She's a beautiful dog, and she'll be well cared for. I had one just like her when I was a boy, but she died a few years ago of old age."

Emmeline looked at Stratford who shrugged. Then she cleared her throat. "Will you promise to take good care of her?"

"Yes, miss!"

"You will feed her and exercise her and all the other things one must do for a dog?"

"Yes, miss!"

Emmeline gave the groom one last long look. The man straightened his shoulders. He must be ten years her senior, but she was undeniably in charge. "Then you may have her." She bent, took the dog into her arms, and handed the spaniel to the groom.

Stratford closed his eyes and rubbed the bridge of his nose. This was why Emmeline was still unmarried. She was impossibly dictatorial, though she had a regal way of going about it. Still, no man wanted to be treated like a subject to the queen, and most men were no match for her. He'd watched her at countless societal gatherings over the years. She could dismiss a man with a single look. The braver men abandoned her when they realized she had a mind of her own and was not afraid to express it. As he mounted his horse and steered the animal in the direction of the inn, Emmeline right behind him, Stratford noted that she was unlikely to marry any time soon, if ever.

Why that thought should please him was a mystery better left unexplored.

\*\*\*

*Duncan*

Duncan rose early, as usual. He hadn't been able to accustom himself to the hours the English kept in Town. Highlanders were always up with the sun as were soldiers, and he was both. He'd slept hard and heavy, a dreamless sleep that left him feeling refreshed this morning. And yet as he made his way down to the public room, where a gray-haired woman hummed to herself as she dusted chairs and wiped down tables, Duncan couldn't stop himself from looking just a little too long in the direction of the door leading to Beatriz's chamber.

Though they did not speak the same language, he couldn't help feeling she had wanted more than a curt *good night* the evening before. The way she'd looked up at him with those dark, brown eyes made him want to kiss her full lips. But he was probably imagining things. He'd just spent weeks in London, trying his damnedest to catch the interest of just one lady, *any* lady, and he'd failed spectacularly.

Though he wouldn't admit it publicly, his pride was bruised. He didn't need to damage it further by soliciting rejection from a woman who had no choice but to stay with him.

There were lasses in Scotland who would be more than happy to catch his interest. They would not call him a barbarian or back away when he walked into a room as though he were some sort of murderer after their blood.

Duncan sat at a table by the window and looked out upon the cobbled street running through the center of the small village. In some ways, it reminded him of home. He too had grown up in a small, simple town, where he knew everyone and where life was simpler. But he was the younger son of the brother of the laird. He'd tried his hand at farming, then at raising sheep, then at several other professions. Nothing seemed to fit him. Nothing seemed to quell the roaring in his mind and his soul that had begun when he'd gotten his father killed all those years ago. No, the only time the pain and agony of that loss subsided was when Duncan used his fists.

And so his mother had suggested—insisted more than suggested, really—that he join the army. And what Lady Charlotte wanted, she got. But Duncan hadn't fought her on it. Like most Highlanders, Duncan had no love of the redcoats, but when he'd been given the opportunity to fight the French on the Continent, he had gone. And then when he'd been approached by Lieutenant-Colonel Draven after a bloody battle and asked to join his suicide troop, Duncan hadn't understood why he'd been selected.

Colonel Draven had merely cocked his head and said, "I need men who are not afraid to die."

Duncan had snorted. "Everra man is afraid to die."

Draven had nodded. "Some more than others. I just watched you, on foot, take down three mounted officers armed with bayonets."

"I lost my horse," Duncan said, "or it would have been more."

Draven had leaned forward then, his blue eyes boring into Duncan. "Your commanding officer calls you the Lunatic. I can't say as though I dispute his assessment. Answer me this, Lunatic. Are *you* afraid to die, Mr. Murray?"

Duncan had shrugged. "Nae verra."

"Good. Then you're one of mine now."

But Duncan hadn't died, though he'd been sent on missions that had killed others in the troop, and he'd done things that should have resulted in his death. It seemed the French forgot to fire if a man ran toward them with his face painted red and screaming like a banshee. Perhaps the soldiers who went into battle calmly were the real lunatics.

Duncan stiffened as he became aware of someone moving behind him. For a moment, he thought it might be the woman come to offer him refreshment, but the steps were too heavy. A familiar voice spoke, "Old habits die hard, soldier."

Duncan smiled. "One of these days I'll sleep past six." He turned just as Stratford Fortescue slapped him on the shoulder and took the seat across from him. The two had served together in Draven's troop and had lately spent several weeks causing trouble in London. Duncan was glad to see his friend. "I thought I'd finally rid myself of ye when ye left London."

"And I thought you'd be on your way back to Scotland by now. What are you doing in—where the devil are we?"

"How should I ken? This isnae Scotland. I plan tae be back on my way home after a wee detour tae see Nash."

Stratford sat back in his chair. "His estate isn't far from here, is it? Now, that's an idea."

"I can see by the narrowing of yer eyes, ye have a plan swirling aboot in that brain of yers. Leave me oot of it. I have a lass I need taken back tae London, but she doesnae speak English. I need Nash tae translate."

Stratford set the legs of his chair on the floor. "I have so many questions that I'm not sure where to begin."

Duncan waved a hand. "Then dinnae. She speaks Portuguese and so does Nash."

"Do I want to know how it is you ended up with a Portuguese woman in the middle of the English countryside?"

"I'm still wondering that myself. What are ye doing here?"

Stratford covered his eyes with his hands, a gesture Duncan had only seen him make on a few occasions when he had to plan a particularly difficult sortie against the enemy. "It's one of the Wellesley sisters."

"Yer almost cousins, the ones ye've been squiring aboot the last few weeks?"

"Yes. Emmeline Wellesley ran away."

"Which one is she? Nae the mannish one?"

Stratford stiffened and lowered his hands. "She's not mannish."

"I dinnae mean in appearance. I willnae argue that she has a fine pair of—"

"Eyes?" Stratford said coldly.

"Those too. But any man who spends three minutes in her company kens that she has her own mind and wants her own way."

"Yes, well, apparently she has decided she's attended her last ball and has run off to God knows where. I need paper and pen to let the baron, and through him her mother, know I have her and will return her today."

"Ye think she will go so easy?"

"I think I'll have to drag her kicking and screaming."

The woman who had been cleaning the tables approached with a basket of warm buns and asked if they'd like tea or coffee. Duncan would have preferred whisky, but he settled for tea. He and Stratford were on their third cup of tea and their fourth basket of bread when Beatriz made her way down the stairs. Duncan hadn't exactly been looking for her, but she caught his attention as soon as she stepped onto the landing. She wore the same yellow-and-white striped dress as she had the day before, and her hair was secured in a simple tail down her back. Her coffee-colored eyes swept the room, and he felt his throat go dry when her gaze landed on him.

Duncan didn't make a sound, but he must have done something because Stratford turned in his chair and looked at her. "Is that your problem?"

"Aye." Duncan stood, grabbed a chair from a nearby table and gestured for her to come over. She did, her cheeks pink when she looked up at him. She looked far too pretty with those pink cheeks and her simple yellow gown in the morning sunshine. Duncan made the introductions and pushed the breadbasket and pot of tea toward her. Stratford tried the two or three Portuguese phrases he knew, but her answers were unintelligible to both men.

"I need Nash," Duncan said. "I have nae idea what she's saying. Her family is probably worried aboot her."

"Perhaps she'd like to write them a letter," Stratford suggested. "You can send the letter when you see Nash and either take her back yourself or send her back in a mail coach."

"Good idea," Duncan said then sat straight. "Dinnae look now, but yer cousin is on her way over."

"I'll just go fetch the paper," Stratford said, rising.

"Ye would leave me here undefended?"

"It appears I would." Stratford rose and was gone. A moment later Duncan rose and offered his chair to Miss Wellesley.

"I trust ye remember me, Miss Wellesley," he said.

"You are hard to forget, Mr. Murray." She gave him an odd look when he introduced Beatriz, and then she did something even stranger—though nothing Emmeline Wellesley did could really surprise anyone.

"Would you leave us alone for a moment, Mr. Murray?"

Duncan cocked his head. "Leave ye alone with Beatriz?"

"That's what I said."

"But why? The lass doesnae speak any English."

Miss Wellesley just stared at him, and finally Duncan sighed, stood again, and went to find Stratford. Apparently, it wasn't just Portuguese women he couldn't understand.

# Four

*Emmeline*

"Do you want to tell me why you are pretending not to speak any English, Miss Neves?" Emmeline asked.

Miss Neves lifted her teacup and took a long sip. "Thank you for not saying anything, Miss Wellesley," she finally said. "The moment I saw you, I thought my ruse was at an end."

Emmeline could understand why. Miss Neves was well-known among the ladies of the upper classes. Emmeline, along with every other fashionable lady, had patronized the lace shop Miss Neves's sister owned in Town. Catarina lace was à la mode this Season.

Emmeline put a hand on the lacemaker's arm. "I assumed you had your reasons. Has Mr. Murray abducted you? Is he holding you against your wishes?"

The lacemaker gave her a wistful smile. "Nothing like that, unfortunately."

Emmeline sat back. "Unfortunately? Do you *want* to be abducted?"

"Some days I think so." Miss Neves turned toward the window, watching the scattering of townspeople walking past the brown stone houses and shops. "It seems vastly more romantic than working with thread and bobbins all day."

Emmeline could understand that. Though the creations the lacemakers crafted were beautiful and exquisite, the work was undoubtedly monotonous at times. As someone who had embarked on her own adventure just yesterday, Emmeline was in no position to judge anyone else. Still… "But surely you don't want Mr. Murray to abduct you. He'd take you back to Scotland with him."

"I hear Scotland is quite beautiful. And who would not want Duncan Murray to sweep her away?"

Emmeline smiled. "He's a bit wild for my taste, but I can see you like that sort of thing. He might be big and brawny, but he's no fool. He will find out who you are sooner or later."

"And then he will take me back to my sister as quickly as possible."

Emmeline stared out the window as a mother led her daughter by the hand along the other side of the street. "Perhaps I can help you."

Miss Neves gave her a sharp look. "You would do that, Miss Wellesley?"

"Who am I to stand in the way of romance?"

The lacemaker laughed. "I would not say it is a romance. Yet. Oh, but forgive me. I did not realize you had married. I should wish you happy."

Emmeline shook her head violently. "I haven't married." The idea was ridiculous. "Mr. Fortescue is not my husband. He's my—well, it's difficult to explain, actually. He's a distant cousin, I suppose. Our mothers are close friends."

"Oh, I see." But Miss Neves wrinkled her delicate brow. She was such a small, slender thing that Emmeline felt like a giant beside her. "I thought because you were traveling together, you must be…"

"We're not traveling together," Emmeline said. "I am running away, and he wants to send me back."

"Why are you running away?"

"I suppose because this is my fifth Season, and I don't see the point anymore. No man will want to marry me. Not any man I want to marry, at any rate. And the more years I have spent at balls and dinners and soirees, the more I realize that I am wasting my life hoping for some man I don't even know to notice me. What do I care if some man notices me?

Why can't I do as I please and hang what any man says or thinks." Why should she ever marry and give a man control over her? She'd had enough of being controlled for twenty-three years.

"Oh, you are wildly inappropriate," Miss Neves said. She grinned. "I like it."

Emmeline laughed. "Thank you, Miss Neves."

"You should call me, Ines, *sim*? May I call you by your given name?"

"It's Emmeline, and of course. If we're to be friends, it seems only fitting. Now, how can I help you?"

Ines thought on this for several minutes. "I am not certain. Mr. Murray plans to take me to see his friend who speaks Portuguese. The man lives on an estate not far from here."

"Then I will travel with you and assist if I can."

"Will Mr. Fortescue agree to that?"

Emmeline shrugged. "I don't see as he has much choice unless he plans to abduct me." Both women laughed then went instantly silent when Stratford approached. He looked far too handsome this morning. His rumpled hair and sleepy eyes made her belly flutter.

He gave them wary looks. "Why do I have the sense that you are laughing at me?"

Determined to make that fluttering stop, Emmeline struck hard enough to push him away. "Because, like all men, you are vain and self-centered and believe everything is about you. Do you know where Mr. Murray is taking this young woman?" She gestured to Ines.

Stratford's gaze cut to the lacemaker, which was preferable to him looking at her. Finally, the butterflies in her belly subsided.

"Our friend Nash Pope lives on an estate not far from here," Stratford said. "Nash spent time in Portugal during the war. He should be able to communicate with the lady."

"And does this Mr. Pope live with his family? His mother? Sisters?"

Stratford ran a hand over his blond hair, trying to smooth it down. It had a habit of always sticking up, which she hated to admit she found rather endearing.

"I can't say. I've only been there once, and that didn't go well."

"What do you mean?"

Stratford gave her a long look, seeming to consider what to reveal to her. Mr. Murray, who must have been watching from across the room, took this as his invitation to return. "Did ye have yer private chat with Miss Beatriz?"

Emmeline fixed her gaze on the Scotsman. "We did."

"And how did ye manage that? Do ye speak Portuguese?"

"I do not, sir, but much can be said without words."

His brow furrowed. "If ye say so."

"I'm given to understand you are taking her to the estate of a Mr. Pope."

The Scotsman narrowed his eyes. "How'd the lass tell ye that?"

"She didn't so much tell me as I put two and two together. I was just asking my dear cousin here whether there is an appropriate chaperone at this estate."

"I dinnae need a chaperone. I'm nae going tae touch the lass."

Ines made a sound of disappointment. Emmeline ignored her. "A statement like that might be good enough in the Highlands, but it will not suffice in England."

Murray turned to Stratford. "Are ye listening tae this? Tell yer cousin I can be trusted."

Stratford gave his friend a pained expression.

"Och, no. Yer not on her side?"

"It's not about you. It's about the appearance of things, and you know Nash as well as I do. He's most likely alone on that estate but for a servant or two."

"Alone?" Emmeline said.

Stratford shrugged. "He was wounded in the war and lost most of the vision in his right eye and all of it in his left."

"Oh, I'm sorry to hear that," Emmeline said. Her stomach dropped at that news. So many men had been wounded in the war. How awful to have to live with an injury like that for the rest of one's life. "But if he's all but blind, how can he live so alone?"

"He's driven everraone away," Murray said. "Nash was a sharpshooter during the war, and he dinnae take it well when he lost his sight. A few of us went tae visit him once, and he ran us off with a rifle."

"But I thought he could hardly see."

"Exactly," Stratford said. "That's why we ran."

Emmeline looked at Ines, who was listening intently. As soon as Emmeline caught her eye, she looked down and pretended to be engrossed in her own thoughts. Oh, it would not be long at all before Duncan Murray discovered the truth. "And this is where you think to take Miss Beatriz? Is it even safe?"

"That was months ago," Murray said. "Besides, I've never ken Nash tae refuse a friend in need." But he didn't say it with much conviction.

"I see." Emmeline straightened her shoulders. "I will come with you. In my opinion, that's the only way to ensure this lady's reputation is not harmed."

"What?" Stratford roared. "Absolutely not. Out of the question."

Emmeline ignored him. "I find I have little in the way of luggage at the moment, so I am ready to leave when you are, Mr. Murray."

Stratford stepped in front of her. "Wait a minute, Emmeline. I haven't agreed to this."

"You needn't accompany us."

"You know I must accompany you. I wrote to your mother last night and said I would return you today."

Emmeline shrugged. "I suppose you had better write again. This time I suggest you tell my mother that I will not be coming home until after the Season." She moved around him, and Ines stood and linked her arm with Emmeline's.

"Be reasonable, Emmeline. You cannot run off with Murray."

"Listen tae yer cousin, lass."

Both Stratford and Emmeline turned on Murray. "Stay out of this."

Emmeline turned back to Stratford and held up a finger. "One, I am not running away with Mr. Murray. I am accompanying Miss Beatriz. Two, I *am* being reasonable. What is unreasonable is wasting everyone's time and money by forcing me to be in London for the Season. I'll save everyone a good deal of trouble if I stay with my grandmother."

"And how will you reach your grandmother with no money, no coach, not even a change of clothing?"

"That's not your concern."

Stratford shook his head. "You are the most aggravating female I have ever met," he muttered under his breath. But he seemed to notice, as she had, they'd attracted the attention of everyone at the inn. "We'll talk about this outside."

"I have nothing more to say." She turned on her heel and marched out of the inn with Ines right beside her. Once outside, the two of them dissolved into giggles.

"I do not know why you laugh," Ines said. "He is very furious."

"He's always furious when a plan of his doesn't work out. What he will soon understand is I am not one of his plans."

"That may be, but you realize he will be accompanying you to the home of Mr. Pope. He will not allow you to go without him."

"I'll make the best of it," she said. Ines laughed. "Why are you laughing now?" Emmeline asked.

"Because you knew all along he would never let you go alone. You *want* him to come."

"No, I don't. I couldn't care less what he does or where he goes."

"I see. That is too bad."

Emmeline would not further the conversation by asking what Ines meant. At least she tried not to ask. Finally, she gave in. "Why is it too bad?"

"Because he obviously has the feelings for you."

Now Emmeline rolled her eyes. But the fluttering in her belly began again. "Ines, I know you fancy yourself half in love, but that doesn't mean the rest of the world is as well."

"I do not know if he is in love with you, but there is no doubt he finds you attractive. The entire time we were talking, he could not keep his eyes off you."

"He was undoubtedly trying to figure out what we were saying. Either that or plotting how to take me home in the most efficient manner."

"I do not think so. His expression was not that of a man scheming."

Emmeline looked at Ines. She was barely a woman and quite obviously in love with love. Nothing she said should be given any weight. But Emmeline couldn't stop from asking, "What was his expression, then?"

"A man who likes what he sees and is trying to puzzle out exactly what to do about that."

Emmeline was spared from making any sort of comment when the men exited the inn a moment later. Stratford declared he would be accompanying her to the Pope estate, and Emmeline tried not to feel a burst of happiness. But just because Ines had been right that she wanted him to accompany her today did not mean she was right that he had feelings for her.

And even if he did, so what? It was not as though Emmeline had feelings for Stratford. Did she? Was that why her belly fluttered when he was near?

No. They were friends, nothing more. Why, she could remember when he had been but a boy of eleven or twelve, all gangly arms and long legs. He would come home from playing with his older brothers, his shoes and trousers covered with mud. Emmeline remembered looking at him and feeling jealous that he had such freedom, while she'd had to sit in the drawing room and sew tiny, straight stitches in an old piece of cloth. It hadn't been Stratford's fault he was a male and she a female, but that accident of fate didn't stop her from sticking her tongue out at him when no one was looking. And it didn't stop him from pulling her hair when she walked past him on the way to dinner.

Of course, she'd noticed when he'd grown up. It seemed he went away to school one autumn and when she saw him the next summer, he was all but a man. She'd actually been shy around him at first because he'd become a handsome man, with that thick blond hair and those intelligent blue eyes half-hidden under his thick honey-colored lashes. But then he'd pulled her hair when she walked into dinner, and she'd known he hadn't changed a bit.

If Ines noticed him looking at her, it was probably because he was trying to find some fault with her or plan when he could pull her hair again. She'd caught him watching her at times when he escorted her to an event during the Season. Once she'd asked him what he found so interesting, as she mostly stood against the wall and waited to go home, and he'd said he was ensuring no scoundrels tried to lure her onto the dance floor.

She'd laughed and told him that most rakes were the sort of men who reached for the low-hanging fruit of widows and courtesans. He'd looked shocked at her response, but he hadn't argued. The next time she'd caught him watching her, she'd stuck out her tongue at him. They were friends. That was all.

Mr. Murray's coachman finally brought the vehicle to the front of the inn, and Murray offered his hand to Ines, who took it and climbed inside. Stratford then offered his hand to Emmeline. But she lifted her skirts, climbed in on her own, then stuck out her tongue at him. Smiling, she sat next to Ines. When Stratford entered and sat opposite her, she expected him to give her an annoyed look. Instead, something in his eyes made her collar feel too tight and her belly flutter. She quickly looked away, out the windows of the coach, as the conveyance made its way through picturesque town and then sped away.

\*\*\*

*Ines*

About a quarter hour into the journey, Ines realized it was more difficult than she'd anticipated to pretend she did not understand English. Miss Wellesley or one of the gentlemen often said something she was tempted to comment about. More than once, Miss Wellesley gave her a pointed look when Ines was paying too much attention to the conversation. She knew how one behaved when one did not know the language. She hadn't known Spanish when her sister had first taken her to Barcelona. When one didn't understand what was being said all around, it was easy to ignore the conversation and focus on one's surroundings. But now she was having difficulty ignoring what was said. One method that seemed to work was to watch Mr. Murray speak and notice how his lips moved or his amber-colored eyes crinkled when he laughed.

But she'd obviously stared at him too long because he gave her a questioning look, and she was forced to go back to staring out the window again. Though Ines had been disappointed the Scotsman hadn't tried to take advantage of her the night before, she realized it was probably for the best. Benedict would kill Murray if he ever found out, and Ines didn't want that blood on her hands. But Draven would probably only lecture Murray if he *kissed* Ines. Surely, she was worth a lecture.

The Scotsman caught her looking at him again, but this time he nodded out the window. "If ye look before we start down this rise, ye can see Wentmore below."

Ines waited until Mr. Fortescue and Miss Wellesley looked out the window, then followed their example. She winced a bit at what she saw. Wentmore had probably once been a lovely manor house. It was still lovely, though the stone of the front face was three-fourths obscured by the overgrown ivy that seemed to have wrapped itself around the house in a choking embrace. The front lawns were also poorly maintained. The grass was yellow, and the hedges and topiary were overgrown. Along one side, she caught a dark stain on the stone. She almost forgot herself and asked about it, but Miss Wellesley asked first. "What is that mark on the side of the stone? It looks like a burn."

"I think you're right," Fortescue said. "There might have been a fire." He looked at Murray. "I hope we can go inside to see how bad the damage is and if Nash needs assistance."

Murray snorted. "He wouldnae take it even if we offered."

"Then maybe we don't give him the chance to refuse. I have a plan."

Murray sighed. "Of course, ye do."

He spoke low so only Murray could hear. Ines exchanged a look with Miss Wellesley, who seemed annoyed to be left out of the conversation. A few moments later, the coach slowed, and Mr. Fortescue opened the door and jumped out. No one emerged from the house to greet them and after Murray exited the coach, the coachman called down, "Are you sure this is where you wanted to go?"

"This is Wentmore," Murray said. Then he looked back at the women. "Stay here while we go inside and do a wee bit of reconnaissance." He started away.

Emmeline turned to Ines. "This looks worse than I imagined."

"It doesn't appear anyone lives here," Ines murmured.

"Or if someone does, he does not welcome visitors."

Just then a crash echoed from inside the house, and the women exchanged worried looks. The crash was followed by the sound of raised male voices. Then the door banged open and Murray flew out. When he turned to look at the coach, blood ran down the side of his cheek.

"*Caramba*!" Ines said. She jumped out of the coach, but Murray had already gained his feet and was running back into the house. The door closed behind him. Miss Wellesley joined Ines on the weed-filled drive, and they listened to more shouts and then the sound of a rifle or pistol firing.

"I've had enough of this," the coachman said. He jumped from the box, untied the trunk and various boxes strapped to the back of the coach, and dumped them on the ground.

"You can't leave us here," Emmeline argued.

"Oh, yes, I can. I agreed to drive the man to Scotland. I didn't agree to this." He jumped back on the box, called to the horses, and drove away before the women could say another word.

Ines watched the coach disappear around a bend in the road. "I don't know whether to be terrified or thrilled."

"I feel a bit of both. Should we go inside and tell them?"

Another crash made both women jump. "Perhaps not quite yet," Ines said.

The door burst open again, and this time Murray fell out. He clutched his arm, blood seeping through his hand. Ines gasped, and he held up the bloody hand. "Dinnae fash, lass. It's a scratch." Then he winced and sank to his knees. Ines ran to him and put her arm around him to steady him.

"Is it your arm?" she asked, though she already knew. Her head was spinning and panic seeped in.

"Aye."

"What happened?"

"The bastard shot me."

Ines gasped then stared at him in stunned silence. Emmeline was not so passive. She looked at Ines and Murray then seemed to make a decision. She straightened her shoulders and stomped past them. "This has gone on long enough."

"Dinnae go in there, lass!" Murray called. But she ignored him and opened the door then closed it after her. Murray looked at Ines, who suddenly realized she had no idea what to do next. She'd never seen a pistol ball wound before.

She had no idea how to treat it or help Murray. She just knew she could not allow him to die. He stared down at her for another moment, and she became increasingly aware of the warmth of his body and that her arms were wrapped around it. She should let go, but she needed to steady him. Or perhaps she needed him to steady her.

"Did that scratch on my heid damage my brain, or did ye speak tae me in English?"

Ines opened her mouth, but it was too late. As Catarina always said, Ines's face was an open book, and Murray had read the writing there.

"So ye *do* speak English."

"I—" But what excuse could she give?

He held up a finger, cutting off her stuttering reply. "We'll talk aboot it later. Right now, I need tae fall over." And he did, taking her with him.

He landed on top of her, pinning her to the drive. It had once been a gravel drive, but she was thankful for the overgrown weeds to cushion her. Still, she could feel jagged pieces of gravel cutting into her back.

And yet, Ines didn't mind the weight of him. He was warm and solid, and he smelled woodsy and clean. There was no trace of the scent of cologne so many men in London wore. Mr. Podmore had favored a strong fragrance with a cloying sweet scent, and it had made Ines want to gag when she was in a closed room with him for too long. Conversely, now she had to resist the urge to bury her nose in Mr. Murray's chest. Except she really couldn't breathe with his weight pressing into her. She gave him a push, then a harder one, and she managed to free her torso from beneath him. Then after much tugging of her dress and her body, she freed her legs and finally her feet. She had to pause to catch her breath.

One look down told her this was a mistake. Her dress was soaked with blood, the material was dusty and dirty, and she could see pieces of her hair fluttering over her forehead. She blew them out of her eyes. The blood was not a good sign. She could see the crimson coloring the drive beneath Murray. She was no nurse, but she knew the bleeding must be stopped.

Ines pushed the Scot's good arm, trying to heave him onto his back. But he was heavy and large, and he didn't move. She adjusted her position, and with a grunt, pushed again. She raised his body just enough that she could wedge her shoulder underneath and push him higher and then onto his back. Panting heavily and wiping perspiration from her brow, Ines decided she would never manage to free him of his coat on her own. Instead, she took a breath then lifted the hem of her dress and ripped a good portion of her petticoat. She quickly bound the Scot's wound over his sleeve and tied another piece tightly around the arm of his coat to staunch the bleeding. Once inside—if they were ever allowed inside—they could remove his coat and clean the wound and see it clearly. She had no medical experience, but surely a surgeon must live nearby.

Resisting the urge to fall back and close her eyes for a moment, she instead looked up at the house, listening. All was finally quiet. That was either a good sign or a very ominous one. Ines ripped another section of petticoat and wiped Murray's face. The wound on his temple looked as though it came from a sharp object. She dabbed at it, determined it was not serious, then tried to clean the blood from his cheek. She had almost removed it all when his hand came up and caught her wrist. She screeched in surprise, and he shushed her.

"Dinnae fash, lass."

"I will fash!" Whatever that meant. "You scared me." And not just by grasping her when she'd thought him unconscious. All that lost blood terrified her. What if he died? He'd used his good arm to take hold of her wrist, and it comforted her that he was still so strong. No one this strong would die, *não*? He would live, *sim*?

"Help me up, lass," he said. "I have tae go back in."

The man was certifiably mad. What was it the English said? Daft? He was daft. "You need to lie down," she said. "You are bleeding, *senhor*."

"I told ye, it's a trifle."

"It is more than trifle if you fall over. Now stay here and be still until Mr. Fortescue and Miss Wellesley come out. They will either have tamed your so-called friend or you will need your strength to run." She could imagine the wild Mr. Pope bursting through the door any moment and firing at her with his rifle.

Murray let out a surprised laugh. "I willnae run. Nash needs a wee dose of convincing. That's all."

"From the sound of it, he needs a whole barrel of convincing." She cocked her head again. "Things have gone silent since Miss Wellesley went inside. I cannot decide if they are all dead or listening to reason."

He didn't respond, and she looked down at him to find his amber eyes were on her. "Why did ye pretend ye couldnae speak English?"

She should have been prepared for the question. She'd known from the beginning she'd have to answer it at some point. It was just that the shock of seeing him with blood streaming down his face had made her forget her ruse. She'd forgotten, too, how nervous he made her. All of a sudden, her belly began to flutter, and she felt her cheeks grow warm.

His brows came together in concern. "I'm not angry with ye, lass. I'm after an explanation."

That was a relief. Not that she would have been afraid if he'd been angry, but it was already difficult enough to speak to him. "I did not want—"

"Speak up, lass. A moment ago, ye were yelling in my ear."

She took a breath and spoke louder. "I did not want you to take me home."

"Why nae? Where's home?"

But she was saved from answering when the door opened again. Ines and Murray both ducked, but it was only Emmeline.

"Mr. Fortescue and I have the matter in hand now. I think you had both better come in. In—I mean, Beatriz, let me help you with him."

Ines was trying to help Murray to his feet. He swayed once but caught himself. He cut her a glance. "Why do I have the suspicion yer name is nae Beatriz?"

"We can discuss it inside," Emmeline said, taking his good arm and lending support. Ines ducked her head carefully under his bad arm and the three of them hobbled toward the house.

As far as Ines was concerned, she would put that conversation off as long as possible. Except she knew it wouldn't be possible much longer. She'd been seen at the inn in that little village and surely Draven was out looking for her by now. If he didn't know she was with Murray, he would know soon, and he'd find her too. Then it would be back to London and Mr. Podmore or some other awful suitor. She'd have to bid her brief taste of freedom goodbye.

She stepped into the house, turning so Mr. Murray could squeeze in after her, and then stared at the wreck around her in horror. The paper curled off the walls, the rug was torn, and the furniture was smashed into pieces. When Emmeline finally moved in through the door, Ines caught her eye. "Are you certain this is safe?" Ines gave the cracked ceiling a worrying look.

"Safe?" Emmeline shook her head. "Most certainly not, but I'll try to keep you alive until dinner."

# *Five*

"Then we're tae eat dinner?" Duncan asked. Stratford, who was in the dining room, pistol pointed at his old friend Nash Pope, rolled his eyes.

"He hasn't changed much," Nash said from the chair where Stratford had finally thrown him. "He always could eat more than the rest of us. Except maybe Ewan."

"We're fortunate he can eat at all, after you shot him."

"It was an accident."

Stratford narrowed his eyes. Nash might be mostly blind, but Stratford was inclined to believe he didn't need his sight to hit a target. "We are in here," he called. Slowly he circled Nash, pistol still at the ready, until he was behind the former sharpshooter and facing the door. The ragged trio that entered immediately alarmed him. Duncan looked fine. He had a bandage wrapped around his arm and blood on his cheek, but Stratford had seen him in far worse condition.

The Portuguese woman, however, was also bloody, her dress was torn—possibly to make the bandages—and she had dirt in her hair and grime streaking her cheek. Emmeline was not much better. She had fewer blood stains, but she was also disheveled.

"Mr. Pope," Stratford said. "Meet my cousin Miss Wellesley. She was the one who ordered you to drop your weapon and sit down."

Emmeline curtseyed. Nash hadn't actually obeyed her, but he'd been so surprised at a female ordering him about that he'd lowered his weapon long enough for Stratford to act. He gestured to the rest of the party. "And this is our new friend Miss Beatriz. You know Duncan, of course."

"Bastard shot me," Duncan complained. Stratford saw him sway and the ladies struggle to hold him upright.

"If you do not mind, Mr. Fortescue, we need somewhere to lie him down." This was from the Portuguese woman and uttered in perfect, if accented, English. Stratford felt his brows rise, but the woman waved a hand. "*Sim*, I speak English. Is there a couch nearby?"

"In the parlor." Nash waved a hand lazily toward the entryway. When he spoke, Stratford could smell the gin emanating from him like a distillery.

"Thank you." Beatriz and Emmeline shuffled back out, Duncan still between them. Stratford looked at Nash, whose head had fallen back, and whose breathing had deepened. If he sat too much longer, he'd probably fall asleep.

Stratford tucked the pistol into his coat and crouched down beside the chair where Nash sprawled, his black hair falling over his scarred left eye. "I don't suppose you have any food in this house?"

"No idea," Nash slurred. "I didn't expect to have guests. You should leave and go find somewhere more hospish— hoshpit—more welcoming."

"And leave you to drown yourself in gin?" Stratford asked. "I don't think so. Besides if Duncan lives, he'll want to kill you with his bare hands for taking a shot at him. Who am I to deny him that pleasure?"

"Flesh wound," Nash muttered. "I could have blown his head off, if I'd wanted."

"Duncan is right," Stratford said. Nash looked up at him in confusion. "You are a bastard."

He marched out of the room, closing the door behind him. Nash was too drunk to go looking for other firearms now that Stratford had taken his pistol and rifle. Still, Stratford wanted to move Duncan to an inn—if there was one close by—as soon as possible. The last thing they needed was Nash popping up with a musket and taking shots at them while they ate whatever food the house might hold. Judging by how thin Nash looked at present, it wasn't much.

Stratford stopped at the door of the parlor and studied the scene. Duncan was seated on the couch and the two ladies were struggling to remove his coat. Stratford would have been jealous if he couldn't see how much the action hurt Duncan. Stratford walked toward them. "Let me hold him up. His clothing is ruined at this point anyway. You might as well look for something to cut it off. That will hurt him less."

"Good idea," Emmeline said. Her words surprised him. He was so used to her arguing with him. More than that, he was unused to anyone connected to his family praising him at all. He was always the one teased or made to feel as though he didn't belong. The teasing was supposed to be all in fun, but Stratford had to grit his teeth and force a smile. Of all his children, the baron had always considered Stratford *the hopeless one*.

Try as he might to ignore the sobriquet, it stung.

Stratford had never understood what was so hopeless about him. He preferred thinking over action, true. And he preferred solitude over company, yes. He was the youngest of his brothers, so he did not have land from their father. A few years ago, Stratford's great-uncle had died, and Stratford had been surprised to learn he had bequeathed a small estate to Stratford. He had a tidy income from it, but the baron had encouraged him to do as most younger sons did and join the army. Stratford hadn't needed to join, but he'd thought that perhaps this one thing would make him worthy in the baron's eyes, would make his mother not look at him with such remorse.

But even coming home from the war a hero hadn't impressed the baron, who'd taken one look at the newly returned Stratford and said, "But when will you do something useful?"

Useful. Stratford supposed the baron meant something like his oldest brother who oversaw the family estate. Or something like his brother Edmond who had invented a new system of irrigation and received dozens of letters from farmers asking about it, and who was currently writing a paper to explain it. Or perhaps something like his eldest sister who had married an earl and borne two children, one of them a boy who would be the next earl. Stratford could go on. Still, he had thought saving England from Napoleon was useful, but apparently not useful enough. And now he had retired from the army, and Stratford was not quite sure what he should do next. He certainly couldn't spend the rest of his life escorting Emmeline and her sisters to balls.

While Stratford took her place and propped Duncan up, Emmeline had gone to the desk and was rummaging through it. "Ah ha!" She lifted a pen knife and started toward them.

Duncan turned his head to look at Stratford. "Don't let the lass stab me. It's bad enough being shot."

"I won't stab you. Now hold still. Miss Beatriz, hold the cloth away from his body while I cut."

Stratford watched her, only half a mind on what she was doing. She seemed capable enough, and he only need concentrate on holding up the big ox of a Scot. Stratford adjusted his grip as Beatriz stripped the shredded coat off Duncan's back. Then Emmeline started on the shirt.

"Christ and all the saints, woman!" Duncan yelled. "Are ye trying tae murder me?"

"Don't be such a baby," Emmeline told him as she removed the shirt. It had been stuck to the wound by the dried blood, and Stratford winced, imagining how much tearing it away had hurt.

"Oh, dear." Beatriz ripped another section of her petticoat and began to staunch the blood that was flowing again. Stratford slowly let Duncan down then straightened.

"Let me take a look at it," he told the women. He put his hand over the petticoat, which was quickly turning scarlet, and when the women had stepped back, he lifted it and examined the wound. A moment later he replaced the bandage and Ines moved back into place.

"Well?" Duncan asked.

"It went in cleanly," Stratford said. "The problem is it didn't come out."

"So it's still in there? Can ye get it oot?"

"I can't see the ball, so no. You'll need a surgeon."

Duncan started to rise, but Ines put a hand on his chest and pushed him back down.

"I dinnae want a sawbones poking at me with his knives."

"Well you don't have a choice," Emmeline told him in her no-nonsense tone. "You can't leave the ball inside. You'll get an infection."

"I'll probably get an infection anyway."

No one argued because it was true. Men had died from lesser wounds. Everyone knew it often wasn't the pistol ball that killed but the fever and infection afterward.

"The sooner I fetch a surgeon, the better," Emmeline said. "Do you think your Mr. Pope will tell me where to go or will I have to guess?"

"*You* go?" Stratford shook his head. "We'll send the coachman to Milcroft."

"There is no coachman," Emmeline told him. "He drove off once the shooting began."

Stratford cursed.

"That was my thought as well," Emmeline said.

Stratford gave her a rueful smile. He had to admire the way she had stayed calm and not panicked. Beatriz looked pale as a sheet and shaky. Her hand on Duncan's chest was trembling, but Emmeline had probably forbidden her from falling apart. "I suppose I will have to go," Stratford said. "If I can't find a horse, I'll walk."

"You can't go," Emmeline argued. "What if your friend decides to start shooting again? You have to stay here and keep them safe." She nodded at Duncan and Beatriz.

"*You* can't go. I'm responsible for you, and I won't have you walking all over the countryside alone." He pointed at Beatriz. "You either."

Beatriz held out a hand. "Then give me the pistol and both of you go. If Mr. Pope so much as steps foot in this room, I will shoot him. I know how to protect myself. "

"How do you know that?" Stratford asked.

"I worked in a shop for many years. One learns to fend off thieves and unscrupulous men." She wiggled her fingers. "Give me the pistol."

Stratford handed it to her. "Just in case," he said. "But you won't need it. Nash is done for today."

She nodded and set the pistol on the floor beside her knees.

"Well, then, shall we see if Nash can tell us if Milcroft houses a surgeon, or shall we choose a direction and start walking?" Emmeline asked.

"I'll go in and ask him," Stratford said, escorting her to the doorway. "You wait in the entry hall." He looked over his shoulder and found Duncan watching him.

"Don't put your dancing shoes on just yet, Lunatic. I'll be back soon."

Duncan smiled. "The devil isnae strong enough tae take me. Nae today."

"Good."

Emmeline gave him a bewildered look as they walked down the hall. "What was that about?"

"It's something we always said during the war, right before we went on a dangerous mission. *Put on your dancing shoes, lads. Time to dance with the devil.*"

"That's macabre."

"That's war. Now go stand over there." Stratford waited until she had moved away then opened the dining room door again. Nash was still sprawled in the chair where Stratford had left him. He did not look up when Stratford entered. Stratford approached and nudged Nash's foot with his boot.

"Wha?" Nash grumbled, eyes still closed.

"Your idiotic behavior necessitates the services of a surgeon. I don't suppose you can direct me to one nearby. Apparently, all the shouting and shooting scared the coachman away, and now I must go on foot."

Nash snored. Stratford kicked him again, harder this time. When Nash looked up at him, blue eye bloodshot, Stratford said, loudly, "Surgeon. Where can I find one?"

"A surgeon? Why do you need a surgeon?"

"Because you shot Duncan, you idiot. Now tell me which direction to walk."

"I shot Duncan?"

"Psst!"

Stratford looked about for the source of the sound.

"Psst!" The servants' door to the dining room was cracked, and he could just make out the sliver of a woman's face peeking through. She waved to him then closed the door. Stratford stood for a moment, wondering if he should follow, then shrugged and went through the door, leaving Nash still mumbling about shooting Duncan.

This was partly Emmeline's fault. She had insisted upon coming with Duncan, against Stratford's advice. Stratford had known it was a bad idea, but would Duncan listen? Of course not. Duncan never listened to reason. He always rushed into everything without thinking of the consequences. He was too impatient to wait for anyone to make a plan. He was hellbent on taking action. Now see where it had gotten him. And, as usual, it was up to Stratford to figure out how to save everyone.

Once through the door, he saw the woman was dressed as a cook, with a white cap on her graying hair and a clean apron over her plain dark blue dress. She bobbed a curtsy. "I'm sorry to call you back here, sir. I didn't want Mr. Pope to hear."

"That was a wise decision, Mrs.—?"

"Brown, sir. Mrs. Brown. I'm the cook here. At least I used to be. I haven't been paid in several months, but I come a few times a week and try to see that Mr. Pope eats."

"That's very good of you, Mrs. Brown. Have you written to the earl to ask for payment?"

She shook her head. "The last time he was here, Lord Beaufort told Mr. Pope he never wanted to see him again."

That was a hard thing for a son to hear from a father. Not that Nash hadn't probably deserved harsh language, but for the father to give up on a son altogether did not speak well of the man.

"I see. And how do you acquire food to prepare?"

"The orders were made in advance and already paid. Of course, that won't last forever, sir."

"No, it won't. What else?" he asked, as he could see the cook had a great deal to tell him.

"It's just the farmers know Mr. Pope isn't himself and give him the poorest selection. That doesn't seem right, when they've already been paid."

"I will speak to the earl when I return to London and see what can be done. In the meantime, there is a young lady and a gentleman in the parlor. Would you be so good as to prepare them something edible? I think soup for the gentleman as he is wounded."

She swallowed. "Were that because of the shooting?"

"Yes." Stratford had precious little coin left, but he pulled two coins from his pocket and gave them to her. "If there is nothing edible in the pantry, then go purchase something. Otherwise, keep it for yourself and your trouble."

She curtseyed again. "Thank you, sir."

"One more question, Mrs. Brown. Where might I find the surgeon? Is there one in Milcroft?"

"Oh, yes. You will want Mr. Langford. He is about three miles to the south, right over the bridge to the village. Just follow the road."

"Thank you." He turned to go back through the door, when Mrs. Brown said, "He wasn't always like this, you know. I knew him when he was a boy, before the war. He was a good lad. Not a bit of temper in him. Always smiling and laughing. Always with a kind word. It was the war that did this to him."

Stratford nodded without looking back. "I know."

The war had done a great harm to many men. Some, like Lord Jasper, bore the visible wounds. Some, like Neil Wraxall, suffered internal anguish. And some, like Nash Pope, suffered both.

Stratford went back through the dining room, past the snoring Nash, and back out into the entryway.

"What took so long?" Emmeline demanded.

"Pope was less than helpful. I did meet his cook, however, and she was good enough to tell me where to find a surgeon. Apparently, the village of Milcroft is about three miles south of here. I remember it vaguely now. The surgeon lives just over the bridge. We're to follow the road, and it will take us straight there."

"Three miles?" Emmeline sighed.

"You needn't accompany me. The cook is preparing dinner."

Her eyes lit at the mention of food. Then she shook her head. "I said I would fetch a surgeon, and I will. I do think it wise for you to remain in case your friend decides to finish Mr. Murray off."

Stratford blew out an exasperated breath. He didn't mind that she tried to order him about as long as she understood he wouldn't follow those orders. "Mr. Pope is sleeping and will remain so for several hours, I suspect. If you're coming, we should leave now. Assuming the terrain is not too difficult, it will take us an hour to walk the three miles, and then, God-willing, the surgeon will have a gig or a dog-cart and drive us back."

She had removed her bonnet, but she put it on again, tying the ribbons under her chin. Then lifting her skirts, she started for the door. Stratford barely reached it in time to open it for her. He made her wait while he moved Duncan's trunks inside the house. Then he joined her, and they walked side by side down the drive.

He had to slow his stride to accommodate her, but not nearly as much as he would have had to with most women. It helped that she wore boots and a sensible dress. But Emmeline was the sort of woman who always walked with a purpose. Some men might say her walk was inelegant or even mannish, but Stratford preferred a lady who knew where she wanted to go and did not wander or dawdle to stare at this flower or that bush.

"It's a pleasant day for a walk," she said once they'd left the drive behind and were on the road, walking along the side, she closest to the fields and he on her right, protecting her from any passing conveyances. "It's not yet too warm, but the sun is out."

"A pleasant enough day, yes. Too bad Duncan had to ruin it by getting himself shot. But then that's the sort of thing one expects from him."

She tilted her head to look up at him. "He is the one you call the Lunatic, yes?"

"Yes. Now you see why."

"I do. Is he completely mad or just very brave?"

"A bit of both, I suppose."

"I see."

They walked in silence for a few minutes. "How did you know the woman with him spoke English?"

"Does she?" Emmeline asked.

Stratford stopped, and Emmeline paused too. "You know she does. She spoke it before we left. But you knew before. You were speaking to her at the inn this morning. How did you know? Duncan said she didn't speak English, and that's why he wanted to see Nash Pope. Though God knows the man probably doesn't remember a word of Portuguese."

Emmeline blew out a breath.

"You might as well tell me. I will find out sooner or later anyway."

"That is one of your more annoying traits. You are always looking for information and asking questions."

"I don't see why that should be considered annoying." He began walking again. "Far more annoying would be a man who has no interest in anything or anybody save himself. Those are the men who never ask questions."

"I cannot argue with you there," she said, probably knowing exactly the type of man he meant. "The truth is I knew she spoke English because I have met her before, in London."

"Where?"

"She works in a shop we ladies frequent, and I have spoken to here there on more than one occasion."

"And her given name is not Beatriz?"

"No, it is Ines Neves."

Ines was not a common name, but Stratford could not help but think he had heard it before. He hadn't met the woman before—at least he didn't think so—but something about her was familiar. Ines. Ines… Perhaps he had seen the lady in passing. He'd had to accompany his sisters often enough when they went shopping. "Which shop employs her?"

Emmeline was looking out over the fields and did not meet his eye. "She is more an owner than an employer."

"She seems rather young for that. Which shop?" he asked again, determined not to be distracted from his question.

She didn't answer, and Stratford paused again and grasped her arm, turning Emmeline to face him. He'd always avoided touching her in the past. He'd learned that if he touched her, he wanted to touch her again. If she took his arm as they entered a ballroom, he'd spend the rest of the evening wanting the night to be over, so he could offer his arm again. Just now he hadn't been thinking and it was too late when he realized what he'd done because he stood before her, touching her, looking into her eyes. Her eyes were so blue and lovely. Her dark hair and dark brows contrasted with the blue and made them stand out that much more. The exercise had made her cheeks pink and she was breathing as one might after a brisk walk, her full lips parted.

Stratford realized he wanted to kiss those lips. It was not the first time he'd realized this, but it was the first time he'd acknowledged the thought instead of stuffing it deep down and burying it before he could see more than a flicker of the idea. But now he was looking at her lips and wondering how they would feel against his. He wondered too what she would feel like under his hands. Those full hips and generous breasts made his hands ache to move over their curves.

"You won't like the answer," she said.

For a moment Stratford thought she knew what he had been contemplating. But then he realized he hadn't asked if he could kiss her. He'd asked which shop the Ines woman was associated with.

"Then you'd better tell me quickly," he said, his voice a bit rougher than he had intended.

Her eyes closed briefly, then opened again to gift him with another glimpse of tranquil waters and clear skies. "She's a lacemaker."

Stratford's eyes narrowed. "A lacemaker." He only knew of one lacemaker. And he only knew of her because all the ladies were wild over Catarina lace. Catarina lace—

named for the designer, Catarina Draven, who was married to his former commander, Lieutenant-Colonel Draven. "Which lacemaker?" he asked calmly.

"The one who makes Catarina lace," she said.

"No," he said.

"Yes."

"No, that would mean she is associated with Colonel Draven, and I am not harboring a fugitive from my former commander."

"I'm sorry to say that is exactly what you are doing, though I hardly think you can be blamed as you had nothing to do with her running away. You are an innocent bystander."

Draven would kill him anyway. "Who exactly is she? Tell me she is not Mrs. Draven's sister."

"She is Mrs. Draven's sister."

"God damn it, Emmeline! I told you not to tell me that!" But he'd known. The moment she had uttered the word *lacemaker* he'd known exactly who she was. He'd heard Draven complain more than once about his mischievous sister-in-law.

"Where are you going? The surgeon is this way," Emmeline said. Stratford had started back the way they'd come. Panic tore through him now, and he couldn't think clearly.

"I can't leave her alone with Duncan. She can't be left alone with a man not her relative." It wouldn't matter if he'd left her alone or not because Draven would kill them all anyway. He was undoubtedly on his way to finish them off at this very minute.

"She's been alone with him for at least a day already. Besides, he's wounded. What can he do to her?"

Plenty, Stratford thought. Plenty. But he had to stop and think. He had to use his brain, which was something he had not been doing enough of else he would have figured out the truth before now. Emmeline was correct in that turning back was not an option. They had to fetch the surgeon if for no other reason than to save Duncan so Draven could kill him.

He turned again. "Very well. We continue on."

After a moment of silent marching, she finally caught up to him. "What is wrong? We will see to Mr. Murray then return Miss Neves to London. She will be back home tomorrow or the next day. No harm done. She's a lacemaker. Her reputation is not in jeopardy."

This was true. Society really only cared about the spotless character of ladies of the upper classes. The other classes were not held to the same standard.

"So you think Colonel Draven is sitting home in London hoping someone brings Miss Neves back? Do you think

Catarina Draven is unconcerned about her sister running away with Duncan Murray?"

"For what it's worth, I do not believe Mr. Murray intended to run away with Miss Neves," Emmeline said.

"Perhaps Draven will listen to that explanation after he kills Murray."

"How can he listen to him if—"

Stratford stopped again. "The point is, Emmeline, Draven will be on his way here by now. It's too late to return her."

"How on earth will he find her here?" She extended her arms to indicate the poorly tended road and the green-stalked wheat, its tips just now turning golden, waving in the breeze.

Stratford shook his head. "He's Colonel Benedict Draven. He was instrumental in defeating Napoleon. He can find a woman in the English countryside."

He began walking again, and Emmeline hurried to follow. "Do you think anyone will come after me?"

He looked at her, but her face was shielded by the brim of the bonnet she wore. But to him the tone of her voice had sounded hopeful. As though she wanted someone to come after her. As though she wanted someone to care.

"*I* came after you," he said.

"I meant, will anyone *else* come?"

And that about summed up their entire acquaintance. As children, he'd played skittles or croquet with her on the lawn, and later he'd hear her tell one of her sisters that no one had played with her all day. Years later, as her chaperone, he had asked her to dance at balls. Yes, it was obligatory, but she was the only one of her sisters he didn't mind dancing with. Once home, her mother would inquire if anyone asked her to dance, and Emmeline would say, "No one."

She obviously didn't see him as anything more than…well, he didn't really know how she saw him. Perhaps she didn't see him at all. "I've written to your mother and kept her informed of events. I'll send another letter as soon as I can, explaining the reason for our delay."

"Your delay, you mean. I told you, I am not returning."

"If you think I will leave you alone on the road to Cumbria, you must be dafter than I thought."

"Because your father sent you, and you hate to disappoint him?"

He stopped, but she continued walking. He reached forward and grasped her arm, spinning her around. "No one sent me. I came on my own."

She looked up at him, and he could see her blue eyes cloud with confusion. "But I thought—"

"And furthermore, I've already disappointed the baron more times than I can count. I'm not worried about disappointing him again. It's inevitable." Stratford only wished he'd known that when he'd been younger as it would have saved him years of grief. "But I do worry about you, Emmeline. I would never forgive myself if something happened to you."

She stared at him for a long moment, and in that moment, he thought the mask of indifference she'd worn to protect herself for so many years dropped away. Her expression was one of longing but also disbelief. She couldn't believe anyone would genuinely care for her.

"Emmeline—"

The quiet was broken by the sound of boys yelling and a dog's high-pitched yelp of pain. Emmeline turned toward the sound, and together they began to run.

# Six

*Duncan*

His arm hurt like the devil had sunk a fang into it and gnawed for hours. Duncan had been shot before. It was an occupational hazard of being a lunatic. One didn't run toward armed soldiers or take on odds like three against one without sustaining some hits. Both times he had been shot before, the pistol ball had only grazed him. One grazed his side and the other his shoulder. A glass of whisky had dulled the pain of those injuries, but Duncan thought it might take a bit more than whisky this time. It didn't hurt to try, though.

"Lass," he said, opening his eyes. He hadn't realized they were closed until he'd tried to look for her and only saw blackness.

"I'm here." She looked down at him, her deep brown eyes staring into his, her soft hand caressing his brow. Where had this beautiful woman been when he'd had those flesh wounds and could have enjoyed these ministrations? "I think you were sleeping," she said.

"I was dreaming of whisky. Do ye see any?"

She looked around, and he wished he hadn't asked. He wanted her eyes to stay on his. "I do not see anything to drink in this room. No doubt your friend has consumed every ounce of spirits within a mile. Shall I see if I can find a kitchen or any servants?"

"No." He reached with his uninjured arm and took her hand in his. "Stay with me, lass."

"I will stay as long as you want, Mr. Murray." She smiled at him, and he hoped he was not dreaming.

"Did ye already explain tae me how it is yer speaking English?"

Her cheeks colored. "I have not, *não*, but I suppose I should confess now that I lied earlier."

"Ye dinnae say." He closed his eyes and found it difficult to open them again.

"I do speak English. And Portuguese and Spanish. I lied because I did not want you to take me back to London. Not right away."

"Yer husband beats ye, does he?"

"No. That is to say, I do not have a husband. I cannot complain of any ill treatment."

Duncan opened his eyes, and she was staring at a point on the far wall. Hearing her speak didn't make the pain go away, but the sweet sound of her made it bearable. She did not have a husband. That pleased him.

"I did not know the carriage I climbed into was yours. I did not know you were leaving London. But when you woke me, and I realized what had happened, I did not want to go back right away."

He closed his eyes again, the lids too heavy to keep open. "Why is that?"

"I suppose I wanted a taste of freedom. I was almost trapped once, and I was beginning to feel trapped again." Her voice lowered to a whisper, and he had to concentrate to hear her. "And if I am really honest, once I realized I was in your carriage, I was hoping for PED."

"I dinnae ken what PED means."

"Passion, excitement, and danger. I hoped to combine all three and steal a kiss."

His eyes opened wide, and she stared down at him. She moved away, trying to pull her hand out of his, but he wouldn't let go. "Ye wanted to kiss me?"

"I thought you had fallen back asleep." She tried to tug her hand away again.

"Do ye always go aboot kissing strange men?"

"We are not strangers," she said, giving up on trying to free her hand. "We have mutual acquaintances."

"Who?" He tried to sit then immediately regretted the action. As soon as Duncan could stand again, he would flatten Pope and then kick him for good measure.

"Benedict Draven."

Duncan did not know what he expected her to say, but it was not to mention his former commander. It made sense, though. He had left the coach outside Draven's home, and that must have been when the lass climbed in. But what had she been doing at Draven's? She was not dressed as a servant. She must be a friend of Mrs. Draven's. That theory fit because they both spoke Portuguese. Except with her shop so busy, he wouldn't have thought Mrs. Draven would have time for friends. Besides, she was always in the company of her younger sister.

"Christ and all the saints!" Draven hissed. Now he did sit, the sharp pain in his arm punctuating his alarm. "I ken who ye are." She winced. Duncan lowered his voice. "Miss Neves, isnae it?"

She nodded.

He released her hand as though he held a viper. "Why am I asking ye for whisky? Ye might as well bring me a knife."

"You cannot possibly cut the ball out of your arm yourself," she said.

"I meant so I can slit my neck."

She gasped.

"It's a far better proposition than waiting for Draven to show up and rip my..." He looked into her face, and her eyes were wide.

Duncan sank back down.

"I am so sorry," she said. "I did not think. I wanted an adventure and a romance—"

"Romance? With me?"

"Why not you?"

"I'm nae poet, lass. The most romantic thing I do is throw a lass over my shoulder before I carry her tae bed."

Her brows went up. "Really?"

Christ, but she actually seemed intrigued by that idea. And he must be delirious from pain because he could imagine tossing her onto his bed and having his way with that mouth of hers.

"Then what do you do to her?"

This woman would be the death of him. Literally. "I read her a bedtime story and tuck her in," he said.

She let out an annoyed breath, clearly wanting more salacious details. Just then they heard footsteps outside the door, and Duncan jumped to his feet. He swayed slightly before he steadied himself and pushed Draven's sister-in-law behind his back.

"Mr. Fortescue said Mr. Pope would not trouble us," she said from behind him.

"Just stay behind me, lass."

The footsteps stopped at the parlor door. Duncan tensed, while behind him he felt the woman fidgeting. "Stand still," he said.

"I am trying to ready the pistol," she said.

"The pistol!" He'd forgotten about that. He turned, found her with it pointed right at him, and snatched it out of her hands. The door opened. He spun around and pointed the weapon at the older woman carrying a tray into the room.

She stopped. "I take it you are not hungry then?"

Duncan lowered the firearm. "Forgive me, missus. I thought ye were someone else."

"Oh, Mr. Pope is quite harmless at the moment. But you, sir, had better sit down. You are injured."

"Good idea." Duncan sank down onto the couch, closing his eyes to make the world stop spinning.

The women were speaking now, both of them fluttering about him, but he couldn't hear what they said above the buzzing in his ears. *Dinnae pass oot,* he told himself.

Suddenly, he felt the cool rim of a glass at his lips. He opened his mouth and sipped. It wasn't whisky, but gin was the next best thing, he supposed. After a few more sips, the buzzing ceased. Unfortunately, his eyes also refused to open, and he couldn't stop his body from tumbling down and down and down.

*** 

*Ines*

Ines removed her hand from the back of Murray's head and studied him with concern. "I believe he is unconscious."

The servant peered at him. "Best thing for him, if you ask me, miss. He won't feel the pain so much." She gave Ines's dress a wide-eyed look. "But you are hurt, too, miss!"

Ines glanced at her blood-stained dress. "It is Mr. Murray's blood. I am uninjured."

The servant sighed in relief. "Oh, good. I will try to find you something clean to wear." She looked at Murray. "And something for him as well."

"His trunks are here," Ines said. "He has clothing in there. What should I do to help him? It seems like Mr. Fortescue has been gone hours. I am anxious for the surgeon."

"It looks like you did a good job of binding the wound and stopping the blood flow. But we could clean the wound."

"How?"

"I'll fetch more gin. In the meantime, I made you soup. Go ahead and eat."

"Are you the cook?"

The woman bobbed a curtsy. "Mrs. Brown, miss. Do you mind if I ask your name?"

"Ines Neves. I am from London."

"And who is this?" She gestured to Murray.

"Duncan Murray. He served in the war with Mr. Pope. He came to see him because"—she waved a hand—"never mind why now. Can you please fetch the gin?"

"Right away, miss."

Ines looked at the soup. She didn't think she could eat it. Her belly disagreed and growled. Ines decided she would be of no use to anyone if she was fatigued from hunger. She touched Mr. Murray's forehead, still no trace of fever, then lifted the spoon and ate a few mouthfuls of soup. It was not particularly good soup—the vegetables were soft, and the broth had little flavor—but it was something.

This was all her fault. Murray would probably die, and it was all because of her. They'd only come here because he needed someone who spoke Portuguese. If she'd just told the truth from the beginning, she would be on the way back to London and Murray would be unharmed. Mr. Fortescue and Miss Wellesley wouldn't be running about the countryside looking for a surgeon, either. No wonder Draven said Ines could not live above the shop. He knew that given half a chance, she'd cause more trouble than she was worth.

Hadn't she done that and more in just two short days?

But it was very hard to feel contrite for long. One glance at Mr. Murray's bare chest, and she quite forgot she was partly to blame for his injury. Of course, she didn't want him to be injured, but was it wrong to enjoy the benefits of touching his brow, sliding her eyes over his broad chest, and following the trail of hair on that chest to the waist of his trousers?

It was most certainly wrong, and she was probably doomed to an eternity of hellfire for the direction of her thoughts. In which case, what was the harm of one more? She allowed her gaze to shift to Murray's face again and wondered, for the hundredth time, what it would feel like if he kissed her.

Mrs. Brown returned, and Ines focused guiltily on her soup again. "I'll just ready everything on this table, miss," the cook said as she set the gin down on the table beside the couch.

Ines forced herself to watch Mrs. Brown and not Murray. As a respectable young woman, she should not be imagining kissing a man like Duncan Murray. Perhaps she wouldn't think of it so much if she had been kissed before. It was very hard to be nineteen years old and unkissed. If she'd stayed with her father in Portugal, she would have been long married and the mother of children by now. Of course, she would have had to kiss a cruel, old man. As she'd grown older, she had appreciated her narrow escape more and more. She'd also realized she had a chance many, if not all, of the women she knew would never have—to make her own destiny. Why could that destiny not include Duncan Murray tossing her over his shoulder?

"Are you alright, miss? Is it too cold in here? You're shivering."

"Oh, I am fine." Desperate to change the subject, Ines stood and went to stand beside the cook. "What should I do?"

"One of us needs to douse this rag in gin and apply it to the wound. The other needs to hold him down."

"Hold him down?" Ines suppressed another shiver. "I will do that."

Fortunately, Murray's injured arm was the one most accessible to them, and it was a simple matter to remove the bandages. He groaned but did not open his eyes.

"Should we give him more gin?" Ines asked.

"Best just to do it while he's unaware. We risk a stronger reaction if we wake him first." The cook held the clean rag to the mouth of the gin bottle and wet the cloth thoroughly. Then she set the bottle back on the table, moved the table out of the range of flailing arms, and nodded to Ines.

Ines was not at all certain where she should place her hands. She settled on his shoulders, setting one knee on the couch in case she needed to leverage her full weight to help hold him down.

"Ready?" Mrs. Brown asked.

"Ready." Ines nodded.

Mrs. Brown moved quickly, placing the hand holding the rag over the wound, and squeezing the cloth so gin ran into the injury.

Murray reacted like he'd been stung by a bee. He yelped and jumped. Even using all of her weight to push his shoulders down, she was no match for him. He seemed blinded by pain, and his flailing arm almost hit Mrs. Brown, who struggled to keep the rag in place.

"Lie still!" Ines ordered. He stilled for an instant, seeming to listen, and it was just enough time for Ines to throw a knee over him and sit on him to keep him down.

"That's it, love!" Mrs. Brown said through clenched teeth. "Give me one more minute."

Murray bucked beneath her, but Ines held him as still as possible. Finally, when she was certain he would throw her off, Mrs. Brown removed the rag, reached for the bottle of gin, and put it to Murray's lips. Instantly, he stilled and drank. His good arm reached for the bottle, and Mrs. Brown nodded at Ines to allow him to take it. When he'd taken another drink, he lowered the bottle and looked up at her. "Are ye trying to kill me?"

"We had to clean your wound."

"Why? In Scotland we rub a bit of dirt on it and grit our teeth."

"Thank the Lord you are not in Scotland, then," Mrs. Brown said. "Now be still while I bind your arm again with clean linen."

Murray looked up at Ines. "Who is this now?"

"That is Mrs. Brown, the cook."

"Nash has a cook?"

"Yes," Mrs. Brown said, "and there is soup over there for your enjoyment once I have finished my work. Almost done."

She tied the bindings neatly, far more neatly than Ines and Emmeline had, then stepped back and nodded her head.

"I'll just bring these soiled cloths to the laundry." She took the gin bottle from Murray's hand. "I had better take this too."

Murray made a sound of protest, but with Ines still sitting on top of him there wasn't much else he could do. A moment later, Ines realized she was still straddling him and from the way he was looking at her, he realized it as well.

"I dinnae usually complain when I find myself in this position, but I'd rather Draven killed me quickly, and if he were tae see ye now, lass, he'd make sure I met a slow, horrible end."

"I should stand up," Ines said. But she made no move to do so. How could she when she could feel the warmth of his body between her legs, enjoy the sight of his muscled chest, look into his amber eyes?

"Any time now, lass," he said.

Her cheeks heated, and she slid off him, not trying to keep her skirts from showing too much of her ankles. He winced. "Did I hurt you?"

"Nae. Ye moved a wee bit slower than I expected."

Ines raised her brows. "You liked it?"

Murray sat gingerly and shook his head. "I dinnae like anything tae do with ye, lass. As far as Draven knows, I never touched ye. I dinnae even look at ye."

"You worry too much about Benedict. It is me he will be angry with, not you. Here, let me help you." She reached to take his arm and assist him to the table with his bowl of soup, but he yanked his arm back.

"I can do it." He slammed a heavy hand on the table, steadied himself, then lowered his body into the chair.

"Do you think Draven will find us today?"

Murray ignored the spoon and lifted the bowl of soup. "It depends," he said, when he'd finished it.

"On?"

"How long it took him tae find Jasper. Jasper is the best tracker I ken. He'll find us like that." He snapped his fingers.

That meant she was quickly running out of time. "And you think because you are not touching me Draven will see no problem with this scene." She gestured to his bare chest.

"I cannae help that. Ye and that she-wolf tore my clothing to shreds. Come tae think of it, I wouldnae mind a blanket. There's a draft in this room."

Ines stared at him. The room was actually a bit stuffy with the windows and doors closed on the summer day. And after she'd had a few bites of the hot soup, she'd needed to fan herself. How could he be cold? His face had gone pale, the dark bristles of his days' growth of beard, standing out. She touched his face, and it was cool and clammy.

"Lass, I told ye—"

"Let me help you lie down, Mr. Murray."

He nodded. "I wouldnae argue."

She put her arm around his waist, ignoring his bare flesh, and let him lean on her as she helped him back to the couch. Once he was on his back, she searched the room for a blanket. Unable to find one, she looked at the heavy draperies. They would take too long to pull down. What about a tablecloth?

But Pope was in the dining room. Did she dare risk it? One glance at Murray, who was shivering, told her she had better. Moving quickly but quietly, she crossed the room, opened the door a sliver, and peered out. The entryway was empty, and Mrs. Brown was not to be seen.

The dining room door was closed. Ines took a breath and tiptoed across the entryway to stand before the doorway. Hoping the hinges had been oiled, and knowing full well they had probably not, she lifted the latch and pushed the door open.

It creaked like the telltale stair in a Gothic novel. Ines winced, but when she looked inside the dining room, Pope was seated in a chair, his chin on his chest.

Ines let out a shaky breath, took in another, and slipped into the room, careful not to touch the door lest it creak again.

The table was not covered with a cloth, but the sideboard behind Pope had drawers that looked promising. Additional linens might be kept there for quick access. But she had to walk past the sleeping Pope to reach it. Fortunately, he was on one side of the table, and she could walk along the other side. She did this quickly, reaching the head of the table, and then realized Pope was only a couple of feet from the sideboard. She slid behind him and quietly opened the cupboards. She found pieces for serving and candleholders, but no linens.

Looking over her shoulder to make certain Pope was still unaware of her, she grasped the drawer handle and pulled the first one open. It did not creak, but the sound it made as it slid along the wooden frame of the sideboard seemed deafening. Thank God it held linens. She was tempted to grab a corner and run, but she lifted one out and found it was only a napkin.

That meant she had to open the other drawer. Fingers shaking, she pulled it open, spotting an embroidered tablecloth right away. Just as she reached for it, a low voice said, "I would have thought you'd take the candlesticks."

Ines spun around and found Pope staring at her with one bloodshot blue eye. The other was hidden under a lock of dark hair that had fallen over his forehead.

"I was not stealing, *senhor*. I needed something to cover him."

Nash frowned, his eye not quite focused on her. She remembered that the men had said he was blind in one eye and almost blind in the other. "So you are a woman. I thought I was hallucinating. What's that accent?"

"I am from Portugal. Please, *senhor*, he needs a blanket. He is cold."

"It's a long way from Portugal."

"I live in London." And then, in case he was considering violence toward her, she added, "My sister is married to your Colonel Draven."

At the sound of that name, Pope straightened in his chair. "Draven sent you to steal my linens?"

"No, *senhor*. Mr. Murray is in the parlor. You shot him, and he is cold. I could not find a blanket."

"I shot..." He rubbed his forehead. "Oh, right. Came storming in here like barbarian invaders."

"It was an accident?"

"We can call it that." Gripping the arms of the chair, he rose. Ines moved back a step, putting more distance between them in case she needed to run. "Don't forget your tablecloth," he said, gesturing to the drawer. "I'll go with you and see how he is."

Fearing it might be a trap, but desperate to make sure Murray was not shivering alone while she hesitated, she grabbed the linen and pulled it out of the drawer. Then she walked quickly to the exit. But Pope, for all that he smelled like a distillery, was quick as well. He reached it just before her and paused to allow her to go in front of him.

She swallowed and squeezed past him, walking quickly to the open door of the parlor. Once inside, she went to Murray, shook out the tablecloth, and covered him with it. She knelt, put a hand on his cheek, and felt how cold he was.

"How does he look?" Nash asked.

"He is pale and shivering," she answered.

"Any fever?"

"*Não*, thank God. But his skin is cold."

"The shock is setting in. Fever will be next. Stratford went for the surgeon?"

"Mr. Fortescue did, *sim*."

"How long ago?"

She couldn't say. She felt as though she had been inside this room for weeks. "Let's see about getting you a real blanket. Brown!" Pope yelled. "Brown!"

Ines winced, but the noise did not seem to faze Murray. He didn't move, and that concerned her even more. As she held his hand, Pope directed the cook to fetch a blanket and build up a fire as well as boil water for when the surgeon arrived. Ines watched him with interest, and finally he raised a brow and asked, "What is it?"

"You are not behaving as I expected."

"The good behavior is temporary, I promise you. The sooner he is better, the sooner all of you will go away."

Ines nodded, wondering why he wanted to be alone so much and why he needed to drink so much. She wondered if his injury pained him. His hair had moved slightly, and she could see a scar cutting across his closed eye. But he seemed to get on well enough with only limited vision in the other. She probably would not have known he had any vision limitations, if she had not been told. There were very few telltale signs.

Mrs. Brown finally returned with the blanket, and Ines covered Mr. Murray while the cook built up the fire. Looking down at the Scot, Ines did not like what she saw. He appeared pale and still. He'd always been such a robust and vibrant man, and this sudden change made her uneasy. She looked over her shoulder at Mr. Pope. He was not facing her and didn't appear to be paying her any attention. She leaned down and brushed the hair off Murray's forehead.

"Do not die," she whispered. "You must fight. If you die, I will be very angry and upset. I still have not been kissed by you. By anyone, if you want the truth. But it is you I want to kiss."

His expression did not change. She might have said more, but Mrs. Brown was telling her how to best arrange the room for when the surgeon arrived.

"I'll get out of your way," Pope said. "It would be more gentlemanly to offer assistance, but I'd just be in the way. Besides, no one calls me a gentleman anymore." He went out after Mrs. Brown, walking slowly and deliberately to avoid bumping into anything that might have moved since the last time he'd been in the room. Ines watched him go, then started to do as Mrs. Brown had suggested. As she worked, she said a prayer that the surgeon would hurry.

# Seven

*Emmeline*

Emmeline ran toward the sound of what must be an injured dog. She was fairly certain that Stratford was running after her.

"Stop, Emmeline!" he called after her. "Wait a moment! It might be dangerous."

But the dog yipped again, and she could not wait. That sound resonated within her heart and pulled her closer. She broke through a cluster of trees not far from the road and burst upon three boys surrounding a gray dog, hunched and growling. As she watched, one of the boys threw a rock, hitting the dog on the flank and causing the animal to emit a high-pitched cry before lunging toward the boy then turning and licking the blood that had risen where the rock made contact.

Another boy lifted a rock, and Emmeline roared, "Put that down! Now!"

All three boys turned to stare at her, and the dog looked at her too, cowering even lower. The boys were twelve or thirteen in age and looked to be from the nearby village farms. They were dressed in simple clothing, but she could see their attire had been cared for and mended in places.

Stratford stopped just behind her, and the boys stared at him. And no wonder. She had dressed to travel and her dress was rumpled and dirty, but even after a day and night in the same clothing, Stratford looked every inch the gentleman, pressed and perfect.

"I said, put that down." Emmeline pointed at the boy who still had his hand raised, rock at the ready. The boy dropped the rock, and all three boys glanced at the dog as though remembering he was there and began to back away. The dog still cowered, looking more frightened now than ferocious.

"What is the meaning of this?" Stratford demanded, gesturing to the obviously wounded dog. "Has no one taught you any better? Where are your parents? I would have words with them."

Emmeline let Stratford go on chastising the boys as she really had no interest in them other than doing exactly as Stratford was in that moment. And he would scare them more than she ever would. Instead, she moved toward the dog.

Slowly, using a low voice, she told the frightened animal she was a friend.

He was a Staffordshire Terrier and quite a large one, though he was painfully thin at the moment. He was what people often called *blue* in color with a white streak on his nose and white on his chest and belly. His beautiful coat looked dirty and, after the boys' cruelty, bloody.

He eyed her warily but did not growl or show his teeth, so she moved closer, still speaking in that low tone.

"Emmeline!" Stratford hissed. "Stop!"

She ignored him.

"Sir, that dog is a killer. He'll eat her for lunch," one of the boys said.

Emmeline tilted her head to look at the dog. He didn't seem like a killer. He seemed like a scared dog who had been hurt by humans and was now hesitant to trust another. She moved closer.

"Emmeline, no!" Stratford said, his voice louder this time, causing the dog to crouch lower.

Emmeline looked at Stratford with a glare she usually reserved for moments when one of her younger sisters did something especially irritating. "You are frightening him. Hush."

She looked back at the dog. "Ignore him," she said even as Stratford stuttered protests behind her. She placed her hand very low to the ground near him. "You see, I am a friend."

Eyes never leaving her face, the dog moved tentatively forward, then back, then forward again to quickly sniff her hand. Then he backed up again.

"You see, nothing happened. Try it again." She moved her hand slightly closer and said, "Come." The dog's ears pricked up, and he cocked his head. "Oh, you know that word, do you? Let's try it again. Come."

The dog moved forward a little then seemed to lose his courage.

"What is she doing, sir?" one of the boys asked from behind her.

"Trying to get herself killed," Stratford answered.

"Why don't we try another?" Emmeline said to the dog. "Sit."

The dog's bottom immediately hit the ground.

"Good, boy," she said. "Good."

His tail wagged, and she reached forward and stroked his head. He allowed it, even leaning into her when she scratched his ears. Satisfied, she looked at the boys and Stratford, standing a few feet away and staring at her. "Well?" she asked.

Stratford gave her a look that said quite plainly he thought she was mad.

"Did you find out who these children belong to, so we may be certain they are punished?"

Stratford looked at the boys as though just remembering they were present.

"Begging your pardon, miss," one of the boys said. He'd worn a brown cap, but he held it in his hands respectfully now. "But it was our parents told us to come after the dog."

Emmeline's hand stopped stroking the dog's head, and he nudged her to continue. "Do you expect me to believe your parents condone throwing rocks at an innocent dog?"

"That's just the thing, miss," a boy holding a dark green cap said. He was a bit younger than the first, but they looked similar and Emmeline assumed they must be brothers. "He isn't an innocent dog."

"Oh, really? What did he do?"

The third boy removed his gray cap and shuffled his feet. "He stole my mum's fresh baked bread."

"This is *your* dog?" she asked.

"No, miss. He stays near our farmhouse, though, and my mum put some bread on the windowsill to cool, and he took it and ran."

"And she told you to go stone him to death?"

"She told me to chase him away and make sure he didn't come back." The lad pointed at the other two boys. "I saw them as I was running, and they came with me. We didn't want to kill him. But we had to make sure he didn't come back."

Stratford gave a sigh. "Why did you not go to the dog's owner? He is responsible for the dog's behavior. Anyone can see the dog has not been properly fed. You cannot blame him for taking food when he is starving."

"He doesn't have an owner," said the older of the two brothers. "Leastways, I don't know who it is."

"That's right," said the boy with the gray cap. "He just showed up one day, and no one could chase him away."

"Well, you may go home and tell your parents that Loftus will trouble you no further," Emmeline told them. When they found the surgeon, they would need to buy some food for the dog as well.

The boys looked at each other. "Who is Loftus, miss?"

"That's the dog's name."

"Is he your dog, miss?" the younger of the boys asked.

"He is now," she said. "Go on. Go home and tell your parents." She made a shooing sign and the boys donned their caps again and ran off, chattering like birds.

Emmeline looked at Stratford, who was shaking his head. "No," he said.

"You don't like the name Loftus?" she asked, knowing that wasn't at all what he meant and also knowing he would be annoyed by the question. She was not disappointed.

"I don't like the name," he said, his jaw twitching in that way it did when he tried to repress a feeling and couldn't quite manage it. "It's a ridiculous name for a dog. But moreover, no to the dog. We are not taking him with us."

"You may not be taking him with *you*, but he *is* coming with me. Aren't you, Loftus?" In response, the dog thumped his tail, and his tongue lolled out of his mouth. "Come, Loftus!" She began walking, and the dog followed, giving Stratford a wide berth.

"I agree to find him something to eat and have the surgeon look at his wounds. But a dog like that is not safe. Those dogs are trained to fight." Stratford soon caught up, walking on the side opposite the dog.

"Then we should punish the trainers, not the dog." There she went again. She could not seem to stop her Very Bad Habit of being Impertinent. But how could she agree with something she did not believe?

"Emmeline." His voice was tight.

She could see the road just through the bushes ahead, and she continued walking.

"*Emmeline*." Stratford grasped her arm. Emmeline heard Loftus growl, and Stratford released her again.

"Sit," she told Loftus. She smiled at Stratford. "He is already protecting me."

"Only because you promised him dinner."

"I know the way to tame savage beasts." She winked at Stratford, and he furrowed his brow.

"In all seriousness, you cannot keep it. You can bring it back to Nash's, but we can't take it back in the coach with us." He was giving a little more each minute that passed.

Emmeline put her hands on her hips. "Two things, Stratford. One, we do not have a carriage at the moment. Two, Loftus is not an *it*. He is Loftus."

Stratford closed his eyes and made a sound like someone was strangling him. Emmeline left him to it and headed back toward the road. He caught up soon enough and then overtook her. She had to lengthen her strides to keep up, but she did not ask him to slow down. They had wasted precious minutes helping the dog, and they were both in a hurry to return to the injured Scot.

When they had walked for a few more minutes, Stratford looked back at her. "Why Loftus?" he asked.

"What do you mean?"

"The name. Why that name?"

"I like it. I've always wanted a dog named Loftus."

"Of course, you have." He shook his head, but he didn't seem quite prepared to let it go. "But that's a man's name, not a dog's name."

She pressed a hand to her side, which was developing a cramp from walking so quickly. "Are there rules for naming dogs?"

"I don't know." He slowed slightly, obviously to accommodate her. She would have walked more quickly just to prove that she did not need accommodating, but she worried Loftus needed to take a slower pace. He really did not seem well.

Stratford glanced at the dog. "I've never named a dog before."

"But you've always had dogs. Those little brown ones your mother likes to adorn with bows and such."

"And my mother has always named them."

"Well, what are their names?"

"Not human names. One was Trumpet because he had a bark like a trumpet. Another was Floppy because of her ears."

"How on earth did you end up with the name Stratford if that is her naming protocol for dogs?"

"It was her mother's maiden name," Stratford said, looking back at the road and then ahead toward where Emmeline hoped a village would soon appear. Her feet were beginning to hurt.

"I never knew that. I always thought you were named after the village."

"That's what everyone thinks. But I suppose my parents used all the names they really liked on my siblings. The baron has told me more than once that he had nothing to do with naming me."

Emmeline stopped. She stopped so abruptly that both Stratford and Loftus continued a few paces before realizing she had stopped. Loftus realized first and loped back to her. She scratched his ears. When Stratford looked back at her, she said, "I have a confession to make."

"Oh, God." Stratford looked pained.

"Not that sort of confession. My confession is that I have never liked your father."

"What a coincidence. Neither have I." He put his hands on his hips. "Why don't you like the baron?"

"Honestly, I never liked the way he treated you."

He scowled. "Is this more of how you feel sorry for me?"

"No."

He arched a brow.

"Maybe?" She shrugged. "It always seemed you tried so hard to please him, and nothing you did was ever good enough." She raised her hands to ward off the dark look he gave her. "Perhaps I am mistaken. I only spend a few weeks a year with your family."

"You are not mistaken." His voice was low, and she thought she detected a note of anguish.

"I never understood why," she said quietly.

Stratford's head jerked up. "It's no matter." He spoke quickly now. "This journey has already taken too long. We had better hurry before Nash wakes." He started away. Emmeline watched him for a moment, then hurried to catch up. She didn't speak. She could tell by the set of his shoulders the topic was closed. Emmeline did not know how to reopen it or if she even should. What did she know about fathers? Her own had died when she was thirteen. He had always been kind to her and her sisters, but he had been distant, preferring to allow her mother to deal with the little girls.

As Emmeline trailed Stratford, she tried to remember if her father had ever shown any preference for one sister over another. Marjorie and Hester were the most conventionally attractive. Abigail had been only five when her father had died, and she had been an adorable baby and toddler. It was only Emmeline who had been made to feel as though she did not quite measure up.

But that was all her mother's doing. Her father had always seemed to love each of his children the same. He hadn't cared that Emmeline was plump. In fact, when her mother had forbidden her from having the sweets the other girls ate on special occasions, her father usually sneaked her a slice of cake or a candied almond. He'd told her she was *his beautiful Emmie*. And Emmeline had believed him. Why should she starve and suffer in too-tight underclothing because her mother wanted her to look a certain way? Emmeline liked her body as it was.

Once she finally reached her grandmother, she would write to her mother and tell her she'd endured her last Season. Then she would eat what she liked, wear what she liked, and no one would tell her she had the body of a strumpet and had better take care not to look like one. She almost laughed. Some strumpet she was, considering she spent most of her evenings standing or sitting by a wall while other ladies danced or mingled.

Now Emmeline looked at Stratford again. Perhaps they had more in common than she'd thought. He too must know something about feeling left out and not measuring up. Not in the same ways as she. He was very handsome with that blond hair and those piercing blue eyes that seemed to look right through you. Ladies were always pretending to be Emmeline's friend so they could have an introduction to Stratford Fortescue. It annoyed her to no end when he flirted with them. But she never saw him do more than that. He wasn't a rake or womanizer. He never tried to seduce innocents or made promises he wouldn't keep.

Not that he was a saint. She did not believe that, but he was an honorable man—a man forced to follow her around the countryside and try to persuade her to go home. He must know she would never agree.

As soon as they brought the surgeon back to Pope's house, she would tell Stratford to go home. She would order him to go home. She did not want to be his or any man's responsibility.

"That's it," he said, breaking her concentration. "Milcroft village."

He was right. She could see a stone bridge ahead and beyond that a cluster of brown stone houses. Window boxes filled with flowers in bloom adorned the homes and shops. Emmeline admired the splashes of red, pink, yellow, and white. "Do we know which house is the surgeon's? There are several just across the bridge."

"We'll ask the first person we see," he said. Once they'd crossed the bridge, Stratford waved to a man pushing a wheelbarrow full of lettuce. The farmer's weathered face grew wary when he caught a glimpse of Loftus. "Stay here," Stratford ordered, as he crossed the street to speak to the man. Emmeline petted Loftus, who sat with his nose in the air, probably trying to scent his next meal.

Stratford returned a moment later and pointed down the street. "The surgeon, a Mr. Langford, is just there." He indicated a building that looked like all the others but without the flower box. "If we're lucky, he's in right now. Apparently, he's the only medical man in the area."

"You go ahead," Emmeline said. "He won't want a dog in his rooms. Loftus and I will wait outside."

Stratford looked as though he would object, but he must have seen reason as he agreed. After leading her to the door of the surgeon's home, he ordered her not to move an inch.

As soon as he went inside, she said, "Come, Loftus." Emmeline led the dog to a shop with bread in the window. She ordered Loftus to *stay* while she went inside. Hopefully, the dog obeyed orders better than she did. Once inside, a woman with frizzy brown hair greeted her, wiping hands covered with flour on her apron.

"May I help you, miss?"

"Yes, thank you. I would like to buy some food for my dog." She indicated the dog sitting outside. Loftus had pressed his nose to the window glass.

"That beast is your dog?" the woman asked. "I've seen him skulking about, looking like he wanted to steal my bread."

Emmeline wanted to ask why the woman hadn't given the dog bread if she could see he was hungry. Instead, she smiled. "He is mine now. My cousin and I are staying with Mr. Pope—"

"Mr. Pope!" This news seemed even more incredible than the fact that Emmeline owned the dog.

"Yes, my cousin fought in the war with him. Come to think of it, I should buy bread for dinner as well. Might I have two loaves and…do you have anything heartier for the dog?"

The woman finally closed her mouth. "I just make bread, miss."

Emmeline took the few emergency coins from the inside pocket of her dress. Thankfully, she always kept a few coins separate from her purse. "I have coin to pay."

The baker looked at the coins then at the dog. "I might have something in the back."

The baker retreated, and Emmeline made the sign for Loftus to wait. He licked the window. She tried not to laugh.

When the baker returned, she offered Emmeline a meat pie. Emmeline bought it and the two loaves of bread for all the coins she had, more than she thought was fair, but Loftus was hungry, and so was she, and she did not want to waste time haggling. She paid the woman, left the shop, and offered Loftus the pie immediately. He ate it in two bites and looked at her hopefully.

Emmeline sighed, broke one of the loaves of bread in half and gave him his portion. She started back toward the surgeon's house, eating a bit of bread herself, just as Stratford came marching toward her.

"I told you to stay right there." He pointed at the surgeon's stoop. "I told you not to move an inch."

She swallowed. "We were hungry."

"Good God, but you will be the death of me."

She offered him the loaf of bread, and he looked like he might refuse. Then he broke off a piece and ate it. Loftus gave a plaintive whine, and she gave the dog more as well.

"What did the surgeon say?"

"He is gathering his things and will drive us in his dog cart." Stratford eyed the dog. "He will have to ride in the box. It will be a tight fit as it is with the three of us."

Emmeline did not answer. She had no idea if Loftus would object to climbing into the box beneath the driver usually reserved for hunting dogs. If he did, she would walk back. Loftus would keep her safe from any harm.

They met the surgeon behind his shop just as he finished harnessing two horses to the cart. He was a man of about forty with a clean-shaven face, light brown hair, and the observant eyes so common in men of his profession. He eyed the dog warily but gave Emmeline a very polite bow.

"Miss Emmeline Wellesley, this is Mr. John Langford."

She curtsied. "A pleasure, sir. You have treated pistol wounds before?"

"I have, although usually they are the result of inattention while hunting. I'm curious as to how your friend was injured, Mr. Fortescue."

"Inattention was most certainly a factor," Stratford said easily. "Shall we be on our way?"

"Of course, how should we…"

"The lady and I will squeeze on the back." Stratford opened the door to the dog box. "Get in, dog."

Loftus looked at him and sat.

"Come!" Stratford ordered. "Get in!"

Loftus did not move.

"He doesn't seem to want to climb in," the surgeon observed, wryly.

Stratford looked at her as though to ask if they could leave the dog to follow, but she shook her head. Loftus was too thin to run all the way back. Stratford sighed. "Fine, I'll help you in." He started for the dog, reaching for him, but the dog backed up and bared his teeth. "Or not." Stratford moved back.

Emmeline moved forward and stood beside the box. "Loftus, come." The dog stood, his ears pricked up. He took a step forward then hesitated. "Loftus, come." Still he hesitated. She looked at her last loaf of bread. Here was to hoping Mr. Pope's cook found some food in the pantry. She broke off a piece of the second loaf, threw it in the box, and watched as Loftus went in after it. Then she closed the door and smiled at the two men.

"And there you have it," the surgeon said. He climbed onto the box, and Stratford offered his arm to Emmeline. She climbed up behind the surgeon on the seat facing away. It was a seat made for only one person, and as soon as Stratford climbed onto it, she wondered how they could both possibly fit.

"I don't think this will work," she said, eyeing the seat. "My bottom is too wide."

"Your bottom is perfect."

"What was that?" She could not have heard him correctly.

He cleared his throat. "I said, we will just squeeze together."

"I will walk back."

He grabbed her wrist before she could climb down. "We will squeeze together." And he yanked her onto the seat beside him. Or more accurately, he situated her onto a sliver of the seat and a large portion of his lap. "Ready!" he called, putting his hands on her waist to hold her steady.

Emmeline swallowed and tried not to think about her bottom touching Stratford's thighs. She tried even harder not to acknowledge the persistent fluttering back in her belly. This time it seemed to be spreading to other parts of her.

She tried to balance her weight, so she was not fully sitting on him. The dog cart started away, and Emmeline fell back, settling all of her weight on Stratford. His hands closed around her, pulling her back against his chest and securing her bottom against his, er—male parts. At least, that's where she imagined her bottom was resting.

"Mr. Fortescue," she began.

"Oh, I'm Mr. Fortescue now, am I?"

"This does not feel entirely proper."

"It's only for a few minutes. The horses will cover the distance in no time."

"Still." She tried to wriggle away from him, to put some space between her body and his.

He leaned his head close to hers and said in her ear, "Stop wiggling or this will become quite improper."

From what she felt against her bottom, things had already become quite improper. Was she really responsible for causing that reaction in him? Was it possible he did not mind having her bottom on his lap? She went very still then and though she tried to concentrate on the fields rushing by, it was difficult not to notice how his arms felt warm and strong around her and how his chest was hard…as well as other parts of him. She wished he would speak to her again, his lips against her ear, his mouth so close to her neck.

"You're trembling, Emmeline," he said, his mouth right where she had wished it a moment ago.

"Am I?" Even her voice trembled.

"Do I make you that nervous?"

The truth? Yes, he did. She had known him all of her life, known his brothers and sisters all of her life. She had conversed, argued, laughed, and played comfortably with all of them—except him. She'd never been comfortable with Stratford. When he walked into a room, the hair on the back of her arms stood up. She seemed to sense him even before she knew he was there. For his part, he seemed not to notice her at all. He didn't ignore her, but neither did he make any effort to speak to or engage her. They never had a conversation alone until the first time he escorted her to a ball and was obliged to ask her to dance. And then she'd been so nervous that she couldn't remember what she'd said or if it had been anything more than one- or two-word phrases.

She'd become more used to him, of course. He'd escorted her to many social events, and she'd developed a sort of careless persona with him. She acted as though she barely noticed him, which was how he had always behaved with her. Except he was actually a very good escort. Stratford was attentive but not so attentive as to chase away any potential prospects—not that she had any. On occasion a less than honorable man would approach her, and Stratford was excellent at intercepting the objectionable man and steering him away.

And then of course it had been Stratford who had come after her. How she wished it had been any of his brothers or his father. She could have easily run away from them. She'd had a dozen chances to run from Stratford. She told herself she did not take advantage of the opportunities because it was not safe for a woman to travel alone. But if she'd wanted to be safe, she would never have run in the first place. The problem was she did not want to leave Stratford. She enjoyed his company. She enjoyed sparring with him. She enjoyed seeing his frustration when she insisted on taking Loftus with them. Sometimes she thought she behaved in certain ways just so he would *have* to notice her.

And now it was clear that he had noticed her. At least parts of him had noticed her. And though she was flattered and thrilled, and her body was all but quivering with arousal, she was also vaguely ill. She had tried very hard not to feel anything but friendship for him. Now that he touched her, held her, whispered in her ear, she would be devastated when he forgot about her again. It would be better if he never noticed her.

"You? Make *me* nervous? Of course not," she lied. He could not help his body's reaction to a woman pressing against him. She should not make more of it than there was.

"May I make a confession?" he asked.

She turned her head to look at him. That was not the sort of thing he usually said. It didn't seem possible, but his words made her more nervous. "If you must," she said cautiously.

"*You* make *me* nervous."

She burst into laughter, and the surgeon actually turned to look back at them, which caused her to cover her mouth and try to tamp down her mirth.

"It's true," he said when she had regained her composure. "I never know what you will do next. Even as a child I found your behavior impulsive and erratic. Unpredictability makes me nervous."

Emmeline straightened. "I was neither impulsive nor erratic. I always had reasons for everything I did. I still do."

"And what reason do you have for the dog under the box at the moment?"

"He needed help. Anyone would help an injured, hungry animal. That is quite a predictable behavior." She turned her head to look back at the fields they passed. Looking into his eyes for too long made her nervous all over again.

"If you believe that, you are more innocent of the world than I thought."

She huffed in response. "I suppose I should take that as a compliment."

"If you are not erratic and impulsive, explain to me your reasoning that summer at Odham Abbey when you jumped into the pond."

"I jumped into the pond?" She could not stop herself from looking back at him again. "I don't remember that."

"I do. We had gone for a walk and you and Marjorie had come along. You wore a pale blue dress with a white pinafore over it, and your mother had put a blue ribbon in your hair. It had come loose, and you swung it in your hand like a whip."

Emmeline stared at him. How on earth did he remember all these details? She had no recollection of the dress or the day at all. "How did I end up in the pond?"

"That's just it. None of us knew why you did it. One moment you were pulling your sister along and the next you scampered to the pond, grabbed the rope we'd tied to the tree branch, swung over the water, and jumped in."

It was coming back to her now. The memory of swinging on that rope had remained with her. It had been so freeing, so exhilarating.

"My brother and I almost went in after you, but you came up laughing." He still sounded bewildered.

"As I recall, the water was not very deep. I could stand on the bottom."

"Which was a good thing because it saved us from having to go in after you and receiving a scolding for ruining our clothing. Yours was bad enough."

She gave a rueful smile at the memory. Her father's brows had lifted in surprise when he saw her, and her mother's face had gone crimson with embarrassment. Emmeline seemed to always be embarrassing her mother.

"It was that sort of behavior that made me nervous. One could never anticipate what you might do next. There was no rhyme or reason to it."

"Oh, there was a reason for it," she said. "Several, in fact."

He turned her sideways so her legs fell between his, her bottom on one of his knees. "What could possibly be the reason?"

"I was cross and hot. What you may not remember was that I was all of about seven. That would have made Marjorie only four, and my mother had probably told me I was responsible for her. And here was my chance to play with the older kids, and I had to take care of a whiny baby who could not keep up. That was my thinking, at any rate."

"I suppose I understand that reasoning, but why jump in the pond?"

"I knew you boys swam in it, and I was jealous. I wanted to swim in it too, but of course girls aren't allowed to strip off their clothing and swim like boys do. So when we came upon the water, it looked so cool and inviting. My sister was annoying, and I was hot. And there was the Great Forbidden Pond."

He chuckled. "It was more of a watering hole than a great anything."

"Yes, well to me it looked very large. Marjorie tugged on my sleeve one too many times, and I ran away and jumped in." She gave him a self-satisfied look. "So you see, there was a reason after all."

"I would have never put all of that together. We all thought you quite mad."

"And then you became frightened of me."

"I never said frightened. I said you made me nervous."

She leaned close and tapped his nose. "And a little bit scared. Admit it."

He looked into her eyes, and she realized how close they were. For a moment she thought he might kiss her. The idea terrified her, and yet she wanted it more than anything else. Except if he kissed her it would probably be as much a disaster as her foray into the pond had been. That had been thrilling in the moment and something she was made to atone for even weeks later. If Stratford kissed her, everything would change. Would things become awkward between them? Or would they behave as perhaps they'd always been meant to? And how could she not be disappointed if he did not kiss her?

"Whoa," the surgeon said to the horses as the dog cart slowed. Stratford looked away from her, and she followed his gaze until she saw they were on Pope's drive.

"Whoa now," the surgeon said.

Emmeline sighed. It was probably for the best. How scandalous would it have been if he'd kissed her as they rode on the back of a dog cart? It would have been—dare she think it?—erratic and impulsive behavior. And there was one thing she knew about Stratford Fortescue. He was never erratic or impulsive.

# *Eight*

Stratford had to allow Emmeline to descend first. It would have been a feat of acrobatics to change places so that he could climb down and assist her. Chivalry was only appropriate insofar as it was useful. Besides, the additional time gave his body a chance to stand down. The feel of Emmeline's soft round bottom against his nether regions had been more arousing than he'd anticipated. That and the scent of her so close to him. She smelled so light and sweet, lemon infusing every one of his senses until it was driving him mad not to bury his nose in her hair and her skin.

She must have noticed his reaction. She must have thought it odd, too, considering she'd always made it clear she thought of him as a brother, if she thought of him at all. Is that why she had been trembling? Because he was not behaving as a brother ought? Well, he hadn't lied when he'd said she made him nervous. He could recall countless stories of her outlandish behavior when she'd been a child. He'd been fascinated by her and drawn to her. But she'd always been younger than he by almost five years, which made her still very much a child when he was already an adolescent.

Until one summer when they were both at Odham Abbey and she was not a child. She must have been thirteen or fourteen, but she had grown since the last time he'd seen her, and she'd grown in all sorts of places where he could not allow his gaze to land much less linger. It had been impossible not to notice her large, plump breasts. But he'd made a concerted effort to look only at her face or above her head.

He was a man now and much better able to control his gaze, but it hadn't been easy to sit with that lush derriere on his lap and not slide his hands down from her waist and over her rounded hips. It helped to remember her as the sopping wet child she had been. Except he could picture her as a sopping wet woman, her dress clinging to her curves...

Stratford forced his thoughts back to Duncan and the crisis inside Pope's house. That cooled his ardor enough that he could climb down. Unfortunately, he had taken a bit too long, and Emmeline had already released the dog from the box. The dog ran about sniffing here and there and marking the perimeter. In the meantime, the surgeon gathered his bag and looked to Stratford for guidance. "This way then," he said, leading the party toward the front door. Emmeline whistled to Loftus as a man would, and Stratford added that to his list of Surprising Facts about Emmeline. The most recent version of the list now had three items.

1. She can communicate in Portuguese. (He supposed he would have to take that off as the Portuguese speaker in question had turned out to be fluent in English as well.)
2. She can calm wild beasts.
3. She can whistle like a man.

At the door, Stratford motioned for Langford and Emmeline to stand back. He hoped Nash would still be in a drunken stupor, but he could not be certain. They didn't need Pope killing the surgeon before he could use his skills. He opened the door a crack, waited for the sound of a hammer cocking. When he didn't hear one, he opened the door further. The entryway was empty, and he breathed a sigh of relief.

Until Pope stepped out of the parlor where Stratford had left Miss Neves and Duncan.

Pope looked in the direction of the door. "Who the devil is that?"

"It's Stratford returning with the surgeon. I have my cousin Miss Wellesley with me. Don't shoot."

Nash squinted. "Why would I shoot you? We've been waiting for you. Hurry up then." He reached for the door and made his way back into the parlor. Stratford stepped into the entryway followed by Emmeline and the dog. The surgeon lingered for a moment outside.

"Are you certain it's safe?" Langford asked.

Stratford was inclined to tell him the truth—he was certain of nothing. But Emmeline must have sensed what he was about to say and chimed in first. "It's perfectly safe. Come along now."

She led them to the parlor, and Stratford immediately saw the situation had worsened while they'd been away. Duncan lay on the couch, covered by a blanket. His eyes were closed, and his face was pale. Stratford must have made some sort of sound because Emmeline took his hand and squeezed it. "The surgeon is here now," she said quietly. "All will be well."

Mrs. Brown moved forward to greet the surgeon. "Oh, Mr. Langford, thank you for coming. There has been an accident."

Stratford glanced about the room for Nash, but he hadn't returned to the parlor. That was probably for the best.

"I have everything ready for you," Mrs. Brown said, ushering the surgeon to a table that had been cleared but for linens and a pitcher of water.

The surgeon set his bag on the table and opened it, then looked about the room. "It's best if the ladies wait outside. Perhaps you too, Mr. Fortescue. Mrs. Brown can assist me, and if the patient becomes unruly, I will call for assistance."

"I am not leaving."

Stratford noticed Draven's sister-in-law for the first time. She had been sitting quietly beside the couch where Duncan lay, her hand on his uninjured arm. She looked as though she'd been in a war, in her blood-stained dress.

"Miss, have you been injured?" the surgeon asked, his eyes wide.

She looked down. "No, this is Mr. Murray's blood."

"I see." The surgeon looked relieved. "Then I think it's for the best you leave. Too many people can be a hindrance."

She stood, a petite woman who looked quite formidable despite her small stature. "Then send Mrs. Brown away." Her voice was firm and unwavering.

"Miss Neves, I have had some practice with this sort of thing," Mrs. Brown said. Her eyes were kind. "I know what I am about. I will take good care of him." She linked her arm with the reluctant Miss Neves and led her to the door.

Emmeline tugged at Stratford, and he followed. A moment later they were outside, the door closed in their faces.

"I don't trust surgeons," Miss Neves said.

"Neither do I." Stratford had seen his share of men die from surgeons' quick, dirty work. But this was not a severed leg or a shattered arm. This was a simple pistol ball in the arm. "But if the surgeon had a bad reputation, Mrs. Brown would have said so or we would have heard it in the village."

"It's out of our hands at any rate," Emmeline said. "I don't know how to remove a pistol ball. Should we go wait in the dining room?" She released his hand, and Stratford had the urge to pull it back. But she put an arm around Miss Neves, and anyone could see the young lady needed shoring up more than he. The doors of the dining room stood open, and as they neared it, Stratford saw Nash standing at the table, pouring drinks.

"Brandy?" Nash asked as the three approached. "You look like you could use it."

Stratford took two snifters and handed one to Emmeline and offered the other to Miss Neves. She shook her head and pointed at Nash. "This is your fault. I want nothing from you. If he dies, his blood is on your hands."

Nash shrugged. He obviously couldn't see how the gesture angered Miss Neves even more. The color on her cheeks deepened to scarlet.

"I have a lot of blood on my hands, miss," Nash said. "More than any one man ought to have."

"You are not even sorry, are you?" Miss Neves demanded. Emmeline tried to calm her, but she shook the other woman off. Stratford thought this might be a good time to down her snifter of brandy if she didn't want it.

"Why should I be sorry? Duncan always was a lunatic. I'm surprised he survived the war."

"Nash," Stratford warned. Nash had always been callous and devoid of any sentimentality. But there was no reason to upset Miss Neves any further.

"I should shut up now?" Nash asked, looking in Stratford's direction.

"I think that would be best."

"Then I'll leave the field to you." He felt along the back of the chairs until he found his way to the door of the dining room. "I will extend my hospitality to one night. But I expect all four of you gone tomorrow." He closed the doors with a thud and walked away.

"What an awful man!" Miss Neves cried, taking one of the full snifters and downing it. She began to cough and sputter, and Emmeline had to pat her on the back. When Miss Neves seemed somewhat recovered, Emmeline turned her gaze on Stratford.

"I must agree with Ines. Your Mr. Pope is an odious scoundrel. What sort of man shoots his own friend and then throws him out? It's unconscionable."

"Nash hasn't been the same since the war and his injury. He wasn't always so unfeeling." Not that he was ever particularly warm and friendly. But Stratford supposed that anyone trained as a sharpshooter would have to rid oneself of feeling very early on. Else how could he shoot men on a mere order? Stratford had killed his own share of the enemy in battle. That was the nature of war. But those men had been ready to kill him. They'd seen him coming and had a fighting chance. Nash took men unaware, and Stratford had to believe that sort of job, day after day, weighed on a man.

"Why did you bring us here?" Emmeline demanded.

Stratford pointed at his chest. "This was not my idea. It was all Duncan."

"*Não!*" Miss Neves interrupted. "If anyone is to blame, it is me. If I had not pretended I was someone I am not, we would not have needed to come here. If he dies, the fault is also mine." She began to weep, and Stratford poured himself another snifter of brandy. Emmeline gave him a disgusted look and went to comfort the other woman.

"It is not your fault, and he will not die. Hush, now, dear. You have done all you could for him." Emmeline continued to pat her shoulder and comfort her, while Stratford went to the window and looked out at the late afternoon sun. His belly growled, unhappy with only a meal of brandy. He had heard a rumor of soup, but none had been produced. Knowing Duncan's appetite, that did not surprise Stratford. Something nudged his leg, and he looked down to see Loftus looking up at him.

"They make a great deal of noise, don't they?" he said to the dog, patting his head. The dog whined, and Stratford nodded. "I think we all might benefit from something more than brandy. Shall we visit the kitchens?"

The dog must have known that word because his head came up and his tail began to wag enthusiastically. Stratford tried to tell the women he would return, but he couldn't seem to find a moment to break in, so he patted his leg to encourage the dog and went out through the servants' door.

The kitchens were in no better shape than the rest of the house, though there had been some effort at tidiness. The problem, Stratford saw, was that there had been a fire at some point, and the flames had damaged one wall and the ceiling. Both had been shored up with heavy pieces of timber, but they smelled of charred plaster and wood and would need to be replaced before they caved in and hurt someone. Stratford poked about and found a few potatoes and dried meat. He gave the meat to Loftus, who took it to a corner to chew on. Stratford, having been in the army, knew something about cooking, and went to fetch water from the yard. That done, he heated it, cleaned the potatoes, and put them in to cook. It was simple, but no one would go hungry.

He sat, patted the dog, and watched the pot to make sure it didn't boil over. Emmeline found him that way a little while later. "Any news from the surgeon?" he asked.

She shook her head. "He hasn't emerged from the parlor yet. Ines has wept herself to exhaustion. I left her with her head on the table, asleep. Are you…cooking?"

He raised his brows. "Someone had to provide a meal, and Mrs. Brown has her hands full at the moment."

She looked in the pot and nodded. "I had no idea you had such skills."

"I'm full of surprises," he said. She looked at the dog, who was sleeping with his weight against Stratford's legs.

"I see that. It looks as though you won Loftus over."

"Dried meat is the way to a dog's heart."

She took the seat beside him. "You're the strategist," she said, looking at the fire. "What do we do?"

He looked at her. Even after all they had been through the past two days—had it only been two days?—she looked lovely. She looked a bit rumpled, to be sure, but he'd always liked her with her dark hair loose and her cheeks pink from exertion. "Too many variables yet unknown to make a plan," he said. "We wait to see how the surgeon fares and how Duncan looks in the morning and then decide."

"Your Mr. Pope said we must leave tomorrow."

"I'll deal with Mr. Pope. I'll hit him over the head if that's what it takes, but we won't be here long even if I persuade Pope."

"The colonel will find us."

"Exactly."

She shifted. "I don't see how he has any say over what *I* do. I am not his wife's sister."

Stratford had to admire her tenacity. "He is no more likely to let an unescorted lady go traipsing about the countryside than I am."

"I will not be unescorted. I will have Loftus with me."

The dog raised his head and looked at her. She smiled, reached over, and petted him. "That's right. You know your name, don't you?"

"Emmeline," he began.

She held up a hand. "I do not want a lecture. My mind is made up."

"Then you must tell your mother as much. You can't run away from your problems. Believe me, I tried." He didn't know why he'd said that. He hadn't meant to say it. And of course, now she was looking at him with those bluer than blue eyes.

"When you went into the army."

"Most younger sons join the army or navy. That wasn't running away. Joining a troop with a slate of suicide missions? That was running away."

She blinked at him. "I always wondered if what I'd heard about Draven's troop was an exaggeration. People say you were the best and the brightest."

"And the most expendable. No heirs, only a few spares, and very few men with any family. We weren't expected to live, and we were prepared to die."

"I think you probably had something to do with bringing twelve of those men back."

"We all played our parts. The point is my problems did not disappear while I was away. I came home and very little had changed."

She shook her head. "You changed. I could see it the first time I saw you again. You were not as angry. You were more at peace—or perhaps you were looking for peace."

How strange that she saw him so clearly. The war had driven the anger he'd always felt at the baron's dismissal of him away. He'd stopped being defensive and looking for reasons to argue and began to appreciate solitude, peace, and simplicity. He'd always known anger hadn't been logical, but now he could act on those beliefs and put the anger away.

She placed her hand on his arm, and he swore his skin burned through the layers of clothing. "Do you think you've found it?"

He looked into her eyes, and he couldn't help but think that every time he'd ever looked at her, he'd found peace. And then he was moving without thinking. He was reaching for what he wanted, without a plan or a strategy or even the benefit of reason. His hand cupped the back of her neck. Her eyes widened, but she didn't resist. And when he lowered his mouth to hers, what happened next was completely unexpected.

\*\*\*

*Ines*

"Miss Neves."

Ines came awake suddenly and looked up. The room was shadowed, but there was enough of the fading early evening light left for her to see Mrs. Brown. Ines jumped to her feet. "What's wrong?"

"Nothing, miss. I came to tell you Mr. Langford has finished. You can go in and see Mr. Murray, if you like."

Ines gripped Mrs. Brown's arms. "He's alive?"

"Yes, of course. He's awake too and asking for food."

Ines felt her knees buckle, and she had to sit back down. She hadn't killed him. She wouldn't spend the rest of her life punishing herself for his death. She began to rise again and then realized that it was still early. He might still develop a fever and die. But she couldn't allow that to happen. She would do everything she could to keep him from taking a fever. She stood. "I need to see him, Mrs. Brown."

"That's why I came to fetch you, Miss Neves."

Ines followed Mrs. Brown to the parlor, taking a deep breath before stepping inside. Then she squared her shoulders, opened her eyes, and put on a smile. She walked into the parlor and smiled in earnest. Duncan Murray really did look better. He was sitting up, the blanket pulled midchest, with a clean bandage around his arm. His color was better, and he was arguing with the surgeon.

"My father and my grandfather both drank whisky for everra ailment. Everra Scotsman kens whisky can cure anything."

"I am not a Scotsman, Mr. Murray," Mr. Langford said, "but I maintain you have had enough to drink and would be better sticking to tea or broth."

"Christ and all the saints! The man is trying tae kill me." He noticed Ines and pointed to her. "That makes two of ye."

Ines ignored the reference to her brother-in-law. "How is he, Mr. Langford?"

"See for yourself, miss. We revived him a bit with a tonic, but he will need plenty of rest the next few days."

"I am not certain that is possible, *senhor*. Mr. Pope has said we must be out of his house in the morning."

"Oh, dear," Mrs. Brown said.

"Should I speak with the man? Mr. Murray should not be traveling, if it can be avoided."

"It will do no good," Mrs. Brown said.

"I, for one, dinnae want tae be shot again. He'll aim for the heid this time," Murray said. "If we had a coach, I'd leave tonight."

Ines rubbed the throbbing spot between her brows. "But we do not have a coach, *senhor*."

"We'll leave it tae Stratford. We'll need two coaches. One tae take ye and Miss Wellesley back tae London, and one tae take me tae Scotland."

Langford, who had lifted his surgeon's bag, set it back on the table. "You cannot possibly be proposing that you travel alone to Scotland, sir. You shouldn't be traveling at all, much less halfway across the country."

"I will go with him," Ines said.

"No," Murray said even before the words were out of her mouth. "I'll order Stratford tae take ye home."

Ines put her hands on her hips. "You may give all the orders you like, *senhor*, but I will see you home safely. It is my fault you are injured, and it will be my fault if you die on the way to Scotland."

Murray furrowed his brow as though she were speaking in Portuguese again. Langford lifted his bag. "Well, I see that is settled then. Miss Neves, if I might have a moment of your time, I will instruct you on how best to change the bandages and clean the wound."

She went with the surgeon, listened to his instructions, and gave him her assurances she would do exactly as he'd specified.

"I am trusting you with him, Miss Neves. He feels much improved now, but he will need your help for the next day or so. The wound is fairly minor, but even a small wound can become infected and fever may set in. If that happens—"

"I am to take him to a doctor immediately. I understand, *senhor*."

The surgeon looked about, his kind eyes sharpening on the dilapidated entryway. "I always wondered what it looked like inside the great house," he said, almost to himself. "It's a shame, isn't it?" He cleared his throat. "I am aware it is vulgar to speak of payment, but I do not suppose I will receive any response if I send my bill to Mr. Pope. Could you direct me to someone who might be able to pay for my services?"

Ines frowned. She hadn't thought of this, but of course the man would need to be paid. What an idiot she was! And she had no money. She had not expected to travel any further than a street over from Draven's house in London. "Give me a moment," she said, turning to go back into the parlor.

Mrs. Brown was fussing with the pillow behind Murray, and he waved her off when Ines returned. "I hope ye were nae serious aboot traveling tae Scotland, lass."

"Never mind about that now," she said. "I need coin to pay the surgeon. He has no faith if he sends the bill to Mr. Pope, it will ever be paid."

"Typical," Murray said. "First the man shoots me then he makes me pay for the privilege of staying alive." He gestured to his coat, which was in a heap on the floor, having been cut off his a few hours earlier. "If ye dinnae cut it tae shreds, my blunt is in the pocket."

She found the purse full of coins as well as a wallet with notes. She took them both out to the surgeon and paid him. When she was finished, she actually felt quite proud of herself. She had handled all of this business herself. And Draven thought she was not ready to live on her own above a shop. She was perfectly capable of taking care of herself. She had made a mistake regarding Mr. Murray, that was true, but she was doing her best to make it right. She would see him safely home to Scotland. She owed him that much.

And she would not think too much about how she would much rather be in Scotland, facing the ire of Murray's mother, than back in London and stuffed into one of Mr. Podmore's carriages. She was not yet ready for this adventure to end. And she could not possibly go back to London after having spent two days and two nights with Duncan Murray and still not have been kissed. If anyone found out—and this was London, so of course everyone would find out—Draven would have a difficult time convincing any of the stuffy middle class merchants to marry her.

And that thought made Ines smile. Podmore would be absolutely appalled at the idea of her having run away with a disreputable Scot. They would all shun her, which meant she might finally get the freedom she'd been hoping for.

And if she had a little fun on that road to ruination then all the better.

She marched back into the parlor and found Murray alone. He'd managed to send Mrs. Brown away, and now he eyed her suspiciously as she set his money on the table near the couch. "Ye look pleased with yerself."

She nodded. "I have never paid anyone before. Catarina always handled the finances for the shop. I feel happy." She moved a chair to face him and sat. "And since I am responsible for what happened, I will reimburse you the fee for the surgeon."

Murray held up his hand.

"Do not refuse. I have money. Our lace sells well, and I receive a tidy sum every week. Benedict never lets me spend any of it."

"He wants tae take care of ye."

"Not every woman wants to be taken care of, *senhor*. Some of us want a taste of adventure."

Murray's look of suspicion turned wary. "Is that why yer insisting on coming tae Scotland with me?"

"I would be lying if I said that was not part of the reason."

He leaned back. "I appreciate yer need for adventure and yer wanting tae keep me alive, lass. But I'd rather nae be kent as the man who ruined yer reputation."

"Oh, you need not worry about that."

His brow lifted. He looked so handsome when he did that. "Because yer a shopkeeper and dinnae have tae worry aboot reputations?"

"Because I *want* you to ruin my reputation, *senhor*."

He shook his head. "I think more than my arm was wounded. I'm nae hearing ye right, lass."

"You heard me." She slid off the chair and moved to sit beside him on the couch.

"I dinnae think that is a good idea."

"You do not know what it is like to have the most uninteresting men in the world knocking on your door and wanting to walk with you in the park or take you for ices. Then all they can speak of is carriage wheels or shoe patterns. I want to stab my eye out, *senhor*."

"I have some idea what ye mean. I just spent weeks in London looking for a bride. I never kent there were so many ways tae discuss the weather. But I think ye should go back tae yer chair."

"I want to check your forehead and make certain you have no fever." She reached out and he feinted to the right.

"I feel bonny. Nae need tae touch me."

She pressed her hand to his forehead anyway. "I promised Mr. Langford I would check for fever every hour."

He winced, as though her hand burned him. But she didn't remove it. Their eyes met. "As ye see, lass. Nae fever."

She nodded and leaned over him.

"Now what are ye aboot?"

She ran a hand down his shoulder, pausing at the white bandage. "Making certain the dressing does not need changing."

"It has nae been on but an hour, lass."

She made a sound of assent but leaned closer to inspect the linen. She was aware this brought their bodies in contact, and that Murray stiffened. "Do you know something, *Senhor* Murray?" she said as she examined the bandage.

"What's that, lass?" he asked, voice tight.

"I have never been kissed." She heard his quick intake of breath and met his gaze. His expression was pained.

"Why are ye telling me this?"

"Because when you feel up to it, I want you to be the first man to kiss me." Satisfied with what she saw, she straightened and then stood. "I suppose I should find Mr. Fortescue and tell him we will need a coach in the morning. And perhaps Mrs. Brown can help me clean this dress."

Murray just stared at her, his mouth open.

"If I leave you for a moment, you will not decide to walk around, will you, *senhor*? You will sit and rest?"

He still didn't respond, just stared at her.

"Good. Then I will be back in a moment. Perhaps I can find you something to eat as well."

She was almost to the door when he called after her, in a hoarse voice, "And whisky, lass."

"Of course. I imagine you do need a drink."

# Nine

*Emmeline*

Emmeline had not realized how much she wanted Stratford to kiss her. She didn't realize it until he cupped her neck and pressed his lips to hers and moved tentatively over her mouth. His lips ignited her body like nothing she'd ever experienced before. Suddenly, she was warm and tingling and needing to touch him.

She grasped his shoulders then slid her hands up to the back of his neck, curling her fingers in his hair and pulling him closer.

This kiss.

She wanted more of it. She wanted more of *him*.

He hesitated for just an instant at her urgings, and then with one hot motion he pressed her mouth open and entered her. His tongue slid against hers, and she would have gasped if only she'd been able to breathe. But she couldn't breathe, couldn't think, couldn't do anything but feel. And the more she felt, the more she wanted to feel, *needed* to feel. She was thirsty for more of this kiss, for more of him. She imitated his gesture, her tongue mating with his in a delicious slow slide that left her eager to crawl into his lap and get closer. But her kiss must have shocked him, because he pulled back and looked at her.

"Where did you learn that?"

She tensed. She'd forgotten that ladies were supposed to be inexperienced and untried. She should have pretended she didn't know what to do. But she was so tired of pretending. She was running away so she wouldn't have to pretend any longer. Emmeline lifted her chin. "I've been kissed before," she said defiantly. What she didn't add was those other kisses had never felt like this.

"Whoever kissed you like that should be knocked on his arse."

"*You* are kissing me like that." She couldn't keep a smile from spreading across her face. Why had she worried Stratford would want her to pretend? Why had she thought he might expect her to live up to some silly unrealistic expectation? She was three and twenty. Of course, she had been kissed.

And she wanted to be kissed again. By him. "Don't stop." She pulled him back, and her mouth took his with an urgency she could feel all the way down in her belly. If she worried her passion might put him off, she quickly forgot the concern. He deepened the kiss until she feared she would explode from the heat. When he pulled back, he kissed her so lightly that she wanted to crawl into his lap and make him press his mouth to hers and give her what she wanted.

She knew she was shocking him. She knew he was acting rationally. They must slow down or do something they might both regret. That was Stratford—logical. Reasoned.

She understood because she had been kissed before, as she'd said. The first time had been when she was only seventeen. The handsome son of an earl had kissed her on a sunny day in a garden. She'd kissed him back, and he'd pulled away and told her she should behave like a lady. She'd been less eager to kiss anyone after that. She'd given in to a few tepid kisses by men who had soft, clammy lips and who kissed so awkwardly she was embarrassed for them.

Then, of course, there had been Lord Rosemont. He had a bad reputation, and everyone knew he was looking to marry an heiress. Emmeline was not an heiress, and he had never paid any attention to her. Except one night when they were both at a ball and she had gotten lost returning from the retiring room. That had been her story, at any rate. She had not wanted to go back to her spot on the wall, and so she had taken a detour, stopping to look at the family portraits and peek in the music room. He had been in the music room. It was obvious he was waiting for someone, and it was not her.

She should have turned on her heel and left as soon as he made his presence known. He'd cleared his throat, and she'd turned from studying the harp to see him leaning against the pianoforte, all dark, curling hair and sultry blue eyes. But he was so beautiful that she hadn't been able to move. His gaze slid down her dress, his eyes touching her in ways that were wholly inappropriate, and it was as though his perusal touched her.

"Do you play?" he'd asked. She'd frowned in confusion, and he'd indicated the harp. "Do you play?" he repeated.

She shook her head.

"That's too bad. I'd like to see you play."

She'd felt her cheeks heat because he knew ladies did not play the harp. It was considered unfeminine as a harpist had to hold the instrument between his legs. And then Rosemont had not said he wanted to hear her but *see* her.

"Have I shocked you?" he asked, moving toward her. He moved slowly. She could have stepped away at any time. But she stood still until he was right before her, so close their bodies almost touched. "Shall I shock you further?"

She didn't know what made her do it—she supposed she was desperate for distraction—but she nodded.

His mouth had quirked up, and he'd pulled her against him. She'd gasped but barely had time to take a breath before he'd kissed her. And she'd no time to enjoy the kiss before his hand was on her breast. She knew she should tell him to stop, but it felt good. Rosemont knew how to kiss, and when she kissed him back, his thumb found her nipple and circled it. She might have stayed in the music room with him, doing God knew what, if he hadn't broken the kiss to kiss her neck and whisper, "You like that, don't you, little slut?"

All the heat coursing through her drained away, and she'd moved out of his arms. He'd let her go, a quizzical smile on his lips.

"I must return to the ball."

He'd nodded. "Go ahead. You know where to find me."

Emmeline had spent the rest of that evening resisting the urge to return to the music room. And she might have gone if he hadn't called her a slut. Why should she be deemed a loose woman because she enjoyed a kiss?

"We should stop," Stratford said now.

"I knew you would say that." She sat back, her body still vibrating from the feel of his mouth on hers.

"You know me too well. We are friends. Good friends. I don't want to ruin things."

Emmeline supposed that was her cue to agree and shake hands and walk away. But she'd said she was tired of pretending. "Are we?" she said.

"Are we?" he repeated.

"Are we good friends? Do we know each other all that well? Certainly, we have known each other for a long time, but we were never close. We never spent much time together."

He swallowed then raked a hand through his hair, making it stick up. "I suppose that's because of the age difference and because I was a boy and you a girl."

"So then we don't really know each other all that well," she said. "We're not even true cousins."

His eyes narrowed. "Are you arguing that I should keep kissing you?"

She was not arguing *against* it. Emmeline raised her brows. "Do you want to keep kissing me?"

He hesitated then stood and paced away from her. "You might consider there's a good reason we never spent much time together when we were younger. It might be wise to limit the time we spend together now."

Emmeline stared at him. Was he implying he'd wanted to kiss her when they were younger? That he'd kept his distance to keep from acting on his attraction to her?

"Mr. Fortescue?"

Emmeline and Stratford both looked toward the stairway leading into the kitchen. Ines's voice carried down. Emmeline wanted to tell him to keep quiet, to stay with her and kiss her again, but she knew that wasn't possible. The moment had passed, and Ines might need help with Murray.

"We're down here, Ines," Emmeline called.

"Oh, good! I've found you." Her footsteps grew closer as she started down the stairs, and Stratford crossed the room to the stove, where the potatoes Emmeline had quite forgotten about were cooking.

Ines appeared, looking rumpled and tired in her blood-stained dress. "Mr. Murray is awake and doing well." She smiled, and Emmeline smiled too.

"Good. I imagine he is hungry."

"Yes, and he is demanding whisky. That is a good sign, *sim*?"

Stratford lifted a potato from the boiling water and speared it. "That sounds like Duncan. I don't have whisky, but I have potatoes. We won't starve."

"Oh, good! Mr. Murray needs food to maintain his strength. But I have come to tell you we need a carriage tomorrow."

"Is Mr. Murray well enough to travel?" Emmeline asked.

"The surgeon did advise against it, but he can travel if he has a nurse. I have agreed to be his nurse." Ines looked small and young. Murray could probably flick her away with one finger. Emmeline could not see her succeeding as his nurse.

"But you cannot travel with him alone," she said because she knew Ines was as stubborn as she, and if she told the other woman she couldn't do something, she'd be all the more determined to do it.

Ines nodded. "I confess, I did hope you would come too, Miss Wellesley. If he should become ill with fever, I might need help."

Emmeline pressed her lips together at the understatement. "Of course, I will come."

"Bloody hell," Stratford muttered on the other side of the kitchen.

"Pardon, Mr. Fortescue?" Emmeline asked sweetly.

"I knew you would say that. But we cannot go to Scotland with Duncan. I have to take you back to Odham Abbey. I have to take Miss Neves back to London."

"But I do not want to go back to London yet," Ines said.

"And I do not want to go back to Odham Abbey," Emmeline said. "So you may either return without us or accompany us to Scotland." She crossed her arms across her chest. "Unless you think you can force us to go back against our will."

Stratford blew out a breath and covered his eyes with a hand. Emmeline took it as a sign of resignation.

"Scotland is days away, and Duncan is a Highlander," Stratford argued. "Who knows how difficult it will be to reach his home?"

Emmeline cocked her head. "That's all the more reason to accompany your friend. He may need your help."

Stratford shook his head. "Duncan is practically impossible to kill. But you two—I can't send you off alone."

Emmeline tried not to smile. No one liked when winners gloated. "Should you send another letter to your father?" she suggested. "I can finish the potatoes."

"Fine." He stormed away, muttering something about strangling Nash under his breath.

"Do not forget about the carriage!" Ines called after him. A door slammed in response, and Loftus raised his head momentarily before returning to sleep.

Emmeline fished the rest of the potatoes out of the water and began to search for something to use to season them. "Are you certain you want to travel to Scotland?" she asked Ines.

"I am not certain at all, but I am not ready to go home."

"Then we leave tomorrow at first light."

Emmeline did not add that their leaving was contingent upon Mr. Murray being well enough to travel in the morning. That was by no means a foregone conclusion.

\*\*\*

*Duncan*

"Why is everraone so surprised I'm nae yet dead?" Duncan asked the next morning.

"I think it's more that we are wishing you had allowed us to sleep a bit longer," Stratford said, squinting his eyes against the rising sun. Duncan had roused the entire house just before dawn. He'd always been an early riser, and he figured that it was better to leave before Nash decided to kick them out.

Miss Neves had been easy to wake. She'd slept in a chair in the parlor. She'd spent half the night checking to see if he had a fever. That was before he'd yelled at her to go to sleep or he'd bite her hand off. Thinking about it now, that might have been a bit harsh, but he'd been tired and his arm had been hurting and he hadn't wanted to be coddled.

He also hadn't wanted her to stay with him all night. Why was she so caring, so kind to him? He'd done nothing to deserve it, and she was a wee thing who needed her rest. He should have told her to go to her own chamber.

But he'd been selfish and said nothing because he liked having her nearby.

Now she and Miss Wellesley had disappeared to gather supplies, and Duncan sat on the front steps watching the drive for the carriage Stratford had supposedly hired. The broad-shouldered smiling dog Miss Wellesley had brought back with her yesterday sat beside him, breathing his warm breath on Duncan's shoulder. "The day is getting away from us," he said.

"I wouldn't call this day," Stratford said irritably. He turned away from the sun. "I doubt the coach and driver I hired will arrive for another hour at least."

"Then we should start walking toward the village."

Stratford gave him a disgusted look. "You are in no shape to walk anywhere, and I walked to the village twice yesterday. We'll wait for a while longer." Stratford sat next to Duncan, and the dog moved so he could breathe on both of them.

"I dinnae think Nash will take it too kindly if he finds us here when he wakes."

"Then I'll smash Nash over the head," Stratford said. "That's what I should have done yesterday."

"Smashing over the heid isnae yer specialty."

Stratford shrugged. "I learned a few things during the war."

Duncan laughed. "So ye did. I dinnae suppose ye learned how tae talk the two lassies oot of coming with me tae Scotland."

"I tried last night. They seem quite determined and have convinced themselves you will die en route if they do not accompany you."

"More like they'll see me killed. Draven will have my heid when he catches up tae us."

"It's not your fault the woman stowed away in your hired coach."

"And I might convince him of that if he doesnae kill me first." Duncan looked down the drive again, debating whether he should say more. But then why not? Stratford was good at plans and stratagems. He might be able to help. "The problem is that the lass wants tae ruin herself with me."

Duncan could see Stratford's head slowly turn until he was staring at Duncan. "Go on."

"She wants me tae kiss her."

"Tell her no."

"I did tell her nae." He rubbed his arm where the wound ached. "I dinnae ken if I can keep telling her nae," he said quietly.

Stratford was silent so long that Duncan looked at him. "Well, do ye have a plan tae save me?"

"Kissing her is hardly ruining her," Stratford said.

"It's the first step on the path," Duncan said. "And she's a bonny lass. I wouldnae mind kissing her." Duncan frowned. "What's wrong with ye? Are ye nae supposed tae tell me not tae do it? Are ye nae going tae tell me how tae keep her at bay?"

Stratford stood. "I wish I had some advice for you, Duncan. But I think in your position, I would probably kiss her. Ah, there's the coach now." He walked away and waved a hand.

Duncan stared at his friend's back. What the hell had gotten into the man? He was always the voice of caution and reason. In London, when Duncan had been on his bride hunt, Stratford had been the one to steer him away from the tempting widows and the beckoning courtesans. He'd told Duncan to stay focused on his search for a wife. But by the end, Duncan had been spending more time at gaming hells and the Draven Club than at Vauxhall Gardens or Hyde Park, places where the marriageable misses frequented. He'd always known the English looked down on the Scottish, but he hadn't expected to have so many women turn their noses up at him or recoil in either fear or disgust.

His uncle was the Duke of Atholl. His mother was the daughter of the Earl of Montleroy. He was half-English. But to the eyes of the ladies of Society, he was an uncouth Highlander who wanted to steal their daughters and take them back to live with barbarians.

His pride had been hurt. More than hurt, shattered.

Duncan supposed he had expected the English women to behave like the women in Scotland. Duncan had been considered quite the catch at home, and he'd never wanted for female company. There were any number of lasses in Kirkmoray he might have married. He'd argued with his mother for months that a Scottish lass was worth ten of any English lass. His mother, though English herself, had agreed. But she hadn't been swayed.

"Duncan, you know your uncle's struggles with the British government. They take our land, our livestock, our men. Your cousins have found English wives—well, those who have half a brain have. You will do the same. That way we ensure the safety of our land and people."

"But mother, an English lass will never survive up here."

She'd held up one imperious hand. "Then you will find one who is strong and hearty. Bring her home and marry her here. If I find her lacking, I will send her back." And she'd turned and walked away. Apparently, that had been her final word because the next time Duncan brought up the subject, she informed him she had hired a coach to take him to London.

On the trip south, Duncan couldn't help but wonder if Lady Charlotte would send him back if he returned empty-handed. He knew his mother loved him, but since his father died, Lady Charlotte had to run the farm and take care of three small children all on her own. She was a strong woman, and when he'd been young, he had not thought anything could bring her to her knees. But the death of his father, James Murray, had flattened her.

Theirs had been a love match. She'd run away to Scotland with James and married him against her family's wishes. Duncan could only imagine what her life had been like as the daughter of an earl. She had certainly never had to cook or mend or feed pigs before her marriage. And yet she did it all with grace and skill. She transitioned effortlessly from washing clothes in the morning to hosting one of the Duke of Atholl's balls in the evening. It was no wonder that James Murray had fallen in love with her. There seemed to be nothing Lady Charlotte could not do.

Duncan had never questioned his parents' love for each other. His mother had left all of her family, friends, and wealth behind to marry the younger son of a laird who lived on a farm—a rather large, prosperous farm but a farm—in Scotland. And Duncan had watched his mother rail about some problem or other only to end up laughing when James Murray had put his arms around her and pulled her into his lap.

Duncan had always wanted a marriage like theirs. He wanted the happiness he remembered from his house when he had been young. Before he'd killed his father and everyone had come to hate him.

Oh, his mother said she did not hate him, but why else had she urged him to go to war and then, only months after he returned, sent him away to London? Perhaps it would have been better if he'd died here at Wentmore. He was returning home without a potential bride and absolutely no prospects. His efforts at finding a bride had been dismal failures. His mother could add his inability to marry the daughter of an English peer to his long list of disappointments.

"Oh, good! The coach has arrived," Miss Wellesley said as she stepped out of the house. Duncan had braced himself when he'd heard the door open, ready for Nash to take another shot at him and perhaps hit him in the head this time. He looked back at her. She was dressed in the same traveling clothing she'd been wearing, but her hair looked clean and neat. She set down a wicker basket to pet the dog who rushed over to greet her as soon as she stepped out. She looked down at him and nodded. "Last night I confirmed with Mrs. Brown that your trunks will be sent on to Scotland separately. You have all you need from them?"

"Aye." Duncan had retrieved clean clothing as well as a few other necessities. He'd even made use of his razor.

"You look better this morning," Miss Wellesley said.

Duncan did not want to look behind her for Miss Neves. He wanted to turn back around and watch Stratford converse with the coachman. He could tell the two men were discussing the best routes to take north.

But Duncan didn't turn around. He watched the door until he spotted Ines. He shouldn't think of her as Ines. She hadn't given him leave to use her Christian name, but it was not a name he had heard often, and he liked the way it sounded in his head. She wore a clean dress now, one not covered by his blood. It looked like it might have been a maid's livery as it was a plain, dark blue without any embellishment. But the simplicity suited her, showing her slender figure to advantage. Her hair was neat and swept into some sort of coil that tucked in upon itself. Duncan didn't know the name of it. He knew he would have liked to unravel it, though.

She carried two bottles, and when she saw him, she lifted one with a smile.

Duncan rose slowly to his feet, aware that if he fell over now, it would cause a stir. "Dinnae tell me that's whisky," he said.

"It is for medicinal use," she said primly.

"It always is, lass." He reached for it, but she swept by him, holding the bottle out of his reach. Of course, she only came to his shoulder. If he'd really wanted the bottle, he could have easily snatched it away from her. "Do ye ken what's in the other bottle?"

"Gin," she said. "To keep your wound clean."

Duncan snorted. Now that he was feeling better, he wouldn't allow anyone to waste gin cleaning the scratch on his arm.

"Mr. Murray, should you be standing?" Miss Wellesley asked.

"He should sit until we are ready to depart," Ines said, giving him a disapproving look. Duncan couldn't say why he liked it so much when she frowned at him and scolded. He supposed it was because he'd just spent months with women who ran the other way when he entered a room. He liked a woman who didn't fear him.

"But he will not listen, Emmeline. He never listens."

"I might listen," Duncan said. "If *ye* tell me."

Miss Wellesley looked from Duncan to Ines and then cleared her throat. "I had better bring this basket to Mr. Fortescue to load." She went down the steps, the dog trotting after her.

Ines put her hands on her hips, the bottles resembling strange panniers. "Last night you threatened to cut my hand off if I touched your forehead again. Now you are willing to listen to reason, *senhor*?"

Duncan shrugged. "I can be a bit of a bawbag when I've nae slept enough."

Her brow wrinkled.

"But I've slept now, and I'm in better spirits."

"Fine. Then I suggest you sit down and rest until we are ready."

"Och, lass. Where's yer fire? A bairn wouldnae sit if ye spoke in that tone."

"Sit down, Mr. Murray. Do not stand until I tell you," she ordered. Oh, but the hair rose on the back of his arms when she spoke like that. Still, he didn't sit.

"Come make me, lass." He was playing with fire, and he knew it. She'd already threatened to make him the first man she kissed. Why was he flirting with her? For a moment she looked as though she did not know what to do. Then she raised the whisky bottle.

"I would, but I fear I might drop this bottle of whisky."

Duncan sat, and Ines laughed and followed Miss Wellesley to the coach. "That was a rank trick, lass!" he called after her. "There's nae reason tae threaten the whisky!"

She handed the bottles to Stratford, who looked at them, and then stowed them in the coach with the wicker basket. The horses pawed the ground, and Duncan wondered if Nash was priming his pistol right then. The ladies and Stratford conversed with the coachman a bit longer and then finally

Ines and Miss Wellesley climbed into the coach, followed by the dog. Stratford walked back to Duncan.

"Ye lost that battle, I see," Duncan said, inclining his head toward the coach. Stratford offered his hand and pulled Duncan up.

"I lost the battle but not the war. I need a new strategy."

"Aye, well perhaps ye can devise one while the dog breathes in yer face all the way tae Scotland."

Stratford gave him a disgruntled look. "No wonder Nash shot you."

# *Ten*

*Ines*

An hour into the trip, Murray had fallen asleep. Ines watched him struggle to keep his eyes open, but he was clearly still fighting to regain his strength after the loss of blood and the injury he'd sustained. Ines and Emmeline sat on one side of the coach and the gentlemen sat on the other. The dog lay on the floor between them.

Mr. Fortescue tried several times to shift Murray's weight back toward the door, but the big Scot continued to slide toward Fortescue until his head rested on the other man's shoulder. Ines could imagine that head on her shoulder, or better yet, in her lap.

"Shall we trade places, *senhor*?" she asked Mr. Fortescue.

"I'm fine," he said, shifting uncomfortably.

"Very well," she said, trying not to show her disappointment. Then to her surprise, Emmeline spoke up.

"There's barely enough room there for the two of you, Stratford. Miss Neves is small and will not be troubled by Mr. Murray. You will be more comfortable next to me."

Fortescue looked like he would argue, but then the Scot snuffled and burrowed closer, and he pushed the man over and rapped on the coach roof. He called for the driver to stop for a moment as they would need to step out of the conveyance in order to change places. The dog made it difficult to maneuver inside the vehicle.

A few moments later, Ines settled beside Murray, who had not even opened his eyes when the coach stopped. He slid closer to her until his head lolled onto her shoulder. At which point, she lowered his head into her lap and stroked the hair off his face.

He was not a traditionally handsome man. His features were too stark, his expressions too fierce. He usually needed a shave and a haircut. She was almost sorry he had shaved this morning, as she liked to imagine shaving him and running her hands through his hair. She didn't know what it was about him that had made her knees weak even the very first time she saw him. He always had a wild look about him, except his eyes. Those amber eyes were calm and full of humor. And when he looked at her with those beautiful eyes, her legs began to tremble every time.

Of course, he would never look at her the way she looked at him. To him, she was Benedict Draven's responsibility. But before she had to go back to her predictable life in London and the tedious men her sister introduced her to, Ines would have her PED. She would kiss one man who truly excited her. She could survive years on the exhilaration of that kiss. She could wait until she was one and twenty or so, and then her sister would *have* to allow her more freedom and to relocate above the lace shop.

Ines could almost feel the liberty of such a relocation now. She could come and go as she pleased and would not have to answer to anyone. She could stay up all night, eat nothing but sweets, take a secret lover. And perhaps when she had tired of that life, at the ripe old age of thirty, she would marry. She'd have a huge romantic wedding in one of the old churches. She'd wear a beautiful dress, and her wedding breakfast would be a lavish event. Her husband would adore her, would do anything for her.

Ines had watched her mother suffer through life with a man who found any reason to beat her. She'd lived fourteen years in a home where if she said the wrong word or looked the wrong way, she too might be beaten. She did not need to wonder why her sisters had not argued when their father had married them to old, ugly men. They were happy to escape one hell, although in some cases their husbands were no better than their father. Ines had once asked Catarina why their mother had not left their father.

"Where would she go?" Catarina had asked. "With seven little girls and no money? Anyone she asked for help would return her to her husband. Once a woman marries, she becomes the property of the man. She cannot escape."

Far from making Ines wary of marriage, the conversation had made her all the more determined to marry the right man, a man who loved her and would do anything for her.

"I'm surprised Colonel Draven has not caught up to us yet," Mr. Fortescue said after a long silence.

Speaking of men who would do anything for their wife. Ines sighed, thinking of her brother-in-law. "It is not for lack of trying, I am certain," Ines answered. "But when Benedict does find me, I will simply tell him to go home."

"And you think he will listen, Miss Neves?" Fortescue asked.

She shrugged. "No, he will protest and argue, but I shall ignore him. I am determined to see Scotland now. I am determined to see more of England." *Passion, excitement, and danger.* "I have seen only London. That seems criminal, does it not, *senhor?*"

He made a non-committal sound, and Emmeline put a hand on his arm. "No one will try to force you to take a side, Stratford. Ines, I find that I would like to see Scotland as well. I have never been further north than Cumbria."

"God help me," Fortescue mumbled and closed his eyes.

Emmeline leaned forward conspiratorially. "He has not yet found a strategy he can use on me. I outwit him every time." Looking pleased with herself, Emmeline closed her eyes and leaned her head back against the cushion. Ines stared out of the window at the passing green fields and wondered at the lives of the laborers they passed.

It was full dark by the time the coachman stopped for the night. Ines appreciated his determination to put as much distance between them and Mr. Pope as possible. She knew it would still be days before they reached Murray's home, but at least they were making progress. Murray had been awake the last several hours. He'd seemed surprised to wake with his head on her lap, and then horrified. He moved away from her as quickly as if she were a viper.

He'd said very little to her that last leg of the trip. He and Fortescue had reminisced about the war, and Ines had been shocked that the men had seemed to be in so much danger. Catarina had said that Draven's troop was a select group of men chosen for their skills to conduct dangerous missions that would ultimately bring down Napoleon Bonaparte. But she had not realized that so many of the troop had died or that both Fortescue and Murray had narrowly avoided death themselves. This revelation made it all the stranger that Murray had not been able to find a bride in London. He was a war hero. Many women should want to marry a hero.

But then she did not always understand the English.

Fortescue went inside the inn where they stopped to secure two rooms for the night, while Ines, Emmeline, Murray, and the dog waited in the coach. Finally, the arrangements were made, and Fortescue helped the women down from the coach. After a full day of riding and only brief stops to change horses, Ines's legs were wobbly. She walked stiffly then stumbled when she stepped on a horseshoe in the yard. But before she could fall on her face, Murray caught her about the waist and hauled her back up against his chest.

"I have ye, lass."

Yes, he did. "I tripped on a horseshoe," she said, stupidly. But how could she think of anything to say when that clean, woodsy smell was all around her and his large arm was clamped about her?

"Are ye steady now?"

"*Não*," she said. "You had better hold on to me."

He let out a breath. "I dinnae what tae do with ye, lass."

"I can think of a few things." She smiled at him when he released her.

"Why dinnae we walk aboot the yard for a wee bit? Stretch yer legs and work oot the stiffness?" He offered his arm, which was very proper. She thanked him and took it, allowing him to lead her in a circle about the yard.

"How are you feeling, *senhor*?" she asked.

"Still weary," he said covering a yawn. "Though I slept all day. I'm like a bairn who needs a nap everra three hours."

"The surgeon did say you should not be traveling. No doubt you would be stronger if you had another day to rest."

"I would be deader, there's nae doubt."

"Fortunately, you do not have a fever."

"Och." He waved a hand. "I'm made of sterner stuff than tae catch a fever from a wee hole in the arm."

He was lucky, that was all. But men did seem to think they were invincible. They came to the edge of the stable, and she paused to stretch her back. Looking up at the stars just coming out in the night sky, she said, "It is a pretty night. I never see such stars in London."

"Aye. Beautiful."

His tone caught her attention, and she glanced at him. He wasn't looking at the sky. He was looking at her. A quick look about told her the yard was empty at the moment. Fortescue and Emmeline had gone into the inn, and the grooms were settling the horses from the coach inside. "Would you think me too scandalous if I asked for that kiss now?"

His eyes widened but not with shock. With interest. "Verra scandalous. I willnae kiss ye, lass."

"What if I kiss you?" She moved closer, and when he didn't step back, she moved closer yet, so close she brushed his chest. Still he stood his ground, his amber eyes fixed on her face as she reached up and wrapped her arms around his neck.

"I do not know much about kissing," she said, looking up at him. "But I believe you must lower your head."

"I dinnae think I should kiss ye, lass." But his arms went around her waist, and he pulled her even closer.

"Then someone else will," she whispered. "I want you to be the first. I know you will do it right."

"Ye ken that, do ye?" His hand came up and brushed a loose tendril of hair from her cheek. His touch was surprisingly tender for such a big man. The heat in her belly at his closeness flared, and she felt a shock of desire.

"One kiss," she whispered, turning her mouth so her lips brushed his palm. He hissed in a breath, and his grip on her tightened.

"It's never only one kiss, lass."

"Good," she murmured as she tugged his head down. To her surprise, he complied, lowering his head until their lips were only inches apart. She tried to close the distance, but he resisted.

"I've been wanting tae kiss ye since the first time I laid eyes on ye in the coach," he said.

Her eyes widened at the revelation. So he had wanted her from the start too.

"I've resisted yer efforts tae tempt me because I dinnae want Draven tae kill me. But Draven will kill me anyway."

"I will not let him," she murmured.

He flashed a smile. "If anyone can put him off, ye can. But ken this, lass. I kiss ye because I want tae. And damn the consequences."

"*Sim*," she said. *Damn the consequences.* And then his mouth was on hers and she could not think of anything else to say. She could not think.

Like his hand, his mouth was light and tender. The kiss was sweet, a press of lips against lips, just long enough to make her want more.

Then he pulled back. "There. Ye've been kissed."

She was breathless, and her heart hammered so loudly in her ears that she felt like a drummer stood behind her, pounding away. "Again," she said, her voice sounding so very faint and far away.

"That's nae a good idea." But he didn't move away. He didn't release her. She wrapped her hand in his hair and tugged his mouth down to hers again, and he didn't resist. This time when his mouth met hers, she kissed him back, sweet and tender until the end, when she nipped his lip.

He jolted and looked in her eyes. "Christ and all the saints."

She looked right back into his eyes, challenging him to scold her. Instead, he pushed her against the stable, pressed his body to hers, and took her mouth with his. This was not a kiss, but an invasion of the senses. Her hands tangled in his soft hair then slid down his broad muscled back. The scent of him and the horses and the nearby fields was in her nose. The taste of him, wild and untamed, was on her lips. She drank him in as though she were a woman dying of thirst. He parted her lips and slid inside, and she moaned with pleasure. Ines had no idea how to kiss, but it seemed to be a battle of twining tongues and clashing lips. She'd always been a fighter, and this was a battle she was determined to win.

His groan when she slid her tongue between his lips was enough to let her know she had the upper hand. That and she could feel his heart pounding against her chest. He wanted her as much as she wanted him.

And how she wanted.

She did not think she had ever wanted anything or anyone as much as she wanted him in that moment.

Abruptly, he stiffened, and his lips ceased their skillful plunder of her mouth. She let out a small sound of protest and tried to pull him back, but he broke away and stood straight, leaving her too far from his lips.

"I do hate to interrupt," said a male voice with a very cultured English accent. "But if that woman is who I think it is, then someone ought to tell you that your hours are numbered."

Duncan turned to look at the man, and in doing so, Ines had a clear view of him as well. He was tall and slim with honey-colored hair and light eyes. He was dressed in riding clothing that looked as though its cost rivaled some of her best pieces of lace.

"Mayne," Duncan said, his voice wary.

"Murray," the man said, then his gaze slid to her. His expression turned to one of annoyance and then slight exasperation. "Miss Neves, I presume?"

"And who are you, *senhor?*"

Duncan blew out a breath. "Miss Ines Neves, allow me tae introduce the Duke of Mayne."

\*\*\*

*Stratford*

"Oh, no," Stratford said when the door to the private room he'd secured for dinner opened. Emmeline turned and, not seeing Murray or Miss Neves or the innkeeper with the tea they'd ordered, looked back at Stratford with a quizzical expression, her hand on Loftus's head to keep him calm.

"I should have known you'd be involved in this," Mayne said, walking into the room as though he owned it. For all Stratford knew, the duke did own it. He removed his hat and nodded his head at Emmeline. "Miss Wellesley, isn't it?"

She stood. "Your Grace. What an unexpected pleasure."

Mayne took her hand and kissed it, his green eyes meeting Stratford's to gauge his reaction. Stratford kept his face inscrutable. Like most members of the upper classes, they knew each other in passing. What did Stratford care if the duke kissed Emmeline's hand? Although, he didn't see the need for Mayne to keep hold of it for so long.

"I presume Draven sent you," Stratford said, eyeing Emmeline's hand still encased in Mayne's.

"He did." The duke finally released her and pulled out her chair for her. When she sat, he followed. Stratford remained standing. "He interrupted my sister's wedding day, as a matter of fact."

"Lady Philomena?" Emmeline asked. "Oh, you must give her my felicitations."

Mayne nodded. "I'd like to do that, but I've run into a bit of a problem. Miss Neves says she will not return to London. Draven sent me to find her and bring her back. It seems Jasper has gone underground, and no one can locate him at the moment. I told the colonel to go back to London for Jasper, and I would find Duncan and bring Miss Neves home. But when I told her I'd been sent to bring her back, she refused."

Stratford wished he'd ordered something stronger than tea. "She does seem rather intent on traveling to Scotland."

"And why is that, do you think?" Mayne asked, his tone calm. Except Stratford knew the man. He was annoyed as hell. Probably because he was an expert negotiator, and he hadn't been able to negotiate with Miss Neves.

"She wants a taste of freedom," Emmeline suggested.

"Perhaps, but when I came upon her, she seemed to want a taste of Duncan." He leaned back in his chair and eyed

Stratford. "You don't seem surprised. Come to think of it, why are the two of you traveling with them?"

Stratford explained everything to Mayne—perhaps not quite everything—and by the time he'd finished, Duncan and Miss Neves had come into the private dining chamber.

"I told you I did not run away," Miss Neves said, sitting regally in a chair at the end of the table. "*Senhor* Murray did not abduct me. You may go back and tell Benedict as much."

Mayne pressed two fingers to his temple. "I cannot go back and tell him that. You will have to come back with me and tell him yourself, Miss Neves."

"The lass wants tae see Scotland," Duncan said, surprising Stratford. "There's nae harm in that."

"With you as her chaperone? Considering what I saw outside, I'd say Miss Neves's virtue is in danger."

Duncan took a menacing step forward. "Are ye implying I am some sort of rogue who would take advantage of a lass? Is that the kind of man ye think I am?"

Mayne rose. "Duncan—"

Miss Neves stepped between the two men. Stratford gave Emmeline a quick glance, wondering if they should leave the three to discuss the matter in private, but she seemed completely engrossed in the conversation.

"*Senhor* Murray is a decent man. If someone is to blame for what you saw outside, it is me. I have corrupted him. I asked him to kiss me."

Duncan shook his head. "I would have kissed ye regardless. I willnae have ye blame yerself. I was corrupted before I met ye."

That was true enough, but it must have been some kiss if Duncan was now taking Miss Neves's side. This morning he had not wanted her to go to Scotland with him. And if she was forced to go home, Emmeline would have to go home. Which was exactly what Stratford wanted.

Wasn't it?

The door opened and the innkeeper paused. "Should I come back?"

"No," Stratford said at the same time Duncan said, "Aye. And bring some whisky. I need it because my heid is so fuzzy I cannae even speak clearly. I'm nae corrupted, lass, but I'm nae saint, either."

Stratford pushed the innkeeper out of the room. "Why don't you bring some food? Whatever you have will suffice." He pressed a coin into the man's hand. "And keep this discussion to yourself."

"Yes, sir."

Stratford knew the gossip would be spread within hours, if not minutes. Emmeline stepped outside as voices rose inside. Stratford closed the door and moved closer to the kitchen. Thankfully the noise of the cook and the banging of pots and pans drowned out the sound of the duke's verbal duel with the lacemaker. The kitchen door was closed, and the only light came from the public room. Emmeline stood in a shaft of that light, her dark hair curling over one shoulder and brushing the luminous skin of her neck. Stratford had the urge to brush that hair off her shoulder and then perhaps press his lips to the curve of her neck. But he couldn't risk kissing her again. That kiss they'd shared at Wentmore…that kiss. He did not know how to describe it. He didn't have the words to compare it to any other kiss he'd ever experienced. Stratford had always thought of kissing as something one did with a woman before moving to the more interesting activities. But when he looked at Emmeline's mouth, the urge to kiss her was so strong, he almost gave in.

He had been telling her the truth when he'd said he did not want to ruin their friendship—not that they'd ever really been friends. And he'd hinted that he'd kept some distance between them because he had always wanted more than friendship from her. But how was he to keep distance between them when he was forced to sit in a coach beside her all day? He'd been able to smell her lemon scent, feel the warm press of her leg when the coach veered one way or another, catch her looking at him when she thought he was not paying attention.

"I don't think the duke expected Ines to be so stubborn. And Mr. Murray is supporting her. Interesting, as he seemed to want to send her away just a few hours ago."

Stratford shrugged. "He does need a wife."

"An *English* wife," Emmeline corrected. "I think it's best I keep an eye on him. I'm not at all certain of his intentions."

Stratford burst out laughing. He didn't mean to, but it was very difficult to keep a straight face when Emmeline played chaperone.

She frowned at him. "Why do you laugh, sir?"

"Because for a moment I had the image of you scolding Duncan Murray in my head."

"I could scold him," she said, hands going to her hips.

"I would much prefer that you scold me." The tone of his voice was lower than he'd meant it to be. She went still and looked at him from under her lashes.

"What should I scold you for?" she asked, her voice like velvet. His breath caught in his throat and he closed his fists and clenched his hands to keep them from reaching for her.

"Tell me I shouldn't kiss you again," he said. "You are the chaperone."

"You shouldn't kiss me again," she said, stepping closer. There was that lemon scent, making his head spin and ruining his willpower. "You should definitely not pull me into your arms, press me against you, and put your mouth on mine, Stratford."

His breath came in short bursts now, and his short nails dug into his palm. "And if I defy your orders?"

She wet her lips, the tip of her pink tongue visible just long enough to make his knees go weak. "You'll be sorry."

He reached for her, hauled her against him. "Make me sorry then," he murmured and pressed his mouth to hers. Heat instantly flared between them as her mouth connected with his. Her tongue slid against his, making him desperate to pull her closer. Instead, he dug his hands into her hips, which he quickly realized was a mistake. Her figure was as lush as he'd always anticipated, her hips soft and full and perfect in his hands. One part of his mind warned him this was a mistake. The more he kissed her, the more he would want her. And he'd already wanted her for so long, already pushed down that want for so many years that he'd become accustomed to the subtle ache of desire for her every time he saw her or thought of her. But now he had the taste of her on his lips, the smell of her in his nose. That ache would intensify until he did something they would both regret.

He pulled back. "We should stop," he said, trying to catch his breath and release her before the kitchen staff walked by and caught him with his hands on her.

"We should," she said. "I'm not behaving like a proper chaperone."

"You are a terrible chaperone," he said.

"Just for that." She grabbed the back of his neck and pulled him to her again. This time they stumbled back until he had her pressed up against the wall. His hands slid— accidentally, of course—to her backside. God, it was so round and plump and perfect. How was he supposed to stop kissing her when she felt like this in his arms?

She did something with her tongue no innocent woman should know how to do, and he felt himself grow rock hard. He could imagine so many delicious things she might do with that tongue.

And of course, that was the moment the kitchen door opened. The light hit them both, and Stratford pushed Emmeline behind him to shield her from the innkeeper's view. The man's brows rose. "I'm so sorry, sir."

Stratford cleared his throat, feeling like a naughty schoolboy. "No matter. I see you have the food we ordered.

I'll let the others know we may eat now." And he'd tell them to stubble it before the innkeeper heard more than he'd already been treated to.

"Miss Wellesley." He gestured for Emmeline to precede him and tried valiantly not to look at her bottom as she moved in front of him. When she opened the door, she cleared her throat before he had a chance.

"Dinner has arrived," she said, giving them all a quelling look that made him want to push her up against the wall all over again. Duncan and Phineas, who had been at each other's throats, parted and straightened their coats, while Miss Neves, who had been standing on a table, stepped down. They all took seats, Stratford across from Emmeline, Miss Neves at the head of the table, and Murray and Mayne glaring at each other from across the table. The innkeeper set the food down and scurried out of the room, returning a moment later with decanters of wine. Stratford needed a healthy dose of it. Besides the tension in the room from the Highlander and the duke, he couldn't stop looking at Emmeline and imagining lowering her bodice to free those impressive breasts.

God, he wanted to touch her again.

"I have a suggestion," Emmeline said. Stratford sincerely doubted it was the same one he was thinking of. "It has been a long day for everyone, and tempers are short. Why don't we all get a good night's sleep and discuss things in the morning."

"Fine," the duke said. "It's not as though we can start back for Town this late."

Miss Neves said something in Portuguese Stratford didn't understand. Judging from her tone of voice, it was not complimentary. Phineas had been known for his skills as a negotiator during the war. He would need all of those skills tomorrow if he was to persuade the lacemaker to return with him. Stratford looked at Emmeline and wondered what decision she would make. Would she return as well or remain determined to travel north to stay with her grandmother? If the latter, they too would need a chaperone. Stratford didn't trust himself alone with her any longer.

\*\*\*

*Ines*

"Where are you going?" Emmeline asked, causing Ines to freeze halfway to the door. She had been so quiet, but it was almost impossible not to wake someone when they were sleeping in the bed beside you.

"To the privy," Ines whispered, hoping the other woman would turn over and go back to sleep.

"We have a chamber pot." Emmeline sat and peered at her in the low firelight. "And you are fully dressed."

"Fine." Ines pretended to be chastised. "I want to make certain Mr. Murray has no fever."

"The duke said he would stay with Murray." Emmeline's blue eyes narrowed. "You are running away." She threw back the covers, revealing she was still fully dressed. "Are you mad? You cannot leave on your own."

"You look ready to leave yourself."

Emmeline waved a hand, dismissing her concern. "I have Loftus."

The women both glanced at the dog, who was sleeping on a blanket on the floor, snoring softly.

"And I have somewhere to go. My grandmother will take me in. Where will you go?"

Ines felt her shoulders droop and sat on the edge of the bed. "I do not know. I only know I cannot go back yet. I cannot! All my life I have wanted an adventure. All my life I have wanted romance and to fall in love."

Emmeline's jaw dropped open. "Are you eloping with Mr. Murray?"

"*Não*. He does not want to marry me."

Emmeline crossed her arms. "You obviously have not seen the way he looks at you. He'd like to do more than kiss you, and men have been known to marry for lesser reasons."

Ines felt a sudden burst of excitement. "How does he look at me? With lust? Oh, this is wonderful!"

Emmeline shook her head. "You are hopeless. You cannot run away on your own. I had better come with you."

Ines took her hand. "You would do that?"

"Of course." She gathered up her few belongings, and the movement woke the dog, who jumped to his feet, tongue lolling with interest. "Leave the candle. We do not want anyone to see us. Quietly now."

Ines opened the door, but before she could step out, Loftus made a small whining sound. Ines looked down and into the eyes of Duncan Murray, who was lying across the door.

"I thought ye might try something," he said, looking pleased with himself.

Ines peered down the hallway to make sure no one else was there then grabbed Murray's uninjured arm and pulled him into the room. She closed the door then glared at him. "Why are you sleeping on the floor? You are injured, *senhor*! You should be resting."

"I slept all day. Phineas tried to give me laudanum, but I switched drinks with him and now he's snoring louder than a drove of piglets."

Ines was actually impressed. "That means he will sleep most of the morning and perhaps into the afternoon. We will be long gone."

"And where are we going, lassies? Surely the two of ye dinnae think tae cast oot on yer own."

And of course, the idiot had to go and act like a man again. "We can take care of ourselves. For years Catarina and I survived on our own. I am not helpless."

"Well, be that as it may, I will go with ye. I take it ye dinnae plan tae go back tae London. Will ye consider continuing with me tae Scotland?"

"I would not mind seeing Scotland," Emmeline said.

"It's settled then," Murray said. "We go now, before dawn, and we walk until we find a farmer willing tae let us ride in his cart."

Emmeline frowned. "What about the coach and driver?"

Murray shook his head. "Too easy for Draven and Mayne tae track. How do ye think he found us?"

Ines looked from Murray to Emmeline. "What about Mr. Fortescue?"

Emmeline shook her head. "He's only stayed with us out of a sense of obligation toward me. He'd much rather go home. Now he will be able to return."

Murray let out a bark of laughter. "If ye think he will just run home and give up, ye dinnae ken him verra well, lass."

Emmeline gave him a stony look. "Shall we wake him and waste more time in discussions or leave now and put some distance between the duke and ourselves?"

Murray scratched his head. "It's best if we wake him. He willnae take it kindly if we leave him behind."

"Well, I vote we leave him behind." She looked at Ines. "What is your vote?"

Ines knew who her ally was and did not hesitate. "Leave him."

"This is why women are nae allowed tae vote," Murray grumbled. "Nae, dinnae lead the way. I'll go first and make sure all is clear."

He opened the door, and Ines slid behind him, liking the warmth of him in front of her. She'd been ready to go on her own, but now that he was here, she could not stop herself from sliding her hand into his. The Highlander's hand was rough and calloused, and she never wanted to let it go. How could she have been willing to leave him behind just a quarter hour ago? She couldn't imagine never kissing him again, never touching him again. She hadn't known kissing could be like he had shown her. If kissing was that wonderful, why did Catarina and Draven not kiss all the time? Perhaps they did, in private. And that led her to wonder if the other things done in private were as wonderful as kissing. How could she convince Murray to give her a taste of that forbidden fruit?

But she had to be careful not to fall in love with him. How many times had Catarina told her that just because a man desired a woman, that didn't mean he loved her? Ines had seen too many girls in her shop heartbroken because they'd fallen in love with men who did not love them back. She'd seen a number of babies born as well due to men's lies about love and women's willingness to believe them. Slowly, Ines pulled her hand out of Murray's and tucked it in her pocket.

# Eleven

*Emmeline*

Emmeline watched Ines step carefully down the stairs, avoiding steps that might creak. She took hold of the railing herself and prepared to step cautiously when a voice whispered in her ear, "Where are we going?"

She spun around and almost toppled backward and down. She might have fallen head over heels if Stratford hadn't caught her arm and hauled her against him. Her heart had been beating hard from the fright, but it still managed to speed up when her body connected to his. She liked the feel of his chest pressed against hers. She liked it too much, which meant she immediately pushed away and then almost fell right back down again. He grabbed her and pulled her away from the precipice.

"What the devil are you about?" he hissed. "Are you trying to break your neck?"

"You scared me half to death," she accused him. "How dare you!" It was only with a great deal of feigned indignity that she managed to move out of his embrace when everything in her told her to move closer.

"I wouldn't have to sneak after you if you weren't escaping in the dead of night like some sort of criminal." He looked down the stairs and pointed at the two faces peering up at them. "I thought better of you, Duncan."

The Scotsman muttered something about women voting.

Emmeline started back toward the stairs. "If we're to argue, let's do it outside. I don't want to wake the duke or the other guests."

"Fine." Taking hold of her arm, Stratford escorted Emmeline down the stairs, and they followed Ines and Murray outside and into the yard. All was quiet except for the chirp of insects and the rustle of leaves in the breeze. A gibbous moon hung in the sky, the occasional cloud sailing over it.

"I told them tae fetch ye," Murray said.

"You and I will speak later," Stratford said.

"How did you hear us?" Emmeline asked, annoyed now that he stood before her, his expression disapproving. She pulled her arm away, and Loftus, sensing her dismay, licked her hand. She'd lost her gloves at some point on this trip, and it seemed one more indignity.

"I was listening for you," he said. "I went through all the possible scenarios for this evening, and the most likely one was that you two"—he pointed at the women—"would try to flee. I didn't think *he'd* be part of it."

"Because ye kent Mayne planned tae drug me."

"I shouldn't have bet against you," Stratford said. "Where is Mayne now?"

"He's having a wee lie down. If the potion he thought tae slip me is worth anything, he'll be oot for hours yet."

"I don't suppose I can convince the rest of you to go back inside and lie down?" Stratford asked.

In answer, Ines said, "Which way is north?"

Stratford sighed and looked at Murray. "Have you considered throwing them over our shoulders and carrying them back home?"

Murray raised a brow. "And just how far do ye think we would get before they concocted some devious plan?"

"I have a devious plan in mind right now," Emmeline said. "If we don't start walking, I might just put it into action."

Grumbling, Stratford fell into step behind Murray, who led the way, Ines right behind him.

After an hour or so of walking, Emmeline had grown to appreciate the comforts of the coach. She also realized it might have been wiser to sleep a few hours before starting out. She was having difficulty focusing on where she put her feet and every muscle seemed to ache. By now the small party was well away from the inn and village, and she was relying wholly on moonlight to see the road. Emmeline tried to watch where she stepped so as to avoid large rocks or dips in the road, but she could feel Stratford looking at her. For his part, he walked as though he had slept for days and could walk as far north as Dunnet Head without pause. Seeing her looking at him, he gestured to Murray and Ines, walking ahead of them. "Duncan may seem fine, but you can't expect him to walk all the way to Scotland. He'll do it because he's an idiot and then fall down dead on his doorstep."

"I see what you are about," she said.

He gave her an innocent look.

"You worry that I am tired and need to stop, but you think if you behave as though a rest is for Mr. Murray's benefit then I will not object."

"Will it work?" he asked.

"It might if I didn't have a plan already."

"What's that?"

"In the morning"—please, God, let it be morning soon—"we plan to ask farmers if we can ride in their carts," Emmeline said.

He snorted. "I suppose that seems romantic to you. Never mind the manure and chicken feathers."

She tossed her head, even though she knew it was childish. "Then we buy a cart."

"Oh, you have blunt, have you?"

She didn't answer. He knew she'd lost her money on that first day in the dog/baby swindle.

"I spent almost the last of mine to hire the last coach and driver," he said. "You know, the one we have now left back at the inn."

How she mourned leaving that coach behind now. "Is your point that this is not the wisest decision I have ever made?" she asked. "Because I know that already."

"Then why are you doing this? I understand you feel obligated to help Miss Neves, but Draven will catch up to her sooner or later. Sooner if he has already located Lord Jasper."

She continued walking, her back stiff, despite how heavy her shoulders felt.

"But why won't you see reason and go home? You have always been the cleverest and most rational female of my acquaintance. I don't understand what you are thinking."

Her gaze stared straight ahead, anger fueled by weariness bubbling inside her. "Why do you pretend not to know? *You* are the most intelligent and logical man I know. Please stop pretending you don't see what's in front of you."

He jogged until he was in front of her and turned to face her, walking backward. "I always see what's right in front of me. I have always seen you, Emmeline."

"Then you see what a disappointment I am to my mother."

He shook his head, but she saw in his expression that he knew exactly what she was talking about. Just as she knew how little Stratford's father valued him. Of all the people who might question what she was doing, she had always thought Stratford would understand.

"She loves you," he said.

"She does, in her way," Emmeline agreed. "But all my life she has tried to change me, to make me thinner, prettier, more like the daughter she wishes I had been. I do not want to live the rest of my life trying to change myself to make someone else happy." She'd never actually put her feelings into words before, but as she did, it all became so clear. She wanted to be loved for who she was. She'd always been told, in one way or another, she had to change. Emmeline didn't want to change. Just because she was not what a few thousand wealthy and titled people deemed to be fashionable, did not mean she should remake herself to please them.

Before she had run away, she had taken a hard look in the mirror. She liked who she saw looking back at her. She liked her contrary opinions, her curvy body, and even her unruly hair. "I just thought that if I could get away for a few years, until I was firmly on the shelf, then I could live as I want. My sisters could marry and have children, and my mother would be able to focus on tasks other than making me into someone I will never be."

Stratford stopped and held his hands out, locking them around her upper arms. "I had no idea you felt that way."

"No one does. I've never told anyone." She shook her head. "I don't know why I am telling you. Except I thought you might understand."

"Do ye need a rest?" Murray called back.

"Yes!" Stratford answered. "Give me ten minutes or so."

It was she, not he, who needed the respite, but she appreciated that Stratford kept up the ruse that she was not struggling.

"Just wait until we reach the Highlands!" Murray said. "Ye will wish for roads like this."

Stratford moved off the road, still holding Emmeline's arm. "Just wait until he passes out," Stratford muttered. "I'll make him eat his words."

"Such a good friend," Emmeline said.

Pausing under the gently swaying leaves of a tree, Stratford removed his hat. "I am a good friend. Why didn't you ever tell me how you felt? I wouldn't have dragged you to all those balls."

She smiled. "I never blamed you. Neither of us had a choice."

"I had a choice. I just like to keep my mother happy, considering she's the only parent who can stand the look of me."

Emmeline sank to the ground under the tree, the weight of the day and her sympathy for him becoming too heavy. "I'm sure your father and mother love you in their own way, but I hope coming after me is not a means to earn their favor."

He crouched down before her. "Is that what you think?"

She looked away, saw Ines help Murray to sit under another tree on the opposite side of the road.

"No. I think you are here because you wanted to come, but you should go home. I am perfectly safe with Mr. Murray and am in the company of Miss Neves. You can leave me and go back to your own life."

"What if I don't want to leave you?" he asked.

She shook her head and blew out an exasperated breath. "I have told you countless times, I am not going home."

"And I have told you that I go where you go."

"Why?" She lifted her arms in frustration. "So you can lecture me at every turn?"

"No. So I can do this."

He reached for her, and though she could have easily moved away, she let him take her into his arms. That was where she wanted to be anyway. And then because she liked the feel of being pressed against him, she pulled him closer. Of course, that caused him to lose his balance and topple forward, toppling them both, she under him as they fell onto the grass under the tree. He pushed himself up on his elbows and looked down at her for a long moment. She knew his eyes would be that beautiful blue she loved. Her own eyes were probably huge because she could feel his weight on her, and it was more satisfying than she could have imagined to have a man splayed on top of her.

"I must stand up," he said.

She wrapped her hands around his neck. "No."

"Duncan—"

"Can't see us behind this tree and wouldn't care if he could." She tugged his mouth closer to hers. "What were you saying before? About why you want to stay?"

"I really should show you," he said.

"Show me."

Anticipating him, she lifted her lips to his, but this was no gentle kiss. Stratford kissed her hard and thoroughly, effectively robbing her of any semblance of rational thought. She wanted more of his mouth, more of his touch, more of everything.

"Not here," he said, pulling away, his breath as short as hers. "What am I saying?" He rolled off her, leaving her cold and lonely. "Not anywhere. We cannot do this."

"Because we are friends," she said.

"Exactly."

She rolled her head to look at him. "We could be *better* friends."

She saw his throat move as he swallowed. Then he looked away determinedly. "That's not the only reason. You are an unmarried lady. I cannot—"

"Then why don't you marry me?"

She didn't know why she said it. She wished with all her heart she could take it back as soon as the words left her mouth. His expression said it all. He looked shocked and horrified and, well, disgusted at the idea. Emmeline scrambled up. "Forget what I said. I wasn't thinking."

"Emmeline." He was reaching for her, and she jumped to her feet and started away.

"I was not being serious. It was a joke that went too far." She held out a hand to ward him away. "I need a moment alone."

"We need to talk about this."

"There is nothing to talk about. I told you I will never marry, and I especially wouldn't marry you. Now give me a moment alone to attend to my personal needs."

At her cutting words, he slowed and finally paused.

"Thank you. A lady needs a few moments alone sometimes." She pushed her way through some low brush then slid behind a tree and leaned back against the trunk for support. She pressed her hand to her mouth to keep her cries silent as tears ran down her cheeks.

What was wrong with her? Why would she say such a thing? Of course, Stratford did not want to marry her. He didn't love her any more than she loved him. He just wanted what all men wanted, though he had more honor than most. And she knew what that honor would lead to. He would tell her that he was flattered by her proposal but could not accept. He would explain, oh so gently, that he didn't love her.

And that was fine. She would never marry any man because what would be the point of escaping a controlling mother only to wed a man and fall under his control? Then she'd be forced to change to become the woman he wanted for a wife. There was only one way she could ever be her true self—and that was to be alone.

And that was why she had left Odham Abbey. And that was why she hated Stratford coming after her.

Because he made her believe she didn't have to be alone to be loved for who she was. And because he was making her fall in love with him.

\*\*\*

*Duncan*

Duncan watched Stratford chase after Miss Wellesley and wondered when the man would admit he cared for the lass. It was as plain as the day was long that he had feelings for the woman. Duncan had known it even before he had seen them together. Stratford was always quick to defend his cousin, though from what Duncan could see of her, the criticism she received was generally fair.

Ines had held off sitting beside him at the base of the tree, but now she gave in and sat daintily with her legs under her. For such a small creature, she was a lot of trouble.

"Are you still angry with me?" she asked.

"Aye," he said.

"I would have thought you glad to be rid of me. I have caused you problems."

It was as though she'd heard his thoughts. "I should be, aye," he said.

"But you are not glad to be rid of me?" she asked, turning her body toward his. Duncan had to resist pulling her onto his lap. Considering how he was feeling, it was probably best to avoid the question.

"I want ye tae be safe, lass."

She exhaled with a loud. "Safe! Safe! Safe! *Caramba*! I am so tired of this talk of safe." From the way her arms were slicing the air and her voice rose, he could see that.

"Ye've a taste for adventure, I ken." He liked that about her. He liked it very much, though it made his head ache at the moment.

"Yes! And I did not seek this adventure. It found me. I was only trying to avoid Mr. Podmore."

"Who is this Podmore?"

She explained, and Duncan felt his collar grow warm as she discussed her sister's attempts to find a suitor for her. He didn't like thinking of her with another man, especially a man like the Podmore she described.

"I cannae blame ye for wanting tae escape a man like that. Ye'll want a man who kens yer need for adventure and excitement."

She looked at him, and even in the darkness, he could feel her gaze boring into his.

He looked for an escape. "What I mean is—"

"If only I knew of such a man," she said, tapping her chin in a show of thoughtfulness, her eyes still on him. Duncan tried to scoot away, but the tree was at his back.

"Lass, dinnae look tae me." He shook his head and held his hands up.

"What is it they call you, *senhor*? The Lunatic?" She moved closer, trapping him. "Why is that, I wonder. And you are in search of a wife, *não*?"

He grasped her arms and held her at bay before she could crawl into his lap, which was exactly where he wanted her but beside the point. "I *was* in search of a wife. Now I'm for home."

She was no good at hiding her emotions. He saw the disappointment written across her face.

"Lass, did ye nae tell me ye were hiding in my coach tae avoid a suitor and running away because ye dinnae want tae be trapped in a marriage?"

She tilted her head, her gaze seeming to see him clearly through the shadows of the night. "Marriage to you would be no trap, *senhor.*"

He felt a lump rise in his throat, and his lungs seemed to push all the air out so he could not breathe.

"But I am not proposing we marry," she said. Duncan didn't know whether to breathe a sigh of relief or hold his breath in preparation for what she might say next. "It is an excuse for me to travel with you. And if you bring me home, then your mother cannot say you did not find a bride, *não*?"

"Nae." He shook his head. He could see her plan now. It was the sort of haphazard, half-baked idea he would have. He had to admire her. She wanted an adventure and a real or pretend engagement gave her presence with him legitimacy. She probably thought he could benefit too.

But she did not know Lady Charlotte.

"Then you do not want me with you," she said, shrinking back from him. He pulled her back where she'd been.

"I dinnae say that. But nor do I want ye tae reach Kirkmoray and believe ye'll receive a warm welcome from my mother. She willnae accept ye for my wife."

She tensed. He could feel her body go rigid, though he only held her arms. Without thinking, he slid his hands down her arms and back up again, comforting her. He also enjoyed the feel of the soft, bare skin of her forearms under his fingers. "It's nothing tae do with ye, lass," he said. "She wants me to marry an Englishwoman. Nae, not just an Englishwoman but the daughter of a peer." He pulled her closer yet when she tried to jerk away. He didn't want to bruise her arms, so he lowered his hands to her waist. His hands were already firmly about that slim waist when he realized his mistake. Her waist was too close to her hips, which was too close to her bottom, which he desperately wanted to plant two hands on and squeeze. She was a slender lass who looked as though she might blow away in a strong wind, but he'd paid enough attention to see that under the loose folds of her dress, she had a shapely bottom. He wondered just how shapely.

Keeping his hands firmly on her waist, he continued. "Ye dinnae ken the history of England. The English have hated the Scottish for years. They've done all they can tae do away with us. Whole villages struggle with finding enough food tae feed their children. Clans are scattered tae the four winds."

"Not your clan," she said, seeming to relax now under his touch.

"Nae, not mine. And one reason for that, it cannae be denied, is my mother. Lady Charlotte is an Englishwoman and the daughter of an earl. She married a Scot, which lowered her in the Crown's esteem, but she is still esteemed, ye ken?"

"And what about you? You are a war hero, *não*?"

"I'm nae hero, lass." And he wasn't. She wasn't the only one who'd wanted adventure or an escape. The guilt of his father's death—well, Duncan had thought fighting with the English would make him forget it. When it hadn't, he'd accepted a dangerous commission, thinking that perhaps in death he could forget. "But I will admit that my service is another protection for the clan."

"But not enough for your mother. I am not good enough." She looked away. Duncan had to wonder how his mother, a woman Ines had never met, was able to extend the long arm of disapproval all the way into England and Ines's heart. Duncan began to wonder if perhaps all the years of living with his mother's disapproval meant he carried it with him and spread it like pollen. Only what grew were not flowers but weeds and thorns.

"Nae lass is good enough for her," he said. "But then she never did ken what tae look for."

She slowly turned back to him. The sky behind her had lightened to a steel gray, pearling her olive skin and making her brown eyes look even darker. Duncan lifted one hand to touch her soft cheek. "She doesnae appreciate the desire for adventure or escape."

"*Não?*" she whispered, leaning her cheek into his touch. Duncan seemed to have always known Ines would respond to his touch this way. He hadn't been surprised at her response to his kiss. She was a sensual creature, one who craved connection, touch, passion. He recognized that part of himself in her. "What else does she not appreciate, *senhor?*"

"Duncan. Nae senhor."

She smiled, probably at his poor accent on the term.

"What else does she not appreciate, *Duncan?*"

He liked the way she said his name. It sounded exotic and foreign. The English always seemed to make it flat and squish it together. He preferred the lilt of the Scots brogue for his name, but if he had a second choice it would be Ines's soft way of breathing it.

"She is a woman who is always skeptical. She doesnae trust anyone. Ye, ye trust easily. Perhaps tae easily." His hand slid from her waist to the small of her back, pulling her closer to him.

"I can trust you. Benedict trusts you."

"Aye, ye can trust me. But only so far, lass."

"Can I trust you here?" she asked, gesturing at the space between them.

"Aye."

She scooted closer. "Here?"

"Aye." But his voice had grown gruffer and deeper.

She moved onto his lap. "Here?

All but gritting his teeth, he said, "Aye."

"What else does Lady Charlotte not appreciate?"

"Passion," he said above the pounding of his heart. He wanted to pull her the last few inches until she was pressed against him, her mouth on his. "She says tae much passion makes a man—or woman—unpredictable and…dangerous."

Ines's mouth curved slowly into a smile. "Dangerous. Do you think I am dangerous?"

"Oh, aye. Ye are a hazard, lass."

"Oh? Am I?" she whispered, wriggling closer. That made his cock sit up and take notice. Just a little further and she'd be warm and cozy over it.

"A hazard tae my good intentions."

"I detest good intentions, Duncan."

"So do I." His hand slid from her cheek to the back of her neck, where he grasped a fistful of her disheveled hair and drew her mouth to his. He hadn't intended to plunder her, but as soon as their lips touched, the craving he felt for more of her, all of her, gripped him and would not let go. She opened to him without protest, and her tongue met his with a fervor that nearly drove him over the edge. He yanked her against him so she straddled him, that warm place between her legs resting over his hard cock, which strained at his trousers. He resisted the urge to lift his hips and press his erection into that warm spot, but he could not resist allowing his hand to trail down over the swell of her bottom. He'd pulled her forward, and she was lifted just enough that he could run a hand over its roundness and firmness. It was high and tight, a good bottom for a playful slap or where a man could grab a handful and hold on.

Her arse moved under his hand, probably testing the feel of it, and he could not resist sliding his hand lower until he slid between her cheeks for a moment. He thought she might stiffen or gasp in shock, but instead she gave a moan so wanton that he almost came. Duncan couldn't think clearly any longer. He just knew he needed to hear that moan again. He needed to see her face when she climaxed. She was the kind of woman who would burn bright and so hot a man might incinerate if he came too close.

Duncan was a man who liked a risk like that. Releasing her hair, he slid both hands to the middle of her spine and eased her back. Much as it pained him to break their kiss, to tear his mouth from her warm, inviting one, he did so. She drew in a breath, her back arching and her small, round breasts close enough to his mouth that he could kiss them over the fabric of her gown. Instead, he anchored her with one arm and slid the other down her neck and between her breasts. "Can I touch ye, lass?" he asked.

She looked down at him, eyes unfocused, expression one of confusion. His hand moved down further to her belly and then lower, and her eyes widened.

"Can I touch ye, lass?" he asked again.

"Please," she said, and the word was barely a puff of air. He tugged up her skirts until he had the hem then slid his hand underneath. The warmth of her thigh met his flesh, and he cupped it, allowing his hand to heat to her temperature. Their eyes met now, her expression clear to him in the growing lightness. How long had they been sitting here? A quarter hour? An hour? Three? Where was Stratford?

And why did he care when she was looking at him like that, like a lioness watching her prey, waiting for the hunt, the catch, the pleasure of the kill.

His hand slid higher and there was that moan again. Her slim body trembled beneath his touch, her knees gripping his thighs tightly as if to hold on and anchor her. He inched higher, closer to her heat, to the core of her. Her breathing grew rapid, her tongue wet her lips, and Duncan's own breath rasped in his throat.

His fingers brushed moist hair and she made a sound like *Oh*. He brushed against her again, and her hips rocked so his fingers slipped over her outer lips. Her entire body shivered, and she moaned.

*Christ and all the saints*, he'd never heard a woman moan like that. It was the sort of sound that came from somewhere deep within, a well of passion he did not think most women, nor most men, even possessed. And he'd barely tapped it.

His fingers caressed her now, learning the shape of her sex, the creases and folds and the heat of her.

And then he found the wetness. He drew it along a finger and slaked it over her, making her flesh slick and slippery. She was gasping, soft little moans, but she went silent when he found her channel. She tightened with anticipation as he moved his fingers up until he found that wet, hard bud just waiting for him.

"*Oh!*" Her exhalation seemed to echo about them, and Duncan had a fleeting thought of Stratford again, but one look at Ines's face and he could think of nothing but her. She was an attractive woman, no one could deny that, but the expression of pleasure he saw on her face made her absolutely radiant. He could hardly breathe at the sight of her.

Somehow, he knew she possessed a short fuse. If he stroked that tight bud, she would climax quickly. He wanted to give her more than a quick burst of pleasure. He slid his finger back to her wet channel, entered it a fraction, and stroked. She was mewling now, moving against him. He tried to keep her hips steady, but she managed to take more of him inside her—one finger to the knuckle. He felt her tighten around him. He slid his finger out and then back in again, and her mouth opened soundlessly. She wanted more, and he wanted to give it to her—two fingers, three, his cock. But someone had to be in control here. Later Duncan would be amused that he was the one to hold back, to keep from rushing in. It was so utterly unlike him.

Duncan tightened his grip on her waist, pulled her close enough so that their eyes were mere inches apart. "Look at me, lass," he said.

Her unfocused eyes landed on his then her gaze flitted away as her body reached for pleasure. He stroked her, slid his finger to that tender nub, and pressed lightly. Her gaze fastened on him.

"Duncan," she breathed.

"That's right. Look at me, lass."

He rubbed the nub again then slid away and entered her. "*Não! Sim! Por favor.*"

"I'll give ye what ye want, lass, but ye have to give up control. Do ye trust me?"

She shook her head. "I do not trust any man."

Duncan would explore that sentiment later. For the time being, he would try a different tact. "Do ye think I ken what ye want?"

Her hips bucked as though to show him, her face an agony of waiting. "Then believe me when I tell ye that my way will make it better for ye."

She gave a brief nod that conveyed tacit agreement. Duncan didn't mistake the nod for trust or a complete relinquishing of control. But for the moment, she would allow him to show her how it could be.

He stroked her with the finger still inside her, pulled out, then entered her slowly. Her eyes closed, and he whispered, "Eyes on me, lass."

She stared at him, her beautiful brown eyes so dark and large they seemed to take up her entire face. Slowly, he slid his thumb over her sensitive bud. She inhaled sharply, but he kept his touch light and teasing. She bit her lip as he circled her. Her hips began to move, and he stilled. She glared at him but remained still until he began to tease her again, his movements so slow they must be torturous. They tortured him. She was so warm and tight. He wanted to replace that finger with his cock. But he also wanted to live, and Draven would kill him if he deflowered her. Draven would kill him for what he was doing now.

But Duncan would rather die than stop.

He flicked at the bud, circled it, felt her shiver. She was close now and he withdrew just for a moment then returned. Her breathing was hitched and loud. Her entire body trembled in his arms. Her gaze was hot and sharp as it bored into his. He gave her a slow smile as he slid his thumb over her center of pleasure one more time. The touch was light, but the pressure was just enough that he knew it would send her over the edge.

Her mouth opened but no sound came out. Her body stilled, though, as if it were drawing tightly into itself. Her legs gripped his thighs as he pleasured her. And then with what seemed like almost an explosion, she let out a moan erotic enough that he might have come just from hearing it if he wasn't so focused on what he was doing. Her inner walls tightened on his finger and her body jerked convulsively as she climaxed. As he'd instructed, her eyes never left his, and he saw in them the wonder and pleasure and surprise of the experience.

He saw the beauty too. This was what the experience should be—beauty and bliss and a reach for something just beyond oneself.

Finally, she threw her head back and pushed her hips forward, pressing harder against him to take all of the pleasure she could. Her hands held fast to his shoulders and though her nails were short, her hands were those of a woman who worked. As she dug her fingers into him she caused just a small bite of pain.

Finally, she fell forward, and he caught her against his chest. Her breathing was rapid as though she took in gulps after a long run. Her face against his neck was hot and...wet? He pulled her back and looked at her face. Tears ran down her cheeks.

"What's this now?" he asked. He removed his hand from under her skirts to hold her in place while wiping the tears away with his other hand.

She said something in Portuguese, and though he didn't understand he understood the shrug of her shoulders and shake of her head. She did not know why she cried. She was overwhelmed by the emotions.

He was overwhelmed as well. He'd never been so enraptured by a woman before. He'd never gotten so much pleasure from giving pleasure.

And though he did not want to cry, he was having trouble making sense of all the emotions he felt in that moment. Rage, he understood. Exhilaration, he understood. Impatience, he understood. Lust, he understood.

But this was none of those. And for the first time in many years Duncan felt something that might have been fear and just beyond that an emotion he dared not name.

# Twelve

*Stratford*

Stratford gave Emmeline a good quarter hour before he went after her. She might need a few moments of privacy, but he wouldn't leave her alone in the woods. When he found her, she was leaning against a tree, Loftus beside her, both of them looking up at the canopy of branches above. She held up her hand as soon as he began to approach. She'd probably heard him coming as he hadn't tried to move silently.

"I do not wish to discuss it," she said before he could even speak.

"I think we should," he said.

"No. I am not myself lately. I say things without thinking."

He could believe she was not herself lately. After all, she had run away, she had adopted a dog, and now she was insisting on traveling to Scotland. But he'd never known her to say something she did not mean. In fact, the opposite was usually the problem. She said too much of what was on her mind.

But if she did not want to discuss her comments about marriage, who was he to force her? It wasn't as though he wanted to talk about it either. She had spoken out of a moment of passion—she didn't want marriage, she wanted one benefit of marriage—and he didn't think she harbored some secret love for him. Until the past few days, she had never shown any particular affinity for him.

He knew because he had always hoped for a sign of affection from her, though if she had shown it, it wouldn't have mattered as he couldn't have returned it anyway.

"We should keep moving," she said. "Mr. Murray and Miss Neves are probably wondering where we are."

Based on the sounds that had carried his way while he'd been giving Emmeline her privacy, Stratford rather doubted Miss Neves or Murray were thinking about them at all. "I think we might wait for them to come and find us."

She gave him a puzzled look, and he raised a brow.

"Oh," she said. "Well…clearly Ines is besotted with him. I just did not think he would take advantage of that."

Stratford frowned. He was in the habit of defending Duncan as the two of them had prowled about London together of late, but he did not like to be put in this position. "Duncan is a man of honor. He won't do anything she doesn't want."

"Oh, I think it is quite impossible to find something Ines does not want Duncan to do to her."

Stratford opened his mouth to say that Duncan knew the boundaries of propriety, but then he realized he would be speaking of *Duncan*. The Lunatic. And whatever Duncan was doing, it hadn't sounded at all proper.

"Then he will accept the consequences," Stratford said. Of that, he was certain. Duncan never shirked his duty.

"Of course," Emmeline said with a sigh that caused the dog to look up at her. "As though women are nothing but a consequence."

"That is not what I meant."

She waved a hand. "I know."

They stood together, looking up at the branches limned in moonlight. And as the sky grew lighter, Duncan finally called for him.

"Here!" Stratford said, coming out into the clearing beside the road.

"What are ye doing hiding?" Duncan asked. "We should be going."

Stratford gave him a withering look. "It sounded as though you needed more time to rest. We were waiting until you were done…resting."

Duncan was never embarrassed, and he smiled now. "I've rested plenty. Let's continue." He nodded to Emmeline then waved a hand as though to indicate that they should follow him. Stratford caught up to him, thinking it might not be the best idea to give a man who had been shot recently the task of leading the way.

Ines and Emmeline fell into step behind them, their heads together as they whispered about God knew what. The dog ran ahead and then sprinted back to them, sniffing them each in turn before running ahead again. Dawn began to rise, and Stratford told Duncan he hoped they might see a farmer with a cart soon.

"It would save us time, aye," Duncan replied.

Stratford glanced back at the ladies to make certain they were not tiring. Emmeline looked to have as much energy as Loftus. Stratford didn't know where she came by it. She couldn't have slept any more than he, and even his bones were tired. Still, he'd fought most of a war without much sleep. He knew he could keep going with little rest. He was not so sure about her.

But then why was he worrying about her? She didn't want his worry. She didn't even want his conversation. She hadn't wanted to talk about the marriage proposal she'd blurted out. Stratford knew he'd hurt her feelings. But he hadn't been rejecting her. He had been saving her the trouble of rejecting him.

For while their families were close, Stratford knew that Emmeline and her sisters did not know everything. They did not know the truth about him. They did not know why the baron hated him.

Of course, any fool could make it out. Stratford, no fool, had figured it out when he'd been but nine or ten. He wasn't the baron's son. Stratford looked a great deal like his mother, but he had none of his father's features. He bore a resemblance to his siblings, but whenever they talked about the Fortescue nose, Stratford was aware of his father's gaze avoiding him. Sometimes the baron would just abruptly leave the room.

Once, when Stratford had been quite young—before he'd figured out the truth—he'd asked his mother why his father hated him. She'd taken him into her arms and held him. It was a rare thing as she almost never showed him affection or attention. Then she'd looked into his small face and said,

"It's not you he hates, it's a mistake I made. He hates my mistake, darling. Not you."

But Stratford was keen enough to understand that the sight of him reminded the baron of his mother's mistake, and he made sure to stay out of sight and to be good, perfect, and obedient. He wondered if the sight of him was why his mother did not love him. Perhaps looking at Stratford was a daily reminder to her too of her long-ago mistake.

Of course, as an adult, Stratford had looked into the matter more closely. He'd made discreet inquiries and discovered that his mother had been linked to the Marquess of Wight for several years before his birth. By the time he was born, the relationship had ended and the marquess had retreated to his country home. He hadn't been seen since, and by all accounts the house had fallen into disrepair.

Stratford had thought for a long time about going to see the marquess. He wondered if he resembled the man and if he had any half siblings. In the end, he decided it did not make any logical sense. Wight had not tried to see him and might not even know he had a son. Better to let the past stay in the past. Except now he had to confront the past. He was not who Emmeline thought he was. He was not who anyone thought he was.

The sound of horses and wheels reached his ears, and he and Duncan turned about the same time. A moment later, a cart pulled by two horses appeared with a farmer at the front and a load of what looked like produce taking up most of the back. Stratford waved to the man, gesturing slyly for Duncan to stand back. Duncan would only scare the farmer.

The man lifted his hat and eyed the women first. It wasn't a lascivious look but one of curiosity. Then he gazed with interest at Stratford, his eyes widening as he took in Duncan, who he couldn't really miss. The farmer was a weathered man of perhaps forty who looked closer to nearing sixty. He wore simple, sturdy clothing that had been mended and was clean and fit him well. His hands held the reins of his horses confidently, and he called out, "Whoa," slowing before he reached Stratford. Stratford walked back.

"Good morning," Stratford said.

"Good morning," the man answered.

"I am Stratford Fortescue, and this is my friend Duncan Murray. These ladies are our cousins." Better not to give their names. "We are traveling to Scotland to visit with Mr. Murray's uncle, the Duke of Atholl." Always throw in a duke if possible—that was Stratford's motto.

The farmer's eyes widened appreciatively and predictably. "I am John Bixly."

"A pleasure, Mr. Bixly. We have had to leave our coach behind," Stratford said. Always stick to the truth as much as possible—another motto. "Would you mind taking us as far as you travel today?"

The farmer nodded. "Of course. It's only five miles to the village, but I might be able to help you find someone else to take you further north."

"That would be much appreciated."

Stratford and Duncan started for the back of the cart as did Emmeline and Miss Neves. The farmer called, "Do the ladies want to sit up front?"

Stratford looked at Emmeline, who looked back at him. He could see she was tired. Her eyes had faint smudges under them, and her shoulders were slumped. But she might just ride next to the farmer to avoid being with him.

"I will sit in the back, *senhor*," Miss Neves said. "Thank you."

Bixly looked perplexed by Miss Neves's Portuguese accent. Really, Stratford wished everyone would just let him do the talking. Emmeline climbed in beside the other woman. "I will ride back here too."

"I'll ride on the box," Duncan said, and the farmer looked startled as the Highlander climbed up beside him.

Well, that left no room for Stratford in the front. He climbed in beside Emmeline, who scooted closer to Miss Neves.

The cart started away, and after they'd been jerked this way and that, Stratford leaned closer to Emmeline. "Listen, I want to say—"

"I think I shall lay down and rest," Emmeline said, not looking at him.

"I will too," Miss Neves said.

Stratford sighed but handed them empty burlap sacks to put under their heads. They both laid back and closed their eyes. With their dirt streaked gowns and tangled unbound hair, they looked like they belonged in the back of the cart, though this farmer probably had daughters who looked more presentable. Still, since Emmeline's eyes were closed, Stratford gave her surreptitious looks. Even though he'd escorted her to balls where she wore expensive silk gowns and diamonds about her neck, he thought she, lying in the cart with her black hair spread out under her and the dappled sun dancing over her cheeks, was more beautiful than he'd ever seen her.

She looked peaceful in sleep, for it hadn't taken her very long to succumb to sleep. Miss Neves, on the other hand, had her eyes closed but was still wide awake. But Emmeline looked like the very picture of repose. He liked seeing her like that, liked not having to worry that she'd catch him looking at her and snap at him with one of her cutting remarks.

He wished she would understand she did not have to be defensive with him. He did not want to hurt her. Except he had, hadn't he? She'd let down her guard for just a moment, and he'd rejected her.

But how was he supposed to know she would suggest marriage? She couldn't have been serious, but still his first response should not have been *no*.

And though he kept trying to apologize to her, what could he really say? *I'm not who you think I am? I do want to marry you, but I don't think you'll want me if you know the truth?* And why need he say any of those things? She hadn't really meant it when she'd said she wanted to marry him. It had been said in a moment of passion. Women's minds always went to marriage when their passions were enflamed. But even if Emmeline would marry him, her mother would certainly not approve the match. She knew the truth about him.

Better to stick to the status quo and keep Emmeline at an arm's length.

And that would have been easier done if she would just go home already.

\*\*\*

*Ines*

Ines looked over at Emmeline and knew her friend was already asleep. She wished she could fall asleep as easily. But tired as she was, her body would not relax.

That was Duncan's fault. Every time she closed her eyes, she remembered the way he had touched her, the way his rough voice had caressed her, the way he had made her feel.

She wanted to do it all over again. As soon as possible.

And that made her quite wicked. She didn't need Catarina looking over her shoulder to tell her that.

Did it matter if Ines was half in love with Duncan, had always been infatuated with Duncan?

Probably not. Duncan wouldn't marry her, and that was what everyone cared about. But at least she had discovered one important piece of information—Duncan *did* want her.

And she wanted him. And so she was wicked. Ines expected to feel horribly ashamed of the realization that she was a wicked, immoral girl. She waited for the feeling and waited and waited. But she didn't feel shame or guilt or even remorse. She wanted Duncan to do what he'd done all over again. The rules could go to the devil. Did they really even apply to her? She was a lacemaker. No one cared who she fell into bed with.

Ines opened her eyes. Was she really considering taking Duncan to her bed or going to his bed or, realistically, fornicating on the ground in the woods?

Why yes, yes she was. She smiled.

"What are you smiling about?" Mr. Fortescue asked.

Ines glanced at him. "Oh, nothing," she said, proving once again what a bad liar she was.

"That wicked, eh?"

She rose on her elbows. "How did you know?"

He shrugged. "I might have heard a few revealing... shall we say, sounds, in the woods."

"Are you shocked?" she asked.

"I've been in a war, Miss Neves. Nothing shocks me. Furthermore, life is too short to forego what makes you happy."

Ines glanced at Emmeline, whose chest was rising and falling in an even rhythm. "You should take your own advice, *senhor*."

He gave her a rueful smile. "I walked into that one, didn't I?"

She frowned. "Walked? But we are not walking."

He laughed. "Yes, I see what Duncan likes about you. But, if I may be so bold, might I give you some advice?"

Ines laid back and sighed. Heavily. "If you must."

"I suppose everyone gives you advice."

"It is a favorite pastime, *não*?"

"Not mine, no. But I do know Duncan Murray very well. Maybe better than almost anyone else. And I can tell you a few things about him." He glanced up at the box and she followed his gaze to see Duncan surveying the passing trees as though he were poised for an attack by bandits.

"What can you tell me?" she asked.

"He is gruff on the outside, but inside he has a heart like any other man. It can be bruised and broken."

She waved a hand. "I have seen this already."

"No doubt. You have also noticed that he has an interest in you."

"And I in him," she said boldly.

He shook his head. "Poor Draven."

She sat. "Why *poor Draven*? Why not *poor Ines*? I am the one who has to live with all his rules? Is it so wrong of me to want a little pleasure in my life?"

"I don't begrudge you or Duncan any little piece of happiness or pleasure. As I said, life is too short. But if you look at this situation logically, if you trace it to its inevitable conclusion, I think you will see what I am trying to say."

She stared at him for a long moment. He was an attractive man with blond hair and intelligent blue eyes. She thought perhaps he lived *too* much inside his head, though.

"Shall I spell it out for you?" he asked, raising his brows.

"Spell *it*?"

He rubbed the spot between his eyes. "Shall I explain myself?"

"You probably should, *senhor*. I do not know what you speak of."

"Duncan can't marry you. His mother wants him to marry an English lady, and Duncan's mother is a force of nature. Even I have heard of Lady Charlotte, though I have never met her. She has bested the British army. She has a Highland clan eating out of her hand. And she will make sure Duncan does as she wishes. She will never accept you."

"Perhaps I can win her over. I am charming, *sim*?"

"You are charming, but you are not English. And Lady Charlotte cannot be charmed. I don't want to see you with your heart broken. It might be better if we all just turned around now and went home. Duncan can go on without us."

Ines looked away, pondering what he'd said. She could go back to London now. That would be the safe path. Her heart would not be broken. Her heart would be untouched. But she did not want a heart that was untouched. She wanted a heart that felt all the emotions. And if pain and loss was to be one of those, then she would take it. To lead a life avoiding anything that might ever give her pain was not to live at all.

"I am willing to risk the pain, *senhor*." She looked at Emmeline. "But perhaps you are not?"

He stiffened and turned away. "I was trying to help."

"You were trying to use your—what is it? crafty?—yes, crafty way to convince me to go back to London. That is what you want, *sim*?"

"If you go back that does benefit me, but that does not mean it is not also the right thing for you," he said.

"Oh, *senhor*, you are good."

He closed his eyes with a look of frustration.

"But I am crafty too. And you will have to make better strategy than this to convince me to turn around."

"I have no doubt I am up to the challenge."

That didn't make Ines feel any better. Because, more than ever, she wanted Duncan Murray. She had thought that one kiss would be enough. But that kiss had only stoked the fire of her desire. And then when he had touched her last night—well, she must feel that again. Ines understood what Fortescue was telling her. She would be burned. She had been burned before.

Catarina had often been exasperated with Ines—as had Ines's mother—because Ines had been the sort of child who had to test everything herself. No one could tell her she would lose her ball if she threw it in the pond. She must see for herself and cry when her toy sank to the bottom. No one could tell her the coals in the fire were hot. She must see for herself and inevitably burn her hand.

It had been the same way with lacemaking. Catarina would tell her a pattern would not work, but Ines must try it on her own and waste hours of effort only to discover what Catarina had said was true.

And Ines knew that Duncan Murray would never love her, and his mother would never allow her to marry him. He could never be hers.

But that didn't stop her from wanting to try. That didn't stop her from risking scorching her heart. She must learn for herself.

She glanced at the Highlander again. He was so handsome with his loose brown hair and strong jaw. He was brave and honorable and exciting. He was everything she had always wanted, and he was worth all the risks she had taken and would take. If it meant he would touch her again, she would burn her heart until it was a black, shriveled thing.

Unfortunately, for the next several days there were no opportunities for stolen kisses or embraces. Ines existed in a twilight world of trading one cart for another, one farmer or tradesman for another. She was given food and drink. She was able to sleep, if uncomfortably, and she was steadily moving northward. She had stopped looking at the passing scenery. It all melted together in her mind. There was nothing to see. Duncan and Mr. Fortescue made sure they traveled on roads that were rarely used to make it more difficult for Draven and his men to find them. Duncan said he would not be surprised if he arrived home to find Lord Jasper sipping tea with his mother, waiting for them.

Ines was not certain who this Lord Jasper was, but she was a little afraid of a man who could move so quickly when the journey seemed to take them years.

Finally, late one night, when they had coaxed a Scottish merchant returning home with an empty cart to allow them to ride with him, Ines was shaken awake. She'd been asleep, her head on Emmeline's lap. Ines looked up at Emmeline to see her blinking the sleep away as well. Duncan was pointing behind them at the landscape bathed in a soft morning light.

Ines sat. "What did he say?"

Emmeline rubbed her eyes. "I'm not certain."

Fortescue, who had been riding in the front with the merchant called over his shoulder, "He said tell England goodbye. We're in Scotland now."

Ines sat and stared into the darkness. She didn't know how anyone could see to stay on the road, much less note that they had moved from one country to another. But if Duncan said they were in Scotland, they must be. He looked absolutely elated. He sat, back straight, arms tight on the side of the cart. She could see anticipation in every line of his tense body. She touched his back, and he jerked to look at her then relaxed.

"I'm well and truly home now, lass," he said with a smile.

Oh, how she liked that smile. She wished he would smile like that more often.

"How long until we reach your village?" she asked.

"Oh, a few days, if the weather holds and we don't encounter any problems."

Ines frowned and drew back. "What sort of problems?"

"Nothing for ye tae worry aboot, lass."

But, of course, that was not at all true.

# Thirteen

*Emmeline*

"We'll just be a few minutes," Emmeline called over her shoulder as she and Ines moved into a wooded area to attend to their needs. When she was finished, Emmeline found a small brook and knelt beside it, plunging her hands into the cold water. She braced herself for the sting before splashing icy water on her face. Ines crouched beside her and did the same.

"Why is Scotland so cold?" she asked. "It is summer, *não?*"

Emmeline smiled. "I remember when I was a little girl visiting my grandmother in Cumbria. It was cold there too until July or August. In a few days you will be used to it."

Ines wrapped a blanket one of the farmers had given her around her shoulders. "Duncan does not mind the cold. He does not even wear an overcoat."

Emmeline sipped water from her numb hands then stood and tucked them into her skirts to warm them. "That is because we cut his overcoat off him."

Emmeline was beginning to think she would need to do the same with her dress as it was ruined beyond repair. It had once been white, but now it was dingy with dirt and green with stains from grass. A few spots were soiled where muddy paw prints had landed. As if summoned by her thoughts, Loftus raced by her and plunged into the brook. Emmeline winced at the splash of water, then could not hold back a laugh. The dog looked to be enjoying the swim immensely. But Emmeline could only imagine that she would soon smell like wet dog, among the other unpleasant smells she had accumulated these last days of travel.

"I must have a bath soon," Ines said, rubbing her arms to warm herself.

"I was thinking the same thing. I want a meal as well."

"Oh, *sim*! A warm meal and a warm bath and a bed. We will have all of that when we arrive at the home of Duncan."

Emmeline hoped that would not take long. She had been doing her best to avoid speaking with Stratford the past few days, but it was not easy when they were constantly together. And she was constantly reminded of what a fool she'd made of herself—suggesting marriage. She was such an idiot!

She'd thrown herself at the first man who found her attractive and stirred her desire.

But, of course, that wasn't true. She'd known Stratford for years. It seemed so natural for their relationship to change as it had. Natural to kiss him. Natural to touch him. Natural to think of marrying him. Which was ridiculous because the whole reason she had run away was to escape all the talk of marriage. But it seemed she'd been running away forever.

"How many more days until we—" she began. "Loftus!" Emmeline frowned as the dog's ears pricked up and he trotted to the bank of the brook and then away from her. "Loftus!"

"Let him go," Ines said. "He has probably scented a rabbit. He will come back to us when he tires of the chase."

But Emmeline heard Loftus growl, and she had not heard him do that since the day she had rescued him. She moved deeper into the woods and finally caught sight of him. The fur on his back was raised, and he had his mouth open and teeth bared.

Emmeline knew better than to speak now. She felt Ines stop beside her, the other woman also sensing that silence was best. "A wolf?" Ines whispered.

Emmeline shook her head. There were not wolves in Scotland. Were there?

Emmeline turned to look into the trees, studying the shapes and colors for anything amiss.

And then she saw it—a splash of red where there shouldn't have been one. The shape slowly came into focus for her. It was a man with red hair. He had a dun-colored cap pulled low over it, probably to hide the color, but it was too bright to conceal. He was crouched near a log, a bow in his hand with an arrow nocked.

The arrow pointed at Loftus.

"Call yer dog off, *Sassenach*, or Angus will shoot him through the heart."

Emmeline gasped and moved only her eyes to see the man. His voice had come from her right, where Ines had been standing, and now she saw he had one arm around Ines's shoulders and a knife to her throat. Ines looked pale and shaken, her already wide brown eyes even wider. But Emmeline also saw a trace of exhilaration in her expression. That girl certainly loved an adventure.

Only this adventure would see her killed.

"I can try," Emmeline said. "I only acquired him a week ago." Had it been only a week? It felt like years had passed. "He might not listen to me."

"Pray he does."

Emmeline cleared her throat. "Loftus!" she said in her sternest voice. "Loftus, want a treat?" That usually caught his attention, but this time he did not even look her way. "Loftus!" she tried again. This time his ears twitched, and she knew he had heard her. "No. Come here." She patted her leg. Loftus eased back again, but his attention remained on the man called Angus.

"Loftus!" she all but yelled. Surely Murray or Stratford would hear her and come to investigate. If they did not and she did manage to call Loftus off, what would these men do? Emmeline had no idea if there were only two of them or more. And what were they doing hiding in the woods? Were they bandits? Escaped criminals? Poachers?

"Loftus, come."

Finally, thank God! The dog looked at her, his expression clearly one of annoyance. He did not want to be called away, but he was, at his heart, a dog who wanted to please. "Loftus, come!" she said again.

Moving sideways, never taking his eyes off the man with the bow and arrow, Loftus started toward her.

"Good job, *Sassenach*," the man said as Loftus whined then sat at her side. Emmeline grabbed the fur at the scruff of his neck to keep him still, though if he really wanted to attack, she wouldn't have been able to hold him back. She might outweigh him, but he was all muscle and strength.

"You may release my friend now," she said.

"After ye hand over yer purse and any baubles." The man's eyes, all that were visible as he wore a scarf around the lower part of his face and a hat over his brow, slid up and down her. Clearly, he could see she wore no baubles.

"I've already had my purse stolen," she told him, using her best authoritative tone. "I have nothing of value, and neither does my friend. Let her go."

"Ye might have nothing of value, but she's a bonny wee thing. I think we'll take her with us. Ye want her back? We'll make a trade for her. Tell yer men to meet us at the old crofter's cottage, a mile to the east at sunset." He began to drag Ines backward, and Ines's eyes widened. She began to struggle, but the man nicked her with his dagger, and she went still again.

"You should not have done that," Emmeline said. "Her man will kill you for touching her. He will tear you limb from limb for drawing her blood." She didn't know where the words came from, but she knew they were true. Ines was the sort of woman men would kill for. Meanwhile, she couldn't even get herself abducted.

"If he dinnae want more blood drawn, he'd better bring a fat purse." The man moved back further and several other men joined him. Just how many had been hiding in these woods? One of them took Ines by the arm, and she gave Emmeline one last pleading look before she was pulled away. Beside Emmeline, Loftus whined.

As soon as the men were gone, Emmeline looked at the dog. "Go get Murray," she said, and Loftus took off in the direction she and Ines had come from.

\*\*\*

*Duncan*

"I think it's best if we hire horses and travel that way from now on," Stratford said as he rummaged about in a sack and assessed their provisions. He was in charge of rationing their food, which meant they always had something to eat and Duncan was always hungry.

"And where will we find the coin for that?"

"How much do you have?" Stratford asked.

"Not enough for four horses."

Stratford seemed to consider. "What about two horses?"

Duncan shook his head. "I have enough tae buy us food and maybe a night or two in an inn, but I cannae hire horses. Unless we want tae do as we did in the army." He raised his brows at Stratford who shot him a disapproving look. In the army they had stolen the horses they needed. Of course, those were the enemies' horses, which was a bit different from stealing from your own countrymen.

Duncan held up his hands. "Yer right. Nae thieving, but what if we—" Duncan looked up when Loftus bounded into the clearing and barked. That was an odd thing as the dog did not bark often, and he was always at Miss Wellesley's side.

Stratford rose and Loftus ran up to him and barked. "Where's Emmeline?" Stratford asked, as though the dog could actually answer.

The dog barked twice and then ran back toward the woods then back to the clearing and then dove into the woods again. "Follow him!" Stratford called. Duncan was already on his feet. Stratford would follow him, but he was no good at navigating woods or unfamiliar places. Duncan followed the sound of the dog through the trees until he heard a feminine voice greet the dog. A moment later, Miss Wellesley came through the foliage, her expression anxious. "Mr. Murray!"

Duncan assessed her quickly, noted she was not injured. He looked behind her for Ines, but Ines did not appear. "Where is Ines?" he asked.

Her face tightened. "That's why I sent Loftus to you. She's been taken."

"Taken?" Duncan yelled. He hadn't meant to yell, but he couldn't seem to stop himself. Of all the things he thought the woman would say, that was not one of them. "Who the hell took her?"

"I don't know." Miss Wellesley was all but crying now. He hadn't thought she could cry. She always seemed so strong and confident. The fact that she was crying alarmed him and sent steel shooting through his spine. She took a ragged breath. "There were men in the woods. They had a knife and a bow and arrow."

Duncan reached her in two strides and grabbed her by the shoulders. He could not think now. The feeling he liked to think of as that lunatic part of himself took over. It scrambled his thoughts and demanded action. "What men? Where did they go? Why did ye let them take her?"

"Unhand her, Duncan," Stratford said.

Duncan hadn't realized he was holding on to Miss Wellesley and shaking her. He released her, and she melted into a heap on the ground, covering her face with both hands. The dog tried to lick her, but Stratford brushed the dog away when he knelt beside her. "Tell me what happened."

Duncan wanted to scream, a primal scream that would scatter birds and shake the boughs of the trees. He wanted to rage against Stratford's calm. His body quivered like a nocked arrow on the precipice of release. He only needed to be aimed in the right direction.

*Ines. Taken.*

Duncan clenched his fists, waiting to be released.

"He had a knife," Miss Wellesley said then blubbered on about something else that didn't quite make sense. Duncan growled low in his throat, his entire body tense and quaking.

Stratford, calm as ever, raised her chin until her gaze met his. "Take a deep breath now. No, don't try to speak. Just breathe." He glanced at Duncan. "Some water, I think. Wine, if we have it."

*Christ and all the saints*! Duncan wanted to shake the information out of her. He wanted answers. *Now*. But the army had taught him some control, and he knew enough about Stratford's methods to trust the man. He stomped back to the clearing, grabbed a bottle they had been using for water, and carried it back to Stratford and Miss Wellesley. She had stopped crying by the time he handed it to her, which was a good sign.

"Drink," Stratford told her. She did. Her small sips seemed designed to appease him rather than slake her thirst. "Better?" Stratford asked.

She nodded.

Duncan folded his arms over his chest and tried not to scowl at her, tried not to think about the precious time being lost while Stratford coaxed and soothed.

*Ines. Taken.*

"Tell us what happened," Stratford said. "From the beginning."

"There's a brook," she said, pointing toward the sound of running water. "We, Ines and I, went to have a sip of water and wash our faces. Then Loftus jumped in and seemed to spot something. He ran away from us, and we thought it was a rabbit, but it wasn't." Her voice hitched, and Stratford offered her the water again.

*Christ* but Duncan wanted the rest of the story already.

"We called him back, and he didn't come. We went to see what he had found, and I saw a man with a bow and arrow pointed at Loftus. And then another man grabbed Ines and held a knife to her throat."

Duncan's arms dropped. "I'll kill him. Where did they go?"

"That way."

Duncan saw only red rage as he cut through the trees. *Ines taken. Ines taken.* He didn't feel the branches snapping against his face or the cut of the brush on his legs. Stratford was beside him a moment later, panting as he ran to keep up. "Emmeline says they want to meet at the crofter's cottage at sunset."

Duncan slowed. "Cottage?"

Stratford nodded, bending to catch his breath. "It's to the east. They'll trade you for her."

"Trade me?" His voice was deadly calm, giving no hint to the rage within him. If Ines had been hurt… If anything happened to her…

Duncan couldn't allow himself to think about it. He couldn't let his emotions take over. This was why he had tried to keep away from her. He hadn't wanted to risk this pain, this loss. But somehow she'd managed to worm her way into his heart because it hurt now when he thought of losing her. "Trade me?" he repeated.

"For a fat purse."

Duncan's vision grew dark crimson. "I'll trade them, I will." He started away again, looking for any sign of the men's movements.

"I'll look for the crofter's house," Stratford said. "You track the men. We need a plan."

"I have a plan," Duncan said. "I'll kill them."

An hour later, Miss Wellesley looked up sharply then relaxed when she saw it was Duncan who stepped into the clearing.

"Reivers," Duncan told her. The shadows had grown longer in his absence. Duncan tried not to think about what the reivers had done to Ines while she'd been away from him.

"What are reivers?" she asked.

"Raiders," he said. "They cross over into England and steal then race back over the border. But they'll steal on this side of the border too."

"I take it you didn't find them," Stratford said.

"Nae. They ken well enough tae keep hidden. Did ye find the crofter's cottage?"

"I did. I have a plan too."

Duncan smiled tightly. "As long as it ends with me killing them."

Stratford explained the plan, and Duncan nodded in agreement. "But Duncan," Stratford said, "if this is to work, you have to follow the plan. You can't go in, ignoring everything I've said, like you usually do."

"I'll already be in, so it willnae matter, will it?"

"Just follow the plan. Wait for my word." Stratford looked at the sky. "We should go soon in case they arrive early."

"You haven't explained what I'm to do," Miss Wellesley said.

Duncan turned on her. "Yer to stay here and nae get in any trouble. Ye've done enough for one day." The moment the words were out of his mouth, he regretted them. It wasn't her fault Ines had been taken.

But instead of looking hurt or angry, she stood and walked to his side. She put her hand on his arm, and Duncan glanced at her warily. "I know you care for her," she said. "I'm so sorry I failed you. I tried. I really did, but they cut her—"

Duncan's hand landed on hers. "What did ye say?" The red was back, and he saw nothing else.

She looked at Stratford who closed his eyes. Clearly, there was something they were keeping from him.

"When I asked them to release her, she started to struggle, and the man holding her nicked her with a knife."

His grip tightened.

"It was only a nick," she said weakly.

"Duncan," Stratford said, his tone thick with warning.

Duncan lifted his hand. "It's nae yer fault," he told Miss Wellesley, his voice cold and deadly, even to his own ears. "It's my fault. I'll make it right."

"I know you will, but Mr. Murray, you can't blame yourself."

Oh, how many times had he heard those words? It might have been a different time, a different circumstance, but the words were the same. But the ending would not be the same. He wouldn't allow it. He was a man now, not a boy, and he had atoned for his past. He would save Ines if it was the last thing he ever did.

"Then who is tae blame?" he asked her, but his gaze was on Stratford. "If they touch her, Draven will kill me. And I'll ask him tae do it."

Duncan gathered his few things, wanting to be ready to follow Stratford to the house. He didn't want to think of Ines right now. He only wanted to think of his plan. He'd been trying not to think about her for the past few days, trying to keep his distance from her. He didn't want a repeat of what had happened that first night under the tree to happen again.

Not because he hadn't enjoyed it. He'd enjoyed it too much. Every time he looked at Ines, he wanted her mouth on his and her body pressed against his. And so he kept his distance.

But now he wished he hadn't. Now he might never see desire on her face or passion in her eyes again. He might not be able to make her his, but he could not be expected to go on if she wasn't alive in the world somewhere. Ines had appeared in his life seemingly out of a dream. Not only was she beautiful and passionate and exciting, she was kind and loyal and steady. He hadn't even known those were things he needed or wanted in a woman. She'd barely known him, but when he'd been shot, she had stayed at his side, alternately coddling him and shocking him. He'd never met a woman like her because there were no other women like her.

Duncan knew a rare gem when he saw it. And he knew things of value needed to be protected.

He should have never left her side. He should have known the dangers about and should have kept her close. If anyone knew what reivers were capable of, it was Duncan.

He couldn't lose someone else he cared about to them.

"Duncan!" Stratford said, and Duncan looked up.

"I've called your name three times," Stratford said. "Are you ready?"

"I'm ready." He glanced at Miss Wellesley. "What aboot her?"

She frowned at him. "Loftus and I are to stay here."

"Good." Duncan nodded. "The dog will keep ye safe, and we dinnae have tae worry aboot them taking ye for a hostage."

She snorted. "They did not want me."

"Only because yer not an easy target, lass. They'll take ye if they get the chance. Stay hidden, aye?"

She nodded. Stratford walked past him, and Duncan looked back, saw he was going to speak to his cousin, and turned back around. This might be farewell. No one knew how the night would turn out. Duncan didn't intend to die, but then neither did the reivers. He moved away, giving the two of them their privacy.

When Stratford finally joined him, Duncan looked at him. "Are ye wearing yer dancing shoes?"

Stratford nodded. "Bring on the devil."

\*\*\*

*Stratford*

Stratford stood in the open area in front of the old crofter's cottage, looking out of place and impatient. At least that was how he hoped he looked. He'd made a show of walking up to the cottage by the main path and then looked all about him, like any man about to meet someone might. He was well aware Duncan was inside the cottage, crouched below a window, keeping watch. He just hoped that, for once, Duncan would listen to him and follow the plan. He hoped Emmeline would follow the plan and stay put as well. She was better at following plans, but only when she wanted to.

Stratford knew she blamed herself, though it was no more her fault Miss Neves had been abducted than it was Duncan's. The men who had taken the lacemaker were the ones at fault. He'd told her that, again, when he'd left her for the crofter's cottage. Her eyes had been wet as he'd said goodbye, and Stratford felt his heart squeeze at the sight of her tears. He hadn't seen her cry since she was a young child, and even then she hadn't cried very often. She wasn't the sort of woman who needed reassuring or comfort. At least that's what he'd thought. But in that moment, he reconsidered.

Maybe that was exactly what she needed.

He'd crouched before her and wiped a tear from her pale cheek. "We'll find Miss Neves," he said, voice low. "I'll bring her back."

She nodded. "I wish they had taken me. Why couldn't it have been me?" she said, her voice breaking.

He cupped her cheek. "I thank God it was not you."

She looked up at him, her eyes very blue. "You do?" And then she sniffed and shook her head. "Of course, you wouldn't want to have to tell your father in those letters you write every day."

"That's not why."

Her gaze snapped to his again, and he saw the anguish in her expression. How could she believe no one wanted her? Was she so desperate for someone to want her that she would accept abduction from a reiver as a substitute? Desperation was not a word he would have ever associated with Emmeline Wellesley, but perhaps he had misread her all these years. Yes, she was opinionated and frank, but she was also no fool. She was amazingly clever. He of all people knew that. And so when she expressed herself so confidently and blatantly, she knew it would scare men away. He'd thought she hadn't wanted to marry. But perhaps that wasn't it. Perhaps her behavior was more a cry for attention. A cry and a test—anyone who could look past what Society would call her undesirable behavior and see the worth of the woman beneath passed the test.

Miss Neves had passed the test. The two were friends, and the lacemaker never seemed surprised or offended when Emmeline began ordering everyone about.

Stratford wondered if he had passed the test. He thought he had, but at this moment, it seemed another was set before him. He must not only pass it but beat the test back into submission.

"The reason I am glad it was not you taken is because I am selfish."

Her brow furrowed. "You are one of the least selfish people I know."

"That's because I hide it well," he told her, still cupping her soft cheek. At least she had ceased crying. "But do you see the way Murray is behaving? It's because he cares for Ines Neves. He's terrified to lose her or that the reivers are hurting her."

"I am terrified of that as well."

"They won't hurt her. They no doubt have wives or sweethearts at home. They're after blunt," he said, hoping he was right. "And even knowing that, if they had taken you, I would be beside myself with anguish and worry and blame." He leaned close. "I am thankful it was not you," he said quietly.

Her lashes lowered then her gaze met his again. "You make me think you care for me."

"I do," he said, his mouth a mere fraction of an inch from hers.

"As more than a cousin," she said.

"As more than a cousin," he said, brushing his lips over hers.

"As more than a sister," she said.

"You're neither my cousin nor my sister, thank God. Because, if you were, I would surely be damned to hell for my feelings." He didn't wait to hear her response. He knew she had one. She always had a rejoinder. Instead, he took her mouth gently and kissed her.

He shouldn't have kissed her. She didn't want to marry, and even if she had entertained the idea of marrying him, she wouldn't once she knew the truth about him. These kisses they shared were exercises in frustration. They just made him want her more, and it was a want that could never be satisfied.

But he kissed her anyway because he was a selfish arse who was happy she was safe and here with him. He kissed her because she needed to be kissed in that moment, shown that she mattered and was worthy and desired. And he kissed her because he needed to kiss her. He needed to kiss her every moment of every day, and at this particular moment, he was too weak to resist.

He kissed her because kissing her was an experience like no other. He'd enjoyed kissing other women. He even fancied himself quite good at the act of kissing. He'd considered his technique and approach and refined it over the years. But he couldn't think about performance or method when he kissed Emmeline. All he could do was feel the way her mouth fit his, the way her tongue flicked over his, the way she tasted. How she kissed him just the way he liked to be kissed—though before the first time they'd kissed he hadn't even known there was a way he liked to be kissed.

He might have lost himself in the kiss if Duncan hadn't cleared his throat. He stood some distance away, far enough away that he couldn't hear what they said, but he couldn't have missed the fact that they were kissing. Duncan probably did not care who Stratford kissed, but the Scotsman was in a hurry to be away, in a hurry to put their plan into action and to save Miss Neves.

Stratford was eager to do the same. He had no desire to die slowly at the hand of Colonel Draven. Besides, he liked Miss Neves. She was a sweet girl who must be scared to death at the moment.

Stratford drew back and looked into the dazed expression on Emmeline's face. *Good*, he thought. He liked her dazed and bewildered. She looked even more beautiful like that. "Stay here with Loftus," he said.

She nodded, unusually agreeable.

"Stay alert and ready. We'll probably need to keep moving tonight. We should put some distance between ourselves and these bandits." He started away, but she grabbed his sleeve.

"Be careful, Stratford," she had said.

He had smiled at her. "I always am."

Now, in the open space before the crofter's cottage, Stratford felt exposed. He wasn't exactly the model of caution, but someone had to stand out front and keep the reivers' attention. A glance at the sky told Stratford the sun was setting. It was late, but this far north, even when the sun set, it didn't get that dark. That was to their advantage as it meant the reivers couldn't hide in the darkness. But it had been cloudy with moments of light rain all day, and the sky was overcast and darker than he would have liked.

He stood with his legs braced, hands on his hips. His gaze scanned the brush and the fields all around until he fastened on a slight movement. The movement became a shape, and that shape was a man sitting in the high grass of the field watching him. Slowly, Stratford let his gaze roam over the nearby area. He spotted three more men, for a total of four. He didn't see Miss Neves, though. They would present her before him, to keep his attention away from the men hiding behind.

And then, as if on cue, a man with a muffler pulled up over his mouth and a hat pulled low over his brow came into view, turning off the main road and walking back toward the house. He held a rope and that rope was tethered to Miss Neves's hands.

# *Fourteen*

*Ines*

Ines spotted Mr. Fortescue in front of the cottage and breathed a sigh of relief. If Fortescue was here, Duncan was nearby as well. She just prayed Duncan wouldn't do anything foolish. She worried, more than anything else, that the Scotsman would be hurt.

So much for PED. She wanted excitement and danger and gotten both plus passion, but she did not want anything if it meant she would lose Duncan.

She knew their party didn't have enough coin to satisfy the men who had taken her. They'd dragged her to their camp, tied her to a tree, and left her alone for the afternoon. When she'd stopped shaking from terror, she had concentrated on listening to them talk. They kept some distance from her, which she appreciated, except that it made it hard to hear them very well. What she did piece together from the snatches of conversation she overheard was that they expected a large sum for her return. If her man did not have it with him, then they would keep her for a few days until he could gather it and pay them.

Ines felt sick at the prospect of having to stay with these men for even a night, but she felt sicker knowing that Duncan would never allow that. He would get her back, no matter the cost. She had already almost cost him his life. She didn't want to do so again.

And so she felt relief at seeing Stratford Fortescue but also dread. Her gaze met Mr. Fortescue's, and he gave her a reassuring smile. She kept her gaze on his, knowing that to look for Duncan might give him away. Better if her captors thought their only foe was Fortescue.

The man leading her, a man she had learned was called Graeme, stopped a few yards from Fortescue, and Ines stopped as well. She knew Graeme had sent men on ahead, but she didn't see them. She wished she could warn Fortescue that Graeme had not come alone.

"I hope ye've brought a large purse," Graeme said, eyeing Stratford up and down. "I'll want a nice sum for the trouble of caring for yer woman all day."

Fortescue looked unconcerned. "If you did not want the responsibility for her, you should have left her where you found her. Now, I suggest you give her back before I am forced to do something unpleasant."

A light rain started to fall, and Ines blinked the water out of her eyes. She was already damp and cold from the rain that had fallen on and off all afternoon, and she dreaded the wet night ahead, especially if she was to spend it tied to a tree.

"I should think ye would be more worried aboot what I might do. I have yer woman, and if ye dinnae plan tae pay me a fine sum tae give her back, I might just keep her. She's a bonny lass."

"If that means she is pretty, you are right. But I can't think she is pretty enough for all the trouble you will cause yourself if you do not hand her over right away."

Graeme made a show of looking about. "What trouble? Ye are standing here alone. If ye had bothered tae look aboot ye, ye'd ken I have my men surrounding ye."

"And if you'd bothered to pull your head out of your arse for three seconds, you'd realize you will be dead in the next quarter hour, if you do not release this lady immediately."

Ines was trying to remain calm, but it was difficult when she still didn't know where Duncan was. And it was even more difficult when she could see Graeme's men creeping closer.

"Oh, I have my heid in my arse?" Graeme yanked Ines's bindings, causing her to stumble forward. "Do ye want the lass or nae?"

Fortescue raised an unconcerned brow. "I said I did, but I won't pay the likes of you for her. Now give her to me and scurry back to the hole you crawled out of." Fortescue held out an imperious hand.

"I ought tae kill ye now," Graeme said as his men moved even closer. Ines's heart thundered in her chest. Soon the men would have Fortescue surrounded and then they would both be prisoners.

"I would like to see you try," Fortescue said, seeming unconcerned by the men moving up behind him.

"Ye dinnae believe me? Then maybe ye'd like tae watch me kill her instead." Graeme yanked Ines to the ground and grabbed her by the hair. She gasped at the bite of pain, her eyes watering.

"You won't kill her," Fortescue began.

And then through the drizzle and her tears, she saw Duncan. It seemed to Ines that he flew out of the crofter's cottage. Of course, he couldn't really fly. Her eyes must be deceiving her, but the way he moved looked like flying. He leapt, his hair streaming out behind him, his handsome face a mask of rage, his arm wielding what looked like a sword, though she could not remember him having one before.

Fortescue yelled, his arms cutting through the air as though giving some sort of direction or rebuke. And then he sagged, seemed to gather himself again, turned to the man closest to him and delivered a hard kick to his hand, sending the dagger he held flying. Impressive as the move was, Ines could not keep her gaze from returning to Duncan. As he came closer, she realized what she had thought might be a sword was actually a sharpened stick.

*Caramba!* He was fighting men armed with real weapons with nothing more than a stick! She knew he had a dagger as well. He had a habit of tossing it when they sat waiting for another cart to pass or a merchant to finish a negotiation. He would hold the handle with the tip of his fingers, toss it in the air, and then catch it by the handle again. But where was that dagger now? He would need it against Graeme. Duncan landed, crouched, then turned his head as a lion might when scenting prey. His amber eyes fixed on his target, and he lunged for Graeme.

Graeme didn't flinch. He met the attack head on. Ines meant to flinch—to close her eyes—but she had to see what would happen. Graeme was on his feet, arms raised for attack one moment, then flat on the ground, the next. Duncan loomed over him, sharpened stick at the ready. Suddenly, that stick looked far more dangerous than any stick had a right to, and Ines could not watch. She had the sudden realization that the rope binding her hands was slack. When Graeme fell, he must have released the end he held. She began to wriggle her wrists in an attempt to free herself. But the knots were tight, and her hands slick from the rain. Around her, men yelled and cried out in pain. Ines tried to focus on her task, but she couldn't stop looking about her.

A man grabbed her hands and Ines cried out. She looked up and into Duncan's leonine eyes. There was no warmth in them now, only hard determination. Duncan pulled her to her feet. The dagger she had seen him toy with on so many occasions was in his hand, and it flashed, freeing the bindings. Ines stared at the crimson liquid that washed briefly over her hands before being rinsed away by the rain, which had begun falling more steadily now.

Blood. Duncan or Graeme's?

"Go," Duncan said to her.

She frowned, still staring at the last droplets of pink on her skin. He shook her, and she looked up and into his face, so hard and ferocious. All of that rage, all of that fury—for her. "Go!" he said and gave her a gentle push.

As though a gear in her mind was suddenly turned, she understood. She looked about, found an opening, and ran.

The sounds of fighting followed her as she tumbled into the brush just out of view of the crofter's cottage. She did not know who was winning, and she could not bear to watch. She heard Duncan and Fortescue's voices in a quick exchange and knew at least they were still alive. They would stay alive, wouldn't they? They had fought together in a war against the French. They could hold their own in a fight against a small group of bandits.

Ines rubbed at her sore wrists and tried to catch her breath. She would simply hide here until the sounds of fighting died away. Then she would hide longer until she could discern a winner. If the bandits won, she would stay where she was and hope they did not find her. It was raining harder now, and the sky had darkened considerably. She would not be easy to spot in her dark dress. But, of course, the bandits would not win. Duncan must win. He must or...

Something moved in the brush behind her. Ines hoped she had imagined it, but she heard a rustling, even the rain could not muffle. She tensed, afraid to move and give herself away. One of Graeme's men must have hidden here. She should have paid more attention to where they'd positioned themselves.

Slowly, she turned to look into the shadows behind her. Something moved, but it didn't look human. *Caramba!* There *were* wolves in Scotland! And then she saw the brown eyes and the patch of white fur, and she sobbed out a cry of relief. "Loftus!" The dog pushed through the undergrowth, his tongue licking her face. Ines much preferred cats to dogs. She thought dogs ill-mannered because they were always licking people they barely knew. But she would have submitted to Loftus's ministrations for another five minutes. She was so happy to see him. He sniffed her, licked her again, and then his ears pricked up as though he were listening for something.

The fighting. Of course, he had heard it. But if he was here, did that mean Emmeline was nearby as well? Ines couldn't imagine Mr. Fortescue or Duncan would allow her anywhere near this place. They would have left her behind with Loftus. Loftus whined, looked at Ines, then back at the sounds of the fight. Finally, seeming to make up his mind, he slid back under the brush and toward the fighting. Duncan and Fortescue would soon have another soldier, but where was Emmeline?

***

*Duncan*

Duncan had to admit Stratford was a better fighter than he would have guessed. The two hadn't fought together often. Duncan and other members of the troop, usually Ewan and Rowden, were sent in when hand-to-hand combat was required. Stratford was usually positioned with Nash to oversee the strategy he'd laid out, while Nash picked off any men Duncan and the others didn't disarm in their first sortie.

Duncan supposed he had seen Stratford fight before. No one escaped the war without some blood on their hands. He just hadn't realized how graceful and controlled Stratford's technique could be. That was the word for it—technique. He didn't fight as Duncan did—with wild abandon. He fought with precision and efficiency. Duncan had to admire the style, even as he tore his own way through the last few bandits still standing. There had only been about seven of them. With their leader down, the others had swarmed. Half had gone for Stratford and the others for Duncan. On the Continent, the men of Draven's had always fought toward each other, until they could press their backs together defensively. Duncan did that now, without thinking. After a few minutes, Stratford's back pressed into his.

"Seems like old times," Stratford said, panting.

"Aye, except I had a sword then." Duncan threw a punch and hoped the man stayed down.

"And I had a pistol." He grunted as one of their opponents obviously landed a blow. Duncan had one more man to take down, then he would finish off Stratford's foes. "You still don't follow plans," Stratford said, obviously annoyed that Duncan had left his position early.

"Make a better one and I might." Duncan dodged his man's right hook.

"The weather is the same," Stratford said.

"Always wet and muddy, aye. I was so tired of the pissing rain." Duncan hit his man across from him with his stick, opening a gash on the man's forehead and causing him to fall to his knees. Duncan kicked him, and when the man went down, Duncan leaned close and said, "Stay down or I'll slide my dagger between yer ribs."

The man stayed down.

Duncan turned to Stratford's last adversary, a big man with dark red hair plastered to his face. He had to weigh two of Stratford, and he had arms like tree limbs. He seemed to have no weapon but his fists, and that was probably all he needed.

This might take a while. The man was obviously besting Stratford, judging by the blood at the corner of his friend's mouth. When Duncan stepped forward, the man smiled.

And then his smile froze. It only took Duncan a moment to realize why. He too heard the growl. With a smile, Duncan spotted Loftus behind the reiver, crouched low, teeth bared.

"Put yer fists down, and I'll call him off," Duncan said. "Otherwise, I'll let him eat ye for dinner."

The man put his fists down, his eyes wild with fright.

"Loftus, come," Stratford said.

Loftus trotted to his side, his eyes still trained on the large Scot. Sensing his opportunity, the man ran. Loftus started to go after him, but Duncan grasped him by the scruff of the neck and held him. "Let him go, boy. He willnae trouble us more."

Stratford bent at the waist, catching his breath. "How do we know they won't lick their wounds and ambush us?"

"Because I killed their leader."

Stratford's head came up. "Bloody hell."

But Duncan felt no remorse. The man had touched Ines. He'd abducted her, bound her, and God knew what he had done to her while he'd had her. And he'd probably terrorized countless other travelers or nearby landholders. The man did not deserve to live.

And he knew that was not the only reason. He'd lost his temper, lost control. He had been worried for Ines, but that was not all. He'd wanted revenge, though of course the man he killed wasn't the one who'd really deserved it.

As Duncan and Stratford caught their breath, the small group of men began slinking away, limping and staggering. Two of them took their leader by the arms and dragged him off as well.

Stratford straightened. "I told her to stay with the dog," he said.

"And when has Emmeline Wellesley ever done as anyone bade her? Take the dog and find her. The roof of the cottage has a few holes, but we can sleep in here tonight. It will be better than huddling out in the rain."

"Where is Miss Neves?" Stratford asked, looking about the gloomy darkness.

"Let me worry aboot her." He knew exactly where she was. He'd seen her run into the brush and duck down. He was pleased she had enough sense to stay there, hidden.

Stratford slapped him on the back and started away, the dog leading him. Duncan started for Ines, covering the ground between them in a few steps. She popped up when she heard him coming. "Is it over?" she asked.

It was so good to see her face, to see her alive and well. His heart ached at the sight. "Aye," he said, his voice gruff with emotion.

"Did you win?" she asked.

"Aye." He reached her, scooped her into his arms, and began to carry her. She squealed in surprise.

"What are you doing, *senhor*?"

"Getting ye inside." And holding her. He needed to hold her in the moment.

He reached the crofter's cottage, kicked the door open, and carried her in. It was dark and chilly inside, but at least it was mostly dry. He remembered the dry corner where he had waited for Stratford's signal—a signal he'd forgotten about as soon as he saw Ines fall to her knees—and deposited Ines there. He'd taken off his coat inside because he'd known he'd want more freedom of movement when he attacked, and it had proved a wise decision as it was still warm. He dropped it over Ines's shoulders and felt around for several abandoned birds' nests he'd seen.

He'd already brought wood inside. He'd used his dagger to whittle one of the sticks into a sharp lance. The others were still in a pile near the hearth. When he'd gathered the bird nests, he used a foot to shove the wood into the hearth, dumped the dry tinder of the old nests on the top of the kindling, and reached into his satchel for his tinder box. A few moments later, he had a small fire started. With a bit of patience and careful manipulation of his kindling, the fire took hold and didn't smoke too badly. The activity was what he needed to settle his emotions and calm his racing blood after the fight.

"Come closer," Duncan said, when he was once again in control of himself. He spotted Ines, still huddled in the corner where he'd deposited her. "Ye look like a wet kitten."

"You look…" Her eyes shone in the firelight.

Duncan swallowed hard. She didn't look like a wet kitten at all. She looked like a beautiful woman.

"You look magnificent," she breathed.

Duncan clenched his hands, steeling himself against the rush of desire her words elicited. Then, against his better judgement, he opened his arms. "Come here," he said. She went to him, burying her head against his chest. He rubbed her back and pulled her close. She was so cold and felt so small and fragile shivering against him. He wanted to hold her until she was warm and safe in his arms. "Did they hurt ye, lass?"

She shook her head, but he needed to hear the words and see her face. He pulled back and looked down at her. "Tell me the truth. Did they hurt ye? Did they touch ye?"

"*Não*," she said, gaze direct. "They tied me to a tree near their camp and ignored me. I heard them discussing me, but they did not come near me."

Duncan touched the small red mark on the side of her throat, and her eyes widened. "What happened here?"

She touched the mark. "I tried to get away at first." She closed her eyes. "I should have fought harder."

"Nae, lass." Duncan rubbed her upper arms, trying to warm her. "Ye were right to go with them and nae tae cause trouble. Men like that have nae honor. They steal what's nae theirs and terrorize small farms and villages rather than eke oot a living like the rest of us. They dinnae care about the pain they cause or the destruction they leave in their wake. I dinnae think they plan tae hurt ye, but they would if ye became inconvenient. Life doesnae matter to them in the least," he said bitterly. He knew that too well.

She wrapped her arms about him again. "You have met men like this before?"

He took a long, deep breath. "They're called reivers, and aye. I have met men like them before."

She clutched him tighter. "They hurt you?"

He did not want to speak of that. Even if now had been the right time. But she was cold and wet, and he needed to take care of her. "I am nae hurt. It's ye I'm worried aboot."

She buried her head in his shoulder. "I am so sorry, *senhor*. Our travel was going so well, and I have ruined everything."

Duncan let out a surprised laugh, and she pulled back to look at him. "Ye think this is going well?" he asked. "We've little coin, we've nae horses or coach, we've angered two of the most powerful men in the country, and we're still days away from my home, where my mother will nae doubt scold me for arriving withoot the one thing she sent me tae London for."

Ines stepped back. "That is one way to look at it, but we are also in the company of friends, we are safe now, and we have met many lovely people who offered to let us ride in the back of carts or wagons. And I have seen the beauty of this country. I will never forget this adventure."

Duncan did not know where she found her optimism, but he couldn't find the will to oppose it. "If I dinnae get ye warm and dry, ye'll never forget the ague that develops. Come closer tae the fire, lass." He settled her before it, and she sighed in contentment. He had a bit of bread in his satchel, and he gave it to her. "Eat this."

She took it, broke it, and offered him half. But of course, she did. "I do not want to eat alone. Sit with me, *por favor*."

Duncan did not think that was a good idea, but he couldn't seem to refuse her anything. He sat beside her, took half the bread, and ate it in one bite. She looked at the piece she had only nibbled and offered it to him. "I think you need this more than I."

"Eat it," he said. "I willnae have ye starve. Draven will have my heid for that too then."

"Is that the last of our food?" she asked.

"Aye. Stratford and I will have tae hunt if we want tae eat after this."

She seemed to consider his words, tilting her head to the side so that her long, damp hair fell over her shoulder and brushed his arm. The feel of it alerted every one of his nerves. He couldn't seem to stop himself from lowering his head to sniff at her hair, which held the faint scent of vanilla and cinnamon. He had to be imagining that. They both must smell like damp wool and smoke.

"You said it is still days until we reach your home?"

"Aye." Duncan could imagine wrapping his hand in her hair and bringing it to his nose to inhale her fragrance more deeply. He'd like to press his face into her neck, taste her skin, touch her until she was not only warm but hot under his fingertips.

"What would make the trip faster?"

"Four horses," he said without thinking.

Ines shook her head. "Three. I do not know how to ride."

"Three then," he agreed, playing along. "Ye could ride with me." He'd like to have her seated before him, wrap his arms about her, feel her thighs against his... His body reacted to that thought predictably, and he tamped down the image. She was speaking again, and he tried to listen. "And what would ye sell, lass? Ye've no jewelry, and even if ye did, I wouldnae let ye sell it."

"I have this," she said, pulling a collar of lace from a pocket under her dress. He remembered she had been wearing it when he'd first met her, with the yellow dress that he'd ruined with his blood.

"A scrap of lace?" he said.

She stiffened, indignant. "This scrap is worth five pounds, at least."

"Nae Scotswoman in her right mind will pay ye five pounds for lace." He looked closer. It was remarkably fine work. "This is Catarina lace?"

She nodded.

The ladies in London had certainly driven up the price of the lace, but it would not sell for enough to provide them with three horses. But it could serve as a gesture of goodwill. "I have an idea," he said. "We might be able tae find a farmer or stableman tae loan us three horses. I can use my uncle's name, promise payment after we arrive. These lowlanders willnae want tae travel all that way to retrieve their horses, not even for a decent price, but if we had this pretty lace tae offer him tae give tae his wife or sweetheart, he might agree."

Ines nodded. "Good. Where is this man? We should speak to him as soon as possible."

Duncan pressed her back down as she'd half risen with excitement. "We'll nae find anyone willing tae do business tonight. Tomorrow is soon enough."

Ines sighed then leaned against him, bringing her hair and that scent he so enjoyed even closer. Duncan was well aware he should move away from her. He should keep several feet between them. But he did not move.

"Where are Mr. Fortescue and Miss Wellesley?" she asked.

"We left her at the camp. Stratford went tae fetch her. I imagine he'll bring her back here, since it's drier than sleeping under the trees. But it will take him some time tae find his way to her and return."

She looked up at him. He didn't like the glint in her eyes. "Then we will be alone for a while longer?"

"A short while," he said, though he thought it could be an hour or even two, considering how hard it was raining now. Water ran through the holes in the roof like a faucet had opened. In Stratford's place, Duncan would have waited for the rain to ease before trying to find his way back to the cottage.

"Then you have time to kiss me again," she said.

He shook his head. "That's nae a good idea. Remember what happened the last time I kissed ye?"

She nodded. "I remember. Do you think I am very wicked if I want you to do that again?"

*Christ and all the saints.*

"I think ye are a woman who enjoys pleasure and is nae afraid tae admit it."

"I enjoy *you*, Duncan," she said. "I want *you* to kiss me."

He was sorely tempted. He knew he should be content to have her beside him, to know she was safe and unhurt. Since the moment the dog had appeared in the clearing without her, his chest had felt tight, and he hadn't been able to take a deep breath. Not until he had her safe at his side again. She was safe and beside him, but he needed more of her.

She touched his face, running her fingers lightly over his cheek, then leaning forward slowly. Duncan did not move, merely closed his eyes when her lips brushed over his. She was so sweet, so soft, and her lips were so tempting. He couldn't stop himself from responding to the kiss. Her hands settled on his shoulders then roamed over his back, gathering fistfuls of his shirt as she deepened the kiss. Duncan felt the sweet press of her soft body against him. He lifted her and settled her on his lap, wanting her even closer. She drew back to settle herself, and he tried not to think about how her legs straddled him and her skirts were hiked up to her knees. Instead, he ran his mouth over her jaw then down her throat, eliciting shivers of pleasure from her as he explored the smooth column of her neck.

She leaned back, and his mouth slid easily to the hollow at the base of her throat and then lower. Her neckline was modest, but he knew where the pins holding the bodice had been placed, and it seemed a natural thing to pluck them out and lower the material. She wore a thin shift under the dress, thin enough that he could see the dark nipples of her small breasts, erect against the linen. With a shaking hand, he loosed the tie of the shift, so it fell open, exposing that lovely swath of skin.

She murmured and then her hand was at the tie. He thought she might close it again. He half-hoped she would. Instead, she drew the material down over the swell of her flesh, revealing pale brown areolas tipped with hard buds that tilted upward, begging for his tongue.

Duncan put his mouth on her, on the top of her breast, then slid his lips down until he circled the center of her. She moaned, that moan that always made his blood race. He had to hear her make that sound again, and so he drew one nipple into his mouth as his hand palmed the other, the tight little peak growing even harder against his skin. She moved against him as he took her into his mouth, whispering words that made no sense in any language—words of encouragement and pleading and pleasure.

Those words were like whisky to him. He savored each one and enjoyed them as he might a fine, aged single malt. He savored the feel of her in his mouth and against his hand. It was difficult not to notice the heat of her sex near his cock as she wriggled to move closer to him. She had all but given herself up to sensation. He loved that she could do that, loved that he could make her forget everything but his hands and his mouth and his body. She arched her small breasts higher, giving him better access to those pretty nipples. He circled them with his tongue and felt her shiver as her fingers dug into his shoulders. His hands ached to reach between her legs and feel the heat and wetness of her. As though she knew what he was thinking, she drew his face up to hers and kissed him. When they parted, she said, "*Por favor*. Touch me."

His hands drifted down to her slim hips and then he drew up her skirts and slipped under the material where he found the softness of her thighs. She was warm, so warm, and he needed to feel the heat of her sex. Sliding closer to her core, he watched her face tense in anticipation. He slowed, drawing the moment out longer until she began to tremble with want.

Finally, his fingers brushed her curls and the wetness there. He slid between her slick folds, making her cry out with pleasure. Christ but he wanted to give her that pleasure. He wanted to feel her climax around his fingers. He pushed her gently back, his hand behind her to cushion her. Arms braced on either side of her, he looked down at her. She was beautiful, with her flushed cheeks, her rosy mouth, and her turgid nipples all but aching for him to kiss them.

"Do not stop." She looked up at him, her brown eyes hazy with need. "I want you."

He gave her a warning look. It would be too easy to be guided by her desire and his cock. Instead, he dug for his meager reserves of restraint. They were limited in the best of times, but now the well was all but empty. "I'll nae take yer virginity on the floor in a dirty cottage. Ye deserve better than that."

"I deserve for my first time to be with a man I love."

Duncan's heart all but stopped. "Lass, ye dinnae love me. Ye dinnae even ken me."

She shook her head. "I know you. I knew you even before you knew who I was. My brother-in-law told me all about your bravery in battle."

Duncan raised a brow. "He said *bravery*?"

She smiled and reached up to caress his cheek. "That is what he meant, *não*? And I confess"—she let her fingers brush over his cheeks then his lips—"I spied on you when you came to call. I enjoyed looking at you."

He grinned. "Did ye now?"

She nodded. "You are tall and strong with this wild hair." Her hand slid over the few pieces of hair that had escaped his queue. "And those eyes that make me shiver when you look at me."

Duncan lowered his forehead to hers. "Lass, that's lust, nae love."

She kissed him quickly. "That was lust, but now I do know you. And do you know what I love about you?"

He should not allow her to continue. She shouldn't love him. He couldn't marry her. He could never be the man she wanted or needed. "I'm nae the man ye think I am, lass." He began to pull away, but she cupped the back of his neck and forced him to meet her gaze.

"The man I think you are never complains, even when he is injured. The man I think you are goes out of his way to help a woman he does not know and cannot talk to just because she is in his carriage."

"Nae, I—"

"The man I think you are hardly sleeps to watch over the rest of us."

"I gave Stratford a turn—"

"I found you sleeping on the floor outside my room at the inn! And that was before you risked your life to rescue me tonight."

"Dinnae make it sound like I am some sort of hero. I should never have let ye be taken in the first place."

She cupped his face. "I know you, *Senhor* Murray. I love you, Duncan."

What was he supposed to say to that? What could he say? He didn't have the words, so he showed her with his actions. He kissed her, and when she kissed him back, there was the proof of her feelings. How had he not known she loved him before? She had told him in so many ways. But he'd wanted to pretend those looks were just the product of an infatuation.

It was more than infatuation. And he should end this now before he let it go too far and broke her heart.

"Kiss me," she murmured against his lips, and his heart lurched. He didn't love her back. He didn't love anyone—he couldn't. But he felt something, something more than what he'd wanted to feel. He'd known it the past few days, and it was the reason he tried to keep his distance from her.

But now here they were, and she was asking him to kiss her, touch her. And Christ but he wanted her. She did deserve to have someone she loved show her what passion could be and should be. He wanted to be the one to give her these first pleasures.

She pressed her hips up, sliding against his erection, and he realized he'd lowered himself over her. As much as his body wanted to join with hers, her virginity was for her husband. That didn't mean Duncan was prepared to be wholly honorable. He was no saint. He lowered his mouth to kiss her throat, and the soft skin there seemed to lead to the soft skin of her bare shoulder and her collarbone and then the gentle swell of her breasts.

Her skin was so soft and sweet. She smelled of rain and starched linen and under all of it the faint scent of vanilla that was her own. He teased her nipple with his tongue while his hand moved under her skirts to mold his hand over her knee then her thigh. She opened for him without him even having to prompt her, and he slid his hand between her thighs. The silk of her inner thighs made his head spin. The heat of her sex was like a beacon calling to him. He slid higher, stroking her soft curls.

Slowly, drawing his tongue over her nipple, he looked up at her. Her eyes were closed, and her chin tilted upward in what looked like sheer pleasure. "I want tae taste ye, lass," he murmured.

Her eyes opened. "Show me."

Duncan tried to stop the world from spinning. This woman seemed to have no fear. She was open to his every suggestion, ready for any adventure. He slid down her body, trailing kisses over the material of her dress until he reached the heap of her skirts. He pushed them out of the way, revealing her shapely legs and the triangle of dark hair at their apex. Duncan parted her legs until the pink flesh of her sex was visible. He expected she would resist, but when he looked up at her, she was propped on her elbows looking down at him with curiosity. "Now what will you do?" she asked.

"What do ye want me tae do, lass?"

"Touch me," she said without any embarrassment.

"Here?" He slid two fingers over her outer lips.

*"Sim. More."*

"What if I touch ye with my mouth. Would that shock ye?"

Her eyes widened. "I like when you shock me."

He chuckled. "I ken ye do. Open wider for me, lass."

She obeyed, and he parted her lips until he saw the small nub that would bring her to climax. Turning his head, he kissed her inner thighs, moving slowly upward until his mouth brushed her downy hair. She moaned and arched her breasts upward, already seeming to be half in ecstasy.

He touched her outer lips with his tongue then slid over them, deliberately avoiding her clitoris, for fear she would come too fast. She writhed and opened wider, welcoming his touch.

"Duncan," she said on a breath. Her legs started to tremble as he opened her and slid his tongue against her inner flesh. She was wet and tasted so sweet. He dipped his tongue inside her channel and felt her muscles clench slightly. He could imagine how wet and tight she would feel against his cock.

"Ye like this, lass?" he asked.

She answered with a moan and some unintelligible words. He didn't think they even made sense in Portuguese. She was lost to sensation, lost to the feel of his mouth against her. Her hips arched as her body sought pleasure. He knew how to give it and slid his tongue slowly upward until he barely touched her plump pearl. She moaned and her head thrashed from side to side. Duncan drew back, then touched the tip of his tongue to her again, this time swirling it over her. Her hands fisted in her skirts as she cried out. Her whole body seemed to vibrate, and he took her hips in his hands to steady her. Her body was tight as a violin string, reaching for the pleasure he could give her.

He flicked at that sensitive bud again, drew back, licked, drew back, and repeated the torment until she was all but begging him *por favor.*

Finally, he pressed his tongue upon her fully, licking her with a deep sweeping motion. He felt her orgasm shudder through her. Her entire body went rigid for what seemed long moments, then she cried out and her hips undulated violently. He kept his mouth on her, feeling the way her clitoris pulsed against his tongue as her hips drove her harder against his mouth.

Duncan had never found so much pleasure in giving a woman release before. He enjoyed a woman's pleasure, but then no woman reacted like Ines. No woman reacted to him as she did. She gave her whole self to him, opening to him, not holding anything back. He sincerely hoped Stratford hadn't come directly to the cottage because her screams were loud enough to be heard outside.

When she finally stilled, only moaning faintly in protest when he tongued her again, he lifted his head and looked at her. He could pleasure her again. She was the sort of woman who could come over and over. He hoped whoever she married realized that about her and gave her many nights full of pleasure. But it was hard to think of her with any other man. It was impossible to imagine another seeing her as she was now. Her lips were slightly swollen and red. Her cheeks flushed, and her eyes half-lidded. Her hair was wild, a tangle of chocolate ribbon beneath her. Her dress had all but come off her arms, and her nipples were still hard and had gone dark. The burn of his beard brushing against her sensitive skin was still visible on the curve of her breasts. She looked thoroughly debauched, a woman well-pleasured. A woman no man could resist bedding.

Except Duncan had to resist.

He moved away from her, and she opened her eyes. "Come here," she said, lifting her arms to him. He wanted to go into those arms. He wanted her to press against him, but if he did, she would never leave this cottage a virgin.

"I need some air," he said, rising to his knees. "I'll be back in a few moments."

She frowned, some of the pleasurable haze clearing from her vision. "Duncan?"

"Just give me a moment, lass." He stood on shaky legs and walked, unsteadily, out into the cold rain.

He shivered in the cool night air, but he knew it would take more than this to cool his need for her. Duncan feared it might never be extinguished.

# Fifteen

*Emmeline*

When Loftus returned without Stratford, Emmeline began to worry. She hadn't worried when Mr. Murray and Stratford left without her. She hadn't worried when Loftus whined to follow, and she was left alone. She hadn't worried when the rain had started pouring down. She'd huddled under a tree with a blanket over her head and stayed, if not, dry, drier than she might have without the protection of the large tree limbs and the thick blanket.

Emmeline was not cold. Her body shivered, but inside she was warm with happiness.

How could she not be when Stratford had all but acknowledged he cared for her—not as a friend. Not as a cousin. Not as a sort of sister.

As a lover?

Emmeline wasn't certain why she was so thrilled at this revelation. A month ago, she would have never once thought of kissing Stratford. He was her escort, someone who had to accompany her on the never-ending list of social engagements. She was miserable and only looking for escape.

But then she had escaped, and Stratford had shown up, and something changed. He wasn't just the man she'd known since they'd been children, not just an escort who endured the Season at her side. He was a Stratford she had never seen— probably, she could admit, because she had not looked at him in so long. Of course, she'd realized he was handsome and well-built. She was not *blind*. Of course, she knew he had been decorated for his service to his country during the war.

But she hadn't known how much she would like his intellect—how talking to him was refreshing and made her feel alive. She didn't agree with all he said, but he made her think. He made her realize that running away from her mother was not the solution to her problems. She would have to face them head on.

Emmeline hadn't known how much she would admire his bravery and cunning and loyalty to his friend. And she even appreciated his cool head and rational way of thinking.

Those qualities had saved them all more than once on this adventure.

But she hadn't thought that he felt the same about her. They had kissed, yes, and she'd known he enjoyed the kiss. But it had seemed he hadn't wanted to enjoy it and hadn't wanted to repeat it. And then they'd kissed again, and she'd said that idiot thing about marrying him. She hadn't meant to say it, but at the time it seemed like such a good idea. If she married him, she would not have to endure any more Seasons. And she could keep kissing him.

But he'd seemed so appalled at the idea, and she'd been humiliated at having said it.

But then tonight he had all but told her that he thought of her in much the same way. Had something changed or had he started to feel something more than friendship for her, as she had with him?

That was when Loftus appeared. She hadn't heard him coming, but with the rain pounding down, it was hard to hear anything. He emerged from the darkness and shook all over, trying to rid his coat of water. Emmeline laughed then looked about for Stratford.

"Where is Stratford?" she asked Loftus, who did not reply, just came to sit with her under the blanket and licked her face. She went instantly cold, afraid the plan to rescue

Ines had gone wrong. But what could she do? She had no idea where the crofter's cottage might be, and she certainly couldn't try to find it in the dark with rain pouring down. She was better off staying here and searching for her friends in the light of day.

She knew it was the wisest decision, but it was not the easiest. As the minutes and then what seemed like hours passed, Emmeline began to wonder if Stratford might be hurt. What if he was lying in a field, bleeding? What if he was cold and wet and needed her?

She could not sit here and wait. She had to find him.

She lowered the blanket and rose, then looked at the dog. He peered up at her mournfully, eyes half-closed to keep the rain out. "Loftus, find Stratford."

The dog whined and put his head on his paws. It was clear he didn't intend to go anywhere. "Loftus, find Stratford!" she repeated. Loftus just looked up at her from those squinted eyes.

Well, what had she expected? That he would bound away and lead her straight to Stratford? That only happened in books. She would have to find him without the dog's help. She knew which way the men had started out.

Wrapping the blanket about her shoulders, she began to walk in that direction.

"And where do you think you are going?" a voice asked.

Emmeline froze. She knew that voice. "Stratford?"

He moved out of the shadows, and she realized he'd been walking toward her, but she hadn't seen him in the darkness and rain. Emmeline couldn't stop herself. She ran toward him and threw her arms around him. He caught her, pulling her close and holding her for a long moment before he said, "Let's find some cover."

She led him back to the tree she'd sheltered under, but he shook his head and moved toward the woods. She followed reluctantly, but once they had entered the darkness, she saw the wisdom of his actions. With more trees clumped close together, the rain was muted. Of course, she couldn't take more than two steps without tripping, but Stratford gripped her hand and kept her on her feet. They settled by a log, and she sank down, her back against it. Stratford took the blanket, draped it over some low-hanging branches, making a sort of shelter, feeble though it might be.

Then he sat beside her, his warmth most welcome as she'd begun shivering now. Loftus came to sit on her other side, and she was a few degrees above freezing.

"Ines?" she asked.

"Safe," he answered. "Unharmed, too, I think. She's with Duncan at the cottage. When the rain slackens, we will go there too."

"How far?" she asked.

"About fifteen minutes. I got turned around, which is why it took me so much longer to make my way back here. Loftus went on ahead. I thought he would comfort you."

She shook her head, her wet hair sticking to her cheeks.

Stratford touched her cheek, brushing the hair away. "You were worried?"

She nodded. He put an arm about her and pulled her close. She buried her face in his shoulder and tried to hold back tears. "I thought—" she began, but her voice faltered.

"Sweetheart," he said, "I'm sorry."

She sniffed and wiped her eyes. "You are safe. That's what's important."

He looked down at her. "I wish this rain would stop, so we could go to the cottage. I hate that we have to sit out in the cold and wet half the night."

"I don't mind," she said. It was the truth. She didn't mind as long as he was with her. "Though I have to say thus far I do not enjoy Scotland."

He chuckled. "We can always go back."

She drew back and hit him lightly on the arm. "Not a chance."

He laughed harder then pulled her close. "Having the time of your life, are you?"

"I'm miserable," she said.

"Well, no one I would rather be miserable with than you." He gave her a quick kiss on the mouth.

At least it started out quick, but then his mouth lingered instead of withdrew. His lips seemed to be questioning hers, asking if she wanted what he wanted.

Emmeline answered by moving her own lips against his in a light whisper of a kiss. His arms tightened on hers, pulling her hard against him as his mouth pressed firmly against hers. When he held her like this, touched her like this, she couldn't think of anything but the way his lips felt against hers. She forgot the rain and the cold and nothing but the heady press of his mouth, the gentle probing of his tongue, and the hardness of his chest under her palms mattered.

He kissed her for what seemed hours. They would pause, come up for air, and then their mouths would be drawn inexorably closer until they began all over again. He lowered her to the soft pine needles on the ground, his body covering hers and giving her warmth. With a sniff, Loftus moved off to the side and put his head down between his paws. As

Stratford kissed her, the heat in her belly caused the rest of her to tingle and ache. She pressed against him, wanting the feel of him in that spot between her legs and against her tender nipples.

He pulled back, lowering his face to her shoulder and catching his breath. *No, no, no,* was all she could manage in the way of forming a thought. She needed his mouth; she needed his body, so hard and heavy, against hers.

"We should go," he said.

"What?" Moving away from this place, from his heat, was the last thing on her mind. But gradually, when he didn't kiss her again, she noticed it wasn't just his body keeping the rain from falling on her. The rain had slackened and now there was only a drizzle. Emmeline began to wonder if there was ever a time in Scotland when it didn't drizzle.

"We should walk to the cottage," he said. "Before the rain starts again."

"It's never stopped," she said, irritably. She did not want to walk to the cottage. She wanted to stay right here, and she wanted him to kiss her again.

"Then before it starts to rain buckets again," he said.

Emmeline wanted to pull him back when he moved away from her. She immediately missed the warmth of his body and his touch. She almost wished it was still pouring rain. But without the feel of him close to her, she was cold and damp and wishing for a fire and somewhere soft to lie down. She almost wished she were home again, except then she remembered how her mother slapped her hand when she reached for a biscuit and how she had to share a bed with Marjorie, who made a show of crying herself to sleep because Emmeline would not be *reasonable* and marry some oaf so Marjorie could marry her one true love.

Emmeline would take Scottish rain and pine needles in her hair over that any day. And she would take Stratford's kisses over pretty much anything else. The warmth of him still infused her, and she could almost forget that she was wet and cold.

He was already gathering his things, and she resigned herself to doing the same. Without speaking, she bundled her few belongings and followed Stratford and Loftus to the cottage. Loftus seemed to know the way and frequently trotted ahead or lingered behind, sniffing something only he could smell before racing to catch up with them. For her part, Emmeline stumbled over her skirts for most of the way and was relieved to see the light in the darkness and smell the smoke of a fire. Her senses detected these signs of civilization long before they reached the cottage. She couldn't tell the condition of the place, but the promise of a fire drew her closer, and gave her strength to stumble along. The first chance she had she would tie up these skirts. The hem had come loose, and she wouldn't be able to stop tripping over them until she found a needle and thread.

When they finally neared the cottage, the door opened, and Duncan Murray stood in the frame. "I'd begun tae wonder if it would ever stop," he said. Giving Emmeline a concerned look, he moved aside. "Come warm yerself by the fire, lass."

She moved inside the cottage, her eyes stinging at the smoke lingering near the ceiling—what there was of it—and her nose wrinkling at the dirt and general ruin of the place. But it was mostly dry and warm, and she could appreciate that. She went to the fire, where Ines was curled up under Murray's coat. The woman was sleeping, her face resting on one cheek. She looked peaceful and unhurt, and Emmeline sat next to her and put a hand on her back. Behind them, the men spoke in low tones, something about horses and lace. Emmeline would normally have wanted to be involved in the conversation, but she was too tired. Her eyelids were too heavy.

The next thing she knew, her back hurt. Her bed was hard and unyielding, and her body ached. She was warm, though, and something heavy was draped over her, keeping her from rolling to her side. Slowly, she opened her eyes and looked into Stratford's face. He was smiling at her, eyes already open.

She started, and the arm he'd draped over her kept her from bolting to her feet.

"Shh," he said. "Miss Neves is still sleeping."

Emmeline looked on the other side of the room, where a small form under a heap of cloth must have been Ines. She looked back at Stratford. "Where is Mr. Murray?"

"He went to surveil the surroundings," he said, sounding very military-esque.

"Why didn't you go?" she whispered.

"I stayed back to protect the women."

She raised a brow. "By lying here and staring at me."

"There have to be some benefits to staying behind." He pushed a strand of her hair off her face, and Emmeline tried not to imagine how absolutely wild she must look—her hair unkempt and frizzy, her clothing rumpled, and her face probably smeared with mud or soot.

"You looked too beautiful for me to look away," Stratford said.

Emmeline stared at him.

"I know it's wildly inappropriate for me to lie here with you, but you smell a great deal better than Duncan."

"I'm sure I smell rank and look just as bad," she said, turning her head away from him. Her cheeks felt hot, and she wished he would move his arm so she could sit up and avoid his gaze. Except she didn't want him to move away so much that she would actually ask him to do so or lift his arm.

"You look a bit…"

She glanced at him, and his brow was furrowed in thought.

"Be careful of your words, Fortescue," she said.

He grinned, and it was such a boyish grin that she was taken back to those summers at Odham Abbey and all the many times she had wished he would invite her to play with him and the older children. "Mussed," he finally said, and she nodded her approval.

"Good choice."

"Thank you."

She looked down at his arm and regretfully motioned at it. "Could you?"

Of course. He lifted it, and she wriggled away, giving her tight muscles some relief. She sat and stretched her back. "I do wish we could find an inn or a bucket of hot water somewhere." She glanced at him when he didn't reply and found him staring at her. He blinked.

"Pardon?"

"Hot water, I said. I would kill for some."

"So would I, but we need horses even more desperately."

Emmeline thought that statement debatable.

"I would like food," said a small voice from the pile of clothing.

Emmeline laughed. "So would I. Are you well?"

Two brown eyes poked out. Emmeline sighed when she saw how pretty Ines still looked. The other woman might have bathed and brushed her hair the night before for all she looked neat enough. "I am very well." She touched her throat, and Emmeline spotted the red triangle-shaped wound the reiver had made with his blade. It was not bleeding, but it looked angry and raw.

Stratford rose to his feet. "Duncan said the men didn't hurt you?"

"They only wanted money," Ines said. She sat slowly. "Where is Duncan?"

Stratford indicated the window. "He went to scout the area. We'll need to find someone with horses to loan."

"And a farmer's wife who likes my lace," Ines said.

Stratford nodded. "It's lucky you have it with you."

"How will lace help us?" Emmeline asked, and the two of them explained the plan to her. A half hour later, the three of them had brushed the dust from their clothes and hair and were pacing impatiently about the cottage. Emmeline was pleased to note the rain had stopped, though the day was gray and overcast. She looked up when Loftus let out a low warning bark and spotted Duncan through the window. He was returning, a smile on his face. He raised a hand to her, and she went to the door and opened it for him.

"Good news, lads and lassies," he said. "I've found a farmer we can negotiate with."

"He has a wife who might like my lace?" Ines asked.

Duncan winked. "Even better. He has two daughters."

***

*Stratford*

Stratford liked Malcolm Campbell right away. He was a short, plump man with an easy laugh and blue eyes that all but disappeared in his round face when he was amused. He also had two plump daughters, all of thirteen and fifteen, who were sweet and pretty enough to turn the local boys' heads.

Campbell had offered them all a meal and hot water to wash faces and hands, and even though he said his great-grandfather had a grievance with someone who was a relation to the Duke of Atholl, Duncan's uncle, he would not hold that against Duncan.

And Stratford had thought the English had long memories.

When their bellies were full, Campbell took Duncan and Stratford to his barn, where he showed them his horses. He had a large farm and several horses. Stratford was as good a judge of horseflesh as any other man, and he nodded in agreement when Duncan picked the best three. The beasts were work horses, to be sure, and Stratford thought they would have little trouble making the journey to the Highlands.

"And ye can do withoot them for a few weeks?" Duncan asked, though now that he spoke to one of his countrymen, his accent had deepened, and Stratford had to strain to understand him.

"Och, the planting is done. I can spare them for a time, and the coin ye promised will buy my seeds for the fall planting." He gave Duncan a rueful look. "Not tae mention, my girls fell in love with the lace yer lady showed them. They'll cry for days if I deny them now."

"Then we should discuss particulars," Duncan said. At least that's what Stratford thought he said.

"Aye." The farmer looked at Stratford, and Duncan looked at him too. Clearly the two Scotsmen preferred to negotiate in private.

"I'll go for a walk," Stratford said.

"There's a pond just a quarter mile west," the farmer said. "It's fed by a hot spring. It's nae as good as a bath in a tub, but it will do tae wash the dust off yer feet."

"Thank you," Stratford said and went off in search of the pond. He didn't believe it would actually be warm—the Scots' idea of warmth and the English's were vastly different—but he'd risk a cold plunge to clean the dust and grime from his body. He could wash out his clothing as well. He'd have to wear them damp, but he'd done that often in the army.

He found the pond easily enough and was a bit surprised at the steam rising from it. The farmer had not exaggerated the hot spring. Stratford wouldn't have called it a proper pond, more like a watering hole about fifteen feet across. At the far end, a group of rocks were the perfect spot to swim to if the watering hole was as deep as it looked to be.

He stripped off his clothing, quickly and efficiently, rinsed them in the warm water—God it would be like heaven when he went in—and laid them to dry on the rocks to the side. He waded into the water. It was deep. The rocks beneath his feet were slippery and dropped off quickly. Stratford went under, dunked his head, and enjoyed the feeling of warmth he hadn't experienced for days. Well, except when he'd had

Emmeline in his arms. Then he'd been warm enough. She seemed to possess a small furnace inside her that heated them both whenever their bodies came together.

But he'd better not think of that now. It had been hard enough to lie beside her all night and mind his manners, harder still when she'd risen this morning and stretched, arching her back and thrusting those glorious breasts out. He'd wanted to touch her so badly, he could taste it. But he'd already done enough damage. He'd given into temptation and kissed her far too much. He'd managed to keep his hands to himself, but if he continued down this path, he wouldn't be able to do that.

Stratford began to swim for the rocks, reflecting that Emmeline had seemed to enjoy his kisses well enough. Considering she hadn't really noticed him much before, that was definitely a change. But of course her thoughts went to marriage, as they probably should, and Stratford knew better than anyone that both their families would frown upon that match. There had been ample opportunity for either his parents or her mother to encourage a relationship between them, but no one ever had. In fact, he'd been tasked with escorting her to balls, where she would be thrown into the path of other men.

Men who were not bastards masquerading as legitimate sons.

He reached the rocks and put his hand on one then jumped back when he felt something soft and pliant. Something that couldn't be a rock at all. "What the devil?"

"Not the devil at all." The pale hand soon gave way to a pale arm and then a head peeked around one of the rocks. It was Emmeline. Her hair slicked back, and her skin glistening with droplets of water. Her cheeks were pink from the heat of the spring. Treading water, Stratford stared at her.

"Where did you come from?"

"The other side," she said, indicating the clothing laid out on the rocks and hanging from the branches of a tree. How had he not seen that before? "I was here before you. At least twenty minutes before," she said.

He would have seen her for certain if she'd been swimming. "Then you've been sitting behind this rock since—"

"Since you appeared and removed your clothing?" She nodded. "Yes."

Good God. He was almost embarrassed, except he was too aroused to be embarrassed. She had watched him disrobe and said nothing?

"You should have made your presence known."

"Yes, I should have." She didn't sound the least bit contrite. "But if I had, you would have left, and I wanted you to be able to enjoy the spring as well. I promise I closed my eyes." She smiled. "Except for maybe one peek."

"Bloody hell."

"You've changed since I last spied on you, swimming at Odham Abbey."

His cheeks felt hot.

"Are you blushing?" she asked. "I promise it was only a very quick peek."

"Well, don't peek again. I'll get out and leave the pool to you." He did not relish putting his wet clothes back on so quickly. He'd thought they'd have a few minutes to dry.

Emmeline reached around the rock and grabbed his arm. His *bare* arm. "Oh, no! Don't leave."

"You know it's not proper for me to stay."

She stuck out her lip. "Then I will leave. I was here first. It seems only fair." She released him and disappeared behind the rock.

"No! You stay," he said, his voice almost frantic.

Her head appeared from behind the rock again. "Why?" Her eyes narrowed. "You're afraid you will peek?"

"No."

"Yes. That's it, isn't it?"

"No."

"Well…" She seemed to consider something. "It does seem only fair."

His breath caught. "What seems only fair?" Why had he even asked? Why was he not swimming to the side and climbing out instead of prolonging this agony? Because even though she was behind a rock, and he was on the other side of it, his mind knew that she was naked. Completely naked. And that meant his body knew he was close to a naked woman—and not just any naked woman, Emmeline. He'd gone hard as the rock between them, and his cock was making it difficult for his head to think clearly.

"That you get a peek at me. I saw you, after all."

"Emmeline, no."

But she continued as though she hadn't heard him. "I admit I really only saw your behind. You had turned to place your clothing on the rocks, and I caught sight of your back and your, er, backside."

"*Emmeline.*"

"It was a very nice backside. Not that I am much of a judge, but—"

"I will swim to the other side and get out now," he said.

"If you must, but I am not about to allow the silly rules I ran away from to ruin this lovely day and a swim in this pool. I may never have this chance again." And she swam away from the rock, passing close enough to him that he felt the push of water away from her feet. And he saw—oh, what he saw. He spotted a long streak of pale skin beneath the dark water. He couldn't make out body parts, exactly, but he could imagine what was what.

And because he was so busy imagining it, he did not move. He stayed exactly where he was as she swam behind him, not close, keeping her distance, and then back around to pause at the rock in front of him.

Now she was close. He could feel the movement of water where her feet and hands pushed at it to keep her afloat. His gaze remained on a spot just above her head except for the one second, he lowered his gaze to catch a glimpse of her face.

She was smiling at him, bemused. "You have more fortitude than I."

"Do I?" he asked.

"I peeked and you haven't."

"It's a fight by the second," he said.

"Then why not give in?" she asked.

His gaze met hers. "Do you want me to look?"

Her blue eyes were clear. "Yes."

Well, how was he to resist now? The answer was that he could not. His gaze lowered to her nose, her lips, her chin, and then the column of her neck. And then the slow perusal ended because there, at the rim of the water were the orbs of her breasts. They were submerged for the most part, but there was no hiding their roundness and fullness. And just beneath the surface he could see the peach of her nipples.

"Are we even now?" she asked, her voice husky. He forced his eyes back to her face, forced his hand to stay at his side as well. "Can we share the pool in peace?"

"No," he said. "We can share it, but not in peace. I'm afraid I'm not feeling very peaceful." He moved toward her, small strokes of his hands and feet bringing him closer to her. She might have swum away, might have ducked under the water or swam off to one side or another, but she stayed where she was until his body slid against hers and those magnificent breasts rubbed against his bare chest.

He groaned. "*Emmeline.*" His mouth came down on hers at the same time that she gripped his shoulders for balance. He gripped the rock behind her, pushing her gently against it and feeling her nipples, large and growing turgid now, press, impertinent, against him. His tongue slipped inside her mouth, and she opened for him, kissing him back with an abandonment that set alarm bells off in his head.

Alarm bells he ignored because how could he think with her naked body against his? His cock pressed against the soft flesh of her belly, and her legs tangled with his until she finally found the ledge that rose beneath the rock and stood on it. That brought her breasts out of the water, and Stratford, no longer needing to keep her afloat, lowered one hand to cup her.

*Christ.* They were perfect. His hand couldn't even fit around the plump flesh, and when he pressed her nipple lightly between two fingers, her head fell back. He had to kiss her then, had to kiss those thick nipples that jutted upward and seemed to beg for his tongue. He ran it along them, took one in his mouth, letting his tongue lave it until she was all but panting and her arms were around his shoulders, her fingers digging into his back.

He lifted his mouth, balanced by his toes on the rock ledge, and looked down at her. If he'd thought her cheeks were pink before, the flush had spread to her entire face, making her eyes even bluer. He filled his hands with her breasts again, kneading them gently. "Do you know how long I've wanted to see you here, touch you here? God, since that first time I saw you and they'd seemed to grown out of nowhere."

"It didn't seem that way to me," she said. "They grew and grew and pretty soon they were so large I didn't know what to do with them."

He kissed her lips. "They're perfect, and I know what to do with them."

"Yes," she agreed. "You're making me feel…"

"What?" he asked.

"Tingly," she said. "You're making me want your hands…everywhere."

"I want to put my hands everywhere." He slid them down from her breasts, over her generous hips, and back up to the wonder of those pale orbs. "But do you know where I really want to put my hands?"

"I don't think I should say."

He grinned. "Yes, there." He rubbed his thigh against the curls he felt between her legs. "But first, here." His hands slid back to her hips and then down and over her bottom. God, he could have come just from touching it. It was so firm and round, and he wanted to see it, bite it, part it and slide his cock…

He took a shaky breath, fighting to find control, even as the decadence that was her body made him all but dizzy with desire.

"Can I touch you?" she asked. And then without waiting for his permission, her hands went from his shoulders down and over his chest. "Where did all these muscles come from?" she asked.

"Fighting, riding, carrying—Emmeline!" He grabbed her hand before it could drift any lower than his belly. "You're playing with fire."

"Oh, good," she said. "I always like to see what happens when I add kindling to a fire." She wriggled her hand free and slid down further until her hand brushed over his jutting cock. Finding it, she closed over it, her grip tentative. "I didn't expect it to be so hard," she said.

"That's what happens when I'm naked with a goddess."

Her eyes met his, and he could see in her expression she thought he was mocking her.

"You're beautiful," he said before she could try and push the compliment away. "Your body is beautiful."

He took her hand away from his cock, which was probably the hardest thing he'd ever done in his life and slid his hands back to her hips then down over her belly to the curls at the juncture of her thighs. "Have you ever touched yourself here?" he asked, his fingers delving into the curls until he found the soft flesh there.

She gasped as he made a V with two fingers and stroked her outer lips between them.

"Yes," she said, not seeming at all embarrassed.

"What about here?" His fingers parted her lips and delved inside, finding her channel and stroking its entrance.

"Yes, but it didn't feel like this." The pink from her face had spread to her neck and the top of her chest. He kissed it, dipping his mouth to kiss the valley between her breasts as he moved his fingers slowly in search of her clitoris.

"And what about here? Have you touched here?" he asked, rubbing it gently.

"*Yes*," she breathed.

"And did you come?" He bit the top of one of her breasts lightly then licked the spot with his tongue. Biting again until her nipple was in his mouth.

"What do you—"

"Did you climax?" he asked. "Did you find pleasure?"

"I don't know," she said. "It felt good."

"Then you didn't come. You'd know if you'd come."

He moved his hand back to her opening and pressed one finger against it. He could feel her wetness, thicker and slicker than the water, against his finger. He pressed into her, just the tip of his finger, and she jerked her hips toward him.

"I like that."

He made a sound of acknowledgement, stroked her again, and repeated the gesture. Then his thumb found the tight bud of her clitoris and circled it. He could feel it swell as he attended to it, felt her body opening to him, her hips angling toward his cock.

"Can you make me come?" she asked.

God, he hoped so. The pink had reached the tops of her breasts now, and he wanted it to spread over them, wanted to see her nipples turn dark with arousal.

"Tell me what feels good," he said. He circled her swelling nub, then flicked his thumb against it.

"*That*," she panted. "That feels good."

"And this?" He dipped his finger back into the heat of her sex, just the tip again, but he pressed his thumb on her clitoris as he did so.

"Oh, *yes*. Oh, *please*. More."

"More of my finger?" he asked, pushing a little deeper.

"Yes, and more…"

His thumb made lazy circles on her clitoris, and he felt her inner muscles tighten against his finger. She was close, so close. Her muscles relaxed, and he pushed deeper. She moaned and thrust her body toward him, taking his finger all the way to the knuckle. She would come soon, and he would enjoy watching it. He would enjoy hearing the sounds she made as he pleasured her.

And then she took his cock in her hand again, and he lost all semblance of the control he'd thought he had. "Emmeline," he half-groaned.

"I like how you feel in my hand," she murmured, her eyes almost closed now.

He liked how he felt in her hand too. He would have liked how he felt inside her, but there were limits to his depravity. It seemed pleasuring her in a pool in the middle of a Scottish farm was not the limit, but he would reevaluate his obviously lacking morals later. Right now she was stroking him and he was stroking her, and her breath was coming very fast. His own seemed to be coming equally fast.

They were both racing toward a finish line, and he knew once he reached it, he'd be too lost to bring her along. He steeled himself to hold his own pleasure in check, but then she let out a small cry of wonder. Her hand tightened around him like a slick glove, and the pressure of it was perfect. He came just as he felt her inner muscles contracting around his finger.

He pushed her against the rock, kissing her hard. Her legs wrapped around him, bringing their bodies into slick, satisfying contact. Christ, he could have started all over again with her. The feel of her body against his made him want her again. He could only think of all the evenings they'd spent together, not touching, not even speaking really. There were so many carriage rides, balls, walks in gardens. Why hadn't he ever kissed her, touched her before?

Because he'd known she thought of him like a brother, if she thought of him at all.

And if she had thought of him, he would have discouraged the interest. He wasn't worthy of her. Hadn't his own mother told him he was nothing more than a mistake? And then Stratford himself discovered he was the son of the Marquess of Wight, who everyone assumed was mad. That meant Stratford had two strikes beside his name. He wasn't good enough for Emmeline. He wasn't good enough for anyone.

He pulled back, and she tried to follow him. "Don't stop."

"I have to stop."

Something in his voice must have gotten through her pleasure-muddied brain because her gaze sharpened. "Have I done something wrong?"

"No," he said pushing back from her. "I have. I shouldn't have touched you like that. I had no right."

She tilted her head. "I think when I begged you to continue, that gave you the right."

"I'm supposed to be protecting you, not debauching you."

"Maybe I like being debauched." Her brows rose. "It's a great deal more fun than being protected."

"Yes, well you won't thank me when your reputation is ruined."

She shrugged, and he realized her breasts were fully visible. He had to get away or he would be drawn back by her body. He couldn't think when she was naked and so close.

"My reputation is ruined anyway."

"We can still salvage it, but you'll have a devil of a time explaining to your husband why you're not a virgin. And you won't be if I stay much longer."

A flash of anger crossed her face. "Since I don't plan to marry, and even if I did it wouldn't be the sort of man who would judge me for something he no doubt had done himself, I don't see how that is a concern. And please do not worry. I know *you* don't want to marry me. This isn't a ploy to trap you."

How could she stand there arguing, looking so magnificent in her nakedness? Was he supposed to think clearly enough to formulate some sort of response? He couldn't.

And then he didn't have to because she plunged back into the water and started to swim to the other side of the pond, where her clothing had been laid out.

Before he could look away, she was climbing out of the pond, her round bottom coming into view. It was even better than he'd imagined, and he was aware that his heart sped up. She looked over her shoulder at him. "I'm good enough to ogle but not to marry, is that it?" she said, her voice cutting through his desire like ice.

Stratford turned his back. He closed his eyes as well to avoid the temptation of peeking. He didn't open them until he heard her walk away, and then he still kept them closed for a long time.

She thought he didn't want to marry her. She thought he considered her not good enough. He would have to tell her the truth—that he was the one not good enough.

# *Sixteen*

*Ines*

She was miserable. It wasn't just the Scottish weather that made her miserable. It had been raining for three days now, and she was cold and wet and wondered if she would ever be dry.

Even worse, her bottom was so sore that she could barely walk—that was when Duncan let them stop long enough to climb down from the horses. The first day they'd ridden on horseback, she'd enjoyed riding behind Duncan. She'd wrapped her arms about his taut waist and pressed her body against his.

He'd stiffened and had not seemed to relax until they were off the beast. It was as though he didn't want her touch. She went over and over in her mind what she might have done wrong.

And she kept coming back to that night in the crofter's cottage. He'd done things she had not known men and

375

women did together. And he'd made her feel…the pleasure was impossible to describe. But then he'd left her, walked away and left her alone.

It was as though he'd felt guilty for what he'd done. And then the past few days, he'd barely spoken to her. She had begun to think perhaps he regretted what he'd done. Either that or he thought less of her. After all, women were not supposed to allow men such liberties with their bodies until after they were married. She was hurt and confused and her thoughts were a tangle.

Why had she been foolish enough to think he would ever marry her? And why had she thought he would fall madly in love with her? Think she was perfect exactly as she was and carry her away to happily ever after? Yes, he was exciting and had shown her a great deal of adventure. But in the end, he wanted a woman who would follow all the rules.

Well, she wasn't that woman. At the start of this adventure, she had thought all she needed was a respite from tedious suitors and hours of lacemaking. But now she could not ever imagine going back. Yes, she loved her sister and wanted to be with her, but Ines couldn't breathe in London. As much as she hated all the rain, she was enchanted by Scotland. The deeper they traveled, and the further north, the more gorgeous the landscape became. It was a rugged country, that much was clear, but the soaring mountains and swaths of flower-filled valleys were beautiful and achingly romantic. It was the sort of place where anything could happen.

And so much had happened, but now Duncan would not even look her in the eye. Well, at the moment, she couldn't see his eyes. He was riding in front of her, toward what looked like an impassable mountain, and she was holding on for all she was worth. Behind them Mr. Fortescue and Emmeline seemed to negotiate their horses with ease. They weren't afraid of being thrown off or sliding off the animal's back.

She risked a quick peek behind her, and Emmeline gave her a reassuring smile. The other woman had been unusually quiet lately, too. Come to think of it, so had Mr. Fortescue. Ines wondered if something had happened between them...

The ground tilted down and though the horse did not stumble, Ines felt herself tilting. She grasped hold of Duncan, and he grunted. "Ye willnae fall, lass," he said, sounding annoyed.

"You would not care if I did, *senhor*," she said.

He gave her an exasperated look. "What rubbish is this?"

"There is *não* rubbish."

He didn't argue, and she almost wished he would. She wanted an argument with him. She wanted something more than this silence and coldness.

Hours later, it seemed, the rain slackened, and the late afternoon sun broke through the low clouds. It colored the mountains purple and dark red. In the sunlight, the terrain looked lush and green. Far in the distance, Ines spotted a brook winding through a valley between two mountains. Were they mountains or hills? She was not certain, but they were captivating.

"We stop here for the night," Duncan said when they'd reached a clearing with another brook running alongside.

"The horses have another hour or two in them," Fortescue said. "We could go further."

But Duncan handed Ines down then climbed down himself. Ines clung to the horse, her legs feeling wobbly underneath her.

"The next leg of the journey is difficult," he said. "We'll all do better with a fresh start in the morning." And that seemed to be the end of the discussion. Ines was happy to be back on solid land again.

While the men unsaddled the horses and turned them loose to graze, Ines and Emmeline rifled through the saddlebags for something to eat. The farmer had sent them with food, and Duncan had bought more in some of the small villages they passed through, but even Ines, who knew little about such things, could see what they had would not sustain four people for much more than another meal or two at most.

When Stratford came over to start a fire, he frowned at the meager rations the ladies had laid out. "We'll have to buy more to eat," he told Duncan. "This won't last us long."

Duncan didn't even glance their way. "We'll be fine."

Ines huffed out a breath. "How do you know?" she asked. "You did not look."

"I ken," he said, not glancing at her.

She called him several unflattering names in her native tongue and a few others she knew. Fortescue stood. "I have to agree with Miss Neves." He glanced at her. "Not about the names she just called you—I speak Spanish." He winked. "But, Duncan, we need more provisions."

Duncan put his hands on his hips and turned to look at them. Ines hated how her heart thudded in her chest and her lungs grew tight at the sight of him. She couldn't help but want him. He was so handsome, so much of what she'd always dreamed of.

But she was not what he wanted. He had made that very clear.

"At least someone listens to me!" she said. Duncan ignored her. Awful man!

"Tomorrow we dine at my mother's table," Duncan said. Ines stared at him then looked at Emmeline. She wondered if her own jaw had dropped open.

"We arrive tomorrow?" Stratford asked. "To Kirkmoray?"

"Aye."

"Why didn't you say something before?" Emmeline asked.

He shrugged. "Nae one asked."

Emmeline rolled her eyes and Ines, so angry, marched away.

"Lass, where are ye going?" Duncan called.

"I'll go with her," Emmeline said, Loftus following at her heels. Ines slowed enough so that the other woman could catch up. The dog bounded on ahead, keeping just within their sights. The two walked in silence for a long while. Finally, Emmeline stopped at a gentle slope and looked down at a winding ribbon of what Ines assumed must be a road. It looked so small from up here. She studied the green hillsides—or were they mountains?—and the clouds racing over them. Here and there a patch of rock was exposed, proving that underneath the beauty was a hard, cold foundation.

"It's very dramatic, isn't it?" Emmeline asked.

Ines was familiar with that word as it had been applied to her on many occasions. She nodded. "It makes me feel small. I look at it and feel so small, *sim?*"

"Yes," Emmeline said, her voice fainter. "It does put things in perspective."

Ines sank down on the grass, which was not as soft as she would have hoped, being that it was mixed with coarse and prickly vegetation too. But she pulled her knees to her chest and tried to ignore the things poking at her. "I do not know this word, *perspective*, but I realize now I should have gone back to London."

"No," Emmeline said, sitting beside her. "Ouch. This looks softer than it is." She tried to find a comfortable spot then gave up and pulled her own legs close, her posture mirroring Ines's. "If you had gone straight back to London, you would never have had this adventure. *I* would never have had this adventure. I've always wanted to see Scotland, and now I have." She took Ines's hand. "I know those reivers were awful, but this journey has not all been bad."

Ines gave her a sidelong look. "There was the time Duncan was shot and almost died."

"That was when we found Loftus," Emmeline said brightly. In the distance, Loftus raised his gray head and looked at them, having heard his name.

"He is a good dog," Ines agreed. "There was the time the Duke of Mayne caught us and almost dragged us back."

"Yes, but we outwitted him!"

"And left our coach behind." Ines wriggled her toes, which were still sore from all the walking they had done.

"You and I have become friends," Emmeline said. "Remember when Murray and Stratford thought you did not understand English?"

Ines smiled. "That seems like years ago. And now tomorrow I will meet his mother."

Emmeline took her hand. "I agree that is a prospect to frighten even the bravest among us. Lady Charlotte is a legend."

Ines tilted her head to see Emmeline better. "You know her?"

"I know *of* her. She was something of a warning to my sisters and me. My mother said that when she was presented at her first Season, all of London fell in love with her. Poems were written about her, songs were composed in her honor, and men swooned." She glanced at Ines. "I rather doubt that last part, but that is what my mother said."

"I see." Ines smiled at the thought of men thirty or so years ago swooning in their wigs and their ornate silk coats. "Why did they swoon? Because she was so beautiful?"

"Yes, but also because she was so shocking. This is the part that was supposed to be a lesson, for me in particular. Lady Charlotte said what she thought and did as she liked. She smoked and gambled and danced with a man three times in a row."

"This is not acceptable? To dance with a man three times?"

"Not for ladies in my circle, no." Emmeline released Ines's hand and clasped her arms about her knees. "She was so beautiful and popular that the hostesses were obliged to continue to invite her to their parties, but after a month or so of this shocking behavior, even the most liberal hostesses had to shun her. Do you know her sin?"

Ines shook her head.

"She had fallen in love with an unsuitable man."

"James Murray?"

"Yes. He was the brother of the Duke of Atholl, which made him good enough to gain admittance to Almack's, but no English lady was to seriously consider him. He was not rich or well-connected or powerful. He was just the younger son of a duke."

"Was he handsome?" Ines asked.

Emmeline laughed. "I asked my mother the same thing, and she told me that was not the point of the story. But I think he must have been. And he liked how Lady Charlotte spoke her mind and did as she pleased."

"It sounds romantic."

"It does, but my mother's point was that only an uncouth Scot would want a wife like that, and if my sisters and I wanted to marry decent men, we should shut up and flutter our lashes and pretend we had not a thought in our heads."

"I am glad I am not part of your world sometimes."

"I no longer want any part of it, either. Neither did Lady Charlotte. She eloped with James Murray. The marriage was not valid, of course. She was not one and twenty, but by the time her family caught up to the pair, she had been thoroughly ruined and the scandal would be less if they simply agreed to the marriage. So they did, and Lady Charlotte, who had been a celebrated debutante faded into obscurity and became"—Emmeline stretched and yawned—"a cautionary tale."

"She followed her heart," Ines said. "I do not see why that is so wrong."

"But by doing so, she lost everything else—her family, her friends, her reputation. I am not one to lecture, Ines."

Emmeline stood. "God knows I have been lectured to enough, but as your friend, you should think about what you are doing. I know you have fallen in love with Duncan Murray."

Ines looked up at her. "It is obvious?"

"It is. But before you give up everything to marry him, consider what you lose. Your sister. Your lacemaking. Your independence. Scotland is beautiful." She made a wide arc with one arm. "But it is rugged and harsh and difficult to survive."

"It does not matter," Ines said, looking back down at the darkening road below them. "He does not want me."

"I wouldn't be so sure," Emmeline said and started away. Ines turned to ask her to wait and saw Duncan approaching. His walk was impossible to miss, even though he was in shadow. He walked confidently, with long, fearless strides. He nodded at Emmeline as she passed and gave the dog a quick pat when Loftus stopped to sniff him before racing off to keep company with Emmeline.

Ines looked back at the clouds, great gray hulks, looming over the Highlands. Duncan stopped beside her. "It's getting cold, lass. Come back tae the fire."

"Oh, now you want to talk to me?" This was not quite accurate. He had not said he wanted to talk to her, just that he wanted her to come to the fire.

"I have nae ceased talking tae ye," he said, crossing his arms over his chest.

"To say, *hold on* or *get down.* That is all."

"Do ye want me tae blather on all day?"

"I want you to say something to me!" She stood, which still only put her to his shoulder. "The night in the cottage—"

"I dinnae want tae talk of that."

"I do. I thought…" She swallowed. Well, why not say it? This might be her last chance. "I thought you cared for me."

"Christ and all the saints!" he exploded. She jumped at his voice, but he grasped her arm and drew her near. "I do care for ye, lass, and that's why I'm angry with ye."

She frowned. He was angry with her because he cared for her?

"I'm angry that yer such an idiot."

She yanked her arm away from him.

"I told ye tae go back tae London, but ye insisted on coming along and have almost gotten yerself killed a half dozen times."

Ines glared at him. "That is...what is the word? Exaggeration!"

"Maybe, but that's how it feels tae me. Yer not safe here. What if those reivers had decided tae rape ye? Yer eyes widen, but dinnae think the thought dinnae cross their minds. What if Stratford and I had lost against them?"

"You would never have lost."

Duncan shook his head. "Anything can go wrong in a fight. And if we'd lost, then what would have happened tae ye? If I lost ye, how could I go back tae Colonel Draven and tell him ye were gone?"

She crossed her arms, mimicking his stance. "And that is your concern? If I died, you would have to tell my brother-in-law?"

"Ye ken that's not the whole of it."

"Then what is the whole of it, Duncan? I love you." She tried to move into his arms, but he held up a hand.

"Dinnae say such things."

"Why not? It is true."

"Then find someone else tae love."

"I do not want to find someone else. I want to love you. You do not love me." Her voice broke. "Just tell me." His face wavered as the tears spilled from her eyes. She had not wanted to cry, but she could not seem to hold them back. She swiped at them angrily, wishing she could control them.

"I dinnae love ye, lass," he said, the words like a knife piercing her heart. She stepped back at the force of them, though he'd said them quietly. "Ye dinnae understand. I cannae love ye."

"Because I am not English."

He laughed. "Nae. Because I have nae heart. It sickened a long time ago, and I have done all I can tae stomp on it and wring it and eke the last bit of life from it. Everra time I killed in the war, my heart died a little more until I felt nothing. I still feel nothing."

She stared at him for a long time. His amber eyes were hard, like the fossils she had seen with the flies trapped inside. But she'd also seen those eyes warm and welcoming. She shook her head. "*Não.*"

"What do ye mean, nae? It's my heart. I ken it."

"I do not think so. There is life in it yet, but you are afraid of it."

His expression turned hard. "I am not afraid."

Ah, she had dented his armor. She could see it now. His eyes were still hard, but there was warmth inside them too. "Not of a battle. Not of an outlaw. But of a woman? *Sim*, I scare you."

"That's right," he said. "I'm scared yer foolishness will get ye killed."

"Then send me back to London," she said. It was a risky statement because he could do it. He could force her to go back if he really wanted her gone. But she had to push him. If she did not, she would never know if he felt for her what she felt for him. "Send me away. Tomorrow we will be at your home. You can arrange for me to go right back. I will probably even meet the colonel on the way back and that will make it easy for you."

"Is that what ye want then?" he asked.

"Is it what *you* want?"

He gave her a long, cold look. "Aye. I want ye gone. For good."

He walked away, and Ines did not cry. But she did not breathe either. She must have taken in air because she did not faint. She did not fall down from lack of air, but her chest hurt so badly she felt as though she could not take in enough, as though she would never take a deep breath again.

And then her heart, like Duncan's, would slowly wither away from lack of sustenance. And when her heart was finally cold, she might be able to do what her sister wanted and live quietly as a lacemaker, married to a man she did not love and could never care for.

\*\*\*

*Duncan*

Duncan knew he was almost home when he saw the familiar landmarks. "I used tae swim in that stream," he told Stratford, who rode beside him. "I used tae climb that tree. I used tae fish in the sea just over those hills."

But he felt home when people he recognized waved and called greetings to him. It was the people that made Kirkmoray home, not the rocks on which he once played King of the Mountain or the bridges he raced friends across. His heart seemed to grow in his chest as people came out of their homes to wave to him.

The party of four, Duncan and Stratford in front and Miss Wellesley with Ines behind her in the rear, had arrived about midday. The farmers and laborers were home for a meal before going back to the fields or their shops. The townspeople called out and greeted him and several of the young boys raced ahead. Duncan assumed they were running to tell his mother to set an extra plate at the table. He hoped they told her to set four extras.

Duncan smiled and waved. He had missed Kirkmoray and missed these people. He'd spent almost a year here when he'd returned from the war. He'd thought after fighting for all those years he was ready to take over his mother's farm and household. His older brother, known as Little James, though he was as tall as Duncan, owned several seafaring vessels that traded all over the world. The Murrays had always been a people connected with the sea, though Duncan's father preferred farming to sailing or fishing and Duncan had always lived more inland than seaside. Little James had his own house and spent much of his time at the laird's keep, assisting the duke with all of his responsibilities. Duncan had spent time with his uncle after the war but found the daily bureaucracy of it all tedious. He had not minded the farming, but he'd also felt as though he were missing something.

He'd been restless and could not seem to settle. He'd gone to London to visit his friends, and then his mother had called him back and sent him to find a bride.

At the thought of a bride, he couldn't stop himself from looking over his shoulder. Ines should have been behind him, holding on to him as she had the past few days, and driving him wild with the way her small hands gripped his waist. But she had chosen to ride behind Miss Wellesley today. She hadn't even looked at him this morning.

Duncan was certain Stratford and his cousin could feel the tension between Ines and himself, but they said nothing.

And Ines said nothing. And everyone said nothing, which should have been just fine except Duncan missed feeling Ines behind him. And when he pointed things out to Stratford, he wanted to be pointing them out to Ines. He hadn't realized how much he wanted to share his land and people with her. He wanted to share everything with her.

But he had ruined that possibility, and it was probably for the best. In a few days, Draven would show up and take her home, and now she would be happy to go with him. Duncan had brought her safely to Kirkmoray, despite a few bumps along the way. He could breathe again when she was back in London. He would never breathe while she was nearby and in danger every minute. He couldn't understand why he had ever allowed her to accompany him. At first, it had been the path of least resistance. She seemed determined, and he wanted to go home. And then, Duncan could admit, he'd wanted her with him. But after the reivers had taken her, Duncan had realized what an idiot he'd been. She was not safe here, not even with him. And if she was in danger, then a part of him was in danger. He would not be able to relax again until she was back where she ought to be.

She thought she loved him, and he'd told her he could not love her back because he had no heart. He'd thought that was true, but even as he'd told her, he'd known it was a lie.

His heart wanted to love her, but he couldn't risk it. He could not risk losing someone else he loved. And then he also knew the futility of loving her. He owed his mother. She had asked one thing of him, and who was he to deny her after everything he had taken from her? He had taken her love, and he must give up his.

Duncan stared hard ahead, hardening his heart and resolve as he did so. "Just over this hill then," he said to Stratford and spurred his horse forward. Stratford did the same and the two men paused at the rise and looked down into the valley below.

"Gad, Duncan," Stratford said. "I had no idea this was what you meant when you said you'd grown up on a farm in the Highlands."

Duncan's mouth curved upward. He tried to see the house as Ines—nae, Stratford—might. It was made of ancient stone, the main section built hundreds of years ago. But that main section, now the dining hall, had been enlarged upon over the centuries until the house now had two wings that boasted six bedrooms, a servants' quarters, a sitting room, a drawing room, and a library. The kitchen was just behind the house, and Duncan could see the doors were open and smoke puffed cheerfully into the gray sky.

In the courtyard below, chickens pecked and a goat milled about. He could hear the sounds of horses stamping their feet in the stables. Beyond the house were the fields and then the tenant farms, the families of which had all pledged fealty to the laird.

Duncan was aware when Miss Wellesley and Ines reached the mountain's peak. He resisted the urge to turn and see Ines's face. He might have wished for a sunny day, as the house looked less dreary and dark in the sun, but what did it matter? She would be here a few days and then back on her way. It did not signify what she thought of the place.

Just as Duncan was about to suggest they ride down, the door to the house opened, and a tall woman in a green dress stepped out. She looked up at the hill. Duncan couldn't see the details of his mother's face from this distance, but he knew the expression she made. It was one of impatience. She did not like to be kept waiting.

"Is that Lady Charlotte?" Miss Wellesley asked.

"Aye."

"She's so beautiful," Miss Wellesley said. "I had heard the stories, but the descriptions do not do her justice."

"Nae point in telling her that," Duncan said. "She's immune tae flattery. We'd best go now. She doesnae like tae be kept waiting."

They rode down the hill, the horses picking their way along the well-worn path. By the time they reached the bottom, Lady Charlotte had gone in again. But two grooms were waiting. "Mr. Murray!" the younger said. "Yer home!"

"Aye, Robbie," Duncan said, dismounting and playfully tousling the lad's hair. "Ye've grown since I saw ye last."

"I hope so. I'm sixteen now!"

"So ye are." He turned to the other groom, who was just a few years older. "Walter, how are things?"

"Verra good, sir. Lady Charlotte will be happy yer home." His gaze strayed to the ladies, who Stratford had assisted with dismounting. "And ye've brought guests."

Duncan smiled wryly. He knew the implication. The lad thought one of the women must be his bride. Duncan supposed he should disabuse his mother of that idea right away, so there were no misunderstandings.

"Robbie and Walter, these are my friends, Mr. Fortescue, Miss Wellesley, and Miss Neves. They've come all the way from England."

The lads bowed. "We'll take good care of the horses," Robbie said. "And the dog." He gestured to Loftus, who was sniffing at the ground and eyeing the chickens nervously.

"Good. Their master will arrive in a few days tae take the horses back. The dog belongs tae Miss Wellesley. He could use a bath before he comes inside." He gestured to the small party. "If ye'll follow me."

They walked across the courtyard, the shadow of the house creeping closer. The chickens scattered as they moved closer, and the maids in the laundry nearby paused in their washing to smile and nod at him. This was home, but after his father's death, it had never felt particularly warm or welcoming.

He stopped at the door, wiped his boots, and lifted the latch. "Mother!" he called as he entered. "I'm home."

She stepped out of the dining hall, which adjoined the entryway. "I can see that." Her voice still held the English accent, though it had been softened a bit by her time in Scotland. Her dark black hair had a wee bit more gray in it, he saw, but it tended toward silver, and the way her maid had swept it into her coiffure only made her look more elegant. She approached as the others crowded inside behind him. Coming close, she took his shoulders and kissed both of his cheeks. She smelled of lavender, as she always had. She looked into his eyes and smiled. "I am glad you are well, my son." Her eyes narrowed. "But I thought I told you to bring home a bride."

# Seventeen

*Ines*

Ines did not know what she had expected Duncan's home to look like. She supposed she had imagined one of those small dwellings they'd passed on the trip here. They were sturdy enough homes, built low to the ground and with thatched roofs. But this was no small dwelling. This was a stately home.

The entryway was long and paneled in wood. A table sat against one wall, a crystal bowl on top of it. Light poured through a window high above the door. Ines imagined if it had been sunny, the blue and green rugs she stood on would have been bathed in light. And then, just as she was accustoming herself to this part of the house and imagining what the rest must have looked like, Lady Charlotte stepped out and into the far end of the entryway.

When Emmeline had remarked that she was beautiful, Ines had tried to look around the other woman to get a look.

She had seen her, but not very well. Years of doing detailed work in dim light meant that she could not see as well far away as she did up close. She saw only a female figure, a tall woman with dark hair, but no details.

But now she saw the details, and Emmeline had not exaggerated. Lady Charlotte was beautiful. Like her son, she was tall, but where Duncan was broad, she was slim and elegant. Her thick hair, a dark mahogany, was brushed with silver that had been swept gracefully into a delicate chignon. Her eyes were green, not amber like her son's, and they looked almost emerald. Ines supposed that she had chosen her dress because it complemented her eyes. It was made of fine wool, and she wore a plaid shawl draped about her shoulders. She'd seen that pattern before, perhaps on something Duncan had worn, and Ines assumed the colors were those of the Murray clan.

Lady Charlotte had greeted her son warmly enough—at first—but then her eyes had drifted to Emmeline and skated over Ines. *Skated* was exactly the word Ines wanted because she felt like a sharp blade had run over her skin. If she had ever wondered if this woman would think her good enough for her son, Ines had her answer.

Not that it mattered as Duncan did not want her anyway. Well—he might want her, but he did not love her, did not want to marry her. Ines squared her shoulders. What did she care what the legendary Lady Charlotte thought of her? Ines and Catarina had been looked down upon in Lisbon then Barcelona then London. Until people discovered their lace. Then they fell all over themselves to buy it.

Catarina always said skill and talent were better than status because with skill and talent one could not only create beautiful things but earn money from the sale of those things. Status only bought one respect, and one could not fill an empty belly with respect. And so even though Ines had never felt more like the daughter of a Portuguese peasant than in this moment, she lifted her head high and looked Lady Charlotte in the eye. She had skill and talent. She had made something of herself. She did not need Lady Charlotte's approval.

Beside her, Emmeline curtsied. Ines glanced at her, then tried to do the same, clumsily, when Emmeline swatted at her. Duncan introduced them, Emmeline first.

"A pleasure to finally meet you," Emmeline said, rising from her curtsy. "I have heard so much about you."

Lady Charlotte raised her brows. "Don't believe everything you hear."

"Of course not," Emmeline said.

"Only the really bad things you've heard about me are true."

Emmeline started to laugh, but when Lady Charlotte did not smile, Emmeline closed her mouth and tried to look serious again.

"Lady Charlotte, might I present Miss Neves," Duncan said. Ines had already risen from her poor attempt at a curtsy and wasn't quite sure what to do when Lady Charlotte's green eyes fastened on her. Her first instinct was to cower. She had not really thought about what she looked like for several days. She had washed quickly with cold water every morning, so she was clean, but she hadn't made much of an effort with her hair, and from the corner of her eye she saw it hung over her shoulders in messy tangles. And then there was her dress. Mrs. Brown had given her a maid's livery she had found at Wentmore, and Ines had been grateful to have clothing not covered in blood.

But now she saw herself as Lady Charlotte did. Far from being dressed in the latest fashion, as she had been when she had left London, Ines wore an ill-fitting maid's dress that she'd caught on a log and whose hem hung lower on one side than the other.

There was nothing she could do about it, though. And it was not as though it mattered what Lady Charlotte thought of her. Duncan wanted her to go. Benedict would track her down any minute and then she would be gone. Who cared if her hem had come loose?

"Welcome, Miss Neves," Lady Charlotte said, her voice formal and far from welcoming. "I do not know the name Neves."

"It is not an English name, my lady," Ines said. Lady Charlotte's eyes widened slightly when she heard Ines speak. "I am from Portugal, though I live in London now."

"I see. And what brought you to London?"

Ines could hear the next question already—and what brings you *here*?

But Duncan interrupted. "Mother, you have nae greeted Mr. Fortescue. Lady Charlotte, Stratford Fortescue."

Fortescue gave a deep bow. "Lady Charlotte, I am honored."

She offered her hand and he took it and kissed it.

"Your father is a baron?"

Stratford nodded. "He is."

"And you fought with my son under Colonel Draven."

"I did, my lady."

"Well, then, you are most welcome." Her eyes slid to Emmeline and then briefly to Ines. "All of you." She ushered them inside and bid them follow her into what Ines soon saw was the dining hall. "One of the little boys from the village ran ahead and told me to expect you, so I have had Cook keep the midday meal long enough so you might settle in then eat. But it appears there is little to settle in." She looked at Duncan. "Your trunks arrived a day or so ago, but no other luggage came ahead of you."

Ines did not know why she did it. Perhaps because she'd grown used to Emmeline's brashness. Perhaps because the high, vaulted ceiling of the dining hall, the huge hearth that took up almost an entire wall, and the flickering candles in the wall sconces all about made her nervous and feel as though she had stepped back in time to when knights roamed the land. Ines said, "We do not have any luggage, your lady. Just the clothes on our backs."

Silence slammed down so quickly that Ines could hear the rattling of pots in the distant kitchen.

"It's a long story," Duncan said.

"It always is." Lady Charlotte gestured for everyone to take their seats and then rang a bell. A footman came in with a tray of steaming towels. Using tongs, he handed each of them one to clean their hands. Ines was impressed. She had not ever thought about such things being done at a dining table, but obviously she was the only one not familiar with the ritual as Emmeline and Duncan knew exactly what to do.

She might have stared at her towel curiously if she had not watched the others. It seemed everyone in London considered Scotland a land of barbarians, but clearly those people had never traveled to Scotland. Aside from the reivers, it was a land of kind and generous people. More than thirty years here had not obliterated all of the social customs from Lady Charlotte.

When the footman collected the towels and exited, Lady Charlotte steepled her fingers and said, "I am breathless with anticipation."

Duncan rolled his eyes. "I can simplify it for ye. Miss Wellesley is Fortescue's cousin."

"We are not technically cousins," Emmeline said.

"Our mothers have always been close, and they called us cousins," Fortescue explained.

Duncan glared at them. "As I was saying," he began again when they quieted. "Miss Wellesley wanted tae visit her grandmother in Cumbria. Stratford went along tae escort her."

Lady Charlotte looked at her son then looked at her guests. "I feel compelled to point out, this is not Cumbria." She looked at Mr. Fortescue. "And you, cousin or not, are not a proper escort for a young lady."

The door opened, and the footman had returned with a tureen of soup. The conversation ceased as he served each of them then placed a basket of warm bread on the table. Ines was suddenly so hungry, she was dizzy with it. She tried to remember her manners, but she feared she attacked the soup as a wolf might a rabbit.

"Perhaps Miss Neves is your companion and chaperone," Lady Charlotte said. Hearing her name, Ines dropped her spoon and lifted her head from the bowl. "Though she seems a bit young for the task."

"Actually," Emmeline said, "it is I who decided to accompany Ines to Scotland. She wanted to see Mr. Murray's home, and I have always wanted to see this country and came along."

"And how do you know my son, Miss Neves?"

Before Ines could answer, Duncan said, "That's a long story better saved for later. How are James and Moira?"

"Your brother and sister are well, Duncan. And I have time for a long story. Now you have piqued my interest. Please allow Miss Neves to enlighten us."

"We have a mutual acquaintance," Duncan said before Ines could say anything. "And there was a mis-understanding."

All of the careful wording and sidestepping seemed quite silly to Ines. Obviously, Lady Charlotte would find out the truth one way or another. She might as well know it now.

"My sister is married to Colonel Draven," Ines said. "I was trying to avoid a suitor and hid in the coach of Duncan—Mr. Murray. Before I knew it, we were outside of London."

Lady Charlotte set her unused spoon on the table. "You stowed away in his coach?"

"By accident."

She turned to her son. "Why did you not return her to London immediately?"

"I wanted tae, but—"

"But I pretended not to speak English," Ines said, breaking a piece of bread in two. Telling the truth was quite freeing. She felt better than she had in days. "I did not want to go back to London right away. I wanted an adventure. And, truth be told, I wanted more time with Duncan. He is most handsome."

"I see." It was difficult to know what she thought of this statement by Ines as his mother's expression did not change.

"I am a lacemaker. A shopkeeper. I wanted an adventure."

"You are young, Miss Neves, and perhaps did not think through your plans. You are related to Colonel Draven. That makes you more than a shopkeeper. Your brother-in-law will insist you marry my son."

Ines shrugged. "I will decline. After all these days with Mr. Murray, I find I do not want to marry him."

Lady Charlotte's eyebrows shot up. Ines did not know if she was more shocked at the idea of her son being forced to marry a shopkeeper or that same shopkeeper refusing to consider her son as a suitor.

"I am certain my brother-in-law will arrive soon, and I will be out of your way." She looked at Duncan. "You will not ever have to see me again."

Lady Charlotte harrumphed. "And if Colonel Draven is half the man the rumors would have him to be, you know that is ridiculous. He will force my son to marry you."

Ines stood. "And if you knew me, my lady, you would know that I do not do anything I do not want. Excuse me." She threw down her napkin then started away. But she quickly turned back, grabbed the breadbasket, and took it with her.

***

*Emmeline*

Emmeline started to rise to follow Ines, but Lady Charlotte pointed at her. "Sit down, Miss Wellesley. It is quite enough to have one guest storm from my table, but I will not have two."

Emmeline started to lower herself again then stood. "I am sorry to disobey, but Miss Neves is my friend."

"Your friend? She is a shopkeeper."

"She is an artist and dearer to me than my own sisters. Excuse me." Emmeline thought Lady Charlotte nodded her head in approval, but she was probably mistaken. Emmeline walked quickly away. In the entryway, she saw the door was open and followed it into the courtyard, where Ines stood near where they had ridden in, a wet Loftus at her side. She was feeding him bread. Emmeline crossed the courtyard to her and put her arm around her shoulders.

"I never thought I would want to go home," Ines said.

"All good adventures must end sometime." Emmeline looked out at the rise and the craggy landscape beyond. It looked like it was raining on one of the peaks not so far away. "At least we will sleep in beds tonight."

"I would rather sleep out here."

Emmeline snorted. "No, you wouldn't."

Ines smiled at her. "You are right. But I do not like her."

"I told you she was a force to be reckoned with."

"She must hate me," Ines said. "The low shopkeeper who dared to look at her son."

"I don't know what she thinks of you," Emmeline said. "But one thing my mother always told me is that society respects those with a spine. You showed her you would not be cowed. I think Lady Charlotte, of all people, respects that."

"Your mother is a wise woman."

"She has her moments," Emmeline admitted. "But she can also be ridiculous and petty and superficial. I hope you will not mind if, when Colonel Draven comes, I ask him to escort me to my grandmother's."

"You will not go home?" Ines asked.

"Not while the Season rages. I won't be stuffed into another silk gown and forced to stand against a wall while men turn up their noses at me because I am too old or too outspoken or too fat."

Ines gasped. "I cannot believe any man would think any of those things about you. I wish I had your figure or your way with words. I thought you had not married because you were in love with Mr. Fortescue."

"I am not in love with Stratford."

Ines just looked at her.

"I am not!" Emmeline closed her eyes. "I was not. And he is not the reason I haven't married. I don't want to marry a man who does not love me as I am. All of my life my mother has tried to change me. *Keep your opinions to yourself, Emmeline. Suck in your stomach, Emmeline. Try to smile, Emmeline.* Why can't I just be myself? And after almost four and twenty years of my *mother* telling me how to behave, why should I give myself to a man who will spend the next four and twenty telling me how *he* would like me to behave?"

"I understand," Ines said quietly. "There are many men who want to dominate and control. But Mr. Fortescue does not seem to be that type of man."

"He's not," Emmeline admitted. "But I do not want to marry him. I don't want to marry any man." This was not quite true. There was a part of her who wanted very much to marry Stratford, but after he'd rejected her in the pool, she could hardly look at him, much less consider spending the rest of her life with him.

"Men are awful," Ines said almost to herself.

"Yes, they are," Emmeline agreed. "We will soon be rid of those two." She tossed her head in the direction of the house just as the door opened and a servant emerged and waved to them.

An hour or so later, Emmeline was settled into a large room with a window that overlooked green fields and, in the distance, the shrouded peaks of the Highlands. It was like a painting, she thought. It was so beautiful she could not quite believe it was real. Staring out of this window, her life in London seemed very far away. The Season seemed like a distant memory, something that had happened to some other woman.

When she had left Odham Abbey, Emmeline had feared she would turn back. Not because the journey was difficult. Oh, she had not anticipated how difficult a journey this would be or how unprepared she was for a world beyond her sheltered sphere. She had feared she'd turn back because she would come to find that she missed her old life. It was one thing to believe one could do without servants and four-course dinners and days full of lawn bowls or battledore and shuttlecock, but it was another to actually experience it.

And Emmeline would acknowledge that she wouldn't mind a clean dress or a maid to do her hair or a long nap, but she did not need them. And the only things she missed about her old life were her sisters. She missed Hester's preening and Abigail's snooping and Marjorie's cold feet when she climbed into bed at night. She missed the way Robert's face lit up when he saw them after a month or so away at school.

Truth be told, she even missed the way her mother kissed her goodnight and the smell of roses in her hair. She did not miss her mother's fussing and scolding, but she wouldn't have minded someone giving her a hug right about now.

Emmeline wiped her eyes and blinked at the watery scene outside. For once, it was not raining outside, but she couldn't seem to make her eyes stop watering. She knew why. It wasn't hard for a woman with a modicum of intelligence to ascertain the true reason for the tears. Thinking of her family had stirred up her emotions, and those emotions had opened the door to the emotions she had tried to lock away—her feelings for Stratford.

What did she feel for him? Attraction? Definitely. Lust? Absolutely. Friendship? Always. But love? Did she love him?

She feared she was falling in love with him. Or perhaps she *had* fallen in love with him. She couldn't say when it had happened—sometime between that walk to Milcroft Village and that—whatever it was—in the spring-fed pool. She hadn't thought she would ever fall in love with him. If she'd had to choose one of the Fortescue men to fall in love with, it probably would have been the middle brother who was always making amusing comments and coming up with entertaining diversions.

But when she really thought about it, it wasn't Stratford's brothers she remembered from her childhood. It was Stratford. She had a memory of him helping her up after she'd fallen and skinned her knee and promising not to tell anyone she'd cried about it. And he hadn't. She remembered him playing spillikins with her when none of his other siblings had time to teach her the game. And she remembered more recently, too. He'd dutifully escorted her to balls, and when her mother had criticized her for saying something impertinent, Stratford had always defended her by saying that she was right. Of course, whether her opinion was accurate was never her mother's point. But Stratford understood that Emmeline didn't need to be right—although she usually was—she needed to be heard.

Stratford heard her. He saw her. He had always been there for her. How had she not fallen in love with him long ago? And how had she not seen that he had feelings for her for what must have been some time now. But if he had feelings for her, why did he reject her? Why did he keep pushing her away?

A tap sounded on the door, and she opened it to a middle-aged woman she'd seen moving about efficiently in the hall after the midday meal. "I'm Mrs. Freskin. Lady Charlotte asked me tae bring ye this."

The housekeeper's accent was thick, and it took Emmeline several seconds to comprehend what she'd said.

When the woman held out the dress draped over her arm, it helped make matters clear. Emmeline opened her door wider, and the woman brought the dress in and laid it on the bed. She had a pile of clean underthings as well as a towel and soap. "Lady Charlotte has sent the tub and warm water." There was another tap at the door and the footman who'd served at the meal brought in a small tub that Emmeline might fit in if she pulled her knees up to her chest.

"He'll be back with the water."

An hour later, Emmeline was clean and dry in a simple wool dress whose style was old-fashioned—the waist being too low—but was soft and warm. Her hair was still damp, the fire not being sufficient to dry the thick strands, but Mrs. Freskin had secured it in an elegant topknot, and when Emmeline passed a mirror in the entryway, she smiled at the results. The cut of the out-of-fashion dress actually suited her better than the newer style with the waists practically under her breasts. The full skirt but closer-fit bodice made her body look shapely, not like an amorphous potato sack, and the blue, though faded, had always been a good color on her. She'd taken a shawl in the clan colors and wrapped it about her shoulders and gone outside to find Loftus.

He was lying in the courtyard, watching the chickens with interest, but when he saw her emerge, he stood and trotted over to her, giving the fowl a wide berth. "They won't hurt you," she told him.

He sniffed at her then buried his nose against her leg to beg for a scratch behind his ears. He too was clean and dry, and she would bring him in with her to make sure he stayed so for at least a day. But right now those distant mountains were calling to her. The rain she'd seen earlier had moved over the water of the sea, and streaks of sunlight burst through the clouds in shafts that looked like a picture out of an illustrated Bible.

"Come, Loftus." Emmeline lifted her skirts, heavier and longer than she was used to, and started out. She'd walked perhaps a quarter mile when she realized the mountains were further away than they looked, and she was wearier than she'd thought. Perhaps tomorrow she would make the long trek. The grass on the small rise where she stood was dry, and she spread her skirts on it and sat, feeling the breeze on her face as Loftus chased birds out of the brush below.

"You always did love a walk," Stratford said. She knew he was close by even before he'd spoken. Her skin had prickled the way it always did when he was near—and that was another thing she was just learning, how aware of him she'd always been.

She glanced over her shoulder to see him approaching from the house. He too looked clean and had changed clothing. The coat was a bit big on him, and she assumed it must have been borrowed from one of the Murray men. His blond hair had been slicked back, still a little damp, and she missed how it had grown long enough in past days to fall over his forehead. She craned her head upward to look at him when he stopped beside her.

"May I?" he asked, indicating the spot beside her.

She shrugged, which she knew was juvenile, but she did it anyway.

"You're still angry with me," he said, stating the obvious. But of course, he would want to identify her emotion correctly before he could strategize a way to approach her.

"I'm not angry, exactly," she said.

He sat beside her, angled so he might see her face. "Then what are you? Exactly?"

Why not tell him? She never liked being vulnerable, but she'd already exposed her feelings to him—more than just her feelings—and this might be her last chance to tell him how she really felt. If Colonel Draven was half the soldier everyone said he was, he would be here in a day or two at most.

"I hurt you," he said before she could say it. She glanced at him, surprised he'd identified her feelings so accurately. Stratford's strengths were logic and reason, not emotion and feelings. "You feel rejected." He raised his brows. "Yes?"

"Yes." She nodded. "But it's my own fault. I should not have—"

"It's not your fault," he said, cutting her off. "That's your mother speaking. You haven't done anything wrong. You are attracted to me and acted on it. I am attracted to you and acted on it. Those are logical behaviors."

"I feel so much better now," Emmeline said. "Thank you for explaining." She started to rise, but Stratford laid a light hand on her arm.

"I do want to explain," he said. "I don't want to hurt you."

"But you don't want to marry me. I would prefer if you didn't keep saying it over and over." She gathered her skirts and pushed to her knees.

"Don't you want to know why I can't marry you? It's not you, Emmeline. God knows, I would marry you in an instant. I've thought of it many times over the years."

She sank back down, staring at him in disbelief.

He nodded. "That's right. You might not have noticed me five years ago, but I noticed you. I've always noticed you."

"I know," she said softly. "I'm sorry I didn't see it before."

"I didn't want you to see it, and I can be very good at hiding what I don't want seen."

"But why hide it?" she asked. "Especially now when you see that my feelings—Stratford, I love you." The words were not easily spoken. They seemed to catch in her throat and then almost as though a dam had broken, came rushing forth. "I think I have always loved you in some way or another."

"I wish that weren't true," he said.

Emmeline swallowed. "That's not exactly the response I was hoping for."

"Then my next words will not be overly welcome either. You are not the reason we cannot marry, Emmeline. It's me. I'm not worthy of you.

# *Eighteen*

*Ines*

Ines hadn't been certain if she should accept the clothing Mrs. Freskin brought, but after her bath, she couldn't force herself to put the dirty servant's livery back on, so she pulled on the soft, brown wool dress and secured her hair in a long braid down her back. She wondered whose dress she wore. Though unembellished, the fabric was too fine for a servant. The stitching was precise and neat and the cut of the dress appealing. If only she had her bobbins and thread, she could have fashioned some lace for the sleeves and perhaps the collar to make it look pretty.

It was the first time she had missed her lacemaking in…well, perhaps ever. Since Catarina had taught her how to make lace five years ago, there had rarely been a day when Ines's back and neck were not sore from bending over the pillow and working the bobbins. Her wrists ached constantly, and her eyesight had worsened when she tried to see at a distance.

Her room was small, but it had a window that looked out on the wild peaks of the Highlands in the distance. She admired it until she realized she was still damp and cold and wanted the fire. She hadn't bothered with stockings or her tattered half boots and was sitting cross-legged before the fire when three loud raps startled her out of her thoughts. The door opened.

Without waiting for an invitation to enter, Lady Charlotte stepped inside and closed the door behind her. To Ines, the sound of the door shutting was like the clang of a dungeon door.

"My lady," she said, rising from the floor and trying to curtsy.

"That's not necessary, Miss Neves." The woman's green eyes traveled over her, pausing on Ines's bare toes. "That dress was my daughter's," she said.

Ines looked down at the plain dress she'd been thinking of altering.

"She wore it when she was fourteen," Lady Charlotte said. "Now the hem would brush her calves and the bodice would burst the seams. How old are you?"

"My family is fine-boned," Ines said, avoiding the question of her age.

Lady Charlotte huffed. "You're a wee thing, as the Scots would say. I'm amazed you survived the journey from London."

Ines fisted her hands in the material of the skirts. "I am petite, not weak."

Lady Charlotte lifted her brows dismissively then circled the room. It was a small room, only about a dozen steps across, so this did not take her long. "I see why he is attracted to you," Lady Charlotte said.

"Who?" Ines asked, but she knew.

Lady Charlotte ignored the question. "I send a drab brown dress made for a child and you manage to look beautiful in it. In my younger days, I would have envied you."

Ines took a step back.

"Yes, it's true. I'm taller than many men and if I am not careful about the style of my hair and the colors I wear, I look hawkish and severe."

That look would have suited her personality, Ines thought.

"But you—in your bare feet and braid—look pretty as a picture. Any man who saw you in this moment would want to seduce you. Did he seduce you?" she asked.

Ines couldn't stop her jaw from dropping. How dare this woman?

Lady Charlotte waved a hand. "Do not pretend I offended your delicate sensibilities. What do you want? Money? Prestige for your shop?"

Ines knew when she was being called a whore. "You offend me, *senhora*," Ines finally managed, her voice shaking with rage. "Please leave or I shall."

"Did he tell you he would marry you?" Lady Charlotte asked. Though the question was asked casually, the woman's eyes told a different story. She desperately wanted to know the answer.

"What does it matter?" Ines asked, sidestepping the question. "I am certain you would never allow him to marry a lacemaker."

Lady Charlotte looked away. "Of course not." The silence between them grew and then Lady Charlotte paced away from Ines. "So he has not asked for your hand in marriage?"

Ines had no intention of telling the woman that Duncan hadn't asked anything of her. "If Duncan cares for me then that is between the two of us. You have no say in what I do."

"Then you love my son." Lady Charlotte turned and looked intently at Ines.

Ines tried to stand straight and stare down the other woman, but the mention of love made her want to crumple. It hurt to think of her feelings for Duncan. "He does not love me, so you need not worry. I will leave very soon, and you need never think of me again."

Lady Charlotte nodded slowly. "Perhaps the colonel's arrival will be the best thing for all of us." She moved to the door and opened it. "Please wear your shoes to dinner." She glided through the door and closed it after her.

Ines wanted to throw something at the door. She would have if she'd been holding anything. *Wear her shoes to dinner.* As though she did not know what was appropriate! She had been warned about Lady Charlotte. The woman was a dragon—a grumpy dragon who only looked for fault in others. If Ines had thought she might win the woman over, she saw the error in those thoughts now. But she would not give her the satisfaction of telling her that Duncan had not asked for her hand in marriage or told her he loved her.

Duncan had told Ines his mother would never accept her, but if he loved her, she did not think that would have been enough to keep him from her side. She did not want to believe he did not love her. The way he had touched her, kissed her, whispered her name. The way he had fought the reivers for her and the way he blamed himself for not keeping her safe. He loved her, but he was afraid to lose her. He might say he had no heart, but she saw otherwise. Something must have happened to injure it, to make him afraid to be hurt again. Given time and patience, Ines thought she might be able to help him mend his heart. She might be able to show him that she would never hurt him.

But she did not have time. Benedict would be here soon, and Lady Charlotte would do all she could to keep Duncan from her in the meantime. And perhaps that was for the best. If he would not fight for her, risk his heart and the wrath of his mother for her, then he was not worthy of her. Ines would not force him to love her. She'd almost been trapped in a marriage herself. She would never trap anyone else or allow herself to be trapped with a man who could not reciprocate her feelings.

And she definitely did not want to be trapped with a woman like Lady Charlotte.

Tears sprang to her eyes as she thought of the long journey back to London. Without Duncan. And then there would be the days and weeks and months of lacemaking and sympathetic looks from Catarina and long hours where Ines tried to hide her hurt. But she would survive. And even if she never found a man to sweep her off her feet or throw her over his shoulder, she would have the memories of this adventure to hold on to.

It would have to be enough.

Ines would have preferred to stay in her room all day and avoid Lady Charlotte, but she hadn't eaten much at the noon meal and she was hungry. She ventured downstairs, hoping to be able to sneak into the kitchen or find a servant who would bring her tea and toast. Instead she heard her name as she tiptoed past the drawing room.

"Miss Neves," Lady Charlotte said in her loud, unmistakable voice. "Join us, please."

Ines paused just out of sight and blew out a breath. She was still not wearing shoes. She'd wanted to move quietly. And her hair was still plaited and hanging down her back. There was nothing for it now. Besides, Lady Charlotte already thought of her as a peasant. She threw back her shoulders and moved to the door of the drawing room.

"I do not wish to trouble you," she said, her gaze finding Lady Charlotte near the fire. Unfortunately, it also found Duncan seated in a chair near his mother. He was looking at Ines, his amber gaze warm. She looked away before her body persuaded her head she should go to him. "I only wanted tea and toast. I will find a servant."

"We have tea here," Lady Charlotte said. "Come in."

Ines let out a breath and moved into the room. There was a tea service beside Lady Charlotte. A tray had been set on the table, and it was filled with small sandwiches and cakes. Ines's belly rumbled audibly.

"Sit there." Lady Charlotte pointed to a couch on the other side of the table, across from the fire. Ines sat, trying not to look at Duncan. She glanced at him anyway, and he seemed to be trying very hard not to look at her.

"How do you take your tea?" the lady asked.

"Sweet," Duncan said, "and with a splash of cream."

Ines flicked her gaze at him. How had he known that? When had he heard her ask for tea and how had he remembered?

Lady Charlotte said nothing, prepared the tea, and handed it to her. Ines's hands were shaking, and she set the tea on the table so she would not spill it. She eyed the tray with the sandwiches, and Lady Charlotte handed her a small plate. "Eat, little bird."

"She may be small, but she can eat as much as Fortescue."

"I do not," Ines said, piling her plate with sandwiches. Of course, taking half the tray of food probably contradicted her words, but she didn't care at this point. "Is it not rude to speak of a lady's appetite?"

"It is," Lady Charlotte said. She gave her son a long look. "You seem to know Miss Neves quite well."

"Nae really," he said.

Ines tried to swallow the bite of sandwich in her mouth, but it seemed to stick in her throat. How could he say he did not know her well?

"She tells me she is a lacemaker," Lady Charlotte said as though Ines were not sitting right there.

"She is. Her lace is coveted in London. All the ladies are after it. We gifted a wee scrap of it in the lowlands and the farmer's daughters were so pleased, the farmer gave us loan of his horses."

"My mother taught me how to make lace," Lady Charlotte said. Ines raised her gaze to the lady. She pointed to a table in the corner with a lace covering. "I made that."

"Brussels lace," Ines said, glancing at it. "Very nice."

"Ines—Miss Neves makes Catarina lace," Duncan said.

"I have never heard of that. Is it Portuguese?"

Ines should not have been surprised that word of Catarina lace had not spread as far as Scotland. And she should not have been pleased to know something of fashion that Lady Charlotte did not. "You are obviously familiar with Brussels and Chantilly lace?" she asked.

"Of course."

"Catarina lace is more coveted."

Lady Charlotte set her teacup on the saucer. "Doubtful."

"It is. In another six months, we predict Catarina lace will surpass blonde lace in popularity, and even your English royalty wear blonde lace."

"Ridiculous prediction."

"All the ladies in London wear it," Duncan said.

"Why is it called Catarina lace?" Lady Charlotte asked, seeming genuinely interested. But Ines would not lower her guard.

"Because my sister invented it. As you must know, Barcelona is where all of the best blond lace is made. My sister studied there with a master. She learned enough in six months to create her own lace. It was so in demand that she opened her own shop."

"What makes the lace so special?" Duncan asked. "It's verra pretty, but I dinnae see how it differs from other lace."

Despite her wish to remain cool and remote, Ines could not help but warm to her topic. "Like blonde lace, there is a contrast between the patterns and the ground, *sim?*" She looked at Lady Charlotte to see if she was understood.

"Of course. But blonde lace is inferior," Lady Charlotte said, lifting her haughty chin.

"Yes, because the pattern is not as perfect and regular. But Catarina not only created the new patterns, she designed a process to ensure the patterns were more regular than Chantilly or Lille lace."

"I do not believe it," Lady Charlotte said. And then to Ines's surprise she rang a bell. "Show me."

The woman Ines had seen earlier, and thought must be the housekeeper, entered. She wore a simple dress and a white cap with lace around the edges. She carried a pillow, a set of bobbins, and thread. She cleared the table before Ines and set the materials there. Ines lifted the bobbins. They were made from light wood and each had been painted with a different flower. She could identify lavender and roses and daffodils. Of course, there was the Scottish thistle. The varnish over the wood had preserved the painting and made the bobbins smooth to the touch. "These are lovely," she said.

"Will those materials do?" Lady Charlotte asked.

Ines studied the cylindrical velvet pillow, suitable for making lace edging for small items like handkerchiefs. Then she lifted the thread. It was good thread, not as fine as she and Catarina liked to use, but it would do. "*Sim.*"

She lifted the materials and moved them to a card table near the window. The light would be better here, and she would not have to sit at an odd angle to work. Ines was surprised at how eager she was to work. Since she had arrived in London, she had not found as much pleasure as usual in making lace. It had seemed like a daily drudgery when there was a new city to be explored. But perhaps she had explored enough for the time being, because the prospect of sitting in this cozy room near the window with the lovely view and creating something beautiful appealed to her immensely.

She laid out her materials, arranged the pillow, threaded the bobbins, and then looked out the window, hoping for inspiration. She knew a dozen patterns she could easily recreate, but she wanted something uncommon. And what to make? Edging for a handkerchief or a cap? A lace doily?

"Well, she has threaded the bobbins well enough," Lady Charlotte said to Duncan. "But now she sits and stares."

Duncan didn't respond to his mother, and Ines could feel his gaze on her. His amber eyes were very gold in the firelight, and she looked down to avoid meeting his gaze. She knew his mother was watching both of them, but she could not allow the dragon to make her nervous.

Ines studied her hands and her wrists, the plain sleeves of the drab gown. She could make lace to edge those sleeves, not lace that would hang down but lace to sew on the cuff and make them pretty.

Then she noticed the flowers again. She was in Scotland. Why not a pattern where she incorporated the thistle? Perhaps a pattern of lines reminiscent of the weavings of a plaid?

Almost without thinking, the bobbins in her hand began to move. Her progress was slow at first. Beginning was always the most difficult. She had to find a rhythm and that would not come until after she was sure of her design. She tried to ignore Duncan and Lady Charlotte, to concentrate on even movements that would create the fine lace her sister had become known for.

"She does know how to make lace," Lady Charlotte said, as though the matter were ever in doubt.

"What are ye making, lass?" Duncan asked after a few minutes had passed and she was beginning to feel the rhythm.

"A decoration for the cuffs of this dress," she said, not looking away from her work.

"Why that dress?" Lady Charlotte asked.

"Because this pattern is Scottish, and because this dress is special to you, *não*?"

"I would hardly allow you to wear it if it was precious," she said with a huff. But Ines did not think the woman would have kept the dress all these years if it hadn't meant something to her. Perhaps it simply reminded her of when her daughter had been young.

Lady Charlotte rose and moved closer, and Ines forced herself not to stiffen. Her hands seemed to move of their own volition now, and she did not want to think too much and make a mistake. Creating lace was simply a matter of the placement of the bobbins. This one crossed that one and then the rose crossed the lilacs and under the heather and all the way to the jasmine. Of course, her hands moved quickly, pulling the threads taut and shuffling the bobbins so quickly it was almost a blur. She felt the familiar ache in her shoulders, but it was only a small nuisance as the pattern beginning to emerge on the pillow pleased her.

Gradually, she became aware of Lady Charlotte standing over her. She had been standing there for some time, but Ines had been wrapped up in her work. She continued moving her hands but glanced up at Lady Charlotte. The woman's eyes were as sharp as ever, but her mouth was lax and even parted slightly.

"I chose a thistle for the flower," Ines said.

"I see that," Lady Charlotte remarked. "It's very clear. And that is supposed to be a plaid on the border?"

"Yes. Of course, I cannot use the clan colors."

Lady Charlotte did not speak and another twenty minutes or so passed. Ines did not know how long it had taken, perhaps an hour, before she finished the first cuff, tied it off, moved it from the pillow and stretched her back before readying her materials for the second cuff.

Lady Charlotte's hand covered Ines's, and she looked up in surprise.

"Wait," the lady said. She took the cuff Ines had made and lifted it, studying it in the light from the window. Then she brought it to Duncan and showed him. He had been watching Ines, but his gaze shifted to the lace, and he nodded appreciatively.

Lady Charlotte turned back to Ines. "I would not have believed this if I had not seen you create it with my own eyes. This is the finest lace I have ever seen."

"I could do better," Ines said. "The thread we usually work with is finer and thinner."

Lady Charlotte looked at the scrap she held in her hands. Then she set it down and walked out of the room. Ines stared after her, confused. Since she appreciated the lace, Ines would make a gift of it. It was the least she could do to thank her for feeding and sheltering her while they waited for Draven to arrive.

"She dinnae want tae like ye, lass," Duncan said.

Ines had not forgotten he was there. It would have been impossible to ever forget he was in a room with her. He was not a man one could ignore. Ines started the second cuff, her movements slow, as usual at this beginning stage. "I wanted very much to like her."

"She's nae an easy woman tae like. She scares most lasses. Christ, she scares grown men. But she doesnae scare ye."

"She does not scare me. You forget I am a shopgirl." She yanked the lace a bit too tight and had to maneuver the bobbins to compensate. "I serve the upper classes day in and day out. Most of the ladies are accustomed to being treated as though they are the only people in the world."

To her surprise, Duncan laughed. The sound was warm and throaty, and her body seemed to heat in response to it. "That is a good way tae describe them." He stood and started toward her. Ines wanted to keep her hands moving, but her fingers fumbled, and she dropped one of the bobbins.

Duncan stopped. "Do I distract ye?"

*Distract* was too mild a word. Ines bent to retrieve her bobbin then began to untangle the threads that had gone awry. But her fingers shook, and she seemed to make no progress. In frustration, she looked up at him. "What do you want, *senhor*? Two days ago, you would not speak to me. Now we are friends again?"

"We were never friends, lass."

She nodded, her gaze on his. "I never wanted to be your *friend*."

"And friendship is all I have tae give ye."

She waved a hand. "Give it to someone else. Now leave me. I wish to finish my cuff and present it to your mother as thanks."

He gave her an odd look, and she would have sworn there was a tinge of sadness in his gaze. But she looked away before she could be certain. And then he murmured that he would take his leave, and he was gone. Tears swam in her eyes, blurring the threads before her. But she swiped at them and willed them away, and went back to work

\*\*\*

*Stratford*

Stratford saw the way Emmeline's expression went from anguish to confusion. She'd told him she loved him, and he'd told her it was futile. He hadn't told her he'd loved her back. There was little point in saying those words. He could not act on them, and they would only hurt them both more.

He wished he could tell her. This seemed the ideal setting, here on the grass in the shadow of the Highlands. Looking about, it seemed the whole world was laid before them and went on and on, an endless wave of green and brown and, above, blue. He would have liked to lay her down on the grass, spread out her hair, and kiss her. He would have liked to run his hand over her body and feel her soft skin under his fingertips again.

But this was good-bye. This was the end because Draven would be here in a day or so, and then Stratford and the colonel would escort Emmeline to her grandmother's. Her mother could retrieve her from there. Emmeline would be safe, and that was what mattered.

"That's the most ridiculous thing I have ever heard," Emmeline said, shattering the lingering image of her naked on the soft grass. "How are you unworthy of me? If you do not want me, just say it. Don't give me silly excuses." She began to rise, but he caught her arm.

"It's not an excuse. I am unworthy."

She crossed her arms. "You are the son of a baron, and my father was not even titled. He was a gentleman, yes, but if rank and status are your gauge, then *I* am the one who is unworthy."

"I am not the son of a baron," he said.

Emmeline's tight expression softened slightly. "What do you mean?"

But the way she'd said it—he knew she had heard the rumors. "Don't pretend you do not know. You have heard and you are clever enough to put things together. I am not the baron's son."

"Are you certain?" she asked.

"Yes. My mother admitted it, and my father has always made sure I knew it."

Her hands fell back to her sides. She reached for him, but he moved away. She swallowed and seemed to consider her words before finally speaking. "I often wondered if the rumors were true, and if that was why he treated you as he did."

"I wondered as well and when I came of age, I hired an investigator to look into it." He stared, unseeing, at the mountains towering in the distance. "The rumors are true."

"Who is your father then?" she asked. He did not think many people would have come straight out and asked. But then this was Emmeline, and she almost always said what she was thinking.

"The Marquess of Wight."

She shook her head. "But he—no one has seen him in more than twenty years. Everyone says he is—"

"Mad?

She pressed her lips together. "I was about to say *eccentric.*"

He gave her a rueful smile. "Now you want to be tactful? Say it like it is, Emmeline. I'm the bastard son of a madman. Your mother surely knows it. Half of Society knows it."

"And why should they care? How many of them have by-blows walking around?" She put a hand on his arm. "I know that is not the point."

"No, it's not. Not only am I not legitimate, if I am anything like my father, I may go mad."

She gave him a long look. "A little madness might be an improvement."

He gave her a horrified look, and she squeezed his arm. "You will not go mad, Stratford. You are as sane as the day is long."

"You can't know that."

She lifted her hand from his arm. "No, I can't, but that is not the real issue, is it? The real issue is that you are illegitimate, and all of your life you've been made to feel less than."

It was as though she had shot an arrow straight into his heart. Her words pierced him, and the pain bloomed, spreading throughout his body. He'd felt so much shame his entire life. He'd done all he could to hide the truth from everyone, even though he knew, every time he walked into a room, that some of the whispers were about him.

"That is why you went off to war, even though your uncle willed you that property, and you could have lived off the income. You had to prove yourself."

He'd never thought of it that way, but it was true. He had felt the need to prove himself.

"Do you know the terror I felt, we all felt, when we learned you had joined Draven's troop? By then Lord Jasper and the Duke of Mayne had joined—not that he was the duke yet—and we all knew it was little more than a suicide mission. And when you joined, no one could understand it. I couldn't understand it. How could you have so little regard for your life?"

The hills in the distance became something of a blur as he stared at them, harder than ever. "Perhaps I valued my country above my life."

"Or perhaps you felt so unworthy that you needed to do something extreme. Oh, Stratford." She put her arms around him, but he could not seem to return her embrace. His limbs felt paralyzed. "You are not unworthy. You do not have to jump every time your parents say *up*."

"I tried to make myself useful," he said, though the words sounded thick and clogged in his throat.

"You tried to earn their love, and it's not something you should have to earn."

He could not do this. He could not sit here and allow her to dissect his entire life. Stratford rose. "We should go back."

She rose as well. "Do you see now why I told you, over and over, that I did not want you to come after me? I do not want to be another way you try and prove yourself to your father and mother. I don't want to be a path they can use to hurt you more. Because Stratford—they will never love you. Not like they love your brothers and sisters."

He stared at her, knowing it was true. But he hadn't come after her to prove himself to anyone. He'd come because he cared for her.

"Your mother makes me the angriest. She made the mistake of lying with Lord Wight years ago. Not you. You should not suffer for it."

He knew the truth of those statements, but hearing someone else voice them brought up all the old pain. He felt the sting of tears prick behind his eyes. "I should go back now," he said, his voice strangely devoid of emotion, when inside he churned with so many feelings, he could not possibly name them all. He started away and she moved in front of him, blocking his way.

"But I love you, Stratford. I think I have always loved you in some form or another. You can have the love you want, if you'll just accept it from me."

"And do you think I feel nothing for you?" he said, his heart pounding and his blood rushing so loudly he could hear it like a waterfall in his ears. "I love you, Emmeline. I always have, and that is why I will not marry you. Do you think I would saddle you with a husband whom no one respects? A man who doesn't even respect himself?"

She took in an audible breath and stepped away from him. "That's not true. You think no one can look past the circumstances of your birth? Your true friends do not care. Murray and Mayne and Colonel Draven and I'm sure all the rest of them. They have the utmost respect for you."

He stared at her. She was right, but he couldn't seem to let himself accept it. He could not believe himself worthy of it.

"I respect you too. I love you, but I'm beginning to agree that we should never marry."

Stratford didn't think he could be wounded again, and yet her words were a sword to his gut.

"If you really know me so little—if you really believe that the circumstances of your birth matter to me...well, then you do not know me at all. After all we have been through. After all the years when I have never once treated you as anything less than a friend and equal, if you really believe that I wouldn't want you because your father was not married to your mother, then you are correct. You are *not* worthy of me."

And with that final twist of the sword, she walked away.

Stratford let her go, though some part of him screamed to go after her. But he couldn't. Because she was right. He'd thought her just like everyone else, when she, like he, had never fit in. Of all the people he knew, she was one of the few—outside of the Survivors—who knew him and saw him for who he really was.

And now he had lost her, and it had nothing to do with the Marquess of Wight or his mother or the goddamn baron.

This was all on his shoulders.

# Nineteen

*Duncan*

His brother James came for dinner. Duncan and James had their share of fisticuffs as lads, but they got along well enough as adults. Of course, James was far more pleasant than Duncan would ever be. He always had a ready smile and an amusing story and made everyone feel at ease.

Duncan appreciated those qualities immensely this evening when the table felt like a heavy shroud had been laid over it. Ines sat quietly at one end, hands in her lap, saying nothing. Duncan assumed she'd finished the lace cuffs this afternoon, but he did not yet think she'd given them to his mother. Miss Wellesley and Stratford sat across from one another, but they tried so hard not to look at each other it was almost painful to watch.

Duncan didn't know why Stratford didn't just propose to his cousin and have it over with. It was obvious to Duncan, whenever he'd seen them together, that Stratford cared for her. Watching them over the course of their travels to Scotland had only made it clearer that Miss Wellesley felt the same way about Stratford. The two of them seemed a perfect pair—friends since childhood, close families, and an obvious attraction.

Duncan and Ines had attraction—they had more than attraction. Ines loved him, and he—Duncan would not allow himself to think too much about what he felt for her. He'd wanted to avoid the pain of loss. It was a pain he knew well from losing his father. But try as he might to keep Ines at arm's length and far from touching his heart, she'd found a way in. Duncan didn't know how she'd done it. No other woman had ever even breached the drawbridge of his heart. If a woman drew near his fortifications, it was easy to scare her away with gruff words or an outrageous act.

Ines had seen him at his best and his worst. His most outrageous—well, perhaps not his *most* outrageous—and his most gruff. And she still wanted him. But the fact was Duncan could not have her. Even if Draven agreed to allow them to marry, Lady Charlotte would never accept her. And how could he go against his mother? Hadn't he caused her enough pain in her life?

"Isnae that right, Duncan?" James said, and Duncan realized his brother had been telling some anecdote in which he played a part.

"I would caution the party nae tae believe everrathing my brother says," Duncan said, feeling that was the safest response.

"Dinnae believe everrathing *I* say?" James countered. His eyes were bright and his cheeks ruddy. With his beard, he looked very much like Duncan remembered their father. Duncan glanced at his mother, and saw she wore a wistful look as she listened to James entertain the party. He knew she was thinking of her late husband too.

"Och, well, Duncan is the war hero. But do ye think we can get even one story oot of him? Nae. He's like my oldest son. He goes tae school all day, and when I ask what he learned at the evening meal, he says *nothing.*" James looked at Stratford. "But perhaps ye have a story tae tell us of my brother's bravery."

Stratford looked at Duncan, and it was easy to read Stratford's expression. They had lost eighteen men of their troop. Eighteen brothers. Nothing they had endured was fodder for dinner conversation. Stratford could undoubtedly tell stories of Duncan rushing into a fight. Of course, if Duncan had saved one man, there was another story of when he had not been fast enough. The Survivors had an unwritten rule that they did not tell each other's tales.

Stratford cleared his throat. "Duncan and I had very different orders," he said. "We didn't work together often enough for me to have any stories about him. I'm sorry."

The shroud James had been trying so hard to lift descended again. The footman came in with a plate of candied and sugared nuts, and Duncan breathed a sigh of relief that dinner was almost over.

"I have a story," Ines said.

Everyone looked at her. She'd said only a few words at dinner and then only when someone had spoken to her directly.

"I am not a storyteller like you, *senhor*," she said, looking directly at James. "But I do know your brother is brave. He saved my life."

Duncan felt heat climb up his neck to the freshly shaved skin of his jaw. He knew what she would say, and he wanted to take her arm and pull her out of the room—anything to stop her from telling this story in this place to these people.

"Och, do go on," James said, motioning for the footman to fill his wine glass. "I would like tae hear this. Dinnae ye want tae hear, Mama?"

"I do." Her eyes shone with mirth. She did not know what was coming.

"It's late," Duncan said, standing. "The ladies must want their beds by now."

"Sit down," Lady Charlotte said. "We have time for one story."

Duncan looked at Ines, but she did not return his gaze. He knew what she was about. She wanted to say something about him that would impress his mother and brother. She wanted to boast about him. That was the type of person she was—kind and giving. She couldn't know this story would not have the effect she anticipated.

"Ines," he said.

James waved his wine glass. He was half-drunk or he might have caught at least one of the cues Duncan was sending. But then James had always been a bit of an arse, so maybe he would not have cared. "Let's hear the story, lass."

Duncan glared at him and James smiled, knowing exactly what he had done to raise his brother's ire. "Forgive me. Miss Neves, proceed with the story."

She gestured to Miss Wellesley. "We had stopped for the day near a river, and Miss Wellesley and I had gone to wash our hands and faces. We had taken the dog with us…"

She went on, telling the story of how Loftus had chased after a noise and how the ladies had followed and thought it might be a wolf. Duncan sat stiff and straight-faced while his mother and brother smiled at the idea of wolves and then watched as their faces slowly drained of color as they realized what the ladies had thought were wolves were actually reivers. Ines noticed, of course. She was used to watching people closely as any good merchant was. She obviously thought his family's reaction was one of concern, so she hurriedly told them how Duncan and Stratford had ambushed the men and saved her. She gave Loftus praise as well, but when she had finished, no one spoke or smiled.

Miss Wellesley tried to fill the silence. "Thank goodness for Mr. Murray and Mr. Fortescue's quick thinking else we might not all be here."

"And I'm certain you were terrified, Miss Neves," Stratford said. Duncan winced as his two friends dug his grave deeper.

"*Não.*" Ines said. "I knew Duncan would come for me."

"Of course, he would," James said. "He's always looking for trouble, aren't ye, brother?"

Duncan said nothing.

"Ye see, this isnae his first experience with reivers," James went on, his face red now, but not from drink. "Years ago, he decided tae run away and had a run in with a group of reivers. He soon found himself their prisoner."

"That's enough, James," his mother said, but her voice was barely a whisper.

James did not seem to hear her. "My father went after him, but he was nae as lucky as ye were. He was killed in the skirmish."

"Excuse me," Lady Charlotte said, rising and leaving the room.

Ines looked pale. "I am so sorry. I did not know—"

James waved his cup before refilling it. "Why would ye, lass? Duncan likes tae play the hero. He doesnae like tae talk aboot the time he got his own father killed."

"Now wait a minute," Stratford said, rising.

Duncan shook his head, and Stratford frowned at him. But why should his friend defend him when everything James said was true? Duncan was the reason his father was dead. His stupidity, his impulsiveness—traits that had earned him the playful sobriquet Lunatic in combat—were also the reason his father was dead.

"Nae worries, brother," Duncan said. "I willnae stay home long. I dinnae want tae be a constant reminder of the worst day in yer life."

"Yer such an idiot," James said. "Ye think any of us want ye gone? It only hurts her more when ye leave." James pointed to the ceiling, presumably indicating his mother's room above. "But then ye always were a selfish bastard."

Duncan did not even realize his feet had moved until he was on the other side of the room with his hand wrapped about his brother's neck and James's head pushed against a wall. For all his strong words, James was not a fighter. He had always been the diplomat of the family. Undoubtedly that was why their uncle valued him so much and why James was always at the laird's castle. Now James struggled under Duncan's grip, and as much as Duncan wanted to slam his fist into his brother's face, it would not make his father come back.

He stared at James, and James stared back at him, and then Duncan felt a warm hand on his arm. He looked down, and Ines was there. "*Não*," she said. And then, "I am so sorry."

The look of true grief on her face all but undid him. Duncan dropped his brother as the pain tore through him. He felt as though he were being ripped apart. And how could he stand here, in the dining hall, and allow everyone to see his insides spill out? That was how it felt, as though someone had taken a blade and cut across his chest and now his heart was exposed and vulnerable.

With a growl, Duncan stalked out of the room, not seeing where he was going or caring. He just needed to get away. And then he just needed air, to fill his lungs with something other than pain and grief and, yes, guilt.

He stumbled into the night. Even though it was summer, it was still cool in the Highlands, and the chilly night was like a slap in the face. He did not know where to go so he made his way through the courtyard to stand at the edge and look up at the rising mountains and the blanket of stars above. He'd missed this in London. Once he'd been away from the city, he could see so many more stars, but he hadn't taken the time to look at them until now. He remembered all the times he and James and Moira sat outside on a summer night and looked at the stars, the sweet smell of his father's pipe tobacco drifting around them.

How many times had Duncan wished he could bring those moments back? How many times had he pushed the pain of loss away by running into danger? He'd loved his father, loved him as he'd never loved anything or anyone else, and he'd killed him.

The sound of a shoe crunching on a leaf made him turn. "Go back inside, Ines."

"I think you should not be alone now."

"I want tae be alone." He turned away from her, but she came to stand beside him anyway.

"I do not think so. I am sorry my story brought up such painful memories. I meant—"

"I ken what ye meant. It's nae yer fault. Ye dinnae ken."

Her hand was tentative on his arm. He knew he should push it away, but he wanted her touch right now.

"Why did you not tell me? I knew there was something wrong after you saved me from the reivers, but I thought I had done something. Said something."

He looked at her. He should send her inside, shouldn't say anything more. But he was raw now and vulnerable, and he couldn't seem to stop the words from gushing forth. "Ye did do something. Ye made me realize how much I cared for ye, and ye had almost been taken from me, lass. I cannae let that happen again."

"Let what happen again?" she asked, looking up at him. Her expression was so kind, her eyes so understanding.

"I cannae lose someone else I love," he said, his voice low and harsh.

She nodded. "Now I know why you joined Benedict in the war. You wanted to die."

Duncan did not speak, only stared at her.

"Because if you are not willing to risk losing what you love then you are not really living."

He hadn't been living for a long time. He had just been pretending to live. During the war, he'd taken every risk. He'd taken a good deal after the war too, but it seemed pointless. If God had wanted him dead, Duncan would be dead. There had been more than enough opportunities to strike Duncan down. But God wanted him alive, wanted him to continue to suffer. Yes, he'd gone to London, as his mother had commanded, and searched for a bride, but he hadn't really tried. He'd scowled and stomped around so that every lady who met him would be scared away.

Every lady but one.

Duncan looked at Ines. "Go inside," he said.

She shook her head. "I have words, Duncan, but my words are not any you have not heard before. I am sure you tell them to yourself. The death of your father was not your fault."

Duncan took a shaky breath. How many people had said that to him? His mother? His uncle? His sister. Even James. But Duncan had never said it to himself. Could never believe it.

"But you need to say the words," Ines said. "And believe them in here." She lifted a hand and tapped his chest. Her touch seemed to burn through the layers of his clothing. "Only then will you be willing to risk the hurt again."

"And when did ye become so wise, lass?"

"I have lost too. When I left with Catarina, I lost my mother and sisters and friends—the village full of people I had known all of my life. I lost my father, though he was not a good man. I still miss them, but I have met others who I have come to care about—friends in Lisbon and Barcelona." She tapped his chest again. "Friends in London. There has been pain but also joy."

Duncan understood what she meant. The men of Draven's troop had become like his brothers. Losing many of them had caused him pain but knowing them had also given him joy.

He hadn't cared for any of them like he cared for Ines. He hadn't risked getting too close to any of them, knowing anyone he cared for could be snatched away with the flick of a blade or the firing of a pistol.

"I love you, Duncan," Ines said, and her words were like that pistol ball slamming into his heart. "And if you do not love me back, then that will hurt. I have been hurting for the past few days, afraid you did not care."

Duncan hated to hear that he'd hurt her. He hadn't considered that while he was trying to protect his own heart, he had caused her pain.

"I do care," he said. He put his arm about her waist and pulled her to him. He couldn't seem to resist the pull of her, the warmth of her body and the softness of it against his. He needed her touch, had missed it so much.

"Show me," she said. "I want to love you. I want to feel what it is to really live. If only for one night."

Her words robbed him of breath. Desire slammed through him so hard, he had to close his eyes to maintain control. And then he wondered why he was fighting it. He wanted her. Almost from the first time they'd met, their joining had been inevitable, and now it would be so much more than an act of lust. For once he wanted to risk something more than his body. He wanted to risk his heart.

Duncan pushed a loose piece of hair behind her ear, feeling her tremble as he touched her. "Are ye sure, lass?"

She smiled. "With you, I am always sure."

He bent and swept her into his arms, causing her to gasp then giggle. "What are you doing, *senhor*?"

"Sweeping ye off yer feet."

He carried her to the side of the house, used his toe to open a back door, and started up the rarely used staircase.

Ines was no great weight in his arms, and still his heart pounded as though he carried a load of bricks. He was not afraid of making love to her. He'd been with other women. But he had never given any of them his heart, and he had known since the first time he kissed Ines that if—no, when, it had always been a matter of when—their bodies came together it would be a melding of not only flesh but also hearts and souls.

He did not know if his heart was strong enough to risk loving her back. But he didn't know if it was strong enough *not* to love her either.

He reached the top of the stairs and turned to the first door on his right. He'd often used these stairs to sneak out at night when he'd been a boy as they had been so close to his room. Now he shoved a foot against his door, and it flung open. He kicked it closed behind him then walked to his bed and laid Ines on the coverlet.

His impulse was to fall down beside her, strip her, and take her then. He made himself slow down. He needed a moment to slow the pounding of his heart and the shaking of his hands. Duncan went to the lamp, feeling for the tinderbox beside it and lighting a match before touching it to the wick inside the lamp. He opened the shutter further and turned to Ines. He wanted to see her, and he was not disappointed. She was beautiful—lying on the bed, her hair half falling out of the simple style she'd worn, her cheeks pink, and her eyes dark with anticipation. Duncan went to her, kneeling on the bed and looking down at her. She lifted her arms to him, and he went into them willingly.

She was small, but she held him so tightly, so fiercely. His mouth found hers, teasing her lips until she opened for him and he could stroke inside, tasting her. Her smell, her taste, the feel of her was intoxicating, but it was also *right*. It was as though he was meant to kiss this woman, to touch this woman. As though he had been waiting all of his life to find her.

With a low growl, he rose to his knees and looked down at her, her dark eyes, her red cheeks, her now-swollen lips. His gaze drifted to her dress. He was uncharacteristically nervous. His hands fumbled at her bodice, searching for pins or tapes or whatever the hell women used to keep their underthings from showing, but Ines shooed his hands away.

"Let me." She sat, and he groaned. She had that look in her eye that told him she would happily torture him. Slowly, she drew the first dress pin out, placed it on the table next to his bed, then smiled up at him. Oh, this was sweet torture.

"Dinnae stop now, lass."

She reached for another, drew that one out, and placed it neatly beside the last.

"Ines," Duncan said. "Do ye mean tae kill me? My heart is racing like a horse after a long run."

"*Sim*. It is for all the times you teased me." Her voice, low and husky, caused heat to surge through his loins.

Duncan narrowed his eyes. "Perhaps I can persuade ye tae hurry up a bit." He might not know much about how a dress was put together, but he knew what was under one. He sat back, took one of her feet and made short work of her boot. He dropped it on the floor then discarded the second boot. Ines set another pin beside the first two.

Duncan reached under her skirts, found her garters, and loosened one. He tried not to feel how soft her skin was, how silky and tempting. Gritting his teeth, he rolled her stocking down. Ines had paused, with her hand over her heart to watch him. He slid the stocking over her foot, but instead of reaching for the other, he held her foot. Her foot was small in his big hand, and he imagined if she felt anything like him, her feet ached from all the walking they'd done. Lightly, he pushed a thumb into the pad of her foot, and she moaned. The sound of her pleasure almost undid him. It was an addictive sound. He wanted more and more. He continued massaging, working his way over her foot, and watching the way her eyes closed and her shoulders drooped with relaxation.

"Lass, yer supposed tae be removing those pins."

"This feels too good."

As impatient as he was to have her naked, he moved to her heel and pressed his thumb into it. Her head fell back as she moaned again. Christ but she was a sensual creature.

He reached for the other leg, pulled the stocking down, and began to massage that foot. With one leg on either side of him, he was in exactly the position he wanted. He was still massaging, when she finally opened her eyes and plucked at the bodice of her gown. The materials fell away, and she lifted her shoulders and removed the rest. Next she reached for her skirts, but she couldn't drop those with him between her legs.

With a curse, he stood and pulled off his coat and loosened his neckcloth, while she squirmed out of her skirt. He'd just finished with his boots when he looked up and saw her standing only in her shift. She was shivering. Of course, she was. He'd banked the fire and it gave off little to no heat. He pulled her close and kissed her. He could feel her slim body under the thin linen. His hands began to roam, but she kissed him and then moved away. "Take off your shirt," she said.

His brows rose even as his blood pumped harder. "Ye think ye can tell me what tae do now?"

She nodded. "Take it off."

Christ and all the saints, but he liked it when she gave him an order. He was so hard now, it was painful. In a hurry, he pulled the tail from his trousers, unfastened the sleeves, and yanked the linen over his head. Before he could grab her, she held out a hand to still him.

"Wait."

Now he was the one to groan as her hands went to his shoulders, then ran down his arms. Her touch was like liquid fire, making all of his senses come alive. When her fingers slid over to his chest and down to his belly, he inhaled sharply. Her skillful fingers toyed with his waistband. "What is under here?"

"For a virgin, ye arenae verra demure." His voice was a low growl, and he felt like a caged beast, ready to pounce at the first chance of freedom.

She frowned. "What is the demure?"

"Nothing I want, lass. Loosen the placket and see what's there." *Please*. He needed her to touch him.

Bold as ever, she didn't hesitate. She'd told Duncan she wanted him almost from the start, and even though he'd been a complete arse, she hadn't changed her mind. She unfastened the trousers and he sprang free, hard and hot against her small hand. He had to bite his cheek to keep control as his head went dizzy with arousal. She murmured something in Portuguese.

"I hope that was a compliment," he said.

She gave him an enigmatic smile then moved her hands to his hips and slid the trousers down. When his trousers were on the floor, she moved around him, running her hands over his bottom then giving it a squeeze. His entire body quivered at her touch, and though Duncan liked a forward woman as much as any man, he'd been pushed to his limit. When she moved to his side, he grasped her hands and yanked her to him. "Like what ye see?"

"Very much." Her voice was breathless and her eyes hazy with desire.

"My turn." Releasing her hands, he grasped her shift in both hands and pulled it up and over her head. He thought she might try and cover herself, but she stood straight in the flickering lamplight. Her skin was smooth and olive, her breasts small and tilted upward, the nipples dusky and hard. The small triangle of dark hair between her legs beckoned him. "Let me worship ye, lass."

He dropped to his knees and kissed her belly, drawing her close with one hand on her round bottom. He left that hand there, kneading that ripe flesh while his mouth trailed lower, his tongue darting out to learn the feel of her and licking at her sensitive skin. Finally he was between her legs. She smelled of soap and the hint of vanilla that he always associated with her. And when his mouth found her lips, parted them, and then his tongue explored until it came upon that sensitive nub, he tasted *her*. Her body went rigid as he laved and suckled. He put both hands on her hips to hold her steady as she was shaking. Her hips began to move in an instinctual rhythm he knew well, and she moaned in that way that made him all but come just at the sound.

He could have done this all night. He loved the way she felt in his arms and the sounds she made. He'd never known what it was to be wanted this much.

She gasped and her body arched, and he knew if he hadn't been holding her, she would have collapsed. Instead she wantonly pushed her sex against his mouth, and he felt the way she tightened and then exploded with release. Feeling pleased with himself, he grinned and decided to do it all over again. But she went limp. He let her fall over his shoulder then stood, her bottom in the perfect spot for his hand.

"What are you doing?" she asked dreamily.

"Putting ye in bed." He dumped her onto the soft mattress, and she looked up at him in a tangle of limbs.

"That was much more romantic in my mind."

"Imagined me doing that, did ye?"

"I imagined you doing many things."

He wedged a knee between her legs, opening them, enjoying the view of her glistening pink sex. "Ye dinnae need tae imagine any more." He kissed her, and she wrapped herself around him. Her skin slid against his skin, her flesh warm against his. His cock knew exactly where it wanted to be, and he pushed the head against her warm, wet entrance.

"*Sim*," she said, her voice filled with desire.

"I dinnae want tae hurt ye, lass."

She pushed his hair back from his face. "My sister says the pain is worth the pleasure. Can you make it worth the pleasure?"

It sounded like a challenge, and Duncan was always ready for a challenge. He kissed her again, entered her slightly. She was so tight and felt so good as she closed around him. At her moan he had to restrain himself from plunging in. Instead, his fingers found that tight, swollen nub and stroked it. He thought it might take time for her to react. After all, she'd just orgasmed, but a moment later, she was breathing heavily and moving her hips in an undisguised invitation. He slid in deeper, pausing when her channel was too tight, allowing her to adjust to the feel of him and allowing himself to catch his breath.

His lips found her breast, closing in on the nipple and suckling as his fingers danced against her. Her hips arched, and it took all he had not to thrust inside her. He slid just a bit deeper, and Christ but he wanted to sheath himself in her. "Am I hurting ye, lass?" he murmured between teeth gritted against the growing pleasure.

"*Sim. Não.* Duncan!"

He knew what she wanted, knew he could give it to her. He pressed his thumb against her throbbing clitoris, and she cried out and stiffened. Duncan squeezed his eyes shut at the feel of her muscles clenching around him, and then as soon as they began to loosen, as she began to come down, he slid deeper. He expected her to cry out in protest at the discomfort, but she clawed at his back, urging him closer. He moved slowly until he was buried inside her, his face in her neck, her legs wrapped around him.

*This.* Yes, *this.* He had lived all of his life to be here with this woman, in this moment.

He looked down at her, and her dark eyes met his. "Show me," she said.

He moved inside her, watched her wince slightly, then relax. He was careful, gentle, and gradually, she moved with him, learning his rhythm, her breath beginning to hitch when he pressed in just the right places. He might have been able to pleasure her again, but he had restrained himself too long. His own need crested, and he swore. "I cannae wait, lass." With a feral growl, he gave himself to the pleasure, pulling out and spilling his seed on garments scattered beside them. And then he collapsed beside her, gathering her close, needing her near him. His hands roved her body, her hair, her lips. He did not know how he had survived without touching her, without having her scent surround him.

She moved in his arms, rolling to face him. Her leg slid up his body, making his senses wake again even as she kissed him. The kiss was as sweet and seductive as any he'd ever experienced. Her hand cupped his cheek, and the tenderness with which she touched him made his heart constrict. He knew what was coming next. Knew what she would say, and he wanted to hear it. He needed to hear those words from her.

"Duncan." She kissed his cheek, his temple, his nose. "That was…how do I say…amazing?"

"Ye are amazing," he murmured, turning his face to kiss the palm of her hand.

She laughed and kissed his eyelid then his brow and finally his lips. "*Eu te amo*."

Duncan held her closer. "Did ye just say what I think ye did, lass?"

"Do you think I said…what is the English word?"

She was teasing him. He loved that she was teasing him, and he was also incredibly annoyed. He didn't realize how much he wanted to hear that she loved him, wanted her to say it now, when they were close and naked and both still reeling from the pleasure of their lovemaking.

"Say it, lass," he urged, nuzzling her neck.

She giggled. "How can I think when you do that?"

"Then I should stop?" He pulled back, and she squealed.

"Do not stop." She pulled him back.

He nuzzled her again, this time behind the ear. "Say it, lass," he whispered into her ear. She shivered.

"I love you, Duncan."

Christ but his heart hurt. He thought it might burst from happiness and fulfillment and desire. She moved her head so that their eyes locked. "I love you," she said again.

"Lass, I—" Duncan's throat was tight. He swallowed.

A loud rap sounded on the door. "Christ and all the saints," Duncan muttered. Then louder, "Go away!"

"I will not go away." That was the unmistakable sound of his mother. "I know that trollop is in there with you, and I want her out of my house. Now!"

# Twenty

*Emmeline*

Emmeline departed, leaving Stratford to help James Murray up off the floor. Even if she'd wanted to assist—which she did not—the men probably would not have desired her involvement. Men and their pride. James Murray seemed to have a healthy dose of it, and God knew that Stratford had more than his share.

She'd gone to her room, put on the nightclothes Lady Charlotte had supplied for her, and climbed into bed. She'd been longing for a bed for days, but now that she lay down, she could not sleep. She tossed and turned and finally lay on her back and stared up at the ceiling, her fists clenched at her sides.

So Stratford was a bastard. The idea had crossed her mind in the past. She was not one for gossip, but her sisters loved to gossip and share any tidbits they heard. And they had heard the rumors about Stratford, though no one believed it. Emmeline hadn't believed or disbelieved. She hadn't really cared, but she realized that if the rumors were true, it would explain some of what she had seen in the Fortescue family. The baron was a reserved and demanding man. He was not the kind of father she had known. Baron Fortescue was strict with his children and had almost impossibly high expectations. He was not a father a child went to for comfort. Once Stratford had fallen from a tree and his parents had only found out because his siblings had informed them. Stratford had kept a straight, unemotional expression while his arm was poked and prodded. Eventually the doctor was called and determined the arm had a slight fracture.

As much as Emmeline hated her mother's criticism, she had always known her mother loved her. Stratford had not grown up with that assurance. He had been a constant reminder of his mother's mistake. He was the proof of her infidelity and the baron's cuckolding.

Should it be any surprise, then, that Stratford could not believe Emmeline loved him? At times it was hard for her to believe he thought her beautiful and desirable. She'd grown up being told her body and her face were not good enough. But she'd been loved, and perhaps that was enough for her to find some worth in herself.

She turned over again, trying to convince her mind to quiet, when she heard a loud bang and then what sounded like Lady Charlotte yelling. Emmeline thought it was probably best if she pretended not to have heard, but then the sound of Duncan Murray's voice rose and was followed by the quieter tones of Ines.

Emmeline had wondered where they'd disappeared to after dinner. It had not been difficult to speculate, and Lady Charlotte had obviously had little trouble finding them.

Well, Emmeline couldn't leave Ines to battle the dragon on her own. She rose, pulled a blanket over her nightgown, and went to her door. She peeked out and almost went back inside again, but she caught sight of Stratford looking out of his door, further down the corridor. If he had seen her, she wouldn't want him to believe she was afraid.

"Ye cannae put her oot in the middle of the night," Murray was telling his mother, as Emmeline started down the corridor.

"This is my house, and I do what I like. If you do not like it, you should leave." Lady Charlotte, still dressed, hair perfectly coiffed, stood outside Murray's room. As Emmeline neared, she noted Ines was wrapped in a sheet and nothing else. Not much question as to what she and Murray had been up to then. But far from looking embarrassed or humiliated, Ines faced Lady Charlotte defiantly. She might have been wearing the Crown jewels instead of an old sheet.

"We will leave, if that is what you wish. Duncan and I will dress and be gone."

Emmeline passed Stratford's door, and he peeked out of a crack. "You're taking your life in your hands if you go down there."

"Coward," she threw at him.

"Hell, yes."

Emmeline moved forward as Lady Charlotte turned to her son, her gaze piercing him. Clearly, she wanted to see what he would do. Would he take Ines's side or let her be thrown out into the cold and dark? "You will not accompany that trollop," Lady Charlotte ordered, her gaze on her son.

Emmeline too looked at Murray for his reaction, but Ines did not falter. "He will accompany me."

How lovely to be so confident. But Emmeline was not certain her confidence was warranted. Murray, a blanket wrapped around his midsection, looked like a hare caught between two snarling foxes.

"Silly girl. Do you think he loves you? Do you think he will marry you?" She looked at Murray. "Do you love her, Duncan? If you wish to marry her, say so now."

Duncan hesitated, and Emmeline almost wanted to hit him to make him speak. Emmeline did not think Lady Charlotte, terrifying as she was, would shun the woman her son loved. Couldn't Murray see that she wanted to hear him say he loved Ines? She wanted to know what he really felt.

Emmeline had moved close enough to catch Lady Charlotte's attention now. The woman blew out a breath. "Wonderful. We have awakened the entire household. Go back to your room, Miss Wellesley."

Emmeline shook her head. "Not without Ines."

But Ines was looking at Murray. And Duncan Murray was not looking at Ines.

"Duncan?" Ines said. One word. One name, but there were a thousand questions in that word. *Do you love me? Will you stand with me? Will you fight for me?*

"Ye cannae put her oot in the middle of the night," Duncan said again to his mother. "Colonel Draven will come for her in a day or so."

Ines took a step back, as though she had been punched. Emmeline could imagine it felt as though she had been.

"Ines," Emmeline said, and reached out her hand. "Come with me. You may stay in my chamber tonight."

Lady Charlotte might throw them both out, but Emmeline couldn't leave Ines to fend for herself. And if

Duncan was willing to abandon her, as he just had, he should be drawn and quartered.

"Fine," Lady Charlotte said, seeming to crumple a bit. Was she too disappointed? "She is your responsibility, Miss Wellesley. If I find her fornicating with my stable hands, I shall hold you responsible." Lady Charlotte looked at her son. Had the comment been a last effort to provoke him?

Emmeline glanced at Duncan. Surely he would not allow that comment to go unchallenged. He seemed ready to say something, but his mouth did not open. Ines ran to Emmeline and buried her face in Emmeline's shoulder. Emmeline wrapped an arm about Ines's slim shoulders and guided her back to Emmeline's room. When they passed Stratford's door, it was closed.

Once inside, Emmeline seated Ines by the fire and built it up as Ines was shivering. She knelt before the chair where she'd put the other woman and took her hands. "I wish I had some wine to offer you," she said. "You're shivering. Here." Emmeline removed the blanket from her shoulders and draped it over Ines.

"I thought he loved me," Ines said, staring into the fire.

Emmeline squeezed her hands. "He does love you. Anyone with eyes can see that. Even his mother."

Ines looked away from the fire, tears glittering on her eyelashes. She looked so pretty. Of course, she did. When Emmeline cried her face turned red and her eyes became puffy and snot poured from her nose.

"Not enough," Ines said.

Emmeline hugged her. "I believe this is the sort of situation where one says, *It's complicated.*"

Ines pulled back and shook her head. "Lace designs are complicated. That horrid game you English play, whist, is complicated. Love is not complicated."

Emmeline opened her mouth to argue that sometimes it *was* complicated, but then she closed her mouth again. Ines was correct. Murray either loved Ines enough to fight for her, to sacrifice for her, or he did not. The equation was actually very simple.

"You're right," Emmeline said. "Murray has no excuse." And then to herself she murmured, "Stratford has no excuse."

He either loved her enough to believe that she could love him back, that he *deserved* to be loved back, or he did not. She had laid her feelings bare. She had done that one thing she had sworn she would not do—give her heart to a man. It had taken most of her childhood to pry her heart away from her mother and cushion and wrap it so her mother could no longer cause her pain. Now she'd been fool enough to offer her tender, bruised heart to Stratford. Whereupon, he had looked at her gift and returned it.

Stratford might not believe he was worthy of Emmeline, and if he would not fight for her, even if that fight was within himself, then that assessment was all too correct. He didn't deserve her.

***

*Stratford*

Stratford waited until all the noise and voices quieted and the house was still once more. Then he took the bottle of whisky he had slipped in his coat at dinner and went across the hall to knock on Duncan's door.

"Go away," Duncan said.

Stratford tried the latch, found it open, and walked in. Duncan was lying on his bed, dressed in loose shirt and trousers, staring up at the ceiling. When Stratford entered, he half-rose, his eyes looking ready for murder. Stratford paused until Duncan saw who it was and plopped back down. "Och, it's ye."

"Good God, man. That bed is huge." It was one of those massive, carved beds with four posts and half a forest's worth of wood, which had been whittled into elaborate Celtic symbols.

"I'm nae a wee man," Duncan said.

But even for a man of Duncan's proportions, the bed was generous. "Where did it come from?"

Duncan waved a hand. "Some ancestor or other. Why are ye here? Did Miss Wellesley send ye to flay me?"

Stratford held up the whisky bottle. "I thought you might be thirsty."

Duncan sat. "Ye thought right. Where are my manners?" He climbed out of the bed and indicated two chairs near the hearth. The hearth was easily large enough for a child to stand in, perhaps two children.

"You never had any manners," Stratford said, taking a seat, then accepting the glass Duncan offered him. He poured them both three fingers, but Duncan stared at the offered glass until Stratford filled it to the top.

"Now that's a drink," Duncan said, taking it. He lifted it in salute to Stratford then drank half it down. Stratford blinked and sipped his own drink. The whisky was strong and burned his throat. He winced, knowing it would burn less the more he drank. And he would feel less as well.

"Did ye come tae tell me what an idjit I am?" Duncan asked.

Stratford shook his head. "It would be hypocritical as I'm also an idiot." He drank again, winced.

"Ye finally realized ye love Miss Wellesley? Ye mooned over the lass the whole time we were in London."

"Yes, well, nothing has changed since we were in London," Stratford said. It was true. Emmeline had never treated him any differently than the other members of his family. He'd thought that meant she didn't care for him. But perhaps it was because she *had* cared for him. And now she loved him. "She loves me," he said. "And I managed to ruin it."

Duncan held out his glass for more whisky. Stratford looked at it with wonder then poured his friend another glass. "So fix it," Duncan said.

"If only I could, but that would require traveling back in time and preventing my conception."

Duncan furrowed his brow. "One thing I dinnae miss aboot England is how ye English never make any sense. If ye love the lass, then marry her."

Stratford waited just a beat for Duncan to hear his own words through the whisky haze and knew the moment he had when he drank again. "You do know what I am about to say?"

"Nae need tae say it." Duncan ran a hand through his shaggy hair. "I shouldnae have taken her tae bed. I dinnae ken where my heid was." He lifted the glass and studied the liquid in the flickering light from the fire. "I kent my mother would never accept her. I kent Draven would kill me. And I couldnae stop myself." He looked at Stratford. "And I would do it the same way again."

"Then do the right thing and marry her."

Duncan shook his head, and Stratford lifted a hand. "You will be happy, your mother will be happy once she has grandchildren to spoil, and Draven—well, he will never forgive you."

Duncan laughed then looked serious. "My father's death is my fault." He pointed at Stratford when he tried to argue. "I dinnae shoot the pistol, but my father wouldnae have been in the line of fire if nae for me. It wasnae easy, but my mother forgave me. My brother forgave me. My sister—I dinnae think she can ever forgive me. And all these years, I have tried to make it up tae my mother, and she has never once asked me for anything. Until now."

"That you marry the woman of her choosing."

"Aye. How can I refuse that one request?"

"How can you not? Of all people, your mother knows one or two things about love. She ran away with your father and gave up her entire family and all she had ever known.

Could she really condemn you for wanting to marry for love as well?"

"Nae, but I would condemn myself. I owe her this one thing."

Stratford shook his head. "You do not owe her your life and happiness. After all, she lost a husband, but you lost a father. I'd say neither of you owes the other anything."

Duncan stared at him then went back to looking into the fire. He sipped the whisky now, contemplative.

Stratford sipped his own whisky, and when the last fiery drop burned his throat, he said, "I made a mistake."

"Which one?" Duncan asked.

"I misjudged her," Stratford said. "I thought if she knew who my father was—or wasn't, actually—it would matter to her." Or perhaps he wanted to believe it would matter to Emmeline because she was right; he knew her better than that. But, of course, it hadn't mattered, and he was just using his parentage as an excuse. Because she was right. He was a coward. He was afraid he was not good enough for her. He was afraid she would realize that and tell him. He was afraid if he loved her, she might reject him. And he'd been rejected so much over the years that he couldn't bear to risk it again.

But he also couldn't bear to lose Emmeline. He hadn't anticipated how much that would hurt. He hadn't ever felt the stab of pain he'd felt today when she'd walked away from him. And he'd known, *known*, she would not come back. He'd lost her, and he could not lose her. She was the one person he could not bear to lose. If he lost her, then he might as well have died on the Continent in the war. The only reason he'd ever wanted to survive was to come back and see her again.

"I thought ye would have asked her tae marry ye by now," Duncan said.

"I should have." Why hadn't he been willing to take the risk? He'd risked his life daily for years, and now, he was too much a coward to risk his heart.

"So do it."

"I'm not a coward," Stratford said. "If there was ever anything worth fighting for, it's her."

"So fight." Duncan held out his glass. "But first pour me another wee dram of that whisky."

Stratford obliged, pouring more than a dram. "She won't have me now. I need…some sort of grand gesture. Something to prove to her that I love her, that I'm willing to risk all for her."

Duncan chuckled, and Stratford gave him a sidelong look. "Ye want me tae help ye make a plan?"

Stratford had never in his life needed anyone's help making a plan. And Christ knew that he did not want Duncan's help to do so. Duncan was too wild and unpredictable and…perfect. Stratford sat straight. "I do want your help," he said. "I want to do something wild, something outlandish, something…lunatic." He poured more whisky—obviously he needed it—and sipped.

"Ye need tae abduct her," Duncan said without hesitating.

Stratford coughed as the whisky went down the wrong way. "Pardon?" he croaked.

"Ye heard me. I ken where ye can take her too."

"I cannot abduct her!"

Duncan raised a brow. "Too ootlandish? Too wild? Too lunatic?"

Stratford sighed. "I hate this plan, which probably means it's perfect. Where do I take her and what do I do when I get her there?"

Duncan raised a brow. "Lad, if ye dinnae ken what tae do when ye get her there, I cannae help ye."

"So I'm to debauch her." Stratford could do that. Yes, he would have no trouble at all *thoroughly* debauching Emmeline.

"If that's what ye English like tae call it."

"And where do I take her for this debauching?"

Duncan lowered his voice and told him, and it was exactly the sort of lunatic idea Stratford expected from Duncan Murray.

And it might just work.

# Twenty-One

*Emmeline*

Neither Ines nor Stratford came to breakfast. Duncan Murray, Lady Charlotte, and Emmeline—who never missed breakfast if it could be helped—dined in awkward silence, though the looks Lady Charlotte gave her son spoke volumes. Obviously, Emmeline's presence was not wanted. She hastily drank her tea and ate her scone then excused herself. Ines was still sleeping—or pretending to sleep—in Emmeline's room, so Emmeline decided to walk about the courtyard for an hour or so. Perhaps then she could go by the kitchen and ask for something to bring Ines. She opened the door of the house and stepped into the crisp morning. It was sunny, and she had to squint at the unexpected brightness. She took a few more steps then paused as she heard the thundering of hooves. She couldn't quite see where it was coming from and should have jumped back and out of the way, but she couldn't seem to move her legs.

The first thought that crossed her mind was that Colonel Draven had arrived and planned to mow down anyone in his path. Her second thought was, *I am in his path.* And then, when she could all but feel the hot breath of the horse on her neck, she was grasped roughly about the waist, lifted off her feet, and tossed like a sack of grain over a saddle.

Emmeline might have screamed, but she did not have enough air to breathe let alone scream. The ground rushed by in a blur, and she hung on to the horse for all she was worth. The man who had grabbed her held on too. Clearly it was not Colonel Draven. Not only because he would never mistake her for Ines, but also because she recognized the boots she was staring at.

Emmeline tried to crane her neck to peer up at Stratford. She didn't have the air to speak, but she was able to catch a glimpse of him. His blond hair flew back in the wind, his cheeks were flushed, and his blue eyes glittered like gems. Or perhaps that was the effect of the sun in her own eyes. Whatever it was, he looked more alive than she had ever seen him.

Clearly, the man had gone mad.

Emmeline smacked his calf with her hand, but he didn't react. He probably barely felt her pummeling through the thick boot. She smacked him harder and wriggled about, but then realized the last thing she wanted was to tumble headlong onto the ground. Emmeline went still.

Gradually, the road became rockier, and as they descended, sandier, and she detected the scent of salt in the air and could hear, even above the thundering of the hooves, the crash of waves on the shore. Stratford slowed the horse, walking the beast as Emmeline stared down at sand. Emmeline caught her breath, now that she wasn't being jounced within an inch of her life, and called up, "Let me down."

"Not yet," Stratford said. "We are almost there."

Emmeline looked right then left. Almost where? They were on a beach, rocky walls rising around them. The sea was rough, churning black with white caps dotting the waves coming ashore. It was not the sort of sea one bathed in or even dipped toes in. A spray from one of the waves proved to her that the water was as cold as ice.

But as they moved along the beach, the waves seemed to calm, and though Emmeline at first thought it was her imagination, a few moments later the horse passed under a rocky arch, and the crashing of the waves ceased, replaced by a lapping sound.

"Here we are," Stratford said, lowering her to the ground. Emmeline looked about the small cove in confusion.

"Why are we here?"

Stratford dismounted and took the horse's reins. "We are here because we need to talk."

Emmeline shook her head. "I have said everything I wish. And anything you want to say could have been said at the house. Now I am damp and cold and annoyed. Take me back."

"Not yet."

Emmeline blew out a breath. "What else is there to say, Stratford? Why drag me all the way here to tell me the same thing you have already told me? You cannot expect me to continue to bare my soul when you do not trust me enough to bare yours."

"That's why I've brought you," Stratford said. "To bare my soul. To give you my heart as well, if you'll have it."

She stared at him, but he gestured behind her, and she turned to see the opening of some sort of cave. The angle meant it was hidden from view until one was almost upon it. "Shall we?" he asked.

The man was mad. Speaking of baring souls and now expecting her to enter a cave.

"Emmeline, please," he said.

She blew out a breath. "Aren't there bats in caves?"

"Not this one," he said. "It floods at high tide, which is hours away."

She must have looked dubious—bats and floods did not appeal—because he went on, "Duncan assured me the cave is quite deserted but well worth a look." He stepped inside, leading the horse. Emmeline stood outside. It was too far to walk back. And she had never been inside a cave before. She took a step closer and saw that Stratford had brought some sort of torch. He lit the end of it, and the smell of sulphur and pitch stung her nose.

She edged closer, past the horse, who was contently munching from a feed bag now, and further into the cave. Stratford watched her, torch in one hand, saddle bag heaved over the other shoulder. She pointed at the bag. "What is in there?"

"I thought we might have a picnic."

Emmeline could not be certain she heard him correctly. She stared at him, at his smiling face, and shook her head. "You *are* mad. If you wanted to have a picnic, why not simply ask me? Why throw me over a horse and jostle me to within an inch of my life over two miles of rocky road? And all this to persuade me I should eat inside a dark, damp cave?"

"Would you have said yes if I'd asked?"

She stared at him. "Of course not. I have nothing more to say to you."

He offered her a hand. "Which is why I did not ask."

She stared down at his hand.

Finally, Stratford sighed. "Emmie." It was what her family had called her when she'd been a child, and she looked up at his use of the name. "You will have your apology. You will have your groveling. Just let me finish my grand gesture."

Her heart sped up. Did this mean he *did* want to marry her? And if he did, was that still what she wanted? He'd hurt her, disappointed her. Did she really want to give him the opportunity to do it again? She looked past him and into the dark cave, where she could hear water dripping. "That is your grand gesture?"

"Yes?" he said, tone laced with uncertainty.

"Fine." She put her hand in his and allowed him to lead her into the depths of the cave.

Once they were through the initial low, tight entryway, the cave opened up. Emmeline could stand straight and when Stratford lifted the torch, she gasped in amazement at the glittering surface above. "What is it?"

"Duncan says crystals grow on the cave formations. Apparently, they are not valuable, just pretty in the firelight."

Emmeline looked about her at the crystals winking in the glow of the torch. Long, cone-like formations hung down, some of them bare but many almost covered with crystals like a formal robe might be encrusted with jewels.

"Come this way," Stratford said. "There's a place to sit deeper inside."

Emmeline held his hand and tried not to step in the small pools of water gathered in the uneven floor of the cave. They squeezed through another opening and stepped into an even larger room. She immediately saw where Murray had thought they might sit. There was a long, flat ledge at the far end of the chamber. Stratford led her there, opened the saddle bag, and laid down several blankets. The bottom two were thick and would keep the damp and chill from reaching the top two. As he worked the end of the torch into a space in the wall nearby, Emmeline sat and pulled her knees close to her chest. Like the other room, this room glittered with crystals. The cone-like formations were smaller and there were fewer crystals, as though this chamber had been formed later than the other, but the smaller formations meant it looked almost as though the ceiling of the chamber was studded with stars.

"It is so quiet in here," she said. "I cannot even hear the waves." She looked up at him, at the way his blond hair burned almost golden in the firelight, and his handsome face, so familiar to her, was filled with tension.

"I must tell you something," he said.

"I have no choice but to listen."

He winced. "About that. I should have asked—"

She waved a hand. "I like it. You are the last man I would expect to plan something reckless and wild like this. I like it," she repeated.

He sat beside her, took her hand. "I have loved you for as long as I can remember. First, when we were children, I loved you as I loved my sisters, and then as we grew older, I loved you as a friend. But…" His eyes took on a faraway look. "Do you remember your first Season?"

Even the mention of it made her a little sick. She had been such a dismal failure.

"It was before I went to war, before I left for the Continent. I saw you at a ball. I don't think you knew I was there. I wasn't escorting you, but I caught a glimpse of you, and my breath lodged in my throat. You were so beautiful, Emmeline."

She shook her head. "You know that's not true."

He took her hand. "It's true to me. It's what I thought in that moment. You were dancing, your ivory skirts swirling about, and you were telling your partner something—by the look of it, correcting him on some point."

Her Very Bad Habit, of course. She laughed. "That was before I realized men did not wish to be told when they were mistaken."

"No, we do not, but that has never stopped you. You always say what you think, what you mean. And I realized that you were the last person to pretend the circumstances of my birth did not matter if they did. They truly do not matter to you."

Her hands tightened on his, her heart clenching. "Stratford, if I had known, all those years, that you felt so unloved, so unwelcome, I would have done more, said more."

"I know you would have, but that was not your role to play. I wish I had not been made to feel like a mistake, but what I have realized—what you have helped me realize—is that does not have to be my role to play. I do not need the baron's love. I do not need my mother's affection. I have become the man I am without them. But there is one person whose love and affection I do need."

Emmeline began to tremble. She had dreamed of hearing these words—longed for them and dreaded them.

"I need your love and affection, Emmeline. It's you I thought about when I lay in a ditch in France, waiting for dawn to launch an attack and not knowing whether it was my last night on earth. It is you I think of when I see a beautiful painting or landscape. You I want to share it with. And when I think of my childhood—my lonely childhood—the bright spot in that darkness is always you." He released one of her hands, moved off the ledge, and knelt on one knee.

"I know you do not want to marry. I know the last thing you want is a man controlling you as your mother has done. But I swear to you, if you marry me, I will never tell you what to say, what to wear, or what to eat. I just want to love you—*you*, the clever, opinionated, beautiful woman I fell in love with all those years ago."

It seemed to Emmeline the torch grew brighter and the room was filled with warmth and light. The dread she'd felt for so many Seasons at the idea of having a husband—a lord and master—faded. Stratford knelt before her. *Stratford.* She must have loved him almost as long as he'd loved her, only she hadn't realized it until recently. And why hadn't she realized it? He had always been, and was, perfect for her. "Stratford, I—"

"Damn, I forgot to ask you the question." He cleared his throat. "Emmeline Anne Wellesley, will you do me the honor of becoming my wife?"

She wanted to smile at him, at the look of nervousness on his face. He really did not know how she would answer. Foolish man. How could she ever say no?

"Stratford Leopold Fortescue, I will." She pulled him up and off his knees and into her arms. And when he kissed her, it was the sweetest, softest, most respectful kiss she could ever imagine. "Is that the best you can do?" she asked.

He blew out a breath. "Emmeline, I am trying to behave as a gentleman should to his betrothed."

She cocked her head. "Why?"

"Because I love you."

She pulled his mouth back to hers for another kiss. "Then *love* me." This time she kissed him, her mouth taking his in a fervent mating of lips and tongues. Her hands roamed over his arms, his broad shoulders, his strong back. But she wanted to feel more of him as she had that day in the spring. She pushed at his coat, and he pulled back.

"Miss Wellesley, I fear you intend to take advantage of me."

She looked about the cave. "And you brought me here because you are such a romantic?"

"I brought you here because I knew we could talk without interruption."

"That's not all we can do without interruption."

He shook his head then removed his coat and hung it over a nearby rock. "You are a wicked woman, Miss Wellesley."

"You like it." She beckoned him closer.

"I do."

She pulled at his neckcloth until it came loose, and she could unfasten the row of buttons at his throat. She placed small kisses there as she lifted the tails of the shirt from his trousers and moved her hands underneath the linen to the hard muscles of his abdomen and chest. "Unfasten your cuffs," she murmured, loving the feel of his skin under her fingertips.

"I'll freeze in here without a shirt." But he reached for his cuffs.

"I'll keep you warm."

He stood and she helped him draw off his shirt, admiring the way his chest gleamed in the torchlight. She went to her knees and pressed kisses on his neck and chest and down his belly. When she reached the waistband of his trousers, the evidence of his arousal was clear. She reached for the placket, and he caught her hand.

"Not so fast. I haven't had a chance to see you."

She gave him a wary look. "If I remove this gown, I will never be able to find all the pins to put it back on again, not to mention it's far too cold in here."

"I'll keep you warm," he said, echoing her words. He kissed her, his hands making quick work of her bodice, removing several dress pins until he could push it down. Her nipples hardened when the wool bodice was removed, and he pushed down her stays. She was cold with only the linen shift over her skin, but she shivered at the heat in his eyes as he drew that fabric down, revealing one nipple.

"I've dreamed of these," he said, lowering his head and kissing the turgid point. His other hand cupped her breast and kneaded it gently, taking that nipple between thumb and forefinger until she was panting with need. A few more tugs of fabric, and he had her fully exposed, his mouth all over her, making her hot and provoking an insistent tug in her lower belly.

"I want you," she whispered as he laid her back, hands braced on either side of her, eyes full of love and desire.

"I want you." His hand slid under her skirts, cupping her calves then her thighs, then parting her thighs and moving upward until he paused.

Eyes closed, she opened them at his sound of confusion. "What is this?" He touched the material of her drawers, tracing the fabric. "Are these—?"

"Drawers? Yes."

He blinked then laughed. "Good God, I had no idea."

She rolled her eyes. "I will never understand why a woman wearing drawers is considered more forward than going without. How is a woman with a bare arse under her gown demurer than a woman wearing drawers?"

"I don't know, and it's a question I'll have to ponder later." He found the slit in the fabric and his hand brushed against her curls, making her inhale sharply.

"Yes, later," she said.

"Thank God I did not know you wore these before." His fingers found her flesh and brushed over it lightly, teasingly. "I would not have been able to resist you."

"Men," she muttered. Or at least that was her intention. The word came out on a gasp as he found her center and parted her lips.

"You're so wet." He slid a finger inside her, and she arched in response. "God, yes. I could watch you do that for the rest of my life." He withdrew his finger, slid it up to that small nub that ached for his touch, and circled her.

She moaned.

"I am the luckiest man in England," he said.

"We're in Scotland," she said before she remembered to keep her Impertinence to herself.

But Stratford only chuckled. "The luckiest man in England and Scotland. You like that?"

"Oh, yes."

He slid a finger inside her again, his thumb circling her, and making her forget everything except the feel of his hands on her.

"I want to see you come. I've dreamed of seeing you again."

"I want to see you," she said, opening her eyes. She reached for his trousers again, and his free hand stopped her.

"Should we save that for the wedding night?"

She frowned. "When we're both exhausted after a day of smiling at our tiresome families and then we must be quiet because we don't want to wake up the house?" She looked about the cave. "I like this much better."

He pulled back. "I can't take you without marrying you."

Emmeline sighed. She loved Stratford's honor, but sometimes it could be tiresome. And then she remembered.

They were in Scotland.

"Do you have a length of rope?"

He gave her a look that said he thought she had gone quite mad. "No."

"Ribbon then? String?"

He moved to the satchel, untied one of the packages of food he had inside—he really had planned for a picnic—and offered her the string.

"I know this is not legal, but it will be weeks before we can marry in a church." She twined her fingers with his and laid the string over their hands.

"A handfasting?" he asked. "Don't we need witnesses?"

"Don't we need clothing?" She gestured down to her open bodice and his shirtless chest. "Details, my love."

He gave her a wry smile. "Very well. What do we say?"

"I don't know." She gazed up at him. "What do you *want* to say?"

He took a breath then placed his free hand over their joined hands. He took one end of the string and looped it over their wrists. "I, Stratford Leopold Fortescue, do promise before you and before God to love and cherish you all the days of my life. I will forsake all others and love only you." His eyes were locked with hers. "How was that?"

"I think," she murmured. "You are supposed to say something about worshipping me with your body."

His gaze lowered to peruse her body then met hers again. "You're right, of course. Emmeline, with my body I thee worship and with all my worldly goods I thee endow." He pressed his forehead to hers. "And I promise to never doubt your love, to never doubt my worth, and to make certain you feel beautiful and perfect every day of your life." He kissed her gently.

She felt tears sting her eyes. "Thank you." It was a long moment before she could swallow the lump in her throat and say anything further. She wrapped the other end of the string around their joined hands. "I, Emmeline Anne Wellesley, do promise before you and God to love you with my whole heart, to cherish and honor you until we grow old, to tend you when you are sick, to mourn with you when you suffer loss, to swim naked with you when we find another hot spring."

Stratford, who was looking rather teary-eyed himself, laughed at that as she'd intended.

"And of course, I shall worship you with my body and endow you with all my worldly goods. But most importantly, if the baron should ever so much as look at you with disapproval, I will give him such a dressing down that his ears will burn for a week."

He pulled her close and held her tightly for a moment. "You are sure to become his favorite daughter-in-law," he murmured, and she laughed. "What do we say to conclude? There is no one to pronounce us man and wife."

She wrapped her free hand around him. "I think you simply kiss the bride."

"I have been wanting to do that for ages now." He lowered his mouth to hers and kissed her softly and gently. Their hands were still clasped, tied lightly with the string, but he twined his fingers with her other hand, kissing her until they were both flushed and a bit breathless. He took the string binding their hands and tossed it over his neck like a loose neckcloth. Then he led her to the ledge where he'd laid the blankets and lowered her until she was on her back and he lying beside her.

She'd wanted him to continue where he'd left off—his hands under her skirts, his mouth on her breasts—but he began to kiss her gently and sweetly starting at her forehead and moving down. When he reached her mouth, she kissed him back, deep kisses that seemed to go on for hours and said more of what they both felt than words ever could.

Finally, he moved lower, kissing her neck and her shoulder and her collarbone and then the slope of her breast. He laid his head there, then lifted a hand and cupped her, teasing first one nipple then the other into a peak. Heat flooded her sex, making her squirm with need. "Stratford, I want you."

"Don't rush me. This is our wedding night. I want you to remember it."

"We are in a cave in Scotland. How can I ever forget?" But perhaps actions would persuade him faster than words. She reached between them, found the fall of his trousers, and opened it.

"Now you're not playing fair," he grumbled into her breast. With a laugh she took his erection into her hand and stroked. He groaned and pushed into her touch. Then his mouth closed on her nipple, sucking hard and eliciting an equally insistent pull from between her legs.

He seemed to know what she was feeling because his hand slid up to her knees, parting them, then finding the gap in her drawers to cup her sex.

"You're wet and hot," he said, moving to lick her other nipple.

"I want you."

"Then you shall have me." He moved over her, reaching both hands under her skirts to remove her drawers and dropping them beside her. "One day, when we are in a proper bed chamber, I want to see you wearing those—and only those."

"Should I be scandalized?"

"You will be when I show you just what I want to do with you when I have you wearing just those drawers."

Heat burned through her. "What do you want to do with me now?" she asked, her voice barely a whisper.

He pushed her skirts up, edging her legs open with his body as he settled between them. Emmeline had never expected to feel fear, but when he was in that position, she suddenly felt quite vulnerable and uncertain. He kissed her gently. "We'll take things slowly," he said as his hand glided up her thigh and stroked the burning flesh between her legs. "You like this?"

"Yes," she said.

"I won't do anything you don't like." His fingers played her, one moment stroking firmly and the next feathering lightly. She forgot her fear when his thumb found that pearl of pleasure, and she couldn't stop her hips from rocking into him. She could feel his hard manhood pushing against her leg, and when his fingers entered her, she wanted it to be *him*.

"I want you inside me," she breathed as pleasure began to uncoil through her.

"Not yet," he said.

"Soon," she demanded. "Please."

But he ignored her demands and continued his gentle assault, until she was practically crying out with need, and then crescendoing with it until she cried out and bucked hard against his hands. And just when she had peaked, she felt him enter her. Not all the way, just enough that she realized he'd replaced his fingers.

"Am I hurting you?" he asked.

"No." Their eyes met. "It doesn't hurt at all." How strange that women always talked about the pain of their wedding night. When this was all pleasure and—he moved deeper, and she went still.

"Am I hurting you now?"

"It's definitely uncomfortable," she said. "Is that all?"

He lowered his forehead to her shoulder. "No. There's more."

She lifted his face so she could look in his eyes. "How much more?" The look he gave her said this was only the beginning. She nodded and clenched her jaw. "Very well. Go ahead then."

He laughed. "You are the very picture of endurance." He reached between them and stroked the place where their bodies met. Even though she'd just climaxed, the feeling was pleasurable. "I told you I shan't do anything you don't like."

"I like that." She kissed him, and his mouth was warm and inviting. She wrapped her arms about his neck and willingly opened her legs further as he stroked that place that gave her the most pleasure. She felt his hips move, pushing deeper, and though the intrusion stung slightly, she found that she trusted him and that every time he inched deeper, he did something wicked with his hand or mouth that distracted her enough until finally he groaned and had to bite his lip.

"What is it?" she asked. "Are you hurt now?"

"God, no. I'm sheathed to the hilt and you feel so good I can hardly stand not to move."

Emmeline, curious now, moved her hips slightly and felt more than a little discomfort. But the pain was minimal. He pulled back slightly then moved forward again and she gasped. There was the pain.

"Do you have to move?" she asked.

He gave her a pained look. "That's rather the point."

"I see." She considered for a moment. "Perhaps if you distract me…"

"How shall I do that?"

She slid her foot up the back of his thigh and wrapped it around his hip. The pressure lessened when she did that, and his blue eyes darkened to near violet. "With your lips." She nipped at his lip, and he moved in what she thought must be a purely instinctual rhythm.

"Sorry."

"I can see how it will be pleasurable," she said. "Next time."

"Yes." He slid his hands under her bottom, adjusting their position so she was actually a bit more comfortable. But he was also pressed harder against her, and this time when he moved, he slid against that pearl, and she clenched her hands on his back. His gaze was hot on her face, watching her, noting what she liked. He moved again, sliding against that place where she needed him until she was arching to gain more friction.

"Emmie," he rasped. "You have to stay still. I can't—" As though his body moved on its own, he pressed against her again, and she gasped.

"Harder there. Right there. Yes." He thrust deeper, and though there was pain there was also a flash of pleasure.

"Oh, Christ," he groaned. "I can feel you. I can't…" He moved within her, and the pain was there but mixed with the pleasure she was hardly aware of it. Then he cried out, and she looked up at him, at the play of light on his face as he climaxed.

He was beautiful. And he was hers.

Finally, and forever.

# Twenty-Two

*Ines*

"You have to eat something," Emmeline told Ines. She had returned only a couple of hours ago, and she had not stopped smiling. When Ines had asked if Fortescue apologized, Emmeline said they were to be married. Ines had been genuinely happy for her friends, but she did not want to sit across from them and Duncan and his horrid mother for two hours.

"The housekeeper brought a tray earlier," Ines said.

Emmeline gave her a look. "Which you did not touch. I saw it." Emmeline pulled Ines to her feet. "Come down or Murray will probably come up after you. Besides." She reached for Ines's hair, tucking a piece behind her ear and bringing another piece over her shoulder. "When he sees how pretty you look, that will be the best revenge."

"I do not want revenge."

Emmeline raised a brow. "Yes, you do. And if you do not, I do. The man is a fool. Let him see what he is missing."

"He is missing nothing, just a silly girl with silly ideas."

Emmeline took her shoulders. "You are not silly, and neither are your ideas of romance. You made me believe in romance, and that is no small accomplishment. Please, *please* come down to dinner."

"Fine." She had to go. If she stayed, then everyone would think she was ashamed. She was not ashamed of what she and Duncan had done. She loved him. She knew he loved her.

But as Catarina had told her on more than one occasion, love was not everything. Sometimes love could not conquer all.

"You will come then?" Emmeline asked. "Good."

Ines straightened her shoulders and lifted her chin, determined not to be cowed by Lady Charlotte. For the first time since she'd left London, she had wished Benedict had found her. If he'd found her, they could be on their way home by now. She'd never have to see Duncan or his awful mother again.

She and Emmeline reached the drawing room just as Lady Charlotte was leading the party into the dining room. She greeted Emmeline and nodded to Ines, her eyes flicking across the room. Ines followed Lady Charlotte's gaze and spotted Duncan. He was standing beside Stratford, and as usual, he made an imposing figure, especially dressed as he was. She tried not to stare, but she had only ever seen illustrations of Highland dress. Duncan wore a dark green coat and linen neckcloth. The belt around the coat secured the green and blue plaid with faint stripes of red that he'd draped over his shoulder. It matched the kilt he wore, which fell just above his knees. Below his knees were flat soled boots, probably more for show than actual use as they looked too thin to offer much protection in the elements.

He had shaved and his hair was pulled back into a queue. His amber eyes met hers then moved away. Ines tried to slow her heartbeat. Her heart seemed determined to betray her. It still loved him, even when her mind begged it to stop.

Duncan took his mother's arm, escorting her. Fortescue took Emmeline's, and Ines moved to walk behind. But Fortescue shook his head. "I'd be a lucky man to have two such lovely ladies on my arms. Miss Neves?" He held out his free arm. Feeling grateful for his kindness, she took it and allowed him to lead her to the dining room.

When she entered, Lady Charlotte stood behind her chair, her son behind her, waiting to seat her. But Lady

Charlotte was staring at something on the table, and too late Ines realized exactly what it was.

She'd forgotten to tell the housekeeper not to leave the box on the table tonight. She should have told her to give it to her mistress after Ines was gone. But it was too late now. Lady Charlotte lifted the wooden box and looked around the table. Everyone stood, as no one dared sit before Lady Charlotte.

"What is this?" she asked.

Ines did not want to answer, and the rest of the party looked questioningly at each other. Ines did not need to answer. The lady would know soon enough when she opened it, and Lady Charlotte did not wait for an answer at any rate. She flicked the small gold latch aside and opened the box. For a long moment, she stared down at the contents. Ines felt her face flush and burn. She wanted to sink under the floor when Lady Charlotte lifted the lace from the box and held it up. There was no question what it was or who had made it.

"What is this?" Lady Charlotte demanded. Her gaze rested on Ines for what seemed a very long moment. Ines was aware all eyes were on her, and she swallowed. Words deserted her.

Emmeline broke in. "I am certain Ines meant it as a thanks for your hospitality. Her lace is highly prized."

Lady Charlotte looked at Ines again, and Ines took a breath. "It is a gift. They are lace cuffs. I thought they would look pretty on the dress of your daughter. Then I thought why not give them to you as a thank you." She looked at Duncan, but he was staring at the lace in his mother's hands. "I asked your housekeeper to leave it on the table tonight. It was before…" She trailed off.

Lady Charlotte looked at her son, seeming to want him to speak. Was it possible she wanted him to defend Ines?

Ins shook her head. Now she was acting truly foolish.

Finally, Lady Charlotte looked away and her hand shook before she dropped the lace back into the box. Ines prepared for her to return it. Surely, she would not want any sort of reminder of Ines. Perhaps she would throw it in her face or throw it in the fire.

"Christ and all the saints!" Duncan exploded. "I cannae do this."

Ines jumped at his outburst, and everyone but his mother turned to stare at him. Lady Charlotte took her seat, looking almost relieved. "You have something to say, Duncan?"

"Nae tae ye, Mother." He shook his head. He looked at Ines, and she stared back at him, hoping her glare was harsh. She wanted to hurt him as much as he'd hurt her. Duncan's look softened as he stared at her, and then he was moving toward her. Ines started to back up, but Duncan was too quick. He caught her hands and held her. Then, to her shock, he knelt before her.

"Stand up, Duncan!" his mother said, her voice like iron.

Somehow Duncan ignored her. He looked up at Ines, and no matter how much she tried to look away, it was his face that she wanted to see above all others.

"Lass," he began, then shook his head. "*Ines.* I owe ye an apology. I faltered when I should nae have."

Ines did not speak. It was not enough. She wanted to forgive him, but his words were not enough. Her heart still hurt. It still felt hard and unyielding when she looked at him.

"It's strange, aye?" He glanced at Fortescue. "I never faltered when a line of soldiers fired at me, but last night, I hesitated."

Fortescue gave him a sympathetic look, but Lady Charlotte was becoming more agitated. She stood. "Duncan, sit down."

He ignored her and looked only at Ines.

"I love ye, Ines. I love ye heart and soul."

Ines gasped. Or perhaps she sobbed. She just knew her heart lurched hard in her chest.

"I wanted tae tell ye last night. I tried tae show ye instead, but I wanted tae give ye the words as well. I'm giving them tae ye now."

"Thank God," his mother said. Duncan turned to look at her, then put his arm about Ines's shoulders. Ines stood still and frozen, not shying away, but not accepting his touch either.

"Mother, ye ken I love ye and respect ye."

Lady Charlotte blew out a breath. "I know that. I've been waiting for you to tell me what you feel for *her*."

Duncan frowned, looking confused. "I should have said before. I should have stood by her side last night. It's where I should have been from the start. I ken I'm a failure in yer eyes. Ye sent me tae London tae find a titled English bride, and I fell in love with a Portuguese lacemaker. But ye of all people should understand love. Ye felt it once with my father."

Lady Charlotte gripped the table hard then eased down into her chair, looking suddenly older and frailer.

"I've spent years trying tae atone for my mistake. I ken if I hadnae run away that night, yer husband and my father would be at this table now. I never wanted tae disappoint ye or defy ye again, but I have tae. I love Ines Neves, and I want tae marry her." He looked down at Ines. "If she'll have me.

And if ye dinnae approve"—he looked back at Lady Charlotte—"then I'll accept that and we'll leave right now. But I willnae ever leave her side again."

Lady Charlotte sat back, nodding resolutely. The room had gone silent except for the crackling of the fire. Duncan went to his knees again and took Ines's hands. "I dinnae deserve ye, lass. I dinnae ken if ye can ever forgive me, but I swear if ye'll have me for yer husband I will nae give ye a moment's regret."

Ines realized everyone was looking at her. She looked down at Duncan. There was still pain when she looked at him. He'd hurt her, and that would not disappear in an instant. But more than the pain was the love. She loved him too. First, she'd loved the idea of him. Then she'd loved the look of him. And now she loved the man himself.

"I love you," she said. "*Sim.* Yes, I will marry you."

Duncan rose to his feet and pulled her into his arms. And then she was off her feet as he lifted her up and swung her around. She wrapped her arms around him and kissed him, and he kissed her back, and in that moment, she felt her heart soften and melt and she fell in love with him all over again.

Somewhere a door slammed open, and Ines supposed Lady Charlotte had fled the room. But then she heard a familiar voice. "Take your hands off my sister-in-law."

\*\*\*

*Duncan*

Duncan had known Lieutenant-Colonel Draven would arrive. He just hadn't thought it would be during the happiest moment of his life. He broke the kiss and stared at the dining room door where Draven stood, his gaze dark and full of anger. Just behind him, Duncan spotted Jasper, his black mask covering the burn scars on his face.

"Put her down," Draven said. "Get your pistol and meet me outside."

Duncan lowered Ines to the floor and pushed her behind him, wanting to protect her, though she needed no protection from her own brother-in-law. "Sir, I want tae…" Duncan knew that was not the way. He began again. "May I have yer permission tae marry Miss Neves?"

"No," Draven said. "You will be too dead to marry anyone."

"Sir," Jasper said from behind him.

Draven pointed at Stratford, who was now standing at the table. "You here too? Did you formulate the plan to abduct my sister-in-law?"

Stratford shook his head. "Sir, you are mistaken. This is not what it seems."

"Really?" Draven stepped further inside. "It looks to me like Murray has taken advantage of my charge and now feels duty-bound to marry her."

"Nae, sir," Duncan said. "I want tae marry her because I love her."

"So you did not bed her?" Draven asked.

Duncan hesitated, eyeing the pistol at the colonel's side. Then he noticed Ines tugging at his arm, trying to loosen his hold on her. Finally, she pushed herself forward. Duncan could see his former commander brace for some sort of dramatic scene, but Ines only gave him a short curtsy then smiled.

"Benedict, I have missed you."

The colonel's eyes narrowed.

"The truth is Duncan did not abduct me. It was all a mistake." She looked at Duncan and smiled. "Except it was not a mistake, and I love him."

"Ines, move aside."

She held up a hand, turning a withering look on Draven. "And if you so much as hurt a hair on the head of my soon-to-be husband, I will tell Catarina and she will flay you alive."

"Your sister is home and worried sick about you."

Ines looked repentant at those words. "I am sorry about that. But she will forgive me when we tell her about the wedding."

"There will be no wedding!" Draven yelled.

Jasper moved beside him. "Sir, I have met your wife, and she has something of a temper. I beg you not to act in haste. Perhaps if we send for her…"

"Perhaps I can kill him and beg forgiveness later."

Ines moved toward him. "Benedict."

Quicker than Duncan thought a man of his age could move—but then Draven had always seemed as fit as any of the men, despite being fifteen years their senior—he caught Ines by the wrist and thrust her at Jasper. "Hold her." And then he lunged forward, head down like a charging bull. Duncan didn't even try to resist. He deserved this much, at least. The colonel slammed into his midsection, and Duncan stumbled back, crashing against a wall and sending a painting flying off its hook and clattering to the floor.

Colonel Draven pulled his right fist back and plowed it into Duncan's cheek. Duncan winced at the pain but didn't fight back. The next punch brought the taste of blood. His ears were ringing, but he could hear Ines screaming and Stratford yelling and Jasper and Miss Wellesley somewhere in the midst of the fray.

And then his mother's voice rose above it all.

"Cease this at once!" she demanded. She'd sat at the head of the table, watching the scene, but she'd obviously had enough.

Draven, fist pulled back for another blow, paused and looked at Lady Charlotte. Duncan took a breath, which was not easy with the colonel's hand clamped around his throat and his head pushed against the wall. Lady Charlotte pointed at Draven.

"Release him."

The colonel hesitated, but he was a soldier first and Lady Charlotte had been born a commander. Draven released him and stepped back. Duncan almost slumped over but caught himself just in time. The punches had been harder than he'd expected. His cheek throbbed and one eye was swelling closed.

"Now step away."

Draven did as ordered, and Duncan steadied himself against the wall. Jasper must have released Ines because a moment later she was at his side, supporting him. Of course, she was. The lass was one of the few genuinely kind, compassionate people he had ever met. She'd barely known him, yet when Nash had shot him, she'd never left his side. Duncan put his arm about her, pulling her tight against him.

He'd come perilously close to losing her, and only now did he realize how close to the precipice he'd been standing. For once, he did not want to go over. He did not want to risk it. He wanted the assurance that the woman holding him up now would be at his side forever.

It was the sort of predictability Duncan had never thought he'd want, but he now realized—almost too late— that it was what he'd needed all along.

"I do believe you have forgotten yourself, sir," Lady Charlotte said to Colonel Draven. "How else to explain why you have come into my house and begun a brawl as though you were in some sort of tavern."

"My apologies," Draven said. "I was not myself."

She nodded. "None of us have been ourselves lately." She surveyed the room with accusation in her eyes. "But we must maintain some semblance of order. Duncan, introduce your…friends, please." Her gaze dipped to Ines at his side, but Duncan saw only resignation in her eyes.

"Lady Charlotte," Duncan said, taking a breath as his was short after the blows he'd taken. "Might I present Lieutenant-Colonel Draven and Lord Jasper Grantham. We served together in the war."

"You are heroes then," Lady Charlotte said. "Four heroes at my dinner table." She gestured to Stratford and then

Duncan. "I am fortunate indeed. Please sit." She gestured to the empty places at the table. "I will have two more place settings brought in." The footman departed immediately without having to be told.

"Thank you, my lady, but we would not wish to intrude," Draven said.

"Oh, nonsense," Lady Charlotte said, taking her seat again. "I imagine you have been traveling day and night, tracking my son's betrothed." She glanced at Ines, and Duncan started at how easily she used the word *betrothed* for Ines. "And now you have found her."

"And we are anxious to take her home. My wife—her sister—is worried sick."

"Completely understandable. Do sit," she said, ignoring Draven's obvious desire to be gone. "After all, you cannot start back tonight and on an empty stomach."

Draven looked at Jasper, and Jasper shrugged then moved toward the table. The colonel gave Duncan one last menacing look and followed Jasper. Unwilling to relinquish Ines, Duncan held her tight as he hobbled back to the table then seated her in the chair beside his mother and stood behind her. He would not leave her side again.

His mother gave her new guests her best hostess smile, and then looked at Duncan and sighed. "Colonel Draven," she said.

"My lady?" He had sipped from the glass of wine in front of him and still held the glass aloft.

"How long will it take for Mrs. Draven to travel to Scotland?"

"Mrs. Draven?" he asked. He'd removed his hat, and his red hair stuck up, mirroring the lift of his brows.

"She will want to attend the wedding, yes?" Lady Charlotte looked at Miss Wellesley. "And your own mother? We should send to her first thing."

"My lady?" Miss Wellesley looked confused. "I am not sure I understand."

Lady Charlotte lifted her own wine glass and sipped, slowly as though she had all the time in the world to explain herself. "For the double wedding, my dear. I plan to hold it here."

Miss Wellesley stared; Stratford dropped the fork he'd been playing with. Jasper laughed, and Draven's cheeks turned red before he nodded tightly. But Ines...Ines looked up at Duncan and smiled.

That smile was like the sun in the warmth it brought. Duncan smiled back at her then looked at his mother, who was watching them. Duncan thought he saw a suspicious sign of moisture in her eyes. But that couldn't be, because Lady Charlotte never did anything so human as cried.

"Thank ye, Mother," Duncan said.

"Anything for you, dear boy," she said. "I only wanted to know that you loved her, that you would fight for her."

"I do."

"Then I do as well." She raised a hand. "You must promise me one thing, though. You won't go running off to England or to war again. I want you and Ines to live here."

"You do?" Ines asked, her voice filled with shock.

"I do," Lady Charlotte lifted the lace cuffs from the wooden box still before her. "I want you to be here when I wear these."

# Twenty-Three

*Stratford*

Baron Fortescue did not arrive at the Duke of Atholl's castle, where the wedding parties were to stay, with the rest of the wedding guests. The baroness said he was needed in Town and Scotland was simply too far to travel. Stratford did not think his mother would have come if he hadn't been marrying her best friend's daughter. Later Emmeline, Loftus trailing behind, had come to her betrothed, put her arms around Stratford, and simply held him. "I'm so sorry," she had whispered in his hair.

Stratford pulled back and looked at her lovely face—her blue eyes like the color of the Scottish sky on this sunny, summer day. "I wasted years trying to earn their love, and now I ask myself why. I never needed it. Everyone who matters is here." He looked at her with a smile. "My friends are here—Jasper, Ewan, Colin, even Mayne forgave us and came."

Emmeline smiled. "The duke still will not accept any cup Murray hands him. He said he slept for almost two days the last time Mr. Murray gave him a drink."

Stratford chuckled. "Duncan forgets that what would put him out is enough to flatten another man." He pulled Emmeline into an embrace. "I love you, Emmie."

"I love you." She laid her head on his shoulder. "Do you believe you are worthy of it yet? All this love?"

"I'm gradually accustoming myself to the idea," he said. He pulled back and took her hand. "But I wouldn't mind being shown just one more time." He led her toward a hidden entrance Duncan had shown him was the perfect way to sneak into the keep, unseen. He knew he could have her in his bed chamber within minutes.

But Emmeline tugged at him. "The wedding is in the morning. I have to go hide from you. It's bad luck to see the bride before the wedding. Besides, my mother and sisters will come looking for me soon. They brought an entire coach of dresses, ribbons, and lace. I imagine they mean to drape me with it until I teeter under the weight."

"You will look beautiful no matter what you wear. In fact, the less the better."

She swatted him playfully. "Tomorrow," she said, and it was a promise.

The wedding day had dawned rainy and overcast. Lady Charlotte had declared it good luck, but everyone else had declared it typical Scotland. Duncan and Stratford had managed to make it to the church in Kirkmoray. Like the Duke of Atholl's castle, it was old and crumbling, but when Emmeline had said it had charm, he'd agreed. The church had been built overlooking a loch and, in the distance, the Highlands. With the low-lying clouds, neither could be seen at half past seven in the morning, but if the weather ever cleared, the view was spectacular. The stone church looked a bit uneven in places, but the circular stained-glass window and the vaulted ceilings made the inside airier than the squat outside would have led him to believe.

He and Duncan stood nervously at the chancel. The priest, Anglican (though Stratford had a suspicion that Duncan's village might still harbor any number of Catholics), cleared his throat and looked at the papers before him. His hands shook and he muttered to himself, seemingly more nervous than the bridegrooms.

"Do ye think he will make it through the service?" Duncan whispered to Stratford as the guests continued filing in.

"He'd better," Stratford said. "I'm not doing this again."

"Mrs. Wellesley looks happy," Duncan said as his soon-to-be mother-in-law entered with three of her daughters and took a seat at the front beside his own mother. Emmeline's mother was beaming.

"Thinking of all the blunt she'll save not having to send Emmeline to Town for another Season."

Duncan elbowed him, almost causing Stratford to topple over. "She's pleased tae have ye for a son."

"Yes, well." Stratford felt his neck warm at the compliment. "I need to thank your mother again for arranging all of this."

Duncan waved a hand. "She's in her element." It was true. Lady Charlotte stood with the Duke of Atholl, presiding over everything like a queen.

And then as if by some invisible cue, the guests quieted and took their seats, and Stratford realized the brides must have arrived. His belly fluttered as the doors to the narthex opened, and the two women started forward.

Certainly, there were two—Stratford knew this—but he could only see Emmeline. She wore a pale blue gown adorned with ribbons of sapphire. Instead of a bonnet, she wore those same ribbons threaded through her hair. Drops of rain glittered in the dark curls, making a stark contrast beside her pale face and her large blue eyes.

Duncan gripped Stratford's shoulder, and Stratford was not sure if it was to support him or because the Scotsman needed shoring up. Emmeline was finally beside him, and the priest spoke, but Stratford barely heard a word. Emmeline smiled at him and mouthed the words, *I love you.* And Stratford knew he would spend the rest of his life proving just how much he loved her too.

*** 

*Emmeline*

When they'd emerged from the old church, the sun had deigned to peak through the clouds and rays of light streaked across the Highlands beyond the loch. Loftus had been relegated to waiting outside the church, and he jumped up to greet them. Emmeline petted him and looked about her. The scene was so pretty Emmeline could have painted a picture— if she had any talent for painting. Instead, they'd all returned to the duke's castle for the wedding breakfast, held in the keep, which with its tapestries and trestle tables, made her feel as though she had stepped into the Middle Ages.

At the breakfast, Stratford's mother had taken her hand and welcomed her to the family. "I've always thought of you as a daughter," she said. "Now you are one in truth." She'd kissed her cheek, and Emmeline had felt true warmth. She and Stratford were to live at the estate his uncle had gifted Stratford, but she would not mind inviting his mother to visit. Her own mother…

Well, her own mother had not been quite as insufferable as usual. She'd limited her comments on Emmeline's appearance and had only tried to prevent Emmeline from eating cake once. When Emmeline had given her a hard stare, she had withdrawn and murmured, "Well, you are Mr. Fortescue's problem now, I dare say."

"Do you hear that?" Emmeline whispered to her new husband. *Husband*—she liked the sound of that.

"You are my problem?" he said, giving her a wink. "You're a good problem to have."

"Do you think you might take your problem upstairs for a little while? I think I should like to lie down."

His expression turned to one of concern. "Do you have a headache?"

"No, but I'll say that if it means we can have time alone."

He smiled, relieved. "You go first. I'll join you shortly."

She excused herself and left the breakfast, which took a good twenty minutes as everyone wanted to wish her happy and hug her and tell her how lovely she looked. Finally, she escaped up a narrow, winding stone staircase to the bedchamber she'd been given. Stratford's things had already been moved to it, in preparation for the wedding night. She was ready now. Once she had put her mind to it, Lady Charlotte had proved an adept chaperone and ensured she and Stratford had very little time alone. They'd barely been able to steal a kiss under Lady Charlotte's watchful eye.

Now, they no longer needed a chaperone. Emmeline removed what she could—shoes and stockings, ribbons and lace, but she could not manage the dress on her own. She couldn't reach the pins in the back. When Stratford knocked, the bodice hung down and the skirts sagged. She opened the door. "Come in and unwrap me," she'd said, pulling him inside.

"Gladly."

She gave him her back before he could act on any of the other ideas she saw formulating in his mind, and he began to remove pins and untie laces. "Did anyone see you sneak away?" she asked.

"I would have gotten away without notice," he said, "but Duncan yelled out across the room, *Where are ye off tae, Stratford?* And then everyone looked at me and clapped."

Emmeline laughed. "Were you terribly embarrassed?"

"Not so embarrassed that I didn't salute and come here to join you. There. That's all of them I think."

Her skirts slid to the floor, and she removed her bodice and stays, standing in just her chemise. "Now it's your turn," she said, turning to him. She took her time undressing him. First, she stripped off the tight coat, then the neckcloth and waistcoat, and finally the linen shirt.

He had to sit on the bed to remove his shoes and stockings, and when he reached for his breeches, she reached for the tie of her chemise. He eased his trousers over his slim hips as she slid the linen over her breasts and down to her waist.

"I don't know what I did to deserve this," he whispered as the chemise fell to the ground and she stood naked before him. "You're perfect."

"No," she said, looking at his broad shoulders, muscled chest, and slim hips. She could not miss his erection jutting proudly either. "*You* are perfect."

"Turn around," he said, twirling one finger. "I want to see that arse I have been dreaming about."

Normally shy, Emmeline turned around and wiggled her hips.

"You will be the death of me," he all but groaned as he wrapped his arms around her and kissed the back of her neck. His hands slid down over her bottom, squeezed it, then slid back up again to rub her arms, cup her breasts, and then brush over her sex. She moaned as he touched her and turned in his arms to kiss him fully.

He pulled her to the bed, coming down next to her and gazing at her with undisguised admiration. They both took their time exploring the other. She was particularly fond of the feel of his hip under her leg when she threw it over him. He seemed to want to kiss every part of her, twice. When they were both panting and dizzy with want, he entered her. It didn't hurt this time, and Emmeline had to bite her lip to stop a cry of pleasure from the feel of him deep inside her. He moved slowly, locking his hands with hers, watching her face, and murmuring how beautiful she was and how he loved her.

When the pleasure had built to a peak and she was mewling with need, he suddenly rolled her over so that she straddled him.

"What is this?" she asked, breathless. But he nudged his hips, and she could see exactly what he wanted her to do. She took him inside her and moved her own hips tentatively.

"That's it," he said. "Show me what you like."

She moved again, the friction delicious. He gripped her hips as she rocked over him, his face a mask of restraint. And then the pleasure was spiraling through her, coiling up through her belly and radiating out to every limb. She cried out and gripped his shoulders as he thrust into her, deepening her own pleasure. They crashed over the edge together, clinging tightly to each other to steady themselves in the storm.

Afterward, when she lay in Stratford's arms, her head on his chest, listening to the steady beat of his heart. She looked up at his handsome face, his tousled blond hair and heavy-lidded eyes. "Thank you for coming after me," she said. "I think the truth is, I wanted someone to come find me."

"I'll always find you," he said, squeezing her shoulder.

"You'll never need to. I plan to stay right by your side."

"Good." He turned and kissed her. "That's right where I want you, my love."

***

*Ines*

Ines watched Mr. Fortescue start up the stairs after Emmeline and gave Duncan a meaningful look. He smiled and leaned close. "Ye take the stairs over there—"

"Oh, no." Catarina moved behind them. "You are staying right here, *irmã*." She pointed to the empty seat beside Duncan, where Fortescue had been seated. "Move over."

Duncan sighed with resignation and moved. Ines steeled herself for a lecture, but Catarina smiled at her. "Are you happy?" she asked in Portuguese.

Ines smiled. "*Sim.* Very happy. I love him, Catarina. He is a good man," she answered in their native tongue.

"He is not the man I would have chosen for you."

"*Senhor* Podmore will find some other unfortunate woman to bore."

"He already has."

Ines raised a brow.

"He has been courting the daughter of a renowned saddle maker."

"Saddles and coaches. They sound perfect for each other."

"They do, yes." Catarina's smile faltered. "Is that why you ran away?" she asked. "Because I wanted you to consider Mr. Podmore?"

Ines grabbed her sister's hands, concerned at the look of guilt on Catarina's pretty face. "*Não, não.* Well, partly? I told you I was merely hiding, and then the coach started to move."

"I did not believe that story."

Ines squeezed her hands. "It is true. But the reason I did not want to come back? I did not want to meet any more Mr. Podmores. I wanted a Duncan Murray."

Catarina glanced at him. "But you have always wanted love and romance, and he is so…"

At that moment, Duncan drained his wine glass, slammed it on the table, and signaled for another. All to the cheers of the men nearby.

"Scottish."

Ines watched Duncan who winked at her. "I like that he is Scottish. I like this country. It is wild and free."

"You really will not come back to London with us?"

Ines looked about the old keep of the castle and thought about the loch, the sea, and the mountains beyond. "We will come and visit."

"What about our lace shop?"

Ines cocked her head. "That was always your dream, Catarina. I enjoy making lace, but I always made what you showed me. And perhaps I can show some of the women here how to make it. We can sell to some of the shops in Edinburgh."

Catarina's brows lifted. "Expansion of Catarina lace?"

Ines smiled. "I can see the excitement in your eyes already."

Catarina laughed and then her expression turned serious. "I want you to be happy, Ines. I feel responsible for you. You were only fourteen when you ran away with me."

"And you have been a mother and father to me," Ines said. "But now I am all grown up, and you should go live your own life. Visiting me regularly, of course!"

"Of course." Catarina hugged her, and Ines rested her head on her sister's shoulder. Her sister always smelled of home to her, and Ines had to sniff to hold back tears. "You are crying, *irmã*."

"Because I am happy," Ines said. Catarina gave her a look, and Ines conceded, "And I will miss you not bossing me around every day."

"Then you must come to London often so I can keep in practice."

"I will."

"And you," Catarina said, switching to English as she turned on Duncan. "If you do not make my sister very happy, I will come for you."

Duncan scooted back in his chair. "I promise she'll nae have a moment's complaint."

"Good. And do not even think of sneaking away. I want to hear all about your travels. I hear you allowed her to be abducted by bandits."

Ines buried her face in her hands.

She had thought once the breakfast was over, she and Duncan would have time together, but then they had to bid farewell to the guests who were travelling home that day. Emmeline and Fortescue had not been seen again, so the task fell to Ines and Duncan. And then there were gifts to open and sort and the duke wanted to speak to his nephew privately. By the time their parley was over, it was time for dinner. Emmeline and her new husband did reappear for the meal, and they looked very happy. Ines and Duncan could only stare at each other across the table.

Finally, after more toasts than Ines could count, the ladies adjourned to the drawing room while the men had their whisky. Both Emmeline and Ines protested they were exhausted and ready to retire. The ladies hurried up the stairs, giggling and then at the landing stopped to embrace.

"You'll have to come visit us," Emmeline said. "You're like a sister to me now."

"And you will have to come and visit us."

"We will." Emmeline squeezed Ines's shoulders.

"Did you speak to *Senhor* Fortescue about *Senhor* Pope?"

Emmeline pulled back. "Are you still worried about him? Even after he shot your husband?"

"He apologized."

"Before he threatened to do it again!" Emmeline put an arm around Ines's shoulders and paused outside the door to the bedchamber she and Duncan had been given. "Stratford has promised to make inquiries and to speak to Mr. Pope's father, Lord Beaufort, if necessary."

"Thank you."

Emmeline looked as though she would say something else, but she simply whispered, "Write to me," then scurried toward her room. Ines watched her go and then saw the reason for her abrupt departure. Lady Charlotte was approaching.

Ines straightened her shoulders.

"Have you been inside yet?" Lady Charlotte asked, gesturing to the closed door of the bed chamber.

"Not yet."

"Allow me then." Duncan's mother opened the door and held out a hand for Ines to enter. Ines stepped inside and took a breath. The room was huge with a hearth almost as big as she boasting a roaring fire. The curtains to a window were still open, and Ines was drawn to the view of the mountains with the pink of the setting sun behind them. Then she could not help but peek at the bed. It was monstrous in size, with heavy blue velvet curtains hanging about it.

"That bed is famous." Lady Charlotte motioned to it. "'Tis said King James VI slept in that bed."

Ines had no idea who that was, but she tried to look impressed. She motioned to the lace cuffs she had noticed Lady Charlotte wore earlier. "They look well on you," she said.

Lady Charlotte looked at them and then back at Ines. "They are the finest lace I have ever owned. Thank you, and I am sorry for the way I treated you when you first arrived. And after you first arrived. Duncan can be so impulsive, and I had to be sure he really cared for you. I thought I could bait him into revealing his feelings if I—" She sighed. "Well, I should have known he would do things his way."

Ines put a hand on her arm. "We will start over, *sim*?"

"Yes." Awkwardly, she gave Ines a stiff hug. Ines pulled her close and hugged her harder until Lady Charlotte laughed. "We will start over."

Ines pulled back. "Good. And now can you help me take this dress off? I have a wedding night ahead of me."

Lady Charlotte looked surprised at being asked to play lady's maid, but she complied. When she left, Ines poured two glasses of wine from the bottle on the table by the bed, slipped off the robe and then the nightrail she wore and climbed naked into the big bed. She did not think she would have to wait long for Duncan to arrive.

She was right.

\*\*\*

*Duncan*

His mother stepped out of the bridal chamber just as Duncan was reaching to open it. He stared at her in confusion. Had he the wrong chamber? And then he gave his mother a wary look. "Ye didnae kill her, did ye? This is nae time tae play Lady MacBeth."

She glowered at him as only she could. "I did not kill her. I helped her take her clothes off."

Duncan reached for the door handle again.

"Wait."

He stilled and gave his mother a long-suffering look.

"I want to tell you something."

Duncan nodded. "Ye love me."

"I love you."

"Yer happy I have come home."

"I am happy you have come home. To stay," she added.

"Tae stay. Which gives us plenty of time tae talk tomorrow." He reached for the door again.

"Wait."

Duncan heaved a sigh.

"I never blamed you, you know? For your father's death."

Duncan stiffened involuntarily. The topic still brought a lance of pain through his heart.

His mother gave him a sad smile. "The men who killed him bear the responsibility. Not you. Never you, sweet boy. I knew you felt responsible, and I should have said something to you. But I had my own pain, and I suppose I was not a very good mother for not taking yours on as well."

Duncan put a hand on her shoulder. "Ye protected me and yer family. Ye raised the three of us on yer own. Ye were a verra good mother."

"And I intend to be an even better grandmother."

Duncan smiled. "Then I'd best open that door." But before he did, he bent and kissed her cheek. "We'll talk more tomorrow, aye?"

"Aye," she said with a smile.

Duncan opened the door and stepped into the room. The curtains had been closed and the fire banked low enough to give warmth but not overly heat the room. He looked about but did not see Ines. What had his mother done to her?

The bedcurtains moved, and he spotted the glasses of wine next to the bed. "Wife?" he called.

"Come find me," she said. "Naked."

He let out a breath, half laugh half groan. Moving toward her, and stripping off his clothing as he went, he was naked when he parted the curtains and looked down. Propped on one elbow, she too was naked. She looked up at him, her eyes taking him in appreciatively. "Come here, husband, and ravish me."

"Ravish ye?"

"Is that not what you say in Scotland?"

"I dinnae ken what other men say, but I plan to love ye, lass."

She held out her arms and he went to her, pulling her warm body against him. "I plan tae love ye tonight." He kissed her lips. "Then again tonight." His hand stroked her hips and cupped her bottom. "Then again tonight." He gave her a light slap when she laughed. Then he pulled back and looked down at her, her face so lovely in the flickering firelight.

"I'll love ye all the days of my life."

"And I you." She lifted her lips to kiss him, and his mouth met hers. The kiss was searing, and he pressed her legs apart, eager to be inside her.

"There is just one thing," she said.

Duncan who had already found her sex, warm and wet for him, blew out a breath. "Anything, lass."

"You must promise to throw me over your shoulder and carry me to bed again."

He looked up at her. "Ye like that, do ye?"

She nodded. "I like it when you are wild and unpredictable and—oh, yes, when you do that." She caught her breath.

"Then hold on, love, because one thing I can promise ye is more of that." He kissed her. "And this." He pulled her closer. "And…"

But she took his mouth and for a long time no words were needed. He showed her how much he loved her, would always love her—passionate, exciting, and dangerous to the end.

# About Shana Galen

Shana Galen is three-time Rita award nominee and the bestselling author of passionate Regency romps. Kirkus said of her books: "The road to happily-ever-after is intense, conflicted, suspenseful and fun." *RT Bookreviews* described her writing as "lighthearted yet poignant, humorous yet touching." She taught English at the middle and high school level for eleven years. Most of those years were spent working in Houston's inner city. Now she writes full time, surrounded by three cats and one spoiled dog. She's married and has a daughter who is most definitely a romance heroine in the making.

Would you like exclusive content, book news, and a chance to win early copies of Shana's books? Sign up for monthly emails here for exclusive news and giveaways.

*Read Sweet Rogue of Mine, the next book in the Survivors series, featuring Nash.*

*Enjoy an excerpt.*

Someone was in the house. Nash Pope might be half asleep and half drunk, but he knew when someone was in his house. He was a trained sharpshooter, and his body was attuned to even the most subtle changes in atmosphere. Just a few minutes before, the air in Wentmore had been stale and still, the only sounds were of mice scampering in the attic and the creak and groan of the ancient timber beams and floorboards settling.

But now the mice had gone silent and the air stirred. The house seemed to straighten and take notice of someone new, someone far more interesting than its current occupant. In the dining room, the curtains closed against the daylight, the lone candle that burned flickered as though the house exhaled softly in anticipation.

Nash raised his head from the sticky table and heard the shuffle of feet and the squeak of a door hinge.

He reached for his pistol. He didn't need to see it. It was an extension of his arm and his favorite pistol by far. He owned at least half a dozen, including a brace of matching dueling pistols made by Manton, a pepperbox pistol made by

Twigg, a more decorative pistol he'd purchased from the London gunsmith Hawkins—who liked to advertise that the former American President George Washington owned one of his creations—and this one, made by the Frenchman Gribeauval. Gribeauval had made Napoleon's personal pistol, and though Nash was no admirer of Napoleon, he did admire the French armory of St. Etienne.

Nash's thumb slid over the polished walnut gunstock, over the pewter filigree, until his finger curled into the trigger guard as though it were a well-worn glove. He lifted the pistol, not feeling its weight, though it was heavier than some, and then waited. It would do him no good to seek out the intruder. The world, what he could see of it, was gray and full of shadows. Better to let the interloper come to him. He could still shoot straight if he was still.

All had gone silent. Perhaps the uninvited guest had paused to listen as Nash did.

If the game was patience, Nash would win. As a sharpshooter, he had waited more than he had ever fired at the enemy. He often stood in one spot, unmoving, for four or five hours. He stood in the heat or the cold or, if he was fortunate, in the cool, scented breeze of a spring day. The weather might change, but his rifle at his side never had.

The rifle had been put away. He couldn't sight in the rifle anymore, and it was basically useless to him now, but hitting his target with his pistol and one poorly working eye was possible.

"Nash!" a voice called out. If he hadn't been trained as well, he might have jumped. But Nash's jaw only ticked at his name shattering the silence.

The floorboard creaked again. The intruder was in the foyer. He was not directly outside the dining room. The voice was still too distant.

"Put your pistol down, Nash. I came to talk to you."

Nash did not lower the pistol, though the voice sounded familiar now. Stratford? No, this voice wasn't refined enough. Stratford had been here a few months before. Apparently, he'd sought out Nash's father, the Earl of Beaufort, in London and told him Nash needed him. Stratford obviously didn't know that the earl didn't give a damn about Nash. He'd sent his solicitor, and Nash had fired the pistol he held now over the bald man's head and sent him running back to Town.

A door opened and the man said, "Nash?"

It was the door to the parlor.

"Nash, if you shoot me, I'll kick your pathetic arse all the way to Spain and back."

Nash felt his lips quirk in an unwelcome half-smile, as he finally recognized the voice. "And if I kill you?" Nash asked.

"Then I'll come back and haunt you." Rowden was just outside the dining room now, standing at the door. Nash and Rowden had met in Spain, both serving in His Majesty's army. They'd become close friends, even if their skill sets were quite different.

"If I open this door, will you shoot me?" Rowden asked.

"It depends," Nash said, still holding his pistol at the ready. "Did my father send you?"

A pause. "Of course, he sent me." Rowden spoke like he fought—directly and plainly. He did not pull punches.

"Then don't open the door."

"Shoot me and the next to arrive will be men from an asylum. Beaufort is ready to send you to an institution right now. Mayne and Fortescue managed to talk him out of it and arranged to have me sent instead."

Nash considered. The Duke of Mayne would have done the talking as he was the negotiator of the group. Stratford Fortescue would have decided to send Rowden. Fortescue was always the strategist.

"Why you?" Nash asked. Seeing that Mayne was the negotiator, it would have made more sense for him to come.

"I needed the blunt."

Nash winced and set the pistol down. That hurt. His father was paying Nash's friends to intervene. He expected as much from his father, who had given up on Nash a long time ago. But his friends…still, what could he expect when he had shot Duncan Murray this past summer? That misstep was bound to have repercussions.

"I'm coming in," Rowden said, his tone one of warning. The latch lifted and the door opened. In the flickering candlelight, Nash made out a dark form. Of course, he remembered what Rowden looked like. He was broad and stocky with short brown hair and coal-black eyes. He had a pretty face, or he would have if his nose hadn't been broken so many times. Nash remembered what every man he had ever served with looked like. His memory was more of a curse than a blessing, though, as he remembered every woman and, yes, child he had ever shot too.

"You look like hell," Rowden said, still standing in the doorway.

"I wish I could tell you the same, but I can't see worth a damn."

"Still feeling sorry for yourself, I see."

Nash's hand itched to lift the pistol again, but he was not hot-tempered. He would not have lasted a week as a sharpshooter if he had been. "What do you want, Payne? To what do I owe the pleasure of a visit from one of Draven's Dozen?"

Rowden pulled out the chair at the opposite end of the table and sat. Nash saw only a gray, amorphous shape but his other senses filled in the missing information. "Considering you're one of us, I'm not sure why you're surprised. We Survivors take care of our own."

It was a lie, but Nash decided not to point that out. Not yet. The Survivors were a troop of thirty highly skilled military men who had been recruited as something of a suicide band to kill Napoleon or die trying. Eighteen had died trying. Twelve had come home. They had been brothers-in-arms, but Nash did not feel any fraternal affection now. The others were moving on with their lives, while he would be forever alone, locked in a world of darkness.

"You're thin," Rowden observed. To a stocky fighter like Rowden Payne, thinness was a liability. "Don't you eat?"

"You must need my father's money badly if you're playing nursemaid now," Nash said.

Shot fired.

"I want to keep you alive, and no one has to pay me for that."

Missed target.

"I'm alive." But Nash knew that wouldn't be enough. Not after the accident with Murray a few months before. Nash had known some intervention was coming. He supposed he should be glad the Survivors had convinced his father to send Rowden before the men from the asylum. Very little frightened Nash anymore, but the prospect of the next fifty years locked in an asylum drove a spike of fear into his heart. He would put the pistol in his mouth and pull the trigger first. "What do I have to do to keep the asylum at bay?"

"So you haven't completely pickled your brain yet."

"What do I have to do?" Nash repeated. He would do what was required and then, hopefully, the world would leave him alone. After all, he'd given his sight for King and Country. Why couldn't they leave him in peace?

"I don't have a comprehensive list," Rowden said after a pause, during which, Nash assumed, he was looking about the dining room. "Off the top of my head, I would say this old pile needs some repair. It looks like there was a fire at some point."

Nash did not comment.

"And clearly you need to ingest something other than gin."

Nash lifted his empty glass. "This was whiskey." At least he thought it had been whiskey. Maybe it had been brandy.

"You need staff."

"No staff," Nash said.

Rowden let out a quiet grunt. "We'll discuss it. But suffice it to say, I can smell you all the way over here. When was the last time you put on a clean set of clothes or took a bath?"

"Will you scrub my back?" Nash sneered and then was sorry for it. None of this was Rowden's fault. None of this was anyone's fault. Nash had known the risks when he went to war. He just hadn't thought anything would happen to him. He'd been so young. Like most young men, he'd thought he was invincible.

Rowden rose. "I'll make you some coffee. We can start there."

Order it now!

Printed in Great Britain
by Amazon